Praise for *Knots*

"★★★★ A haunting portrait of a Somali-born woman desperate to make a difference in her native Mogadiscio. . . . In diamond-cut prose, Farah—a Somali who has vowed 'to keep my country alive by writing about it'—reveals a world where women are raped and beaten, boys pack guns and Islamic factions threaten. *Knots* is a brutal, beautiful, unforgettable unveiling of a volatile city and a complex woman 'risking her life in order to get the better of her loss.'"   —*People*

"Farah's calm, profoundly humane new novel, *Knots,* makes an ideal and sobering companion piece to [*Black Hawk Down*]. . . . As depicted by Farah, the reality on the ground in Mogadishu—an anarchic, violent, impoverished, unspeakably squalid city he calls Mogadiscio—is every bit as horrifying as the hell on earth that Bowden described. But Farah's Somalians aren't waiting for a helicopter to airlift them out; Somalia is a problem they long to solve. Their country is tied up in knots, and picking away at those knots is what Farah, and his unforgettable heroine Cambara, quietly try to do. . . . The denouement belongs to a fairy tale— or to a great author's heartfelt dream of a happy ending for his troubled heroine and ravaged homeland. A-"   —*Entertainment Weekly*

"An insightful exploration of what it means to come home again."
—*USA Today*

"Of the many things to admire in *Knots*—the unsparing depictions of a war-ravaged city, its vast cast of complex characters—queenly, dynamic and unyielding Cambara stands at the forefront. . . . A woman who subversively used the veil to hide her identity while she fought the hero's fight."   —*San Francisco Chronicle*

"With Somalia back on the front page, its paramount novelist writes of an independent Somali-Canadian woman who returns home to try to make a life in Mogadishu."   —*The Philadelphia Inquirer*

"A beautiful, hopeful novel about one woman's return to war-ravaged Mogadishu, a city most Westerners only see on CNN."   —*Time*

"A powerful dissection of a fragmented societ~ ~ ~iter has to be a dreamer for his people, Farah has said. *Knots* guered people with grave analysis of an impl ascendant Islamists clash with neighboring E offers a salutary reminder of the Islamists' o~

"The anguish of leaving one's homeland is an experience with which Nuruddin Farah, exiled from Somalia for two decades, is intimately familiar. He also knows something about the visceral need to reclaim what has been lost. With *Knots*, the second installment of a trilogy that began with *Links*, Farah traces the painful return of Cambara, a Canada-based businesswoman and actress, to her native Mogadiscio, the unhealed wound of Somalia's civil war. . . . There is beauty in this story of reclamation and resurrection. When Farah's heroine sheds her veil of conformity, it is as if Somalia itself is emerging from a cocoon of despair."
—*TimeOut New York*

"A timely portrait, given Ethiopia's recent military intervention in Somalia to help the interim government rout rival Islamists and American air strikes in the chaotic country aimed at al Qaeda-affiliated fighters. . . . A tale of hope set against a backdrop of seeming hopelessness."
—Reuters

"[*Knots*] sends non-Somali readers to a place and set of circumstances unimaginable elsewhere in the world. And yet, somehow (as in a scene in which gun-slinging boy warriors are unnerved when asked to kill a chicken for lunch), Nuruddin reduced his country's trauma to a scale we can almost grasp. 'One may be lulled into believing that everything is normal,' Cambara thinks. It's not, of course. But such a world does really exist, and the fact that Nuruddin allows us to experience this—even glancingly—is an achievement in itself."
—*The Christian Science Monitor*

"Truly rousing, an inspiration tale of one woman's gradual blossoming through sensitive interaction with a brutalized society."
—*San Antonio Express-News*

"Farah revisits Mogadiscio, the capital of Somalia and the setting of many of his previous works, to discover the humanity in the ruins of that war-torn city. . . . This novel presents another facet of the story of Somalia by one of its most respected writers, now in exile in South Africa."
—*Library Journal* (starred review)

"Spellbinding . . . [Cambara's] journey is mesmerizing. . . . Despite its heavy subject, joy suffuses the novel. . . . Few readers who let Cambara into their lives will easily forget her."
—*Publishers Weekly* (starred review)

PENGUIN BOOKS

KNOTS

Nuruddin Farah is the author of nine novels, including, most recently, *Links*. His novels have been translated into seventeen languages and have won numerous awards. Farah was named the 1998 laureate of the Neustadt International Prize for Literature, "widely regarded as the most prestigious award after the Nobel" (*The New York Times*). Born in Baidoa, Somalia, he now lives in Cape Town, South Africa.

K
N
O
T
S

NURUDDIN FARAH

PENGUIN BOOKS

PENGUIN BOOKS
Published by the Penguin Group
Penguin Group (USA) Inc., 375 Hudson Street, New York, New York 10014, U.S.A.
Penguin Group (Canada), 90 Eglinton Avenue East, Suite 700, Toronto,
Ontario, Canada M4P 2Y3 (a division of Pearson Penguin Canada Inc.)
Penguin Books Ltd, 80 Strand, London WC2R 0RL, England
Penguin Ireland, 25 St Stephen's Green, Dublin 2, Ireland
(a division of Penguin Books Ltd)
Penguin Group (Australia), 250 Camberwell Road, Camberwell,
Victoria 3124, Australia (a division of Pearson Australia Group Pty Ltd)
Penguin Books India Pvt Ltd, 11 Community Centre,
Panchsheel Park, New Delhi – 110 017, India
Penguin Group (NZ), 67 Apollo Drive, Rosedale, North Shore 0632,
New Zealand (a division of Pearson New Zealand Ltd)
Penguin Books (South Africa) (Pty) Ltd, 24 Sturdee Avenue,
Rosebank, Johannesburg 2196, South Africa

Penguin Books Ltd, Registered Offices:
80 Strand, London WC2R 0RL, England

First published in the United States of America by Riverhead Books,
a member of Penguin Group (USA) Inc. 2007
Published in Penguin Books 2008

10 9 8 7 6 5 4 3 2 1

PUBLISHER'S NOTE
This is a work of fiction. Names, characters, places, and incidents are either
the product of the author's imagination or are used fictitiously, and any
resemblance to actual persons, living or dead, business establishments,
events, or locales is entirely coincidental.

THE LIBRARY OF CONGRESS HAS CATALOGED THE HARDCOVER EDITION AS FOLLOWS:
Farah, Nuruddin, date.
Knots / Nuruddin Farah.
p.   cm.
ISBN 978-1-59448-924-2 (hc.)
ISBN 978-0-14-311298-3 (pbk.)
1. Americans—Somalia—Fiction.   2. Mogadishu (Somalia)—Fiction.
3. Real property—Somalia—Fiction.   I. Title.
PR9396.9.F3K58 2007   2006023107
823'.914—dc22

Printed in the United States of America
Book design by Stephanie Huntwork
Photograph by Meighan Cavanaugh

To Abyan, my daughter,
and
Kaahiye, my son,
with all my love

K
N
O
T
S

ONE

Zaak says to Cambara, "Who do you blame?"

"Blame?" Cambara asks tetchily, as she goes ahead of him taking the lead, although she has no idea where to go. As it happens, she arrived in Mogadiscio earlier today after a long absence and does not know her way about, the city's landmarks having been savagely destroyed in the ongoing civil war to the extent where, based on what she has seen of the city so far, she doubts if she will recognize it.

Cambara has had the proclivity to keep a safe, polite distance, the better to avoid Zaak's bad breath, diagnosed as chronic gingivitis. When both were younger and growing up in the same household, the dentist would prescribe special toothpaste with antiseptic and aromatic qualities, in addition to a medicinal mouthwash, and a very soft toothbrush with which he was to clean his teeth. Cambara remembers his gums bleeding prolifically and receding wastefully at a phenomenal rate, the inflammation, combined with the irritation on account of the tartar deposits, causing the loosening of several of his teeth. She remembers his suffering from persistent indigestion ever since Arda, her mother, who is also his paternal aunt, brought him from a nomadic hamlet during his early teens as her charge in order to facilitate his receiving proper schooling in Mogadiscio.

Cambara waits for him to push the door shut, which he does with a squeak, and she watches him as he turns the wobbly handle a couple of times in a futile effort to secure it, notwithstanding its state of malfunction. Meanwhile, she reminds herself that it has been years since she last set eyes on him or was in touch with him directly. Arda has carried words back and forth from one to the other and has persuaded her daughter to put up with him, at least for the first few days, since Cambara informed her of her wish to go to Mogadiscio. At her mother's cajoling, Cambara acquiesced to stay with "her blood," as she put it, for the first few days, until, perhaps, she has made her own contacts with a close friend of a friend living in Toronto. No doubt, Cambara cannot expect her mother to recall her nephew's malodorous breath, nor is it fair to assume that this is reason enough to warrant her daughter's not wanting to share the same space. But how on earth could she, Cambara, have forgotten the awfulness of it, so vile it is sickening? Nor had she known him to be a chain-smoker or a constant chewer of *qaat*, the mild narcotic to which urban Somalis are highly addicted.

"Surely someone is to blame?" Zaak insists.

"Who?"

Zaak lets her go past him and out the side gate—she almost six feet, he a mere five-foot-seven. Scarcely have they left the compound and walked a hundred meters when she slows down, covers her head more appropriately with a plain scarf as the Islamic tradition dictates, and stays ten or so meters behind Zaak. Her eyes downcast—again, as expected of women in Mogadiscio these days—she reaches into one of the inner pockets of her custom-made caftan to make certain that she has brought along her knife, her weapon of choice, if it comes to self-defense. A glance in her direction will prove that she is bracing her courage in preparation for an ugly surprise, to which anyone in a civil war city is vulnerable. Herself, she looks in consternation from the dilapidated tarmac road to Zaak, as she releases her stiff grip around the handle of the knife. Then she tightens her lips and moistens them, her head sending two contradictory messages: the one advising that she remain wary, the other declining, as per her mother's suggestion, to put all her trust in Zaak, because he has firsthand knowledge of how things are likely to pan out. Adopting an indifferent posture as she focuses for a moment on Zaak, she studies his expressions or lack of them, and remarks, with surprise, that he does not appear as if he is expecting an untoward occurrence: the telltale advent on the scene of armed youths intent on launching a virulent mayhem that might end in either of them being shot or killed. She tries to relax into a high state of alert, if that is at all possible, and then picks up Zaak's pungent body odor, the un-washed detritus of a *qaat*-chewer's unhealthy living. The power of the stench hits her forcefully, and she comes close to fainting.

In a belated answer to her question "Who?" Zaak mumbles an un-intelligible remark she is unable to make out. With so angry a face, she nervously scans the horizon, as they turn a sharp corner and are sud-denly face to face with several sarong-and-flip-flop-wearing youths armed with AK-47s. Her instinct tells her to prepare, her hand making renewed, abrupt contact with the knife, even though two of the youths appear indifferent to her and are religiously chewing *qaat* and arguing, bansheelike, about yesterday's match between Arsenal and Manchester United, and agreeing that the referee made a balls-up of the game by unfairly red-carding the Gunners' captain. Her sense of caution re-mains relentless until they are well out of danger.

Zaak asks, *"Et tu?"*

She is in no mood to answer such a question early in her visit, not until she comes to grips with the complexity of what is in store for her. In fact, she is delighted that she has refrained from engaging him in a serious talk so far, worried that this might give him the license to zero in on her scant preparedness for what she intends her visit to achieve beyond perhaps getting reacquainted with the country of her birth and maybe reacquiring the family property now in the hands of a minor war-lord. She is consumed with doubt, wondering if it is possible to ac-complish such a feat without a lot of help from a lot of people. Of course, she is well aware that the warlord will give her kind no quar-ter whatsoever, it being not in the nature of these brutes to show mercy to anyone. What about Zaak, her cousin and current host? Will he ex-tend a protective hand to her if she makes the resolve to confront the warlord? How will he react when she puts his loyalty to the test?

Whatever else she might do, she must not afford Zaak free access to her affairs, at least not before she has consolidated her position and fortified it against its inherent weaknesses, which might come to light after she sets the confrontation with the minor warlord and his armed minions into motion. At any rate, she must not allow Zaak to make her question the motives of her visit, what has prompted her to leave her peaceful life, husband, and job in Toronto, where she has been resident for three-quarters of her life, and come to the war-torn country. She could see questions forming in his head when he met her at the airport, sensing that he wants to ask if she has moved house and relocated to Somalia. Why has she brought so many hefty suitcases filled with all her movable assets?

That she has been unhappy in her marriage to Wardi is no secret—everybody has been aware of this for a long time. Moreover, having once been Cambara's "husband" on paper and having "lived" with her in confined spaces, first as children growing up, then as a couple who entered into a contract of the marriage-of-convenience kind, Zaak has his partisan views. He thinks of her as a woman capable of exemplary generosity, most loyal, above all, to her mother, very devoted to her close friends, especially to Raxma. But she also cuts the figure of an impulsive woman, difficult to please, harder still to pin down, and known, lately, to be off her rocker, understandably so, because of her son's death. Cambara blames Wardi, her husband, and his Canadian mistress for her son's drowning. And even though he has not dared ask her—fearing she might flare up, presuming his question to be provocative—Zaak supposes that she is here for a lengthy period, considering the weight and number of suitcases that she has brought along. She may have been attracted to the idea of relocating here out of her desperate attempt to put an ocean between herself and Wardi, but told everyone else, apart from her mother and intimate friends, that she is here to mourn the passing of her only son. But Cambara hasn't dwelled on her huge loss, not even after Zaak offered his condolences, beyond acknowledging them and saying, "Thank you." Nor has she let the name of her husband pass her lips or alluded to what is to become of their marriage. She has made a point of giving brief responses to his questions, now nodding her head yes and elaborating no more, now shaking her head no and preferring not to expand further. The last Zaak heard, Wardi is doing splendidly: He is finally a partner in the law firm. For his part, Zaak has steered a judicious course, ostensibly avoiding the obvious and the not-so-obvious pitfalls, and has refrained from pressing her. And whenever they have run out of topics of interest, their conversation has taken a detour and led them to Cambara's mother, whom they both love.

However, if there is a subject that neither is comfortable discussing, it is their own shared past as putative husband and wife. Ill at ease, they have reined back from revisiting it, apprehensive that, unchecked, their talking might deposit them eventually at the door to a concern better left alone—the two years spent together under one roof, in her apartment in Toronto, as man and wife—"Only on paper, I'll have you know," she will point out again and again—which had been an utter disaster. Maybe she means to have no intimate talk, none whatsoever.

"Has there been fighting here lately?" she asks, coming level with him. Then, seemingly tired, she squints at the afternoon sun, hesitating before cracking her jaws in the yawning attitude of a passenger in a plane clearing her ears of accumulated air pressure. The sun burns down so harshly that the contours of all visible items melt in its fierceness. She sees the giveaway evidence of civil war devastation wherever she turns: buildings leaning in in complete disorder, a great many of them boasting no roof, others boarded up, looking vandalized, abandoned. The road—once tarred and good enough for motor vehicles—is in total disrepair; the walls of the house fronting the street are pocked with bullets, as if a terrible sharpshooter with assault rifles has used them for his target practice.

"Skirmishes," he says, as if an afterthought.

"How many militiamen died?"

"Only unarmed civilians."

As though out of kindness to Cambara, Zaak holds his cigarette away from her—in his left hand—and he keeps the fingers of his right hand close to his mouth, almost covering it. Moreover, his head veers away from her; she is not clear if he is doing so to protect her from the slightest whiff of his nicotine or if he has lately become conscious of the ill effect his evil-smelling breath is having on her.

All of a sudden, however, he springs on her a challenge with the strident voice of a man of huge contradictions, courteous in one instant, cruel in the next. He says, "Do not tell me that you are frightened."

You might think from the way she takes a step back that she is readying to give him a slap across the face. Not so. All she wants to do is to look down on him from her great six-foot height. She also thinks that there is the bravura of a young boy's dare to his taunting, which irks her no less. She remembers their young years together in the same household—Cambara's parents' house, to be exact—and how she would do anything for a dare and he wouldn't; Zaak was not a rebel by nature, was less inclined to act as wild as she would. After all, she was the beloved daughter of the house and he but a poor relation.

She would throw in his direction all manner of gauntlets, but he wouldn't pick them up. Annoyed, she would goad him, "Three dares for your one." And she would wet her index finger, which is a child's way of timing the retort of the opponent: If the forefinger dries before the response, the challenger will forfeit, and the dare lapses, in which case she would declare herself the winner. He liked to stay out of trouble, preferring living and going to school in Mogadiscio to being sent back to his poorer parents in the hinterland, close to Galkacyo, in Mudugh. Always conscious of their difference in height, he was irritated by her rubbing it in.

She opts for a different tack. She says, wisely, stressing the validity of her point, "Only fools are unafraid."

"Please don't take it that way," he apologizes.

As he prepares to walk away, Cambara remarks that they are close to an open-air market. In fact, they meet shoppers returning, the forlorn expressions of the women swathed from head to toe in cheap veils evident, on occasion with only their eyes and hands showing. The women are carrying their small purchases in black plastic bags. To encounter these women in their miserable state saddens Cambara. Even though the men look equally dour and unfulfilled, they seem relaxed. Maybe it is because the men have preciously tucked away under their arms their fresh bundles of *qaat*, the stimulant that some of them have already started to chew. Whereas the women have nothing of importance to expect, save more war-related miseries and rape and sick children to care for, useless husbands whom they serve hand and foot as they chew to their heart's satisfaction and talk politics.

She thinks of herself as being, already, a victim of the habit. After all, he has dragged her out of bed and forced her to carry the lethargy of jet lag to escort him so that he might buy his daily ration. She has found proof of chewing in the upstairs room where she is staying, which is littered with the dried detritus of the discarded stems of the stuff. For a nonchewer, nonsmoker, she looks upon the upstairs room allotted to her as a hellhole, smelly, the walls green from the spit of the chewers, the crannies stuffed with the plant's unchewed stems.

When Cambara puts urgency into her steps with a view to catching up with him, she trips, loses her balance, and almost tumbles over. Zaak stares accusingly at her sandaled feet, which are now covered with fine brown sand.

"I'll put on walking shoes next time," she says.

"If I were you, I would also put on a veil."

The liberties he allows himself, she thinks to herself, as she reflects on what he has just said. Of course, she is no fool; she has come prepared, having acquired a pair of veils, one in Dearborn, Michigan, the other in Nairobi. But she will don the damn thing on her own terms, not because he has advised her to wear one. She needs no reminding that she is dressed differently from the other women whom they have encountered so far, the largest number of them veiled, some in the traditional *guntiino* robes and others in near tatters. She is in a caftan, the wearing of which places her in a league of one. She wore it, she reasons, because it was close to hand and she hadn't the time to open her suitcases and rummage in them, looking for a veil. Besides, this custom-made caftan permits her to carry a knife discreetly.

He asks, "Shall I take you to a who-die stall? Where you can buy a veil?" She reads meanness in his eyes and interprets the expression as a male daring a woman to defy the recent imposition, which stipulates that women should veil themselves. When she was young, it was uncommon for Somali women to wear one; mostly Arab women and a few of the city's aboriginals did.

" 'Who-die stalls'? Why are they called that?"

"Stalls from where you buy secondhand veils."

Then Zaak explains at length that in recent years, dumping of secondhand clothing on the world's poor has become de rigueur, as many citizens of these countries are in no position to pay the astronomical prices for new clothes.

"I see," she says, nodding.

He is in his element, and goes on. "The who-die stalls are run by local entrepreneurs who buy a shipload of secondhand clothes for next to nothing from a dump house in the developed world and then import these in. The importers and the retailers are all under the impression that everyone is getting a bargain. The truth is, sadly, different."

"Why is that?"

"Because the practice has destroyed the local textile industries, as they can no longer compete with the dumpers. People have dubbed the practice with knowing cynicism; *who-die* clothes from *who-die* stalls!"

Soon enough, a vast sorrow descends upon Cambara, as she remembers how she had taken a suitcase full of her dead son's clothes, and donated them to charity so they might be parceled out among Toronto's poor. Of course she does not know where the clothes that have survived her son have ended up. Years back when she lived here, it was the tradition for well-to-do people to offer the clothes of their dead folks to a mosque. Now, in the harsh light of what she has just learned, she is aware that it won't do to shrug it all off. She will have to think of how best and sanely to dispense with the garments to which she attaches fond memories—her living, active son wearing them. She will wait for a few days before deciding what to do and among whom to distribute them, gratis, no doubt.

He says, "What do you say? Shall I take you to a who-die stall to buy a veil?"

Cambara sidesteps his question, putting one to him herself. "Hadn't you given up smoking many years before you left Toronto?" she asks.

"Yes, I did."

"Then why have you gone back?"

"One vice leads to another," he says with a smirk.

"How do you mean?"

"*Qaat* chewing is the first vice I've picked up coming here," he says, waving his cigarette. "It passes the time."

"What does? Smoking?"

"*Qaat* chewing helps me to bear the aloneness of my everyday life," he says. "You see, Mogadiscio is a metropolis with none of the amenities of one. There is nothing to do here: no nightclubs, no places of entertainment, and no bars in which to drown your sorrows, as even the taverns are dry of liquor. Only restaurants."

"No cinemas?"

"None to speak of."

"No theaters?"

"None," he says.

"What has become of the National Theatre?"

"The National Theatre is in the hands of a warlord whose militiamen have used the stage and props, as well as the desks, doors, ceiling boards, and every piece of timber, as firewood. The roof has collapsed, and everything else—the cisterns, the sinks and the bathtubs in the washroom, not to speak of the iron gates, the computers—all has been removed, vandalized, or sold off."

"What if someone wants to put on a show?"

"It would be a hit, but it will never happen."

"You mean because of the warlords who run the city?" she asks.

"Or the Islamic courts that will step in to stop it going ahead," says Zaak.

"On what grounds?"

"On moral or theological grounds."

"But you reckon ordinary folks will watch it?"

"I reckon they would," he replies.

Cambara's enthusiasm is unconcealed. "How do the armed youths entertain themselves when they have time on their gun-free hands?"

Zaak replies, "They watch videocassettes of Hindi, Korean, Italian, or English movies."

"Surely they are not schooled in these languages?"

"The movies are dubbed into Somali."

"Dubbed? By whom?"

Chuffed, Zaak is clearly pleased that he has for once impressed Cambara with his knowledge about something of which she hasn't an idea.

"There is a burgeoning dubbing industry in Mogadiscio," he says. "There are also kung fu films, locally produced and entirely shot here."

"Where are they shown?"

"In the buildings that once belonged to the collapsed state, which are now free-for-all, run-down, and populated by the city's squatters. The Ministry of Foreign Affairs, the city polytechnics, the second-ary schools."

"How are the films distributed?"

"The Zanzibaris, who have come fleeing from the fighting in their country," Zaak informs her, "have cornered this side of the business. They have total control, Mafia-like."

"Have you seen the dubbed movies yourself?"

"No, I haven't."

Maybe he has time only for *qaat*, she thinks, then she asks, "Do you know anyone who has?"

He shakes his head. "No."

She needs to get in touch with Kiin, the manager of Maanta Hotel, who, according to Raxma, a close friend of Cambara's back in Toronto, is well connected and might serve the salient purpose of Cambara's accessing information about the videocassettes, and building local contacts, including the Women's Network, which may help her with all sorts of matters.

Cambara will admit that she has made a faux pas arriving in Mogadiscio unprepared, with no addresses and no telephone numbers of anyone except Zaak and no personal contacts. Perhaps it is too late to think of ruing her impromptu decision to come. Granted, she mulled over the visit for a long period. No matter, she won't engage Zaak in serious talk until she has been here for a while.

She has no idea what Zaak will think of it, but she cannot help imagining him being more sarcastic than her mother, who reacted with unprecedented bafflement when Cambara informed her of her imminent trip to the country. Asked why, Cambara, in a straight approach to the task informed by a touch of defiance, told her that she meant to reclaim the family property, wrest it from the hands of the warlord. Arda instantly fumed with fury, describing her daughter's plan as a harebrained ruse. "This is plain insane," Arda had observed. Then the two strong-headed women battled it out, Cambara pointing out that those warlords are cowards and fools and that it won't be difficult to be more clever than they so as to boot them out of the family property.

"This is downright suicidal," Arda reiterated.

After arguing for days and nights, Arda consented to Cambara's "ill-advised scheme" with a caveat: that they involve Raxma, who had wonderful contacts in Mogadiscio, and, while waiting for things to be put in motion, that Cambara should either wait in Toronto or go ahead and stay with Zaak. Being a schemer with no equal anywhere, Arda set to work clandestinely on setting up a safety net as protective of her daughter as it was capable of keeping her abreast of every one of the girl's madcap schemes. Only then did Arda agree to "give her blessing for whatever it is worth for a plan as flawed as a suicide note."

A battlewagon hurtling down the dirt road and coming straight at them startles Zaak, who grabs her right arm and pushes her off the footpath into the low shrubs. The vehicle is carrying a motley group of youths armed to their *qaat*-ruined teeth. Cambara picks herself up, dusts her caftan, and has barely sufficient time to stare at the backs of their heads before the battlewagon vanishes in the swirl of sand it has helped to raise.

"Are you okay? You are not hurt?" Zaak asks.

Cambara has already moved on. She asks, "Do the warlords themselves know why they continue the fighting?"

"I don't follow you," Zaak says.

"Are they and their clansmen economically better off than they were when the civil war erupted? And is their position more secure? Why don't they stop destroying what they've illicitly gained?"

Zaak takes his time before answering the questions, but when he does, he adjusts the tone of his voice to that of someone quoting from someone else.

He says, "The warlords make as much sense as the idea of bald men fighting over the ownership of combs, knowing that they have no more use for it."

"What manner of men are they, the warlords?"

"The scum of the earth."

Hot with readiness to do battle with the notion of "dirt" in civil war parlance, Cambara relives with a sense of repulsion the memory of Zaak's creative mess and downright filth in his living conditions. She is appalled to register how his tolerance level has grown since they shared a place, how he abides toilet floors wet with God-knows-what, bathtubs black as though smeared with the soot from the sweepings of a chimney, a kitchen crawling with cockroaches and other bugs, bedsheets brown with repeated use. Maybe the civil war has something to do with Zaak's lowering the measure of his endurance. Maybe she hasn't the right to claim to have known him intimately when she was assisting him in his application to gain his landed-immigrant status in Canada. Even when he first got there, Zaak had unclean ways, above all the uncouth habit of wetting the toilet seat, which made flat-sharing a daily embarrassment. And rather than endure or put up with it, she will have to find an alternative accommodation.

She won't ever forget the shock at meeting him at the airport, when she detected cynicism and hostility both in the expressions on his face and in the remarks he made, as he hauled her half a dozen pieces of luggage to the four-wheel drive. Soon.

"Have you brought a department store?" he said.

Not rising to his comment, she said, "You know what I am like."

"I know what women are like," he chided her.

In a fit of pique, she almost asked him to take her to a hotel—and to hell with what her mother might say. She has come with enough cash and can afford to take a room in one of the best hotels for the duration of her stay, however long that might be. But again, she will only do it under her own terms; she won't be pushed into making hasty, regrettable decisions. Her impatience tested, he knows what she is capable of and how often she takes umbrage at men and allows her anger to act as though it is independent of her.

As soon as they got to his place and he showed her to her room and pointed to the adjoining toilet and bathroom that were to be all hers, Cambara's entire body suddenly went slack, and, in an instant, she was visibly suppressing a yawn, and he was offering to leave her alone for her to shower and settle in and, if she could, sleep off her jet lag. He explained that he had an urgent meeting about a conflict between two warring militias from the same subclan, a frequent-enough occurrence. But he would come back and take her along on her first expedition to the open-air market, where he would buy his daily ration of *qaat*. Then she heard the sound of his steps going down the staircase, a door opening and slamming; she decided to take a nap without changing into a nightgown. She remembers ceaseless noises near enough to lead her to believe that he was hanging outside her room—so close that she imagined sensing his nervous breathing.

Then she remembers him snottily shouting, "Wakey, wakey, rise and shine," when in her drowsy reckoning she couldn't have been asleep for more than five minutes.

Maybe she ought to have slept on, sparing herself a long walk to the open-air market so that Zaak could feed his craving for *qaat*. She is so exhausted that she finds it difficult to keep her eyes open, so overwhelmed by accumulated fatigue that her head feels as heavy as a wet mattress, her tongue as lifeless as the faulty stitching of a quilt. She curses under her breath in Québécois French, knowing he wouldn't understand a word of it.

New, all of a sudden, she awakens to a mélange of fragrances emanating from ancient spices; she is in front of a spice stall at the open-air market where a woman who trades in them is offering to sell her a selection. Other potent scents from a jamboree of mints almost knock her sideways, they are so powerful. Not far from where she is standing as if jinxed, another woman is beckoning to her. The second woman is encouraging Cambara to buy from her spread of edible plants and roots.

"I've brought no money," Cambara says apologetically to the woman, who is offering her fresh cinnamon sticks, cumin seeds, roots of ginger, and cloves of garlic.

The woman is very pushy, and Cambara is more irritated with herself for not bringing some cash. A dollar would make a big difference to any of these women. As Cambara walks a couple of steps away from the stall, feeling foolish, the woman follows her and says, "Take everything that is on the mat for a dollar. This is a bargain."

How has this woman worked out that Cambara is from elsewhere—a dollar country? Amazing.

Finally the woman says, "And since you haven't brought any money today, why don't you take these and bring the money tomorrow?"

But Cambara won't hear of it; she hates the thought of being in debt to anyone, no matter how small the sum. In fact she says it in so many words and as plainly as she can, but the woman won't let her be.

"How can it be that you haven't any money?" the woman challenges. "Tell me where you are from, so I know. Are you from Amriika? Igland? Swiidan? Filland? Put your hand in that pocket of yours and bring out the dollar. Please do not waste my time."

Cambara finds herself automatically putting her hand in the deep pocket as the woman has instructed, and her fingers meet the knife. She brings out her empty hand and rubs it against the other hand. She says, "I have no money today. Not a cent."

"I'll take what is in that pocket in exchange for my entire spread," the woman says.

When Cambara reiterates that she has no money in her pocket, the woman's look forthrightly questions her statement, and the two of them stare into each other's eyes. The woman says, "Take the entire spread of spices and vegetables in exchange for the single item that is in the pocket out of which you've brought your hand."

Cambara searches in vain for Zaak, whom she cannot locate. Curiously, however, she doesn't feel abandoned or threatened. It is because she is among women. She enjoys seeing so many women trading in local produce and wearing colorful *guntiino* robes, the traditional attire, and the fact that they are dominating an entire section of the marketplace. Many are past their prime and don't seem bothered about their exposed breasts; they strike Cambara as easygoing both in the way they carry their bodies and in their attitude toward one another.

She shakes herself loose from the vegetable seller and goes deeper and deeper into the mud-choked portion of the marketplace, pressing on, with one part of her conscious mind hoping to locate Zaak and the other busy working out what she might do if she can't find him. Then she sees a child sitting on a straw mat next to an older woman, presumably her mother. Cambara is grief stricken as an image calls on her. Careworn, drowned in the suddenness of a renewed distress related to her recent loss, she relaxes a little when she identifies the gender of the child—a girl. Next to the girl and sitting in a self-contained way, the woman has a spread of tomatoes, a pile of onions, and some emaciated-looking and nearly dry potatoes.

Zaak is back. He is saying, "Touché."

Cambara pays him no heed. She stares at the girl until she cottons on to the little one's tender adult movements. The girl's expression reminds her of Dalmar, her son, whom she misses terribly and whom she has begun to see in every child of either sex or any age. That's not all; the small girl has only one leg, her second leg having been replaced with a wooden one, crudely constructed out of grainy wood. Furthermore, as Cambara's fragmented memories gather themselves around the girl's grainy wooden leg, she sees Dalmar, who had a keen interest in constructing puppets. The little girl's sweet smile, coquettishly flung in her direction the way an older woman might dart one at a man, takes Cambara back to Dalmar's last day on this earth, as he got into the backseat of his father's car, sweetly making smile-throwing gestures toward her and waving. Such a sweet smile in a girl so young and knowing, formulated in the carefree attitude of one who has suffered hugely at such an impressionable age. The girl is holding in her arms a modestly dressed corn-husk doll, which she is gently rocking to sleep.

Cambara makes herself look into the eyes of the little girl as into the mirrored sorrow of her loss. She feels that, despite everything, the girl has about her a sense of comfort, of being a child and a mother at the same time, and of grimacing at the discomfiture of what it is to be so young and drawn. Cambara stoops over the little girl and then crouches down pretty close to her.

"What's your beautiful name, sweet little love?" Cambara asks.

She stares into the girl's big dark eyes as she might look into the un-fathomable black hole with which she has become intimate since her son's death.

Even though the girl says her name several times, Cambara fails to disentangle the girl's guttural consonants from her mute vowels. Then she looks from the little girl to the woman and then at the surrounding chaos, and back finally to the little girl, who is singing to her corn-husk doll a lullaby about a mother who has been raped, a father killed, an uncle dispossessed of his property, and a sister gone and never heard from again.

"How old are you, sweet little love?"

"I don't know."

Cambara remains in her clumsy crouch, her every bone creaking, her every joint aching, and her thighs enflamed with pain. She can tell that Zaak is close by, chain-smoking and unwrapping the bundle of *qaat* and helping himself to its shiny, leathery leaves upon which he chews meditatively, like a cow attending to its cud. His eyes redden, and his right cheek bulges gradually, chipmunklike.

She says to Zaak, "Can I borrow some money?"

"How much do you need?"

"A couple of dollars' worth in shillings."

He says, "I have less than a dollar."

Her stomach turns at the disturbing thought that he has bought *qaat* and paid money sufficient for several families to live on for a week. How wasteful! She can't bear the thought of receiving the money from him herself, she is so disgusted.

She says, "Please give them the money."

And she extends both her hands to receive the plastic bag into which the woman has stuffed the produce that Zaak has paid for.

They walk back to the house, Cambara furious with herself all the while for having accepted her mother's condition that she stay with him. As they tread along, he stops every now and then to select juicy young shoots of his precious *qaat* and consumes them hungrily.

She looks away, in revulsion.

TWO

Fretful, Cambara is in the upstairs bathroom, bracing for a cold bucket shower, her first in many years. The thought of having one brings on goose pimples. As she readies for the first drop of cold water, she clenches her teeth, closes her eyes, and, standing in rigid expectation of the water descending from above her head, trembles all over. She considers giving up the idea and finding a hotel with warm running water and all the modern amenities she is used to. On second thought, however, she carps at admitting defeat so soon after arriving, conscious of the fact that more civil war–related travails lie in wait for her and that it is high time she took this small challenge head-on.

She remembers talking to Zaak earlier and cannot get rid of seeing the bemused look on his face, as he informed her, almost with a touch of glee, that the geyser in the upstairs bathroom is no longer working, but if she wanted, she could have a warm shower in his downstairs bathroom. Truth be told, she declined his invitation to use his bathroom, because she did not wish to repeat her Nairobi experience years ago when they shared an apartment and she found him wanting. She wonders if the disparaging smile his face wore earlier meant that he hadn't forgotten how much she disliked cold showers. Whatever the case, she thanked him and said that she preferred getting accustomed to the conditions prevailing here right away to postponing the inevitable, for, sooner or later, she would have to confront similar situations and worse. She puzzles over the problem of sharing a small space and living in intimate proximity for a few days. Can she suffer it and for how long? Will they rub each other the wrong way?

Even though she doubts that Zaak will knock on the door on some pretext or another or walk in, she makes sure she bolts the bathroom door from inside, just to be sure. She opens the window wide to let in the early-evening sea breeze, which in its own way weakens her resolve to have the cold shower after all. Her chest rises and falls as she fills her lungs with sea air and breathes in nostalgic memories of the city's salted humidity. The puff of the wind washing over her helps stimulate her powers of recall, and before she knows it, she is in her preteens, mischievously baring her budding breasts in Zaak's presence and daring him to touch them. Because he hadn't the nerve, she accused him of being a shirking coward. Naked and in flip-flops, her right hand resting limply on her hip, her admiring gaze falls on her waist, which is too narrow for a woman her age, especially one who has had a child. Cambara wonders how much the exposure to civil war horrors has affected Zaak's outlook on life and, if so, in what significant ways.

As if asking now the right profile and now the left one to yield up their cheeky confidences one at a time, she stands slightly to the left of the mirror and then to the right of it. She listens to a faucet dripping, a cistern running, a rusty window shakily creaking on its hinges. Then, when she least expects it, she distinctly picks out the sound of a bird calling to its mate, in mourning. She regards the face looking back at her lengthily from the depth of the looking glass with renewed apprehension. She ascribes her inability to compose herself in the way she likes to the fact that, like the bird, she too is grieving.

Her eyes bulge with so many unshed tears, and she senses a sudden, almost blinding rush of hot blood flowing to her head, but she catches herself in time before losing her balance and dropping to the wet floor in a dead faint. She stands upright and breathes in deeply, harder and longer, and more frequently until she is sure that the world won't pull away from under her feet. Now steady, and not likely to founder, she inhales some more sea air, and when she imagines that she has taken in enough, she regains her normal bearing. She first bends down slowly with deliberate willfulness, and then lifts the scoop, which she dips into the bucket filled to the brim with water. Lest she lose her grip, she clutches at the scoop as if making a grab for an item that is, of necessity, an extension of the self. She raises the scoop, preparatory to pouring the water on her head. However, before a globule of liquid has reached any part of her body, her face wears an expectant, tense look, and then ready, set, go. The first drop is insufferable, causing her body to be covered with tiny bumps; the second drop is not so unbearable. By the time she has emptied scoopfuls on her head, she feels she has acclimatized to the inclement temperature, and no part of her body raises a single goose bump. Because she is no longer breaking out in cold spots, she compliments herself for a small achievement, the first since her arrival.

After she has toweled down and gone back to the privacy of her room, which she bolts from the inside, and has chosen what to wear—a discreet dress, decent and not in any way provocative enough to make Zaak wish they had been lovers—she revisits a scene that is permanently etched on the screen of her memory. In it, she and her mother are on an afternoon walk in a park in the suburb of Ottawa where her parents had relocated a couple of decades before Somalia had collapsed into stateless anarchy and where her father, a diabetic, had had two legs amputated in a matter of six months and had been bedridden for nearly two years. At the time, Cambara was not doing as well as she might have hoped in her dream profession, acting. She was worth no more than cameo parts, nothing big, and even then didn't have her name in lights. She had not landed any role that might turn her overnight into a household name anywhere. No one showed the TV commercials in which she had had parts, even though they had been commissioned, and none of her other short skits were ever aired in prime time. In fact, earlier that month, Cambara had failed to get an audition for a role about a young, ambitious Somali woman who is at loggerheads with her in-laws over the infibulation of her seven-year-old daughter, a story that her agent made her believe had been written with her in mind. No wonder she was in a downbeat mood.

"A pity that my biggest fan is in no position to hire me for an acting role," Cambara would remark tongue in cheek to her mother and friends. Arda was so enthusiastic about her daughter's potential that she would delight in speaking gloatingly and praising her to high heaven; she would describe her, preeminently, as an actor who would one day surprise the world, given the chance. When relatives or family friends pointed out that Cambara was getting on in years and hadn't as yet made a breakthrough, married, and provided her with a grandchild, Arda, in her riposte, would speak of the primacy of her profession, which she would place above marriage or childbearing. She would add that Cambara would turn her mind to matrimonial matters only after she had secured an acting contract worth the wait. In the meantime, Cambara worked as a makeup artist for an outfit called The Studio and was very popular among theater folk and among Somalis, who sought her out so she would prepare the bride on the eve of her wedding.

In fairness, Cambara was more realistic than her mother made her out to be. At times, it embarrassed her to hear her mother's over-the-top bragging, her mother who awoke nearly daily animated with the energy derived from the belief that Cambara would one day make it big, and that she would bring a smile to everyone's lips and pride to her own eyes and heart. Arda dreamed of precipitating a profitable scheme that would lead to her daughter's ultimate success. Ever since her parents' relocation to Canada several years preceding the fighting in Mogadiscio, which wrenched power from the dictator's iron grip, Cambara assumed a central role in their lives. She rang them often and called on them whenever she could. When her father took ill, it fell to Cambara to drive to his house and spend her weekends or holidays. And when the old man became bedridden and there was need for round-the-clock care and her mother relied on an elderly Filipino woman for this purpose, Cambara helped out the best she could. Her father's death brought them much closer. How the two women enjoyed their long conversations, complimenting each other, the one a fan, the other, in her self-restraint, refusing to lap it all up like a famished kitten consuming the milk in a saucer. However, seldom did either allow her talk to veer toward the very personal: marriage or babies. Discreet, Arda would reiterate that, in matters of the heart, she had faith that Cambara eventually would make the right choice.

One day, half a year after her father's death, Arda invited her on the pretext that she might have discovered an elixir for her professional problems. Cambara went to Ottawa to humor her mother, assuming that her mother's summons had something to do, most likely, with the strife raging in Mogadiscio and the rest of the land, no more than that. If anything, she supposed that a relative was in some trouble and needing a leg up, or maybe the Canadian government was setting up a commission to help its policy makers come to grips with the Somali crisis, and it was possible that through someone's intercession, Cambara was being asked to join the assembled pundits. Whatever it was, and even though she would not elaborate on it at all, her mother had sounded chuffed. She doubted if the visit would have any bearing on her professional ambitions or would result in her mother's discovery of a panacea, but since, in her experience, Arda's records of intervention were invariably marked by success, Cambara said to herself, "What do I lose?" and drove to Ottawa to hear her mother out.

They got down to the business of talking after a hot bath and a delicious meal prepared and served with loving maternal care. All was good at the initial ground-clearing phase, in which Arda spent a long time on the preliminaries and Cambara listened with due patience and filial deference as her mother untangled the wool gathered from the mesh of her speculative fibers. However, when Cambara finally got the drift of her mother's plan and paid more attention to the nuances being employed, Cambara found out that she could not fight the feeling of nausea gradually coming upon her in waves and eventually overwhelming her with a sense of despondent torpor. The short of it was that Arda was proposing a course of action that would prejudicially undermine Cambara's sense of privacy and encroach upon it drastically.

Cambara was disturbed. Not only was the plan, as her mother conceived it, unworkable, from her own point of view, it broke with a long-held understanding between them, reached during the young woman's teens, that at no time and under any circumstances would either of her parents ever make a decision that might affect her without first talking it over and clearing it with her. In her zealous attempt to remain her own person, Cambara stood guard over her own privacy, allowing no one to intrude upon it and permitting nobody, family or nonfamily, to step past its threshold unless she approved of it. What upset her no end was that she and her mother spoke and met often, especially after her father's death, and she was appalled that the old woman could entertain such a preposterous idea without taking Cambara's feelings into account, in this way entering sensitive territories beyond which she knew she was not to venture ever. Whatever had made Arda barge in without her time-honored thoughtfulness! Yet this was precisely what Arda had done. Cambara could see no sense in her mother's behavior, which was so unlike her. To put it another way, what her mother was now proposing did not tally at all with what she had alluded to when she invited her a couple of days ago to come and talk about the panacea to her daughter's professional success.

The languor that at the moment rippled through her whole body made her want to sit on the first available bench in the park where they were walking. From the expression on her face, you might have thought that someone had held a bottle full of ether to her nose—she was so breathless, and she was becoming drenched with cold sweat. It rankled Cambara that she, who always took exceptional pride in declaiming that she could read her mother's mind as easily as a fortune-teller reads a desperate client's particular needs, was being proven wrong. It was obvious one of them did not make the grade this time, and both would have to revise their views, which she was finding equally disturbing. And when, a little later, Arda seated herself at a small distance from her, Cambara's chest produced something between a chuckle and a snivel.

Emboldened, Arda took this as a sign she could resume speaking. She said, "The long and short of it is that I would like my nephew Zaak to join us here in Canada, legally."

Cambara was sufficiently vigilant to spot the catch, instantly feeling the sting in the tail of the key word "legally."

As irony would have it, planeloads of Somalis were arriving illegally at major ports or airports everywhere in the world, including Toronto, nearly all of them declaring themselves as stateless, and no one was turning any one of them back, not from Canada, anyhow. But Arda did not want her nephew to board an aircraft from Nairobi, where he ended up after fleeing the fighting in Mogadiscio, like tens of thousands of other Somalis, as a refugee. Being Arda, she intended to spread a carpet of welcome for him all the way from Nairobi, which he would leave, if at all, on a flight bound for Toronto, not as a refugee but legally as a spouse. She felt protective toward him, solicitously making sure that he was not vulnerable to harassment at the hands of the Kenyan immigration authorities, who were given to extracting exorbitant corruption money from Somalis relocating to Europe or North America. She did not want him to be apprehended at a midway location between Africa and Canada and returned to Nairobi. Making an already terrible situation worse, Arda, plodding, repeated everything from the beginning for the third or fourth time, as though she, Cambara, were a bit thick: that she would fly out to Kenya on a work-related visit to that country, link up with Zaak, who was waiting for a sponsorship to a third country, and bring him along as her spouse.

Without honoring any of what she thought of as her mother's harebrained plans with a reaction, Cambara stared at Arda, as if trying to puzzle out what her mother meant when she spoke of her making "a work-related visit" to Nairobi. What "work" did she have in mind? But she wished to deal with what bothered her most first.

Cambara said, "Why would I want to become the wife of a man I haven't thought about in that way or seen for a number of years?"

"That way, you'll do me a huge favor."

As she sought succor from the long silence, in which she considered the implication of her mother's statement, Cambara discerned a trace of her mother's fragrance in the form of *uunsi* scent, which Somali women traditionally wear to welcome back their husbands after a long absence.

She said, "Mother, you're too much to take."

"You'll be a wife only on paper."

"What would that make me in other people's eyes?"

"You can act as a wife, can't you?" Arda says.

"I don't want to act like a wife to Zaak."

"In the amateur theater you've been in," Arda said, "I've seen you act as a lowlife, seen you play the role of a wife to a man who is not your husband. Why can't you pretend to be a wife to Zaak? Pretend. Isn't acting your dream profession?"

If you had seen Cambara in her current state, you might have thought that she was strong on the outside and weak on the inside. Could it be that her mother was at last breaking her spirit? Was she about to relinquish all resistance? Admittedly, she had squandered her opportunity to set her mother right; maybe it was much too late to fend her mother off.

"Think of it as a favor to me, as I said."

"I wish you wouldn't ask that of me."

"There is no else I can ask."

"It is unfair."

"Let's think of it as your dare."

"It's unlike you to do this to me."

"A dare to an actor. A wife only on paper. Think."

Since they meant the world to each other, and since the word "no" seldom passed the lips of the one of whom the other requested a favor, Arda relied on the art of persuasion, softening the inner core of her daughter's defiance not with authoritarianism but with pleading. Do me a favor, please, my daughter! Now a species of unequaled sorrow was beginning to take residence in Cambara and was becoming a tenant with full rights. She felt as inanimate as a puppet with broken limbs and no wires to get it moving. Even so, she doubted if acting as a wife to Zaak—pretending and only on paper, as her mother put it—would lend a greater dare to her acting ability or sharpen it. Knowing herself, she might take it on as a challenge, if only to try and turn it into a triumph to revel in. She wished the idea had come from her, then she could have determined the parameters of the relationship and walked out of it when her heart was no longer in it. If the original idea had been hers, then she might have experienced the real thrill from the perspective of her creativity. As things now stood, she would have to think of what Arda might say before instinctually terminating it. Zaak was not worth the candle that her mother was burning.

"I repeat: You won't have to marry him."

Cambara put on a worn smile, exhausted from trying to weather the storm that was her mother. Her head between her hands, she said, "Take me through it all. Tell me what you have in mind, this panacea."

The way Arda explained it, it was all easy. She was to travel to Nairobi on a commission from CBS to interview the Somalis as they arrived and work with a local crew to film them. While there, she was to look up a counselor at the Canadian High Commission who would facilitate the processing of Zaak's application so he could join them in Toronto after half a year.

Cambara said, "Everything is arranged?"

"Everything."

Cambara said, "Still, I can't understand why I can't get him a visa with the help of this person whom I am to see? Why can't you sponsor him and have a temporary visa issued to him? Why his spouse?"

Arda said, "The drag, darling, is that most visas issued locally would have period limitation. Three months, half a year, and two years at most. There is the added hassle that you cannot renew visas issued outside Canada. The applicant will have to go out of the country and reapply to enter."

"Curse the day you became his aunt."

"My sweet," Arda said, holding her daughter's hand, "I have it from good authority that Somalis wanting to come to Canada will find it very difficult to obtain visas, temporary or long term, in Nairobi. I have close friends in the relevant departments, some of them neighbors right here in Ottawa."

"And marrying is the best option?"

"Two of my neighbors are on the case, as we speak, one of them having obtained the commission from CBS, the other liaising with the deputy high commissioner of Canada to Kenya, who happens to have gone to the same prep in Montreal, to make certain that your and Zaak's papers go expeditiously to the relevant desk."

"You've thought it all through, haven't you? Why doesn't he show up at the airport? He'll be granted refugee status the instant he puts his foot on Canadian soil, being Somali. Why can't he come the way the others are coming? He is not counterfeit currency or contraband."

After a pause, Arda says, "A favor to me. Your mother."

"Anyhow, where is the accursed fellow?"

"As we speak, Zaak has an apartment in the center of Nairobi, paid for on my credit card, via a Nairobi-based real estate agent. As his wife, you will be staying with him there."

The Ottawa sky, darkening, made Cambara pause and stare at it as if daring it to rain. She knew that once her mother had made up her mind and had worked out the details of a plan, the likelihood of her backing down or finding fault with it would be minimal.

"You know what, Mummy?"

"What?"

"You wouldn't do this if Dad were alive."

"Let's not go there."

"Would you?"

"I would find a way," Arda said.

"I am not so sure," Cambara said.

In the silence that came after, Arda busied herself, attentively removing dirt from under her nails. This put Cambara in mind of a mother monkey picking lice off her baby's head, then biting and chewing them.

Cambara asked, "Have you thought ahead, Mummy, on what Zaak and I must do about sleeping arrangements, first in Nairobi and then here, assuming that he is allowed to join me?"

"I have, indeed," Arda responded.

"Yes. Go on. Tell me more."

Arda said, "The imagination of most Somalis is prone to rioting as soon as they reflect on a situation in which a man and a woman share an intimate space alone, with no chaperone. They will assume that they are having it off."

"And you don't think we will?"

"I know you are your own woman."

"What does that mean?"

"I trust your judgment."

Talk of the imagination of Somalis going amok about sexual matters, as do all prudish societies. More to the point, could she, Cambara, share an intimate space with a man who might come on to her at the sight of her showered, with her favorite night cream on, walking into the bedroom and lying on her side of the bed, wanting to read? Could she sleep in such physical proximity to him? Will he respect her wishes, or will he pester her until she loses her temper and reminds him of his responsibility to himself: "All for your own good!" Tempted, will she make the first move? What of his bad breath? How would she bear it?

Just before dusk, mother and daughter returned from their long walk and talk, the one content, the other worn out, hot and bothered, and looking half alert to the goings-on, restless like a child having a bad sleep.

Between showers and a dinner together, Arda held out an envelope, which, when opened, Cambara discovered to contain an open return air ticket to Nairobi, a lot of cash in thousands of U.S. dollars, in small and large denominations, a yearlong and renewable insurance policy for two, with one of the parties described simply as "partner."

"Do you have dates by which I must leave?"

Arda replied, "We'll wait for the letter from the commissioning editor at CBS, who has assured my neighbor that she has put it in the post. Meantime I've booked your onward flight, window seat all the way. I'll let you decide on your return date."

"How sweet of you!"

"You'll be a better judge, since you'll be there."

"What else?"

"Damn. I clean forgot."

"What?"

Arda retrieved an envelope from the top of the sideboard, which, sitting down, she passed on to Cambara. "The yellow fever and cholera certificate."

"But I haven't had the jabs."

"It's all taken care of."

"How did you swing it?"

"I know how you hate taking your shots."

"Did you bribe somebody?"

"There are ways to get around such problems."

"You've left nothing to chance, have you?"

Cambara left for Nairobi as arranged. She hired a taxi from the airport and went directly to the place she was to share with Zaak. It irked her to be there exhausted from the long trip, having barely slept a wink because of a neighbor who talked endlessly. When she got to Zaak's door, he was so deep in sleep that it took her and two security men from the apartment complex almost half an hour to rouse him from it. She interpreted irritably the fact that he was unprepared for her arrival. Her irascibility did not augur well, and she knew it.

Within an hour, soon after a shower, she joined him in the kitchenette and right away noticed the telltale disfigurements in body and soul, which she would see more of when she met other Somalis who had just come from Mogadiscio: trauma born of desolation. She could not put her finger on why she felt uncomfortable in his company, maybe because she sensed that he was transmitting to her a flow of detrimental vibes, possibly without being aware of them. She held back and wouldn't get any closer to him, afraid that he might have transported some kind of contagion from the fighting that he had fled. To have the place to herself, she sent him out on an errand to the local general store with cash to buy basic groceries, including coffee, tea, and fresh milk. Then she had a couple of hours' sleep. She awoke to Somali being spoken and was able to work out in no time that it was the BBC Somali Service early-evening bulletin.

They dined out their first evening together at an Indian restaurant two doors away from the apartment complex, prepared to pay for it. Whatever attempts either made to get to know the other or at least to converse bore no positive results: They behaved as if they were a married couple who were under the torment of a recent estrangement and who had no idea how to overcome their mutual antagonism. At some point, she decided that sitting and facing each other in a restaurant when neither was saying much and she was too exhausted was not worth a plugged nickel. She asked for the bill, which she settled, and they left. When they got to the apartment, she retired to her room forthwith, wishing him good night.

From the following morning on, she relegated every other worry to a back burner, determined to throw herself into her work. She got up early and fresh, poised to activate contact with the coordinator of the Kenyan crew, a young woman who doubled as a cameraperson/driver, who told her to wait for her and her Somali-speaking colleague, who had arranged for the interview appointments, at the main gate.

Half an hour later, Cambara, dressed in a discreet manner, eager to get started, and holding her notes in folders in an old leather bag in preference to a showy executive case, was at the main entrance. She introduced herself to the two women in the beat-up Toyota. Compared to the one at the wheel—younger, and guessing from her name, Ngai, Kikuyu-speaking—who looked livelier, the Somali-speaking woman sitting in the back of the vehicle was massive and broad as a cupboard. It was she who said something first, speaking to Cambara in halting Somali that sounded as if she had learned the language in an after-work adult education class, unable to get her tongue flexibly around all the gutturals in Somali. Next to her—in fact, within reach of her stretched hand—were the tools of the cameraperson's trade, including a camcorder and other instruments. It was difficult for Cambara to know where she was from. The huge woman was carrying nothing save a kitschy handbag, pink like her dress and her shoes, the latter also in imitation leather. As soon as she saw her spread in the back of the vehicle, Cambara knew she wouldn't rely on her for much assistance.

Ngai was a bouncy, slim, very friendly and talkative woman in her mid-twenties, dressed in jeans and T-shirt, pigeon-breasted, head recently shaved, and with eyes as huge as stray UFOs spotted over a mountain at dawn. She was easygoing and full of life, and she and

Cambara hit it off immediately, each returning the compliment to the other. But she was a hairy driver and went into the blind bends rather perilously, often speeding when it was unsafe to do so and jabbering away mostly about the Somalis who, according to her, were everywhere, especially in the center of the city, and seemingly moneyed. It was obvious that Cambara took an instant liking to her.

"I kept telling my countrywoman sitting in the back that I am beginning to think that maybe Somalia is richer than our country, Kenya," Ngai said, when they were on the road for a few minutes.

"Why do you say that?"

"All the five-stars in Nairobi show they are booked for months, no vacancies," the thin woman said. "We always thought your country was much poorer than Kenya, kind of desert. You don't have petrol, do you? Like Libya or Saudi?"

She couldn't but shockingly admit how little Africans knew about one another's countries as a result, ironically, of their biased colonial heritage. After all, what did she know about Kenya or neighboring lands? Not as much as she did about Europe or North America. As part of her effort to create a good working relationship, she explained the class nature of the Somalis flying into Nairobi and putting up in five-star hotels and those who were arriving in dhows and overcrowded boats that docked in Mombasa and, because they were poor, were being treated as stateless and therefore as refugees. She placed the two sets of Somalis in the civil war context. "We'll learn more about them as we talk to more and more of them," Cambara promised.

Then her series of interviews started, and she worked from early until late on some days, seeing less and less of Zaak in the daytime and more and more of him and Ngai, who went with the two of them to restaurants, in the evening. Cambara introduced Zaak as her man to some of the Somalis they met, and the two of them put on an act for their own and Ngai's benefit. In private, Cambara kept him at a distance, and he didn't seem to mind that much.

Because of the topicality of the events unfolding in Somalia, Cambara had a select number of her pieces aired on prime time in Toronto, including some in which she interviewed the staff of the Canadian and British High Commissions as well as the embassies of a handful of Arab and European countries, where the Somalis were headed. The notices in the Toronto papers were favorable, one of them, *The Globe and Mail,* describing the pieces as "impressive, the job of a pro." There was a photo of Cambara, big enough to mount on her mother's bedroom wall as a memento.

The local media got into the act too, thanks to an anonymous call and a fax received from Ottawa alerting a couple of the editors to how Cambara's work "done in Kenya" was being received back in Canada. When one of the journalists from the *Daily Nation* rang for an interview, Cambara interpreted this as being part of Arda's string-pulling; the idea was to turn Cambara's visit to Kenya and the interviews she conducted into an article worthy of the front page of Kenya's high-circulation newspaper. A features editor specializing in writing about women's affairs in the continent did a piece on her for the paper, pictures and all.

The Canadian High Commission to Kenya jumped on the bandwagon after the appearance of the piece in the *Daily Nation,* and its titular deputy of mission, who had until then been of two minds whether to see her and for how long, invited her first to tea, which he later upgraded to lunch, because several of his colleagues at the station wished to join in. The high commissioner, who arrived late, was warm in his praise of her and had dessert and coffee with her as they chatted. When the luncheon formalities were over, she went down to the ground floor, where she met a woman whose name Arda had given her, the woman who would help with the speedy processing of Zaak's papers. Back home in Toronto, the woman who did not rate inclusion on the guest list of the deputy said that she, Cambara, was the envy of the fraternity of journalists because of her scoop. Herself, she saw her success as a one-off thing, on a par with the one-off she was doing for Arda by assisting Zaak in getting to Canada. She had no intention of becoming a reporter for CBS or a bed-sharing spouse to Zaak.

Several weeks of living in close proximity with Zaak neither excited nor palled on her. Her mother rang frequently, at one point teasing her that "it is not a bad thing to be a wife, when you think of it, is it? Especially when you are not subject to the tyranny of cooking, washing dishes and clothes, ironing someone else's pants, mending someone else's socks, and having babies and caring for them all on your own, without the husband ever lifting a finger." Three months later, when the news reached her that the papers might be issued any day now, Arda was still wondering how Cambara felt about being "a wife" to Zaak.

Cambara thought she was seeing the humorous side of things as she answered, "It feels like picking up a threadbare skirt at a flea market."

In Nairobi, their living arrangement remained unchanged. She had no room for closeness in private—each stayed in his or her section of the shared space—but when they were in the presence of consular officers, they made frequent use of such endearments that are de rigueur for a couple just married. If she were not a born actor, she thought, these on again/off again intimacies might have been difficult. It took a lot of nerve to get used to the juices of fresh love flowing, only for them to be turned off. This was clearly playing havoc on him. Arda explained, "Because women have more control over their bodies than men have over theirs."

Zaak's carefree lifestyle—never keeping his side of the bargain, never helping in cleaning the toilets or making the beds, cooking or shopping for food—filled her with anger, and on such occasions, she hated their life of pretense. In Toronto, she knew the stakes would be higher; it was her territory, and she had very many friends from whom she held no secrets. The question was, how would she cope?

She was delighted to prove that she could excel in anything at which she worked and was pleased that the TV documentaries had huge political and cultural relevance to all Canadians, more specifically the Somali-Canadians. The idea of having kick-started a belief, until then not prevalent among Somalis, that they could make a success of their presence in Canada was ascribed to her, but she still felt unfulfilled. She wanted to make it at best as an actor or alternatively as the producer of a puppet play, having been interested in puppetry ever since she took a summer course in the art.

As if to highlight her importance, a two-man TV crew from CBS turned up at the airport to interview Cambara. Beaming a smile the size of the cosmos, Arda, wearing a garland, carried a bouquet of flowers in one hand and in the other a placard with two V's traced in black felt pen, the words "Congratulations: Two Accomplishments" as large as the mysteries not yet revealed. That evening's prime-time news alluded to her marriage without mentioning the spouse by name, for neither mother nor daughter would divulge it to friends or relatives until "the lucky man" arrived.

As she combs her hair, which is an impenetrable tangle of kinks and a jungle of curls as dry as Somalia is arid, and as she struggles to persuade them to unknot, loosen up, Cambara remembers how on Zaak's arrival in Toronto, hush met hush. Only one person was there to fetch him from the airport, Cambara, and she was judiciously dressed, her face swaddled in a shawl. She waited in a corner, away from the placard-carrying taxi and airport limousine drivers picking up strangers, or the others meeting their friends and relatives. No journalists. Not even Arda was there. At her mother's suggestion, she condescended to give him a hug, following it with a brief kiss on the cheeks, just in case someone was spying on them, you never know.

She showed him to his room in the apartment, and just as she had said when in Nairobi, he too said, "I'll be okay."

But she asked, "What do you mean?"

"I'll pull my weight," he explained.

She thought of telling him "You are on your own," and then walking out and letting him figure out what she meant, or of challenging him on the practicability of his intentions. In the event she said, "You don't have to pull anyone's weight other than your own."

She expected him to come back with a smart quip. Instead, he surprised her. He said, "You won't have reason to complain."

In her head, she heard his statement differently, the refusenik part of her imagining a conversation between a wife-beater and his victim, the wife-beater vowing never to lay a finger on her and then giving her a worse thrashing the following day. However, the more accommodating part of her mind cast her thought in the generous spirit of a hopeless optimist, knowing full well that he would fail her.

"Same conditions as in Nairobi apply," she informed him. "What is different here is that I have a job to go to and a lot of friends. So be prepared."

She escorted him to the first obligatory interview with an immigration officer: This went well. Then she showed him the way to and from the school of languages, one day taking the bus with him, the following day the subway. She also pointed out where he might buy his take-away meals. He was euphoric for the first few weeks, doing his homework and, on coming home and finding her not there, cooking spaghetti and a sauce distantly tasting like Bolognese. She returned home later and later, way past dinnertime. At times, she would let herself in quietly after midnight, having spent much of the night with Raxma or other friends, only to sleep, then wake up before him and slink out. She took it upon herself to prepare their meals when they were together. Because she could not bear the thought of sharing his.

They put on a show for public consumption, now and then, to wit, when they were attending Somali wedding parties together, they could be seen touching, holding hands, and she would address him as "darling." And they signed cards as wives and husbands do. When they invited friends or acquaintances, she would make a point of almost picking a genuine fight with him, which was how she felt; she presumed others would see it differently: a wife nagging her husband. She was better at playing the part and was more comfortable in the role than he was. Asked by her mother how she was coping, Cambara complained that he was cramping her free-flowing lifestyle, crowding out all her favorite male friends, who wouldn't call her anymore or invite her to the parties she used to go to. Arda knew where she could phone her if she wanted to talk to her—at Raxma's—but she never bothered to enlighten Zaak about any of this.

Cambara soldiered on. Home alone and with no friends, Arda having discouraged him from frequenting the teahouses where Somalis in Toronto gathered and exchanged political gossip, Zaak watched some of the rental videos about Swiss and American immigration officers snooping into the private lives of aliens who applied for citizenship in their countries. He must have seen *Pane e Cioccolata*, in Italian with French subtitles, and *Green Card*, in the English original, to improve his language proficiency, so many times he could recite the exchanges of the actors.

Seven, eight months passed without much of a worrying event, when he gave himself a pass mark and was not so much impressed with his input as he was with the fact that he hadn't messed with Cambara or put her off. When she deigned to come home, cook, and eat with him, she would ask him questions about how he was doing. Not only that, she would not tell him much about herself, neither her work nor where she had been or with whom. He became progressively lonelier by the day, more and more bored, depressed.

One late evening, after he received confirmation that his papers had been approved, Arda rang to congratulate him and also to tell him to pick up a prepaid ticket at the airport counter and fly to Ottawa, where he would spend a few days with her. She must have touched a sore nerve, because he spoke rather uncontrollably about his aloneness, how, although tempted, he had not been in touch or mixed with other Somalis, worried that, in their probing, he might talk and then things might come to a pretty pass because of him letting on what was truly happening to him.

For some reason, maybe because he regretted sharing these confidences with his aunt and wished he hadn't, Zaak did not go. Cambara returned home early, expecting to find him gone, and was surprised to find not only that he was there but also that he was ready to lay into her. By then, of course, he had his papers and had done his language course and knew he could try his luck with another woman and also find a job. She reckoned she knew where his winded anger was taking him to, even though it may have been a one-off burst, an aberration, a detour from his norm.

He said, shaking with rage, "This is your world, and I am made to feel privileged to live in it the way a poor relative lives in the house belonging to his well-to-do kin."

She imagined several months on, when he might behave like a man with a mind to beat her up because he couldn't have his way with her. She saw his unwarranted behavior as being like the red traffic cones in the middle of their journey, warning her that danger lay ahead and that she must act promptly.

She was so incensed she left the apartment without packing even an overnight bag, flew to Ottawa late the same evening, and informed her mother that she wanted Zaak out. Arda agreed—now that he had all she had wanted him to have, his nationality papers—that the time had come for him to make a world where he might be comfortable to be his own man, live his own life, and marry if he had the wish.

He moved out of the apartment into another in a borough that was the farthest suburb from hers. He became an employee-consultant to a Toronto-based NGO, tasked with resolving clan-related conflicts in Somalia, used his first salary to rent a more convenient place, and then a few months later made a down payment for a two-bedroom apartment with a loan from the bank, underwritten by Arda, who also topped up his monthly mortgage payments. When he landed a decent-enough job that allowed him to settle the bills himself, Arda announced it was time that Cambara filed her divorce papers. Two weeks after they came through, Zaak surprised everyone, including his aunt, by taking a wife. Arda was hurt, because she had hoped he would let her in on his decision and consult her. Several years and three children—all of them girls—later, everyone except Cambara was in for another surprise: Zaak appeared before a court, accused of excessive cruelty to his wife and his three daughters, whom he beat almost to death.

Unwelcome among close family and his friends, Zaak relocated to Mogadiscio to be the local representative of the NGO with which he worked. He was made the coordinator of its peace-driven line and, from all accounts, redeemed himself, at least in the first few years.

Showered and dressed and ready to go down, if need be, to prepare a meal for the two of them, since she won't imagine eating his food, she tells herself that Zaak is a hopeless man in a ruined city. In Nairobi, while on the CBS job, she did not benefit professionally from his input on the documentary on the fleeing Somalis, about which he too had a lot to say. It was he who profited from her visit, becoming a husband to her and moving to Canada. Sadly, he reduced himself to a wreck and destroyed whatever opportunities might have come his way. He was a wife-beater, an abuser of children, and an ingrate fool. She supposes that this being the fourth time when chance brought them together— first as children, then in Nairobi, after that in Toronto, and now in Mogadiscio—she will endeavor not to make the same error, however one might define this.

Will she capitalize on her presence here in Mogadiscio and make something of herself, or will she waste the opportunity and return to Toronto empty-handed? If she hasn't let Arda know much about the plan taking shape in her mind, it is because she wants to be her own woman, not a marionette her mother might control from as remote a city as Ottawa. Only one other person is aware of the bare bones of her plan: her closest friend, Raxma.

Cambara hears a knock at the door. The tapping insinuates itself into the gap between the sounds made by the proverbial owl hooting and warning her to take care, and Cambara's recall of what took place between her and Wardi, her current husband.

"You are coming down?" Zaak asks.

She interprets this as "Are you going to cook?"

"Half an hour, and I'll be down," she says.

THREE

Cambara enters the living room, half of which is bathed in amber light, the other curtained away and covered in the somber darkness of a black cloth, similar in color and texture to that of a common everyday chador.

As she walks in, her hand instinctively inches toward and eventually touches her head, which is swathed in a head scarf. She is self-conscious that she did not ease the tangles in her matted hair, considering that she did not succeed in running a comb through its massy thickness before coming down. A smile crosses her face, but whether for her remembrance of Arda scolding her, as a girl growing up, whenever she slept without first neatening her hair and then grooming it or for seeming to have wrapped her head as if she were going into a place of worship, Cambara can't decide. Either way, she steps into the softening hour shaping into the shadowy twilight of a world with which she is not familiar.

After a while, she picks up Zaak's general whereabouts by scenting him in the manner in which a shark might become aware of blood in the vicinity. With pinpoint precision, she identifies his presence by his body odor before she actually sees him. He is the bare-chested, sarong-wearing, heavily perspiring figure with the distended belly sitting on a rug, legs extended in front of him and jaws active. His eyes, which he narrows to the size of the eyelet in a shoelace, are bleary. He leans languidly backward, with his right elbow resting on a cushion and his head, laid back, on yet another, the latter one propped up against the wall.

He is masticating, the pouches of his cheeks filled to bursting. His features retain the inebriated look of a commonplace and homeless alcoholic, chomping his swollen tongue, which now and then he mistakes for food. Her gaze falls on the uneaten, unopened bundles of *qaat*, now delicately wrapped up in wet dish towels to keep the leaves fresh. All around him are Coke bottles, two of them empty and on their sides, a third close to him. This one is open, and he takes sips now and again, and there are two flasks. She presumes one of them is filled with sweet black tea, the other tea with milk. There are also several bottles of imported mineral water.

He tries to get up, as though out of courtesy to her. His attempt to rise to the occasion, however, comes to naught, and he falls awkwardly backward, tipping over like a mechanical device that a child has wound up and that has run its prescribed time, in the process exposing his bare bum and balls before restoring what little there is to his sense of decorum. He lies on his side in obvious discomfort, with the part of his distended paunch that is now visible to her spilling over and spreading in a downward direction. The image of Zaak, relaxed and yet tensely waiting, brings to Cambara's mind the tortured posture of a hospital patient bent over and almost on all fours into whose rectum a nurse is introducing a suppository.

His demeanor discomfited, he pushes the morsel of *qaat* that he has so far chewed out of the way with his tongue, which, for a fleeing second, is visible in all its glory, fumbling, fondling, agitated, and slobbering too. She imagines a baboon fingering the mess of a just-peeled rotten banana and lavishly gorging on everything in sight. It is no wonder that despite the distance she has kept, Cambara, in a state beyond bearing, momentarily suffers a dislocation on account of the odors invading her senses. She has the bizarre feeling that she is at the entrance to a stable reeking of wet cattle dung mixed with horse manure. What is she doing here?

He says, "Will you join me?"

"And do what?" she asks.

She waits for him to say something before she goes off on a tangent in pursuit of her memory, which is now afloat and which leads her back into the murkiness of their time together. She journeys past that to a period after they divorced and he married a semiliterate woman, fresh from Mogadiscio with no family to speak of and no one to advise her.

Zaak fed terrible stories into the rumor mills of Somali Toronto, turning Cambara into a figure of fun. Asked why his and Cambara's marriage did not prosper, he would speak of how he had surprised her late one evening when she was frolicking in the nude with one or the other of her female friends; if browbeaten with persistent demands to tell it all, he would mention Raxma by name. When his fellow *qaat*-chewers would inquire what she was like in bed, Zaak would reply that the two of them did not get it off often, "once every six months, if that." Someone in the select audience, every member of which was from his immediate clan family, was bound to want to know more, and Zaak would oblige. To the questions of whether it was his fault and he had failed her, or whether she was just not interested in sex, period, or was frigid, he would deliver his reply with a cheeky finality: "Because she is a woman's woman, not a man's woman." Not that it bothered her what any of his mates thought of her, one way or another. But to think that she and Arda, through the latter's intercession with her, had done him such a good turn, which made it possible for him to obtain landed immigrant status in Canada on arrival, frankly she expected him to behave differently, at least amicably toward the two of them. Because in his attempt to paint a sullied picture of Cambara, Zaak was alleged to have insinuated that Arda had been the lover of the Canadian diplomat who, while stationed in Nairobi, staffed the Somali desk at the High Commission, the same diplomat, now stationed in Ottawa, who speeded up his own paperwork. He based his innuendo on something that Cambara may have said and that he either misheard or clearly misinterpreted: She had described Arda's relationship with the said diplomat as being "close." Of course, she never let on, nor did she ever breathe a word about this to her mother. What would be the point? Maybe it is in the nature of those who are denied sex or do not have enough of it to be so preoccupied with the subject that they view everything else through its distorted lens.

"What do you say?" he is asking loudly, chewing.

"About what?"

Her voice sounds like that of someone awoken from a deep sleep. Suddenly she comes to know where she is and with whom—the rank miasma emanating from Zaak's corner. I cannot endure it, I will die from this before long, she tells herself. This is torture.

"You see, my fellow chewers, all of them men, have declined to come, knowing that I have a female guest," he says. "You may know it, but I can tell you it is a darn curse to chew alone."

"No, thanks."

"I have a lot of *qaat*. Please."

The thought of joining him leaves her cold, worse than having the earlier shower a second time. All of a sudden, she is furiously scratching her head, her pulse throbbing speedily, and her ears filling with the sound of her deafening heartbeat. She looks at her arm, at which she has a dig, almost making it bleed, and then at him. From there, she looks at the bundle of *qaat* with the string undone and lying spread out, waiting for Zaak to consume it. Time was when only the Somalis from the former British Somaliland protectorate and those in the Somali-speaking Ogaden of Ethiopia chewed it, not those in the southern portions of the peninsula. When Cambara lived here, neither her parents nor any of her friends or acquaintances, in fact nobody she knew ever touched the stuff. Lately, however, the habit has become widespread, to the extent where even at clan council meetings, to which pastoralists are invited, the organizers pass it around, to make certain that no one will question the addled thinking of the attendees, not least that of the warlord and his deputies. Looking at Zaak now, she remarks a worrying dullness in his eyes, reminiscent of the stoned expression her English-language instructor, who was from Hargeisa, used to wear to the primary school here in Mogadiscio after an all-night chewing.

"Are you okay?" she asks.

"I'm fine."

"You don't look it," she says cockily.

"What makes you say that?"

"The unhealthy way you're sweating," she comments.

"You don't like sauna, à la tropics?" he says.

"This is no steam bath, and you know it," she says.

"I like my sauna this way," he says.

"How misguided can you be?" she says.

He is silent—a man alone with his fever.

She takes a measure of the low depth to which Zaak has descended since their last encounter several years ago in Toronto, when he spent a couple of nights in a police cell for beating his wife and maltreating his children. She raised and paid his bail at Arda's behest. When you combine his chain-smoking, his frequent chewing of *qaat*, and his living in unaired rooms stinking as awfully as the armpit of piglets, then you have a recipe for unmitigated dissonance between what is expected from someone you think you've known all your life and the unbecoming behavior they come up with when their situation has changed.

Maybe it all came down to the sad fact that Zaak did not deserve all the help he received from Arda and Cambara, as he could not appreciate their contribution from the time he joined them as a preteen. She was certain that he had been in a state fit to be airlifted from Nairobi and to enter into the contract of the anomalous matrimony soon after he and she ended theirs in an unbecoming acrimony. From the comments attributed to him, you would think that she and Arda had done him a disservice and that they ought to apologize to him, not the other way around. The memory of what he had done cut far deeper than she had imagined, and she hoped that he would be desperate for a sense of self-recovery in the same way she was trying to channel her grief into a positive outlook, which is what prompted her to come to Mogadiscio in the first place.

Now she holds his gaze steadily in hers until his eyes grow rheumy and he turns away. She does not feel sorry for him, nor does she empathize with him, because she disapproves of his current behavior as well as his unwarranted treatment of his wife and children. A bully goes for the jugulars of the weak, and his wife Xadiitha filled the bill: a young divorcée, barely literate and until then with no papers and no supporting family, who, in less than five years, gave him three girls. Cambara later heard unconfirmed reports that Arda had had a discreet hand in setting him up with Xadiitha. Rumor had it that Arda placed the first phone call to the family, from her and Zaak's subclan, with whom Xadiitha was staying—they treated her more like a servant than a valued member of their household—and then managed to remain in the background right until the day of the wedding, to which she contributed financially. That her mother had done this did not bother Cambara any more than it upset her when she first learned that Zaak had shown his true colors: that he was a violent man. If a cloak of indifference were drawn over Zaak's despicable mistreatment of Xadiitha; if it did not trouble Cambara enough either to confront him or to speak about it to Arda; if Arda made judicious interventions by having Xadiitha and the children visit for several weeks, it was because of self-ish reasons, both on her part and her mother's. (Cambara put it to Raxma: "I derive a sense of egotistic relief, knowing that he is no longer a nuisance to me but to Xadiitha.") She didn't need to elaborate that not only was Xadiitha dispensable but also she did not warrant Cambara and Arda's worry. Nor was the poor woman worth a moment's stress. If anything, Xadiitha was expedient, in that she helped them to rid themselves of Zaak, and there was no better way to achieve their purpose. Admittedly, it surprised her that her mother had never cred-ited him with being a wife-beater and a sadist to his offspring. The shame of it: Officials from the social welfare department intervened to move his children out of harm's way and provide them with protection. Looking back on it from that perspective, she did count herself lucky. Why, it might have been her lot too if the two of them had become man and woman.

She asks, "Did you say something about dinner?"

He looks at her in a wicked way, winking, and says, "My ambrosia is here, and therefore I'm not in the mood to eat anything else."

"Maybe because *qaat* has dulled your taste buds?"

She thinks how little we know people when they change and their circumstances alter, especially when the two changes occur concomi-tantly. Like it or not, she has no choice but to adapt to her new situa-tion. It is no easy matter to be in a city with which she is no longer familiar, what with the civil war still unfolding after more than a decade and her long absence from the metropolis. She cannot be sure that Zaak will take up the cudgel in safeguarding support of her if the city's adolescent boys loyal to the warlord occupying the family property turn lethal. He is less likely to offer no help if the warlord refuses to vacate it. Maybe it is the norm for the likes of Zaak to behave abnormally in atypical circumstances.

She says, "You were never friends with food, unless someone else tamed it. I remember you either making do with the same diet every single day or running to the nearest restaurant at the sight of unpeeled onions. I felt you fled from uncooked meat the way some of us might flee a lion."

"I've survived, as you can well see."

"In what condition?"

"I am not complaining."

When she can no longer focus her mind on these thoughts, she asks, "Where is the dinner that I must eat alone?"

"It is by the fridge," he says.

"Not in the fridge?"

"The electricity grid has been off since before midnight yesterday," he explains, "and the fridge is off. No point in keeping it switched on and no point in putting the food in it either."

Cambara looks up at the bulb overhead, burning.

Zaak follows her eyes, nods several times, and then offers an explanation. "The supply of electricity for this—the second phase—originates from a small two-star hotel which generates its own power. The manager has a little ice-making factory. We tap into it."

"How do you do that?"

"I make underhand payments to his workers," he says, pleased with his graft. "The water heater, my bedroom, and this section of the living room are connected to this supplier. I pay five dollars a month for tapping into the system."

"And to cook?"

"I don't cook," he says, as if proud of it.

Taken slightly aback because of the fierceness of his assertion, she makes as if to flatter him. She says, "Surely you've prepared the dinner you're offering me? If offered, I would eat *your* Bolognese, I am so ravenous."

"My dear, I couldn't bear the pressure you place on anyone who deigns to present you with the food they have cooked for you," he says. "You once described the sauce I prepared as looking like bird turd and tasting like chop suitable for a dog."

She does not remember saying that to his face, but this sounds like something she might have said to her mother over the phone, and he might have been eavesdropping on her long-distance conversation with her. It would be very like him to have done that. No matter, his remarks do not produce the result he may have expected, even though they are acerbic, and he delivers them coolly, as though he has rehearsed them with the intention of hurting her; the keenness of his observation seems to dull against her skin, which feels indifferent to its scathing maliciousness. She stares at him long and hard, maybe in an attempt to think of badinage of equal incisiveness. Alas, she cannot.

He goes on. "I've seen you terrorize chefs."

"What're you talking about?"

"Haven't I seen you turn your nose up at good food, lovingly and humbly served to you?"

"I don't recall ever making unfriendly remarks about your cooking," she says, "never to your face, anyway."

"Now we're talking."

He stares back at her in silence, his eyes reddening and his once-over smirking taking a more pronounced shape. He does not have to speak; his look says it all, in fact more than she can take at present or dare to cope with. This is the closest the two of them have ever come to sparring openly. If they have resorted to playing a power game—something they have never done before—then one of them has to concede defeat. There were the days when he avoided confrontations and withdrew into the tight-lipped taciturnity of equivocation, worried of what Arda might say or do to him. He was aware of his beginnings: that if it had not been for Arda, the likelihood of landing as many chances as he had under her patronage would have been either wholly nonexistent or minimal. Perhaps now that he is hanging on to the lowest rung of the ladder, he can't be bothered.

Like a hound that has tasted blood and is closing in for the kill, he says, "Time you grew up, time you began to live in the real world."

She feels her larynx seizing up, with her vocal cords failing to produce the slightest sound. However, she is still capable of processing the thoughts that her memory is transmitting. She thinks that when relationships between two persons who once thought they were intimate undergo major changes brought about by the presence or absence of sex that involve one party or both, the aggrieved one attacks the other with uninhibited animosity. She has been a victim of these types of assaults before—Wardi and now Zaak. She is alert to the contradictions and the unfairness of such reactions. Nonetheless, she understands where Zaak's animosity comes from. Then she imagines herself in the body of an elephant, which puts the animal's unparalleled strength into the equation; better still, given his physical shape, she likens herself to a sumo wrestler who lifts a challenger and drops him with accomplished flair. (Cambara is indebted to Arda, who is fond of comparing the strength of women to that of an elephant, which seldom makes full use of it, either because it does not know the extent of it and what it can achieve employing it or because its generous heart requires that it give more than it will ever receive in return.)

He resumes, "Time I welcomed you to the real world."

"As if I live in a world of my own manufacture."

"You lie to yourself; that's your problem."

"How dare you speak to me in that tone of voice?"

His silence serves as salt on her open wound.

"Tell me, why have you never spoken of this?"

"Because I've had no opportunity to do so."

"Why today?"

Zaak does not say anything.

"Why choose the very first day of my arrival in the city? Is it because you are aware that I am wholly reliant on you for guidance and for protection? Is that how to treat a guest?"

"I've been a guest all my life," Zaak says.

"Not in our house, you weren't."

"How would you know?"

She hurts deeply, her inside aching. "My mother raised you as if you were of her own flesh and blood."

"You're saying it yourself!"

"What? What have I said?"

"As if I were of her own flesh and blood, which I was not. You knew it and exploited it every way you could; she knew it and made a point of reminding me whenever I stepped out of line." He throws the words at her like darts on a dartboard.

"Born a coward, you'll remain one," she says.

She tries to recall a single instance in all the time the two of them lived together—as children raised in the same household or as a couple pretending to be man and wife—when she behaved as uncivilly toward him as he is doing right now. It doesn't surprise her that she cannot find any.

No doubt, she kept him at bay, refusing to share "intimacies" with him. Blame it on Arda for setting the terms. She believes she herself was impeccable in her dealings with him, albeit within the parameters of the contract with Arda and then eventually with him. As for the time spent together in their younger years, there is the matter of her excessive naughtiness. Her mother tried and failed to moderate her wildness or to make her behave as one might expect of a girl of her background. Zaak was such a dunce, only good enough to receive the school's booby prizes; she knew he would not amount to much.

"I want to move out," she shouts. "Right now."

"Go right ahead," he says. "Who is stopping you?"

Silent but not rueful, she stares at him in fury.

"Where will you go to if you leave?"

"A hotel."

"Do you know of one?"

"I do."

Kiin's Hotel Maanta, run by Raxma's friend.

"Do you know how to get there?"

This is a taunt to his tone of triumph, and both know it. She does not respond to it, not only because she has no idea where Hotel Maanta is in relation to where she is but also because she is peering into the ugly face of defeat. Her eyes bore deep into his: how she hates him. When she finally hits the concrete reality of so much unyielding contempt in his come-on leering, she says, her voice sounding like that of an exhausted boxer not returning the licks raining on him, "I still don't want to be here."

"Wise up, woman," he says.

"Don't talk to me in that uppity tone."

"I'll talk as I please when I please," he retorts.

She repeats "I should've known" several times. Then she lapses into the dejected silence of the routed, her tiredness suddenly evident all over her body, the look in her eyes dimming, her features twisted into a grimace. She consoles herself, all the same, that come tomorrow she will fight back once she has studied the lay of the land, and will have fallen back on her resolve to recover her dignity.

"You won't want to be anywhere but here and with me, if you know what's good for you."

"I thought I lived in a world of my manufacture?"

"You do."

"One in which I lie to myself?"

"You do."

"In which case I know what is good for me."

"So, what or who is good for you?"

"Neither you nor your place is good for me."

"Here's what I will not do," he says, bossing her.

"What?

"I will not allow you to compromise your safety."

"Why should my safety matter to you?"

"It matters to your mother," he says.

"And why does my mother matter to you?"

"Your mother thinks of me as your host."

"And so?"

"I don't want her to be disappointed in me."

"My safety, my foot!"

He disregards her fury with a shrug and says, "If you wise up, you will not embark on a foolish adventure into the dark unknown of Mogadiscio's dangers. You will not want to risk your life just to prove a silly point. Be under my roof; be my guest; be as comfortable as you can, despite the adverse circumstances. Consider your safety. If I were you, I would put up with the discomforts that are one with your safety. Tomorrow, I will be more than willing to drive you anywhere you like until you find a good and clean enough hotel, which will serve you quality food and which will meet your approval. And the Lord knows there is no such place in this whole city."

She is not certain if he intends to redeem himself when he advises her not to do anything rash, or if what he wants is to heap further humiliation on her head. Who would have thought that Zaak had it in him to harbor so much resentment, keep so much venom bottled up inside him for so many years? Who would have imagined that he would spring it all on her at the least expected moment? Maybe it was naive to assume that Zaak would remain forever beholden to every member of her family. She is confident that if push comes to shove, she will be able, eventually, to square up to Zaak's comeuppance and will relish the prospect of proving herself worthy of her calling as a woman of high resolve, an actor of tremendous potential. What she can't decide is how much bearing all this will have on her. She says, "Promise to tell me why you are doing this one day. For my own edification."

"Wardi has been in touch," he says.

She says, "That is of no concern to me."

"I think it is," Zaak assures her.

"What is the relevance?"

"I've heard his side of the story."

"So what?"

"What's yours?"

He moves as though he is preparing to launch into another of his skirmishes, but she raises her right arm in time calmly to stop him from saying anything. When she thinks she has imposed her way on him, she touches her fingers to her lips, as if to seal the contract with the silence that is about to become her destiny. She stands stock still, wincing, her arms akimbo, in the likeness of a bird readying to take off. She makes as if to depart.

Then she says, "Good day to you."

"Wait, don't go yet," he says.

Cambara goes to her upstairs room to think things over.

FOUR

How can she cure her grief in the briny condiments of her tears when her secondary fury—directed at Zaak, and consequent upon his churlishness—is so overwhelming that her primary anger at Wardi for what he has done pales in comparison? Truth is, she will at no point question the wisdom of coming to Mogadiscio, nor will she regret it. However, what course of action must she take to undo Zaak's misdeed?

She believes that whatever else she does, she will not want to allow her rage to go on a rampage and thereby ruin her chances of success, compelling her to give in to the allure of remorse. There is no sense in admitting defeat hastily either, especially to losers like Zaak and Wardi, or in throwing her hands up in the air in despair. She is determined not to permit Zaak's declared animosity to dampen her newfound bravado, which is the result partly of her having beaten Wardi in his dastardly game and partly of her deciding to come home, so that among other things she can reclaim her family property.

She wishes she had Raxma close by or had the opportunity to ring her up right away so she could bring her up to speed about Zaak's inappropriate comportment. Of all the people she knows and with whom she might discuss such a sensitive topic, Raxma is the one whom she trusts fully and whom she thinks might advise her on the best approach to extricating herself from the complex tangle of relational webs—as intricate as they are destructive—into which Zaak has led her unawares. Cambara replays in her mind Raxma's emotional valediction, spoken as they hugged each other good-bye at the Toronto airport, to

which Raxma had given her a lift. Raxma had promised that she would
not give up her attempt to locate someone who might have functioning phone numbers for Hotel Maanta, owned and run by Kiin, a very
close friend of hers. However, when Cambara called her from Nairobi,
Raxma had been sorry to report that the two numbers she had often
used to reach Kiin might have become faulty, because they had been
permanently busy. She urged Cambara to set her mind at rest, though.
She was very optimistic that in a couple of days she would call her with
Kiin's coordinates because she was continually ringing the number
she had for Kiin as well as trying to contact some of her business associates in Abu Dhabi who might help. If, in the meantime, Cambara
obtained a local SIM card, then it would be worth her while to try the
numbers herself. Raxma, who was more familiar with matters Somali,
in that she had kept abreast of political events in the country from
which she had been away a mere decade, as compared to Cambara,
who had been away for almost two decades, explained that there were
some telephone network providers based in Mogadiscio with no international connectivity. Alternately, Cambara could call her once she
was connected and had her own number and, if there was need for
her to make a reverse charge, then Raxma would place the return call
immediately.

Now she remembers, with charged emotion, Raxma's words of
farewell. "We are here for you, our darling, you can rely on us," Raxma
assured her. "You want to be flown out at half a day's notice to Nairobi
or anywhere else, let me know. Keep in touch—that is very important."

Cambara counts herself lucky in many instances. Lucky that, to
date, the world has been kind to her by offering her never-ending possibilities. Lucky that she has Raxma, who, short of acting like an older
sister, has taken on a surfeit of tasks and helped out as her most trustworthy ally when the Zaak or Wardi affairs were difficult. Lucky that
Arda, despite her occasional bloody-mindedness in the roughshod manner in which she deals with her daughter's crisis-ridden liaisons, is one
with her unceasing love and her untiring care as her mother. Indeed,
if there was any time in her life when Cambara could very well benefit from the support of someone to advise her on matters highly personal, a friend to whose counsel she would pay heed, then today is
the day.

Cambara was always impressed that Raxma's approach to all the affairs of the heart was, to a large degree, informed by the pragmatic sense of a mother who has had to raise a set of twins when her irresponsible husband abandoned her for a younger woman. A good, patient listener with a long-term outlook, Raxma had a canny way of knowing when the right time to intervene had dawned and how to go about doing so, which words to use and what to suggest, seldom giving in to the schmaltzy side of an argument. Her every action was deliberate, calculated to improve on what was there before she came on the scene, her counsel tailored to be of advantage when or if similar situations arose in the future. Raxma, trained as a medical doctor in Odessa, was turned down by the Canadian Medical Association when she applied for a license to practice in Canada. Because she would have had to requalify, needing no less than three years to graduate, she and her husband agreed that she would give up her profession for the sake of their school-going set of twins, which she did reluctantly.

Her former husband, on the other hand, had marketable qualifications: an undergraduate degree in gynecology, in addition to a postdoctoral in a related subject from Germany. He became one of the few Somalis to whom the CMA granted a license, and he was in high demand, serving as a consultant to two hospitals. Well paid and highly sought after as he was, it was not long before world bodies with UN backing, including WHO, recruited him for assignments here and there, eventually posting him to the Indian subcontinent as its representative. By then, his professional success and her apparent lack of self-fulfillment became the third party in their lives, which he gradually opted out of. He started having affairs, first with the women working with him as assistants and then zeroing in on one of them as his mistress.

On discovering these shenanigans, she went about her business in a mature style, neither letting on that she knew about his infidelity nor displaying any signs of tension or unease in their day-to-day intercourse. She put the two boys in a boarding school and then, thanks to a lawyer, put the screws to her wayward husband, making him agree to a large one-time alimony payment and, in the bargain, taking possession of their five-bedroom family house. Then, with the money in the bank, topped off with a guaranteed loan, she set up an import-export business with an office she ran from home and, when necessary, traveled back and forth between the various cities she had to get to, mostly in the Arabian Gulf. Rarely, however, did she spend more than two consecutive weekends away from Toronto, making certain she was available for her two sons, especially when they were younger. She brought her elderly mother and a younger half sister, almost Cambara's age, to fill in for her in the event she did not get back in time. Now that both boys were at universities—one at Guelph, the other at McGill—the responsibility of looking after their mother and running the house fell to her younger sister. In addition to her important role in their household, Raxma remains the main bedrock to a community of Somali women, among whom Cambara was proud to be one.

The two women first met barely a month after Cambara had set up a makeup studio with seed money from her mother, following two years of apprenticeship at another one similar in conception but different in its clientele. Cambara intended hers to appeal to the up-and-coming young black professional classes, in particular the women, who, as a group, were conscious about their appearance and wanted to "improve" the flow, ebb, and texture of their hair. Many of these women, being of an independent cast of mind, were more likely to be single, even if they were of the view that the reconstructed men with whom they might be prepared to set up a life and a home were seldom easy to come across. Because of the particularity of their status, the women spent a lot of money to look good.

The paint on the inside walls was still fresh, the patrons rare, the business lean, when one afternoon Raxma walked in, not so much to pay for the services of a makeup artist as talk. How she talked, as if at the touch of a button, about the plans she had the moment Cambara had seated her at a chair and, wrapping a white cloth around her front, asked, "And what have we got here?" For one thing, Cambara did not expect Raxma to answer the question, which to her was another way of saying "What can I do for you?" or "How would you like me to be of service to you?" For another, she was equally intrigued, once the flood of words suffused with charged emotion sluiced out of the new client, when, by way of introduction, she presented herself as "Raxma" and mentioned a friend of hers and Cambara's, a name that rang no bell in the memory of her listener. Prompted by Cambara, Raxma talked not as if she were sad or enraged, not at all; she spoke as if she were talking into a Dictaphone from which someone else would transcribe her chatter into decipherable text. Even so, she did not pass up the opportunity and therefore spoke quite openly to Cambara about her agitated state of mind, as if they were old friends. Raxma explained that she had just discovered that her husband of many years had been cheating on her with one of his assistants at the hospital where he worked as a consultant. The expression on Raxma's face, as she talked, seemed snarled up into a sudden tangle of indefinable emotions. Moreover, her wild gestures, now that Cambara had meanwhile removed the cloth from around her and freed Raxma's hands to gesticulate liberally, alerted Cambara to a deep hurt. This set Cambara's mind to do what she could to hearten Raxma, at least gladden her day.

Remaining inside but not drawing the curtains, Cambara put up the "Closed" sign and waved away a couple of potential customers. Face to face with Raxma, she listened some more as her newfound friend elaborated on the agonized articulation of her suffering. Half an hour later, they left the studio and together—with Raxma still talking and Cambara attentively listening—went to a café where Cambara was a regular; sat in a corner, away from all the others; asked for tea, coffee, and cream; and chatted. They remained there until the lights came on, had a light dinner, and then drove in their respective cars to Cambara's apartment, where they had more drinks.

Raxma rang her two boys, addressing them by their pet names, into which she put as much affection as she could into each of the syllables they comprised. It was clear that the two boys were the world to her and that she would not do anything to harm them, including denying them the filial right to live together with both parents. Before ringing off, she suggested, since she was coming home late, that they order a pizza and pay for it from the cash kitty. They were very happy to do that. Of course, she knew they would watch TV all night, if they could, and not, as they promised, do their homework. When she returned from speaking to her two boys on the phone, Raxma was saying "Good riddance to bad rubbish" in the improvisatory manner of an actor rehearsing a part for the first time.

Hesitant to ask what Raxma meant, Cambara looked away, obviously pretending that she did not hear anything. Raxma hung her head in pensive silence, narrowing her eyes into slits of utter concentration. Apparently, she had made a snap decision in the instant between the time she suggested that the boys order a pizza and the minute she got back into the living room with Cambara. Raxma resolved to send the boys off to boarding school, and she shared her impulsive choice with Cambara.

"What will you do with the time and freedom that you earn from this?" Cambara asked.

Raxma said, "Do you know a lawyer?"

As luck had it, Cambara had a lawyer friend, a neighbor she had known for a number of years. Mauritanian-born Maimouna was a die-hard feminist who had experience as a litigator for the cause of women in the Canadian courts. A powerhouse, Maimouna was dedicated, loyal to the wisdom attributed to Simone Weil that if there is a hideous crime in modern society, it is repressive justice against women. She saw her principal role as a fighter for women's causes, especially the Muslim wives who often had a raw deal in Canada. A patron of the studio and someone she had known for much longer, Maimouna frequently dropped in on Cambara both at work and at home.

"When would you like to meet a lawyer?"

"As soon as possible."

"Would you like me to present you to one?"

"Yes, soon, and preferably a woman."

"Consider it done," Cambara said.

"Then I will take him to the cleaners."

"After which?"

"If successful, then I'll work toward settling on an occupation," Raxma said. "The idea of getting into the import-export business appeals to me. I will have to see how much money I am able to raise from taking someone I know to the cleaners."

She did not find it curious or annoying that Raxma never, ever mentioned her husband by name—something, Cambara knew, Somali women who were displeased with their spouses tended to do as a way of self-distancing. Such women referred to their spouse only in the third person, as "he" or "him," without once allowing his name to pass or, rather, sully their lips.

A phone call half an hour later sufficed to get Maimouna to come to Cambara's apartment for a chat and a bit of salad, and before midnight, the lawyer agreed to represent Raxma. All told, it took about nine months to set a date for the preliminary hearing of the case and less than a year for the couple to reach an out-of-court settlement. In the hiatus, Cambara saw a lot of Raxma and her two boys, spending a lot of her free time with them or their mother. All four of them would drive to Ottawa in one vehicle and visit Arda on long weekends. As it turned out, Raxma was the only person other than Arda who was privy to Cambara's true thinking about becoming a spouse to Zaak. It was during these early days that Cambara filled her in on what was happening and Raxma chose to stay protectively in the background, reserving the right to remain circumspect until Zaak's arrival in Toronto. She displayed untiring loyalty to Cambara and held her hand all through her ordeals. When it came her turn to help Cambara, whose life was upended, Raxma stepped in and provided companionship and other forms of encouragement to speed her recovery. She pronounced her catchphrase—"Good riddance to bad rubbish"—on the day Cambara booted out Zaak. Then Raxma filled a designer's clay pot with water, and, to the accompaniment of ululation and loud drumming, Cambara, at her behest, took a stick to it, breaking it, so that the water, now set free, might flow out, a symbolic enactment of a woman's release from eternal bondage. They had a weeklong party, together celebrating their status, two women rejoicing their newly enfranchised respective conditions, with Raxma decidedly backdating the coming of her freedom, because it was time, she argued, that she commemorated the event with a reinvigorated sense of accumulated joy.

Before long, Cambara needed Raxma's wise admonition, having made the acquaintance of a charmer named Wardi, whom she described as her one and only infatuation ever. As Cambara gushed about him in a midnight phone call from Geneva—Cambara did not ring her mother to share the news until several hours later—her advice took the shape of a warning wrapped, with flair, in an offer that Cambara could not refuse. Not only did she reprove her friend to stay clear of the fellow under whose magic spell she had fallen, but she also agreed that were Cambara to respond positively to her own heart's dictates and choose to disregard her advice, then she could rest assured that this would not upset her at all. She would continue to support her, regardless. She concluded, "Don't be deceived by his honeyed tongue, but if you feel you are in love and therefore a fool, then I am all for you, my sweet."

Arda, on the contrary, was unflattering in her first comments about Cambara's choice of love, her negative response being instantaneous, visceral, scurrilous, and as insalubrious as a city surrounded by swamps fraught with ill-favored affliction. When Cambara's pleas to talk about it sensibly met with condescending rejection and Arda resorted to making threats that she would have nothing more to do with either of them if Cambara went ahead with this madness, Cambara found a way of bringing their conversation to an end without being terribly rude. But not before Arda had this to say: "How can you be besotted with him when you've barely known the man for a week? I have other plans in place for you, my love. Unfortunately, my plans have no room for a loser like him. Let's be clear about that."

"It is my life, Mother, and I will do with it what I please, with or without your approval," Cambara retorted, and hung up the phone.

Raxma met Cambara at the airport, welcoming her back from Geneva with flowers and comforting hugs. Then she had her to dinner that very evening, and, for the first time ever, Cambara embarked, sadly, on mapping out a plan that would alter her life from that time forward, without Arda occupying center stage. Raxma had the privilege of providing what assistance Cambara needed to design the framework, which would facilitate Wardi joining her in Toronto as her spouse. Further input, from a legal point of view, came from Maimouna, whom they consulted shortly thereafter. Meanwhile, convinced that Cambara would come to her senses, what with an ocean separating her from her flame, Arda found herself refusing to negotiate her way out of the tight corner; instead she dug in, unwaveringly adamant that they would see which of them would eat humble pie. The impasse was in place—Arda continuing to help financially and Raxma serving as a link in their indirect contact—until long after Wardi's arrival and almost three months after Cambara's visit to the maternity clinic, when she learned that she was pregnant. Then Arda summoned her to visit, alone. Pushing aside their differences, without either alluding to what had transpired, Arda and Cambara got cracking. They did their window-shopping, their arms linked, and Arda showered

Cambara and the unborn baby, sex yet unknown, with gifts galore. Truce holding, Cambara flew back to Toronto, joyous. A fortnight later, Arda summoned Wardi to Ottawa, again alone, to assess his trustworthiness. Pressed to pass her judgment, Arda described him as "crafty, with long-term chicaneries hatching on a back burner." No one dared tell Arda that Cambara had put his name down as a co-owner of the apartment in which they lived. Dalmar's birth brought Arda fully into the swing of things.

Cambara might have relaxed herself into believing that she was on to good stuff, especially after motherhood and Wardi landing a job with a law firm, thanks to Maimouna, if a curse had not looked upon her with the disfavor: He found other women an eyeful and strayed into other beds. She stepped away from confronting him, at times reasoning that neither would win and that Dalmar, their son, would ultimately be the loser, at others thinking ahead about what Arda might say in her riposte. Then, one day, she left her son, by this time an exuberant, bumbling nine-year-old, in Wardi's care, only to learn barely six hours later that afternoon that Dalmar had drowned in the pool while Wardi was giving Susannah, his host and law partner, a tumble.

On hearing the news of Dalmar's death, Cambara froze, at first refusing to bring herself to accept it, not even after she identified the corpse at the mortuary. Her heart stopped in reaction to the gravity of what had happened: that he would no longer be in her dreams, living, active as the young are, loving, and seeing her in his dreams. Wardi was to blame; so was she, come to that. She crumbled to her wobbly knees, screaming obscenities, mostly at herself, for entrusting Dalmar into his irresponsible hands. She felt so incapacitated that she disintegrated, her paralysis complete. No "I told you so" from Arda, who was impeccable in her self-restraint, no self-satisfied remarks either.

It was not long before Wardi wore his crafty colors to the courts, cashing in on the deed declaring him the co-owner of her apartment, which he now proposed they sell. From then, he inspired nothing but derision in her, and she showed her aversion toward him in both private and public. When he got physical, hitting her, and walked away from her with a swagger, she struck him more fiercely, paying him in the currency of his aggression and causing him pain where men hurt most, in the whatnots.

The surprise stunt Zaak has pulled on her now prompts further anger, which works its way into her joints and affects her muscular coordination. By turns murderous—when she thinks about Wardi—and mortally offended—when she thinks about what Zaak has said—her body goes rigid at the thought of resorting to violence, something she has done once before, against Wardi, when he struck her in the face. Her temperature rising, her posture becomes that of a kung fu master balling his hands into fists and gearing up to hit back. Scarcely has she talked herself into calming down when the idea of beating Zaak to a pulp dawns on her. She relives in her memory the one and only occasion when she hit back, in anger and in self-defense. It troubles her to imagine what might become of her if she carries out retaliatory measures every time someone upsets her. How can she square her liking to settle arguments through violent means with her claim that she has come to Somalia, among other things, to put a distance between her and Wardi? And to mourn, in peace, while living in a city ravaged by war.

Looking back on it all, Cambara decides that the one fundamental fault in Wardi's character is that he presumed that just because Cambara was a woman, she was more vulnerable in the event of a fistfight than he was. He discovered to his detriment, however, that fury insinuates itself into the fists of a woman who has been spurned and then struck in the face, with the adrenaline resulting from the spleen so far accumulated turning into brute strength. And with so much suppressed wrath going round, the scorned party might transform the gall gathered in the pit of her pique into brawn as powerful as that of an elephant going amok.

She remembers training in martial arts for years in secret, ever since marrying Zaak, whom she wrongly assumed might one evening have a go at fighting his way into the privacy of her bedroom and then imposing his uncared-for sexual appetite on her. As it turned out, he did no such thing, either because he lacked the necessary pluck and pulled back just in time before pushing his luck with her or because he feared what Arda might do to him if he had. To be sure, there was a great deal of subdued aggression implicit in Zaak's behavior, but he did not take it out on her; he did so only after he separated from her and married a poor woman whom he could ill-treat with impunity. That Cambara eventually let loose the animal wildness of her bottled-up decade-old rage toward Wardi did not surprise those who knew her full story. That she got the better of Wardi, beating him to near death, was a testament to a spurned woman's fury mutating her pent-up anger into strength.

He hit her first, punching her unjustifiably hard in the nose and face, cutting her lower lip in the process and making it bleed copiously. Tasting her own blood, she went berserk, and for a moment behaved wildly, striking him fast, fiercely, and with compound interest. She flipped—no doubt about it—and acted as though possessed of a moment's madness, hers the unfocused gaze of the disoriented. She could not define what occurred, taking hold of her by the throat, as it were, between him striking her, her turning away, and tasting the blood of her cut lower lip. Barely had she apprehended that he had crossed yet another line, smacking her, when she misconstrued what she perceived to be two ants—one crawling up her spine, the other going down the small of her back—which, in reality, were two drops of perspiration of such concentration, not ants. Itching, her fingers searching, she touched the moisture, and then she understood that she had confused an inanimate thing with a living one.

She was concentrating on attending to her bleeding lower lip when he hit her yet again on the back of the head, flooring her, and kicked her some more in the teeth. While she was still down, he informed her that he would be leaving for a long weekend and that when he got back he did not want her to be in the apartment—her own apartment, bought with her mother's money—because he was selling it and collecting his share. Moreover, she knew where he would go and with whom. She felt frustrated at his attempt to swindle her out of what had been legally hers. So that was where trust got her?

She recalls dabbing at her cut lip and staring at her index and middle fingers now coated with her own blood. After a moment's reflection, she snapped, seeing in her blood her own failure and the failing of many a woman. She did not like herself one bit. No, she was not jealous that he was off for the weekend with his Canadian mistress. She was angry. And to her, there is a difference between being jealous and being angry, but she was in no mood then to articulate her sentiments. The fool could have gone where he pleased, alone or with someone else; she did not care. He was after all a despicable creature. She was displeased more with herself than she was with him, for having allowed these and many other terrible things to be done to her, or for things to go so badly that she felt hard done by them. Above all, she found it impossible to countenance that her son had drowned in the swimming pool of his legal partner and paramour while they were having it off in the main bedroom, which was in the other extreme of a sprawling house.

The memory of hitting Wardi now intrudes upon her consciousness. She remembers how she struck him with a passion that contained in it a vengeful rage wrapped in contempt, the consequence of a most terrible upset bottled up for a very long time. Did she train secretly in martial arts for several years in preparation for the day when, their embittered relationship having reached a head, she might administer the knockdown blow at short notice? Of course, she wanted him to know that she was no pushover. And what better way to prove this than to give him back his own bitter medicine, humiliate him because he demeaned their oneness, neglected to attend to his son by keeping an eye on him when in the pool. As she laid into him, the image of burying Dalmar, then running into Wardi's mistress first at the cemetery and later at her home: these gathered in her mind as storms do, culminating in a riotous spleen that deactivated her brain before it exploded in a total breakdown. Maybe this explains it all: why she became dysfunctional, sanctioning the beast in her to take charge.

Dissecting with her now sharp mind the detritus of her rage then, she reasons that maybe she paid him back with higher interest than was his due. She might have killed him if she had not changed her mind at the last minute, stopping just in time, well aware that a knife, however small or dull, is a lethal weapon if one places it in the hand of a mother whose only son drowned in the swimming pool of her husband's lover. She feels that her rage accrued into a motive, justifying the administering of a fatal blow. In the end, she caused him a lot of pain. Wardi lay motionlessly on his back, his body instantly sown with a copse of bruises, some growing as big as grapes, some assuming the hardness of cacti, some becoming as patulous as malignant pustules soon after, and others ending up as knobbly as the fruits of a baobab tree.

After knocking him down with her karate punches, Cambara was at first overwhelmed with a sense of haplessness, not of regret but of indecision. Then euphoria, the excitement of accomplishing a feat of which she had unconsciously dreamt many a night for a long time. When it came to replacing her feeling of remorse, she reminded herself that she had wanted to knock him unconscious one day. In fact, a part of her now wished that Wardi's mistress had been with them and had seen her lover on his knees, begging. This filled Cambara with a considerable sense of elation.

Aware now that their marriage was as good as over, she knew too that there was no possibility of patching things up or salvaging it, no benefit to be gained from displaying kindness to a fool knocked out and wallowing in self-reprimand, no mileage in making rash decisions that would inconvenience her in the end either. Take note: No face-saving ploys, please. The time to dispense with Wardi altogether had come. Only Cambara must do so on a caveat of her own stipulation. What about Zaak? How is she to deal with him? Cambara will have to wait, look at it from many vantage points, and then decide; there is time for that yet, a lot of time.

In her recall, Wardi's misshapen face boasts of swollen eyes moist at the edges, like a Styrofoam cup on which someone has inadvertently trampled. Nor does he dare show his ugly, puffed-up face to anyone, nursing his ego and his physical wounds with a huge sulk, silent, whereas she drives herself to the emergency ward in a hospital in the neighborhood, with her lips as thick as Dunlop tires. The nurse attending to her suggests that she press charges against the wife-beater, but Cambara lies, describing herself as the victim of a mugging. She receives half a dozen stitches, and the doctors discharge her with a warning that, given the viciousness of the cuts, she will do well to look after herself and to call the police if the dangerous man poses any further threat to her.

In the event, Wardi does not go away for the weekend with his paramour as planned, scared she might ask how he came by those ugly bruises. Wardi and Cambara share the same space for a few days, hardly communicating; they eat and cook separately for much of this interim period, but avoid each other. For her, the modus vivendi put her in mind of the arrangement she had worked out with Zaak, each keeping to his or her part of the apartment. They would come together for the sake of decorum whenever one of their relations or friends visited or when they had to honor a friend getting married. Nor did Cambara speak of the fistfight; who started it, who bled more, who won, and who lost what. Privately, she felt she was the one hard-done by what happened, especially after the death of her son.

Then, one morning, Cambara wakes up looking like a cat in distress, and, with her gut troubled, her mind unsettled, and smarting because of her heart, which hurts terribly, she resolves to put the greatest of distances between herself and Wardi. Long discussions ensue to which Arda and Raxma are parties, now with one alone, now with the other, and later with both. Security tops the agenda. Arda is of the view that no property in present-day Mogadiscio is worth the risk involved in its recovery. Raxma is inclined to hold the opinion that a visit now will be all to the good, may even have therapeutic value. But where will she stay? They agree to look deeper into every aspect, think of where she might put up and with whom, and then meet again.

Cambara buys a one-way ticket to Mogadiscio after she hears back from both Arda and Raxma. While Arda insists that she will okay the trip on condition that she stay with Zaak and vow to return immediately in the event of the slightest danger, Raxma promises to contact Kiin, who owns a hotel and who, she is certain, can provide her with backup security and accommodation.

Her eyes half open, clouded from exhaustion, Cambara stirs at the sound of the kettle singing downstairs and calling to her host, saying to him in kettle-speech, "Come and make your early tea, Zaak." She lies motionless in the bed, revisiting her first days with Wardi in Geneva, when love was good, and the two of them made it with the leisure of a man and a woman who could not have enough of it or of each other.

Wardi and Cambara met by chance, in a café. Both had been stood up by the person each was waiting to meet: She had an appointment with a screenwriter working on a script about a Somali refugee being deported from Switzerland, and Wardi was to meet with an immigration lawyer to help him present his case to the refugee authority at the canton of Geneva. Drawn to each other as two lost souls, each sought salvation of some sort in and from the other. For Cambara, it was holiday time; she had just completed a two-week film shoot funded by a Swiss-Canadian outfit. Wardi, for his part, was a penniless Somali, eager to receive the papers on which his refugee status in Switzerland depended. She was charmed with immediate effect, and she felt there was no way to undo that; they were bound to each other.

They left the café feeling each other, touching, holding hands. She was giggly, because she found him funny and lighthearted, and being with him excited her in a way she had not thought possible. Hours later, in the same day, she treated him to a gourmet meal at the first upmarket restaurant he had been to since arriving in Switzerland. He walked her to her hotel, where they sat in the lounge and talked until the small hours of the night. Just before dawn, she exchanged her single room for a double so they could chat some more and get to know each other better. He fell asleep with his clothes on. At nine the following morning—she had not slept a wink the entire night—she went out shopping and returned with the clothes she had chosen for him.

She found him awake, just after a long shower. He stood handsome and desirable in a towel wrapped around his waist. Then she gave him the shaving kit she had bought, plus a pair of trousers and a couple of shirts, which fit him perfectly. He behaved as kept men are wont to do—taking their paramour's continued loyalty and love for granted without ever reciprocating either. This should have sounded warning bells in Cambara's appraisal of what to expect, but no. In love for the first time at the age of thirty-five, she was unwilling to hear anything but the sound of her adoring heart beating in rhythm with his.

When he told her about Raxma and her mother's phone calls from Ottawa, Cambara wore an amused expression, in the secretive attitude of a younger girl having her first date. She did not show interest in knowing what her mother had made of him. Why? Because she knew Raxma and her mother well, knew they could prove to be difficult and uncompromising when it came to Cambara's choices of men, especially after what she had been through with Zaak. Arda located flaws in character, clan affiliation, educational background, or some other shortcoming in all the men in whom Cambara had shown interest.

At some point, Cambara sent him out on the pretext of getting her *Le Monde*. While he was gone, she returned Arda's call. Unsurprisingly,

Arda segued into a song, in which the word "love" chimed not with stars shining most brightly but with the notion "ruse." In short, Arda did not like the way Wardi's voice presented itself well ahead of the rest of him. She had no liking of him, because she felt he was hard at work to make her fall for him. "Crafty bugger" was a phrase she employed more than once. Yet she had not met the man! Arda's advice was: "Fly back home minus him."

For her part, Raxma thought that Cambara was deservedly having a delightful time, and, as such, she would not dare to suggest to her friend, who was swooning in the embrace of her fresh infatuation, to give him a wide berth—not until she met the fellow. Told about Arda's take and how she had inferred the man's character from a single, brief telephone conversation, Raxma reiterated that she would reserve her judgment at least until after Cambara had filled her in on the hiatuses in their story. She concluded that, not knowing enough, she would be inclined to a more prudent approach and cautioned against hasty marriage.

Now, lying in bed in Mogadiscio, Cambara remembers with a good measure of self-recrimination that she did not heed her mother's advice. Cambara returned to Toronto a few weeks later, minus Wardi, but that was not all. Cambara married Wardi at one of the city's registries, unbeknownst to Arda, Raxma, and many of those very dear to her, convinced of her true love. It did not seem to matter to her what other people might say, or if they would or would not approve of the union. The hush-hush affair took place in the presence of two of her Canadian colleagues on the film shoot, who served as her witnesses. Before the ink of their signatures on the forms had dried, Wardi was urging her to file copies of their marriage certificate with the Canadian consulate, "for our family reunion," he explained.

Even though she found nothing terribly wrong with Wardi's request to file the marriage papers the same day, Raxma felt a little uneasy, though she hesitated to describe it as distasteful. Compared with Raxma's reaction, Arda's was over the top. "What did I tell you?" she said. "He is a con man, not to be trusted." Cambara proceeded with understandable caution from then forward, and she resolved not to reveal that Wardi was urging her to draw up a legal document clearly stating in legalese that what was hers was his too. It was her aim to humor him as best she could; that was all. Nothing else to it. Nor did any cautionary bells sound in her unhearing ears. How love deafens!

Back in Toronto, her mother made her position very clear: She wished to have nothing to do with the whole affair and would not help or hinder her daughter's effort to get him to join her. Meanwhile, Canadian immigration took its time, cognizant of the fact that she had been married once before to a Somali and been granted a family reunion on that basis. The waiting took its toll on Cambara, who filled in multiple copies of more forms and more papers with the help of Maimouna, who acted as her lawyer. She rang Wardi almost daily, and if she failed to do so, he phoned her collect, her bills mounting and her anxiety likewise. Although she took no delight in her daughter's misery, Arda hoped that Cambara's enthusiasm for Wardi would wilt, like a tree in unseasonable weather, the longer she had to wait for the situation to resolve itself. To the contrary, Cambara claimed that her love grew and grew the more the immigration authorities put bureaucratic obstacles in her way, which she was confident Maimouna would clear.

She had no satisfactory answers when, in passing, Maimouna asked why she had granted Wardi every demand he tried, offering him more than he had ever dreamt possible. More desperate than she cared to admit, she considered relocating to Geneva to be with Wardi. Arda thought her mad and said nothing, but Raxma would not hear of this. "Why, an unemployed couple—one of them a jobless makeup artist, the other a Somali with no refugee papers—couldn't live on the welfare benefits of meager monthly Swiss handouts."

Finally, Cambara came clean about everything, including the fact that she had put down Wardi's name as a co-owner of her own property in Toronto. Now that the onus was on Arda, she did what she knew how to do best. A fixer, she stepped in, calling up someone in authority. Within a month, Wardi's application moved speedily from the junior desks and landed on much larger escritoires where prompt decisions are initialed at the end of a phone call. Notwithstanding this, Arda stuck to her original guns, in view of Wardi's unhealthy hold on her daughter. She used Raxma to carry her messages, saying that she would remain forever suspicious of Wardi and, given the choice, would not allow him to get within her own parameters.

His papers through, Cambara met his flight alone. With little love lost between Wardi and Arda, Cambara wondered if her mother would at least meet him, but the old woman would not acquiesce to her daughter's request that she bring him to her house. The stand-off lasted for several months, until Cambara became pregnant, which happy event made Arda break with her stance: she rang to congratulate her daughter. Then Arda asked Cambara to visit, and mother and daughter had the opportunity to talk, but not necessarily about their estrangement from each other.

Arda moved in with them a fortnight before the due date, agreeing to accept the fait accompli presented to her: that Wardi, a man she thought of as a rogue, was the father of the baby to whom she would be a grandmother. Raxma was a godsend, in that she took Cambara away for long walks and entertained her when the going was toughest on all concerned. Arda did what she had to do, bit her tongue whenever she was tempted to speak, and learned to live with a man she did not trust for the forty or so days she was there to help look after the mother and the baby. Wardi absented himself often during that period, leaving earlier as a trainee attorney-at-law, arriving late at the most ungodly hours, and staying in the room farthest from his wife and her mother. On many a night, he did not even return home.

That there was a great deal of unease all around was plain to see, and everyone remarked on it. While most of Cambara's friends fidgeted around the subject of the relationship, Raxma was the only one who dared to broach the subject: the full-blown affair he was having with Susannah, the principal partner of the law firm where he was doing his yearlong internship. Cambara, meanwhile, concentrated on giving birth to a healthy child, believing that transmitting negative vibes to the baby before its actual birth might somehow adversely affect it. The baby born, Wardi spent more time away from the apartment, presumably with Susannah, in the office. Cambara, her mother, and Dalmar's moods often lapsed in an equal measure of joy in one another's company and a mix of guilt and anger when it came to Wardi's unspoken-of absence.

Now, as she hears the outside door of the house closing, presumably because Zaak has left for work, the image of Wardi—lying on his back with a tortured posture, his nose bleeding, his eyes runny with a sickly amber discharge, his lips cut and swollen—comes to her. She cannot help wondering whether their relationship would have been different had she not married him secretly. Then a fresh rage, mixed with hurt, rises within her, and she does not know what to do, short of continuing to hate herself for her own weakness.

With her son drowned, her marriage to Wardi as good as over, Cambara is in Somalia, where she has more time for reflection. Has she come to Mogadiscio because she hopes to empty her life of him?

FIVE

It is very early the following morning, and Cambara is already awake, the jet-lagged state of her body demanding that she get out of bed. She walks downstairs and then moves about with the stealth of a burglar, cautious, quiet, and looking this way and that. Finally, as she tiptoes into the kitchen area, certain that she has the place to herself, no strange male odor yet scented, and prepares to make herself tea and a bite to eat, if she can find any food. She discovers that she is face to face with Zaak, who, with an unpleasant smugness on his face, is hiding in a corner, waiting, as if in ambush.

"How is my dearest doing?" Zaak says.

The tone of his voice sounds self-satisfied; he seems to take much delight in seeing her surprised expression and obvious discomposure.

Unsettled, she takes refuge in an all-encompassing silence, careful not to make a tetchy remark that she would later regret. After a moment or so, she grows sufficient pluck to stare at him long and hard, and, as she does so, she affords herself the time to look back on their young years together. She finds it hard to picture ever having had the hots for him.

In those days, Cambara's favorite read was an Italian girlie *foto-romanzo* monthly called *Intimità*. With her and her schoolmates, the *affaires de coeur* took precedence over everything else. Her friends, giggly, many of them spoiled brats because they belonged to the bourgeois classes, would not want to pay him a moment's attention. When on two separate occasions Cambara tried to egg on two of them to dance with him at her birthday party, one of the girls refused, describing Zaak as "the pits." Cambara pretended not to know what her friend was talking about, when that was certainly not the case, and then rose to his defense, saying, "He is just insecure, the poor fellow, but he is nice, once you get to know him." Some of her friends started to tease her, one of them predicting that whoever took a fancy to Zaak was sure to be led to "Endsville." No doubt she has ended up doing just that.

Now Zaak asks, "Did you sleep well?"

"Yes, I did, considering," she replies.

"Are you going somewhere?"

"I have a long day ahead," she says.

"What are your plans?"

Just as she readies to answer him, if evasively, she starts at a sudden noise, which disorients her. She looks in the direction of the kitchen and then up at the roof, hoping to identify the source of the scurrying sound, but she cannot decide if it is that of rats or other rodents, and if this is coming from somewhere up in the ceiling or from the scullery. Finally, she is drawn to an identifiable ruckus: a diesel truck arriving outside, its doors opening and closing, a number of youths alighting, and then the hubbub of human voices approaching.

"That'll be my lift," Zaak explains. He pauses and then adds self-importantly, "The truck comes with its armed escort, six youths and the head of the security unit, formerly a major in the disbanded national army."

He makes as if to get up, taking a good while before he manages to rise to his feet. When finally he does so and moves, it is as if he has metal in his knees, his every step a stumble of sorts; he appears incapable of coordinating his movements. He pauses, straightening his back, and rubs his spine, then his fogged eyes.

He says, "I am late for work, as it is."

"Can your driver give me a lift?" she asks.

"Where to?"

"To our family house," she says.

He shakes his head in disbelief. He affects a smile before looking away, and pretends to be concerned.

"Are you mad?" he asks.

"I won't go into the property," she vows.

"What do you mean, you won't go into it?"

"In fact, not only will I desist from going into the property, but I will also make sure not to show myself to the minor warlord occupying it," she says.

"Exactly what do you intend to do?"

"I just want to see the family property."

"In which you've never lived."

"Because it was rented out to foreign diplomats."

"A property you haven't set eyes on for decades."

"I would like to see it up close," she says, "and get to know where it is in terms of where we are, your place."

"You could do with a bit of help, couldn't you?"

"To be honest I could."

"Tell me more."

"What is there to tell you?"

He asks, "You don't expect the family occupying the house to present you with the keys and apologize as soon as you meet them, do you?"

"Are you taking me for a fool?"

"You'll be acting like one if you do not take into account the fact that you are courting danger," he warns her. "It will not be a walk in the park to gain access to the property, still less to dislodge him." He pauses, grins ostentatiously, and then adds, "He won't give it up without a fight."

"I know it won't be an easy task."

"I've heard of several property owners who've come to grievous harm when they've tried to recover it," he says exultantly.

Her smile reluctant, Cambara sets about changing the subject. So she takes a step away from Zaak and in the direction of the door, making as if she will open it to let in a youth who is hanging hesitantly about as he considers whether or not to knock.

"Where else would you go if you had transport?"

"To one of the big hotels."

"You are not thinking of moving?" Zaak asks.

"I am not," she replies. "Not yet."

"Why one of the big hotels, then?"

Cambara looks at him in apprehensive silence, uncertain whether there is any advantage to gain from deliberately misinforming him as opposed to neglecting to tell him everything. She says, "I am looking for a friend of a friend who works in one of the hotels as a deputy manager."

"What's your friend's name?"

"She is a friend of a friend," she says with finality. Then she is determinedly quiet, content with the vague intelligence she has so far given him.

A gentle early-morning breeze is blowing, the air moist with the saltiness of the sea. With patience, a part of Cambara is waiting for Zaak to run off at the mouth about the dangers of the city and about fatal muggings, and to dwell, for a few sadistic moments, on the large number of women who are raped, men maimed, horror statistics that are meant to keep the likes of her indoors. The other part of her waits for his snide remarks about her naiveté and how she is living in fantasyland. She is resolved not to allow him to put fear into her or to remain his guest and dependent on him. Even so, she will pay attention to the hidden meanings of what he might say and interpret his words in the light of what information other people might volunteer, then collate and compare these in the hope of negotiating a safe course between the perils.

"I'm thinking perhaps I should come too," he says.

She would rather they not go together when she tries to insinuate her way furtively into the family property. She would rather he did not know anything about her plans or how she intends to charm her way, lie if need be, to gain access. He is bound to disapprove of her method and very likely will sabotage her effort.

"I'd prefer if you lent me your driver and car."

"Things are more complicated than you realize."

"What's so complicated about that?"

Waiting for him to explain, Cambara is under the impression that Zaak's faraway look is that of someone racing to catch up with an idea running ahead of him but in the wrong direction.

He says, "We need to make detailed preparations."

"What do you mean?"

"You'll need an armed escort."

"Why?"

Seeing him gloating smugly, she feels immediately shamefaced as she recalls from the few bits of information she has garnered about how Mogadiscio functions that, as a deterrent, it has become compulsory for owners of cars and trucks plying the roads to hire the services of armed escorts not necessarily to ensure the safety of the passengers but of the vehicle, because of the frequent carjackings that take place. She reminds herself that in a civil war setting, she must attach herself, perforce, to a broader constituency from which she may seek succor in the event of life-threatening complications. It is more than obvious that as a woman, alone, she stands no chance of surviving any of the possible civil war–related ordeals unless and until she appends herself to a group, armed and therefore clan-based, or civic in origin and therefore ideological. Hence the need to locate Kiin, an active member of the Women's Network.

"I'll organize the armed escort and the truck."

"I wouldn't dream of being a nuisance."

"It'll be a pleasure, not an inconvenience."

"Please. You have important work to occupy you."

He says, "I insist on coming with you."

After a solemn moment in which she considers her options, she realizes that, like it or not, she has joined whichever group Zaak belongs to and that she might as well benefit from her association with him until she has disaffiliated herself from his clique and become part of Kiin's.

"You come on the understanding that I call the shots," she says. "We drive close to it, we do not stop anywhere, and the armed escort remains inside the vehicle. Is that agreed?"

"We are at your service," he says.

She tells him, "I can't thank you enough."

Zaak is chuffed. She discerns a frisson of joy in his eyes, then an adrenaline rush of excitement lighting up his entire face. There is delight, which expresses itself in his bodily movements, for he makes as though steeling to embrace her, but, thinking better of it, he restrains himself in time before wholly committing himself. Moreover, there is a lascivious look in his shifty gaze. Even so, he focuses less on the upper parts of her body and more on her sandaled feet, like a teenager blushing at the sudden appearance of his paramour. Cambara is wickedly attractive to him. She knows what Zaak thinks of her, how much he has always adored her body. Not only is she aware of this, she is also conscious of the obvious fact that he is in awe of her irresistibility, which probably explains why he is acting in a provocative way, why he has been mean all along: because he hasn't ever had her and never will.

"Why do you look rested and I do not?" he asks.

"Because I did not chew any *qaat*, that's why."

"You look rested and beautiful," he says.

She looks away, smiling. She is in her summer cotton casuals: a pair of stretch slacks—comfortable to wear indoors, especially when relaxing—and a shirt open at the neck, her cleavage temptingly ensconced. She cannot help wondering if Zaak is tempted to take advantage of her situation, which is in upended disarray. Their current circumstances are the reverse of what they were several years ago, when he was the guest and the one in need, and she the host and the one in a position to be kind or unpleasant.

He knew the boundaries then and behaved as well as he could under the prevailing conditions. Some hosts are by nature inhospitable when it comes to their private spaces and are miserly if it is their turn to share it.

He says, "You'll have to change if you want to go out of the house. You won't want to attract unwelcome attention to yourself, which you most definitely will if you are dressed the way you are."

"Would you advise me to change into a veil?"

"Since you have brought one? Yes. By all means."

"I have brought two, as it happens."

"Put on a veil on top of what you are wearing."

"It will be unbearably hot."

Quick to take offense, he turns his back on her and flings the words at her. He says, "It's your call."

She notices a smudge, dry and unwashed, at the lower corner of his lip and pictures him eating and bringing his plate close to him, like a Chinese peasant picking up morsels of food with chopsticks, inaccurately tossing food toward his mouth and missing occasionally. He was always a messy eater, Zaak. The residual smear of an uncooked meal, that is what she thinks she is looking at.

The man is a mind reader; he says, "Breakfast?"

The thought of eating food prepared by him in his house is so disturbing that she can only shake her head no. Actually, she means to pick up something somewhere else, she has no idea where or what. A hotel with a restaurant will do her nicely. There she will inquire if anyone knows how she can reach Kiin, her friend Raxma's friend and cousin.

What attracts her attention is not the state of the kitchen, where she might want to cook, or the piles of unwashed plates, which she might wash, but his forefinger, to the end of which something has attached itself: the brown texture of a sort of waste, which eventually she identifies as mucus. He must have picked his nose with the nail of his index finger, which is the longest and dirtiest nail she has ever seen. Smiling, she sees the inside of his mouth, which is unsightly.

Such is the strong feeling that has come over her that her hair reacts to it, each hair rising in the shape of rashes on her skin, the size of pustules. When she readies to speak of her irritation, her tongue, ineffectual, turns as coarse as a camel's, unimaginably papillary.

"Let us see," she says, talking to herself.

Her movement away from him has the feistiness of a woman angered into action, a woman who cannot hear the loudness of her heartbeat, because her bitterness has gotten the better of her.

"I can make tea for myself," she says. "I suggest you go, as you must not let everyone wait for you here at home, where the armed escorts are, and at the office, where the elders of the subclans engaged in skirmishes are expecting to see you."

She starts washing a teapot, scrubbing it clean with a metal brush until it is almost as shiny as a mirror—before he has had the opportunity to respond to her suggestion. For some reason, he looks off-kilter all of a sudden, as redundant as a piece of furniture no longer of any use to anyone.

She boils water for her tea, which she makes in silence. No milk, because she reckons it will have turned, what with the intermittent power supply, and no sugar, because she has decided she will give it up as of today, thank you. During this long pause in their tentative talk, she replays yesterday evening's rude remarks, which prompted her to leave the room and forced her to seek refuge in the seclusion of the upstairs rooms.

He seems to have worked out a detail concerning how he would like to organize his day and hers. She can tell this from his renewed sense of purpose. Finally, he says, "Give me a minute, please."

He explains to her that he is going out to talk to the driver and the armed security detailed to escort him to and from work and that he will collect the keys of the truck from the driver and ask him to take a mini taxi back to the office.

"What about the armed youths?"

"They'll come with us in the truck to guard it and guard its passengers too," Zaak informs her.

"Might this not send the wrong signal to the warlord occupying the family house, if he happens to see us casing his joint? We wouldn't want him to become aware of us reconnoitering, or of my presence in the country or for that matter in his neighborhood," she says.

"Trust me," he says. "I know what I'm doing."

Then he goes out the back door to have a word with the driver and the armed escort.

"You will bring me back here, and then you will go to work?" she says. "Okay?"

"Okay," he replies. But after a pause, he asks, "But why can't you wait for a couple more days, when we are better organized and can deal with all eventualities?"

"I want to get this out of the way," she says.

"Make your tea, we'll talk some more."

As she does so, in the isolation of the kitchen, now that he has stepped out to talk to the driver and the armed escorts, less unwelcome memories call on her, catching her off guard, memories from their youthful years. To forestall any infelicitous emotions overwhelming her, she strikes the posture of an adolescent girl, impossible to please and hard to get, relaxed, blasé, full of gumption. A bit of a poser, with an undecided expression gathering into a frown as concentrated as a storm, she stretches her body and folds her arms across her chest. She breathes slowly and evenly, lulling herself into a sense of necessary composure. She tells herself that first she must put aside her uncertainties, in order to take a good hold of herself and banish all reservations from her current preoccupations.

She tilts her head to one side and then remembers the curious re-mark Zaak made when he picked her up from the airport, comparing blood relations to rivers in which the currents move in different direc-tions, occasionally going parallel but hardly mixing. "And yet the patches of water belong to the same river, as do the members of a blood community," he said. "There is the matter of choice in regard to which side of the river you stand on. Had you given thought to any of this before upping and coming to Somalia?"

She thought he was fishing. She believed it wise not to tell him much, definitely not before she had her feet firmly on the ground, had her own room in a hotel, and had reconciled herself to her new situa-tion. She would not give in to his badgering, no matter how hard he tried; she would wait until time had done its job and had edged open the door to her secrets gently, without compunction. Meanwhile, she would sit tight and unbothered, impervious to the hateful stirrings within her heart. After all, she would not want to startle herself and em-bark on regrettable action.

Cambara knows that Zaak is an early-to-bed person; he likes to be up with the first dawn. As she takes her first sip of her weak tea, she has unclear memories of a scene she cannot be certain she dreamed or saw in real time, however jet-lagged her state. She recalls seeing him from her window overlooking the partially covered veranda, with his note-books spread around him on the uneven floor, maybe working. Maybe he was up early, preparing for the day ahead, before the sun showed its bright, hot face to the rest of the world. Cambara is a night person, up until late.

Cambara mulls over the day's events and at night eats her heart out until there is nothing left of it to pump her blood around. Cambara and Zaak have known of each other's waking, sleeping, and other bod-ily timetables, their likes and dislikes, since living together first as youngsters and later when they pretended to be husband and wife in Toronto. Now that they do not have to bother about form, she won-ders if Zaak will cope with the tensions that are an integral part of their new condition.

Cambara was born to a happier childhood, with parents who adored her, especially her father, who was very content with an only daughter, on whom he doted. Although of a firmer strain of mind, Arda adored her in her own way from the moment of delivering her into the hands of a world ready to welcome her with adulation.

They were a very atypical Somali couple, her parents, blessed as they were with an unusually bright and attractive daughter. It was unheard of for a man to be as devoted as her father was to his only wife, Arda, to whom he was also faithful. When Cambara grew to be self-consciously lonely, needing a kind of playmate and companion, her parents "invited" Zaak, Arda's nephew, the oldest of six brothers and the smartest of them all, into their home, to keep Cambara away from mischief; he was also to tutor her in her science subjects, in which she was weak. Because Zaak's parents often came down heavily on him in view of his maladroitness, Arda took care not to be on his case even, being all thumbs and no fingers, when he made a hash of things. Arda brought him into their home on the speculation that Cambara would benefit from living in close proximity to a boy very different from her, gambling on the assumption that he would stand her in good stead in the future.

Zaak, in recompense, received material comforts as well as intellectual backup, these being of a piece with living in Cambara's home. He trained his mind for higher things, whatever these meant, and while doing so, kept Cambara busy and out of misconduct. To keep his mind occupied profitably, Zaak would set himself unattainable challenges, including committing an entire dictionary to memory or picking up the rudiments of a new language in a matter of days. She would often catch herself asking, But to what end? He would retort that he was doing these things just for the fun of it. Then he would spend the best part of a weekend reading Tolstoy in Arabic, only to read the same novel the following week in English.

Years later, only after he had spent two thousand days in prison, a thousand and one of them in solitary confinement, would Cambara understand what he meant when he spoke of training his mind for higher things. Everyone assumed, until a decade later, following his marriages to, respectively, Cambara and Xadiitha and then his relocation to Mogadiscio that he had come out of detention unscathed. Not so, apparently. Cambara thinks that maybe his current physical and mental conditions are symptomatic of the country's collapse, a metaphor for it.

When younger, she was the more self-assured of the two, the one with the handsomer demeanor, blessed with everything you wanted in a child growing up. He was weak in the eyes and wore glasses as thick as an elephant's posterior. He had a feeble heart and was given to complaining of sudden flutters. Quite often, you saw him holding on to his chest, doubling up in pain, or coughing nonstop. He was deficient in many physical departments but was very strong in the mind. Cambara's mother admired his mental strength but so often worried enough about his health that she consulted doctors and, on occasion, other types of healers, some quacks of the duplicitous kind, others of the sort who sought cure-alls for ailments in the word of the divine.

Cambara became aware of their physical boundaries when she came in on him one day, naked. His pubes were covered with hair; hers weren't. And he was fondling himself. To this day, she doubted if he had seen her or heard her tiptoe away. She would've been about nine and he about fifteen. She had gone to his room to ask him to help her with a math problem, and she had to slink away quietly. This would have been the first secret she had withheld from her mother. If she had spoken of what she saw to either of her parents, she was sure her parents would not have stopped at blaming him; one of them might have consequently punished him. Years later, as putative spouses sharing living spaces but no intimacies, she would often wonder to herself how much change would have occurred between his youth and then, as a grown man. Not that she was ever tempted to look through a knothole. She feels certain that in his current state—what with his distended paunch and his continuous consumption of *qaat*, said to affect a man's sexual prowess negatively—Zaak's manhood is as lifeless as a hangnail.

Furthermore, she recalls now that later the same morning, while she was alone and brooding, she happened to come across a peacock that was excited at seeing her and which behaved as though agitated when Cambara paid it no mind. The peacock was on full display, with an elevated peacock eye, vainglorious in bearing and gait, and with a most gorgeous train, which he now thrust forward at Cambara, or so thought the then pubescent girl. A nearby harem of peahens kept their safe distance, especially when the feathers of the peacock's tail started to shake and he moved in Cambara's direction, eager to make contact with her.

From where she was, she remarked the shimmering quality of the peacock's feathers at the same time she heard the rustling sound that, aroused, he emitted. She would hear it purported that young girls or women anxious about their own sexuality attract peacocks; these pick up their body odors, which, unbeknownst to them, they release into the biosphere. On that day, in her own dim recall, Cambara, weeping, ran off to her mother. She came close to telling her mother whom she had seen, where, and what he had been doing; she came close to speaking about being aroused at the sight of a peacock in full libidinous magnificence. Was it then, she wondered, that Arda began to think that her daughter and nephew were destined to become man and woman?

Cambara and Zaak's relationship lost its childlike innocence soon after that, and she dared not look at him from then on without remembering these two, in her mind, related incidents. Even though she considered asking that he show himself to her again, she could not bring herself to do so, fearing that he might not. Meanwhile, he became more self-conscious in her presence, often displaying shy evidence that he had discovered his own body. Less voluble than before, he took refuge in sulky silences.

As she washes the dishes in the sink with soap powder intended for clothes, she wonders what his reaction might have been if she had broached the topic. She had never dared to allude to this incident in Toronto. She doubts very much if there is any point in doing so now.

"Tell me," Zaak says. "How is Wardi?"

Cambara is at a loss for elegant words. This is because she wishes to avoid falling into a foul mood, in which her fury may run ahead of her and lead her astray, into a world of rage, remorse, or regret. She thinks it inappropriate to scamper after one's rage, convinced that she will never be able to catch up with it. It is a pity, she reasons, that, because of her wish to exercise some self-restraint, she will not allow herself to express the full extent and source of her sentiments either. Her mother is loath to be around her daughter when her rage erupts, a rage she describes as being hotter than and more dangerous than Mount Etna. In addition, of course, Zaak knows that Cambara's parents raised her in a way that precluded her being straitjacketed into the role of a traditional Somali female. He is doubtful if, having been told of it, he could have located her rage as a recent one, to do with her conjugal relationship. To him, Cambara was fine, until one day you would find her off her noodle, deluded, and highly impractical.

He looks on, expectantly silent, as Cambara speaks cautiously lest her words run into one another, like the felt pen scrawls on a blotting paper. How she wishes she could lean on the very rage that is crippling her; how she wishes she could draw sustenance from it. But her words come out a little too creakily, her voice, even if raised, remaining soft in the peripheries and hard at the center, like calluses rasping on sandpaper. She is aware that she will be talking about a man whom she hates to another whom she equally loathes: two men, both losers, with whom she has had a kind of intimacy, the one foisted on her, the other chosen by her. She has no doubts they are or will be in touch. Let Zaak relay whatever it pleases him to; she does not care.

"It's daunting to explain what has happened," she says, and, pausing, she looks him in the eyes until he averts his gaze. "For years, I have lived with an unarticulated rage that has since become part of me and that has taken a more murderous turn after my son, Dalmar's, drowning. I trace the source of the rage and Dalmar's unfortunate death to Wardi."

She has tears in her eyes, but because she will not let go of a drop of it, she trembles. Cambara is a dyed-in-the-wool rejecter of other people's unearned pity.

Zaak intercepts the course of their conversation, guiding it to terra firma, and asks if she intends to live in the property herself if she manages to wrest it from the hands of the man illegally occupying it. He adds a rider, "As I said before, I doubt very much that the man will go without a fight."

"I have no idea what I will do with it once the property is in my hands," she replies. "I feel certain deep within me that I will wrench it from his clutch."

"You must know something I don't," he says.

"I do."

"Will you share it with me? I'm curious."

She does not repeat what she said to her mother about the warlords being cowardly et cetera; she chooses not to, because this way he will have a counterargument. She says, "I am a determined woman, and determined women always have their way."

A snicker. Then, "Will you rent it or sell it?"

"I haven't figured out what I'll do," she says.

Struck by the sorrow spreading on his countenance, he is perhaps mourning like a man watching the passing of an age. He quotes a few lines from an Arab poet, and imagines seeing a dove struck in midflight and shot at the very instant she gazes upon her destroyed nest; the dove dies. The image of Cambara meeting a sorry end makes him shake his head in disapproval. However, he does not speak of the ruin he envisions for anyone who attempts to dislodge a warlord, minor or major, from the house he occupies.

He asks, "Why wrest the property from those living in it if you have no idea what you will do with it?"

"Because it's mine," she says.

"And you want it back, no matter the risk?"

"What risks can there be?"

He has heard of a handful of property owners who have been gunned down when they tried to repossess what was legally theirs. Some have reportedly been harassed and run out of town; others have been humiliated and their womenfolk raped to teach them a lesson. No longer sure if there is any point in voicing his admonitions, he wonders if her determination to forge ahead with a plan hatched in Toronto, while she was enraged and with no intimate knowledge of the situation on the ground, is tantamount to a death wish. The more he thinks of it the more surprised he is that Arda made no mention of Cambara's intentions. Is it possible that she has no idea how mad her daughter is? Wardi had once been the cause of their separation, when daughter and mother wouldn't exchange a greeting. Could it be that they were barely on talking terms and that Arda had rung him to host Cambara out of concern for her safety, no more?"

"Do you know who the occupant is?" he asks.

"Tell me what you must tell me, anyway."

"His name is Gudcur," Zaak says, "and he is the ringleader of a ruthless clan-based militia raised from the ranks of one of Mogadiscio's brutal warlords."

"I don't stand in awe of any of the warlords."

"Have you worked on the practical side of things?"

"What might these be?"

"How you are going to go there and so on?"

"I was hoping you would point me in the general direction of the place, since I won't recognize it, because of the state the whole neighborhood is in," she says, taking a sip of her now cold tea. "I would appreciate it if you took me round and showed me the outlay of the area. You can leave the rest to me."

"Any contingency plan if you are hurt?"

"I hear what you're saying," she says impatiently.

"I want you to know I'll take no part in it."

"I am aware of that."

A sudden harshness comes into his eyes, and she stares back hard at him. Maybe she is hoping to shame him into withdrawing his pledge not to be party to her lunacy. He absorbs her reproving stare with the equanimity of a sponge taking in more water than it can hold, and, having nothing better to do, he starts to sort the rice from the chaff, preparatory to cooking the risotto for their evening meal.

Growing restless in the extreme, Cambara rises to her full height and then, as an afterthought, bends down to gather the tea things. As she does so, Zaak has a good glimpse of her cleavage, and, fretful, he stirs in his chair. Both are conspicuously nervous, and Zaak, the first to move, takes two long strides in the direction of the toilet, entering it, maybe because the door to it happens to be the only one that is near and open or maybe because he needs a place where he can hide his embarrassment. For her part, she draws her lips back into a huge grin as she says to herself, "In addition to being a loser, he is a wanker."

When, several minutes later, he joins her in the kitchen, she is drying her hands after having washed the pile of dirty dishes. She has her back to him, standing imperiously in front of the sink, her head bent slightly to one side, her body tall as a pole, motionless and in concentration. He cannot work out what is on her mind, in part because of her air of toughness, practiced, and also because of her determination. She will work on regaining the inner calm that she first lost on the day her son died and that she thought she would never ever recover on the morning she beat Wardi up. Then she will prepare for the ultimate battles. She intends to reject death; she means to celebrate life, and she can only do this away from Zaak, not with him. She prays that Kiin will prove a helpful, trustworthy friend on whom she can rely.

Midway through drying the plates, she turns round. Zaak, as if on cue, reassembles his features, adorning his fat lips with a beautiful smile.

"What is on your mind?" he asks.

"It may not make any sense to you, but I am thinking that mine is a life that needs simple satisfactions," she says. "I want my own property back, and I want to put my life together the best way I can, on my own terms and under my own steam."

"Does Wardi figure in any of this, somewhere?"

"I have no wish to factor him in," she replies.

"Maybe that is the problem?"

"How is that?"

The word "problem" has in Zaak's view an erotic edge to it; it boasts of a territoriality, if you will, of things hidden, of sweets binged on, of lies spoken and not owned up to, of the death of a child not as yet satisfactorily mourned. And she? She is wholly unanchored by his use of the word in its erotic sense. Maybe "problems" arouse him.

"Might I suggest something?" he asks.

"Go ahead."

"Think 'danger' before you do something rash," he says. He sounds wise, at least to himself, and he grins from cheek to cheek, euphoric. "Meanwhile, you and I will work on arriving at a modus vivendi agreeable to us both."

She moves about as though she has been cast loose from everything that might hold her back, her eyes twinkling with a knowing smirk, lit with a torch of mischief.

"You are on your own if you decide to visit the property," he says. "I am making it clear for the last time. I'll come nowhere near the place."

"We'll stop half a kilometer away and won't come out of the truck. You will point me in the direction of the house so I can familiarize myself with the surrounding landmarks."

"All set," he says.

"Just a moment."

And she goes to her room upstairs and returns shortly, wearing an oversized veil, khaki-colored, dark mirrored glasses, and on her head, although she doesn't need it, a scarf to further disguise her appearance.

Then they go for a drive to reconnoiter.

SIX

Cambara, reminding herself to ask Zaak to give her a set of keys, gets into the four-wheel-drive truck, clumsily hitching up the bottom end of her veil and eventually reclaiming its loose ends from the sharper corner of the vehicle's door, in which it had gotten caught. She heaves herself up into the passenger seat, first by raising herself on the heels of her palms, her entire upper body leaning forward in a tilt, and then by lifting the rest of her body up into place, voilà! She shifts about a little agitatedly before repositioning herself in an attempt to be as far away from Zaak as possible.

Zaak replaces his house keys in his pocket, breathes anxiously in and out, the words catching at his throat when he starts to say something. He looks at Cambara with an incensed expression on his face. He turns away from her, the better to wait until she has made herself comfortable before he speaks. Then she observes that he is more eager to talk to his captive audience than he is to start the engine and get moving.

He says reproachfully, "You are being rash."

"How so?" she asks.

He holds her gaze. Then he says, "Why the rush?"

Stymied for an appropriate reply, she remains silent.

He says, "We have all the time in the world to plan so that we make things work to our advantage."

"We do, do we?" She singles out the one word, the first person plural in "to our advantage." She is surprised by his feigned keenness to include himself, remembering that he has been saying that he does not wish to have anything to do with her folly.

He scrutinizes her features for a clue and, discerning none, goes on, "The way you are going about it—calling on the man and his family who are occupying the property without having the slightest idea what we will do after the visit—is downright foolish."

She is not responding or reacting to what he is saying. It is as though it has only just now dawned on her that it may make sense to have a rethink and beat a hasty, face-saving retreat. Excited, no doubt suddenly scared, her heart palpitating hard and speedily, she wonders if Zaak can hear it pulsating in disquiet from where he is sitting behind the steering wheel. Even though she is in a fluster, she manages to stay phlegmatic in her bearing, barely betraying her unease. The truth is that deep inside her, she feels like a swimmer who is barely able to keep afloat in a pool of medium size, who is thrown into an ocean. Moreover, her skin is alive with irritability when he releases the brake and his hand meets hers on the way back to his lap, where he has been keeping it ever since getting into the vehicle. She is aware of the difficulty that comes with sharing cabin space. This, after all, has its unpredictable bodily configurations, like being in the same bed with someone you have no desire to touch: unsettling.

He throws his hands around, making nervous gestures whose meaning is not obvious to her. He says, "I would rather we worked together, you and me, on several what-if scenarios before we called at the property and came face to face with the new reality of civil war Mogadiscio, with which you are hardly familiar, because you arrived only yesterday. That's all I am saying."

Cambara can scarcely believe her ears. She thinks that he may mean well, but can she trust his motives for speaking to her this way? How is she to react to a world in which her eyes gaze in a different way on her altered circumstances, into which she has brought along her unease and her long history of diffidence when it comes to men?

He tells her, "People here are sensitive to one's nuances, the hidden and surface meanings of what one says. Every action and every spoken word must be made in an implicit recognition of these. If we do not want the guns dug up from where they have been buried, after the humiliated departure of the U.S. Marines, then we have no choice but to take these sensibilities into account."

She thinks she understands his meaning only partially, and she reacts to that portion. She says, "It is hard to think of these people as sen-

sitive or sensible," she says, her teeth clenched in silent fury. "I think
of them as bloodthirsty, clan-mad murderers. That's how I imagine
them. Maybe I am wrong in my judgment. Of course, there have been
many others—Somalis and non-Somalis—who have described the warlords differently, as clan elders, which they definitely are not. These approaches have been of no avail and have led this nation nowhere, most
emphatically not to the house of peace. I cannot understand how you
can speak of them as sensitive and sensible."

"Trust me," he says. "I am in the business of conflict resolution, and
I spend a lot of my time mediating between warring groups. Easily
hurt, people here carry with them egos more grandiose than any you've
encountered anywhere else. The result is that everyone reacts in a self-
centered way to every situation. That's what I am talking about when
I say they are sensitive."

She waits in the futile hope of further clarification. When none is
forthcoming, she asks, "What are we waiting for?"

"We're waiting for the armed escort."

"Where are they?"

"Somewhere in the back garden."

"What are they doing?"

"Chewing a couple of morsels of *qaat*."

"Even the two that are in their preteens?"

"Every one of them is a chewer."

He might be talking about a heroin addict needing his daily fix. Her
hand instinctively moves to sound the horn, but she does not, as she
realizes that in readiness for this eventuality, Zaak is leaning forward
to prevent her doing so.

"Tell me something."

"What?"

Apprehensive, she asks, "By any chance, are you afraid of what the
armed youths might do if you order them around?"

"Why do you ask?"

"Please correct me if I am wrong."

"We're hostages to their guns, that's true."

"They put the guns to your heads whenever they want to blackmail
you into granting them more concessions than you are prepared to
grant them?"

Zaak nods his head in agreement, adding, "We do their will, bribe them with *qaat*, pay them extravagant bonuses, and humor them as best as we can. With death being near, as close as their fingers are to their trigger guards, we value our life and appreciate every second of it."

"What a sad spectacle," she says.

When he does not react to her throwaway remark, her thoughts move on, dwelling for a few moments on her personal tragedy. She tells herself that when an old person dies, you accept it, reasoning that in all likelihood his or her time has come. That is not the case, however, if a nine-year-old full of life and laughter drowns. This is because you sense deep within you that the boy's time has not come and that calamity has come a-calling. No wonder that at first she felt suicidal and then homicidal the day she learned of Dalmar's death.

Her sorrows, because of the tragic loss with which she has lived up to now, devolve into a moment of intense injudiciousness. She asks, "Can't we go by ourselves?"

"Not without armed escort."

"Why not?"

"Because it is not done."

"How far are we from the family house?"

"Pretty far."

"What about Hotel Shamac?"

"That is even farther."

She unmoors herself from whatever is going on in the truck, whose engine is not running because he has not switched the ignition on, and from the conversation that is going nowhere and says, "What a travesty!"

After an uneasy silence, he says, "What travesty?"

"That because life is so precious, we need a couple of boys in their preteens bearing guns to protect us?" She pauses, then adds, "Do you know I could dispossess them of their weapons as easily as I could chase a chicken away from the grains at which it is pecking?"

"They are tough, these boys."

"Have you seen them in action?"

"I won't want to see them in action."

"I bet you'll wet your pants, come to that."

"Our lives are less precious than a handgun or the vehicle we are driving," he says. "If we hire armed escort, it is because we do not want to die at the hand of other armed gangs more interested in the four-wheel-drive truck than they are in who we are, what our clan affiliations are. To those whose services we hire, pay salaries to, humor, bribe, we are worth more alive than dead, but to all armed thugs, we are worth more dead than alive. Tell me what is so perverse about this line of reasoning?"

She stares at him, her chin raised, jaws clenched, eyes burning with her unengaged rage. Not an iota of empathy informs her hard look; if anything, she does not wish to admit that he has a point. In her surreptitious glance in his direction, she means to convey her fearlessness, despite her altered situation, brought up by his unmitigated cruelty, both when they separated as putative spouses and since her arrival here as his guest. From the way she is looking at him, you might think that she is giving him notice: that she will eventually do away with him, his deceits, and double-talk, as if she intends him to serve as a lesson to all the betrayers of our unearned trust. In her sober moments, when she does not give in to her giant rage or her disapproval of all forms of inactivity, she knows that there is no wisdom in rushing, and no mileage in employing shotgun approaches; these will hardly help her in her desire to stay on top of things or ultimately assure her of becoming a winner.

"Please, let's get going," she says.

He looks expectantly in the direction of where he expects the armed youths to come from, but he just shakes his head, saying nothing.

She tells herself that she must go past the reach of his meanness to stay alive and unharmed. Even so, she cannot help questioning herself anew if her genuine diffidence might bring up the rear of more fatal fears that are yet to manifest their grip on her imagination. In other words, what will happen when, like a child in whose imagination fear has started to dwell, her sleep marks her as disturbed, with bugbears dominating everywhere she turns, and she is wakeful. She surprises herself by speaking the command for which she too has not been prepared: "Can we go? We've waited long enough."

Zaak's response is to take a good hold of the wheel. Appearing lost, he is agitated and more like someone who does not know how to drive. He shifts in his seat, cursing under his breath, and moves backward, rubbing his bum on the seat the way urchins might wipe their hind-parts when they have no toilet paper or water to wash. His apparent discomfort puts her in mind of many a traitor soon after hearing the charges of his treason. She imagines him speaking as though she can deliver him from all blame. In fact, that is what he does, more or less.

He says, "It bears repeating that you are most welcome to stay here. It bears reiterating too that since there is no chance in hell for you to recover the family property from the warlord without a fight, it would be ill advised for us to go there before we make adequate preparations."

She says, "I just want to acquaint myself with the area of the city in which our upmarket family property is located, that's all."

"I've noticed that you haven't mentioned even once the other family property in Via Roma, in which we all lived and in which you and I grew up? Why?"

"Because Mother says that every building in Via Roma has been razed to the ground in the fierce fighting between StrongmanNorth and StrongmanSouth in the early years of the civil war," she explains. "Is this borne out by what you know or have seen?"

"What do we do after we've parked a hundred or so meters away so the family living in the property cannot see us or link us to any conspiracy?" he asks.

"I have no intention of announcing my presence."

"I say we need to plan it together, you and I."

"Point taken," she says, knowing that she will not involve him in any of her doings until she has worked out all the configurations of how, where, and when to act on her plan.

"I insist on this."

"Can we get a move on, please?" she says impatiently. Then she surprises the two of them by sounding the horn, pressing it gently once, then harder, and then much louder and continuously until its sound brings the youths running and panting unhealthily. They arrive, with their guns hoisted above their heads, a couple of them as good as naked and a third stumbling, because of being trapped in his sarong, now loose and around his ankles. Ready for action, their weapons poised, with only one of them lying prone in imitation of some movie or other he has seen, moving his gun this and that way, deciding where to aim or who to shoot. Even the driver is there, his cheeks as full as a camel busy chewing, his lips traced with greenish foam, shading his eyes from the harsh sun. Zaak waves the driver off, indicating that he does not need his services. The expression on the driver's face brightens. He picks his nose liberally, and he stalks away, heavy-footed but also eager.

Cambara says to Zaak, "Why don't you want him to drive us to and back from the house and the hotel? It'll be a lot easier, quicker, and perhaps also safer for all concerned."

"Because he is unhealthily inquisitive."

"Why does that matter?"

"It matters to me."

Finally, Zaak sits up, preparing to drive, his back ramrod straight, and his lips atremble. Maybe he is reciting a brief prayer between switching the ignition on, engaging a gear, and moving on. His breathing strikes Cambara as being bothered, and his posture rigid as that of a pupil taking a test he is certain to fail. Only then does the memory come back to her that he is an awful driver. She remembers how he had to resit the oral and the driving tests several times, managing to pass on his sixth attempt. He sets about his driving with the care of a cattle farmer guiding the erection of a bull into a cow not yet in heat. He cries *Bismillah* twice before instructing the armed youths to get in, guns, *qaat*, and all.

Then Zaak turns the key in the ignition a few times before the engine comes to life, coughing, farting, sputtering cold wind, and spurting white smoke out of the exhaust pipe. He applies more pressure on the accelerator pedal than need be, and this jars Cambara's nerves, irritating her. Again, it takes him several attempts before engaging the clutch. But because he misjudges the biting point of the clutch and removes his foot from the brake, the engine stalls. He curses, starts the engine once more, places his foot heavily on the accelerator prior to engaging the clutch, and the vehicle jerks out of control.

Cambara sits up, and so do the armed youths. They all shift in their seats, anxious-looking, helpless, and not knowing what to do or say to Zaak, who, in his desire to prove his worth, is doing all he can to impress Cambara and failing.

Everyone hears the voice of a man, the driver, who is saying, "Do you want me to come and drive, Zaak? I do not mind, really I do not."

Cambara looks out of the window, amused, her gaze falling on the driver, who is pulling his sarong up with his left hand and whose eyes are red and almost popping with exhaustion, presumably from lack of sleep. In her recall of her dream the night before, during her brief, jet-lagged sleep, she remembers the heavy downpour, remembers running, naked and free, among the fillies on a sandy beach, the sky tropical blue, her shoeless feet feeling tickled and she laughing in the way the happy and the young do. After a while, Cambara wakes from her day-dream to the noisy reality of Zaak rudely dismissing the driver, to whom he says, "Go back to your chewing, and we'll see you here in less than an hour."

She keeps whatever thoughts that come to her to herself, waits, and then watches as Zaak starts the engine yet again. This time, how-ever, smooth as new oil, he gets the biting point of the clutch right and engages it without the engine stalling or disconcertingly jerking out of his authority. She tells herself that being around Zaak, being humili-ated and derided, may become the death of her sooner than the bullet from a gun erroneously going off. To be sure, she does not wish to court danger, nor does she get a kick out of riding with boys in their preteens armed with an AK-47.

It is when she has sat back, starting to destress, that she realizes that the foot brake cannot perform the function Zaak has assigned to it, and the clutch is in fact not an accelerator. Eventually, his foot controls fail him just as before, with too little fuel reaching the engine, which al-most cuts off but does not, or too much fuel and the truck surging for-ward. It is when he mistakes the foot brake for the accelerator that the engine speed does not match the road's, then, all of a sudden, he changes down a gear, then another, annoyingly picking up such a ve-locity that Zaak has no idea what to do and then brakes so abruptly they drive into a ditch and stop. One of the two boys, sitting forward, whose AK-47 trigger guard is off, pulls at it unwittingly, shooting volleys and emptying them into the roof. The explosion in the confined space of the motorcar is so close it feels as if a grenade has gone off. Gathering her wits about her, she sees Zaak, mouth gaping open in shock, sitting stock still as if frozen in fright, but she is alert to the imminent peril in the shape of a couple of armed youths who arrive on the scene from nowhere and who watch from the safety of the wall covering them. Cambara has the calm to inquire if anyone is hurt. No man can find his tongue; all is quiet. Cambara, in the meantime, turns round to check for herself and then figures out that, even though every one is startled, no one has suffered any visible harm.

It is then that a rank odor emanating from within the vehicle insinuates itself into the immense silence. Cambara is able to isolate the source of the putrid stench in no time, identifying its emitter: a boy in the back row who, out of embarrassment, holds down his head, cradling it in his hands. Apparently, the boy has fouled himself out of fright. She is for once undecided what to do, not that she knows what there is to say. It is too far for her to reach out to the boy, touch him, assure him that there is nothing to be ashamed of; too inconvenient to step out of the truck, go round and get back in, and embrace the boy. She looks away, her sense of discretion prevailing. Likewise, the older armed youths, who, covering their mouths and noses with their hands, surprisingly to Cambara, hold their tongues. However, the unfortunate boy's age-mates are rip-roaringly laughing, pointing their fingers at the unlucky boy, one of them calling him Xaar Fakay, meaning "ShitLoose."

Cambara waits for Zaak to move before acting on the instinct to intervene, interceding with the bigger boys to desist from bullying the hapless boy, whom, now that she has had a good look, she refers to as Tima Xariir, for his dark, silky, brilliantined hair. However, Cambara is helpless in the face of this new challenge, because it is one thing to make a fuss over the waste of one's child; it is altogether another thing to clean up the mess of a preteen boy, armed, potentially unruly, and likely to pose a problem later.

Zaak, for his part, does not respond to SilkHair's predicament as a grown man might. Angry and showing no empathy, he puckers his face, an indication that the odor has had more of an effect on him than it might on a woman who has dealt with a baby's excreta. In her mind, Cambara links this incident to the scene earlier yesterday when, being most unkind, he told her, "Grow up, woman." Now she feels like saying the same thing to him, to behave as an adult woman might. Zaak says, "Get out and walk."

The boy raises his head, his eyes popping out, as if he were a goat a slaughterer has readied to kill. No one says anything as SilkHair works out how to get out of where he is without drawing more derision from his mates, knowing that the waste will have run down the legs of his sarong and will have soiled his nether regions too.

Cambara surprises everyone by saying, "There is nothing unnatural about what the boy has done, and I want him to stay in the truck."

"No one wants him to remain," Zaak says.

There is uncomfortable silence all around.

"I would like him to," she says.

Zaak is ill at ease, not certain how to react.

Cambara says, "Or else I'll go with him then."

"Where will *you* go?"

"Where will *he* go?"

In the quiet that follows, she remarks that she does not smell anything. It feels as though the rank odor has been replaced by tension and anger, which make their demands on all her senses.

Zaak backs down. "Let's go back to my place and then plan things better. Since we will need to have the inside of the car washed, I suppose the driver can do it better than we can. Besides, there is no point going forward."

Cambara does not share her thoughts with Zaak, but she trusts he knows that she will turn SilkHair into a cause: clothe him, pamper him with bountiful love, given that she has plenty of it. She imagines that she has as much untaken love as a breast-feeding mother whose baby has died has milk. She thinks that the poor thing is most likely wearing the only sarong he owns and if they get back to Zaak's, he won't have anything to change into. Yes, she can give him some of the clothes that have survived Dalmar's drowning. She preferred bringing them with her to Mogadiscio, rather than sending them along to the Salvation Army in her neighborhood in Toronto. Dalmar's clothes will fit SilkHair nicely. What's more, she will take care of him, disarm him, school him, and turn him into a fine boy, peace-loving, caring.

SEVEN

Cambara steps out of the vehicle with the determined step of someone who knows where she is going and what she will be doing. Before making much headway, she pauses in her stride, slowing down, and soon enough she remarks that she has SilkHair by her side, waiting expectantly. He is smiling sweetly, and, his hand extended out to her, it is as if he is proposing that she take it and hold it; he is nodding his head by way of encouragement, if she needed one. Cambara is under the positive impression that the young fellow has arrived at a conclusion similar to hers: that he wants to join her, walk alongside her, be with her wherever she is headed. Not in so many words, though. A mere glance can tell her how pleased he is to stand physically close to her, as if pointing out that they share more than either has realized until now.

His hand gingerly smooths the gorgy silkiness of his unkempt hair with studied effeteness, and Cambara wishes she could help him neaten it more by running her fingers through it, grooming it. Her sweeping glance registers everything around—from the driver and the other youths to the guns and, farther right, to where Zaak is scampering away, in a huff. At a midway point in a thought not yet matured, she cannot decide what has become of the boy's missing upper tooth; another is already going brown, maybe rotten at the root, an abscess not dealt with in time. Or did the missing tooth suffer a sudden trauma? Cambara intends to ask him what has happened to it and to pay the dentist's bill to have it fixed. Of course, it is possible that he has lost the tooth in fierce fighting or in rough play not so long ago. There is a lot that she wants to know about him—and soon.

"Come with me," she says to SilkHair.

She motions with her head for him to follow her, which he does very willingly. He hesitates for a fraction of a second, however, wondering whether to take along his weapon and, if not, what to do with it. In the event, he acts decisively and stands it against the wall closest to him but not without removing the cartridge, which, he discovers, contains three bullets. He looks politely in her direction and nods apologetically before pocketing them all. Then he indicates that he is ready to go. These well-thought-out moves leave an impression on Cambara, who feels more positive about him than before. She is of the view that he is a responsible lad who she hopes will give her pleasure to look after. She can't imagine her son, Dalmar, ever doing a thing like that. No doubt, SilkHair's and Dalmar's situations are different, the one raised in Toronto in a caring home, the other born in an immense wasteland, filled with civil war gloom.

She says, "Come," and moves as though all of a sudden she has freed herself from every sort of impediment in her way, and walks up the stairway to her room now that she is also convinced that Zaak has retreated to nurse a huge sulk. This is nothing new to Cambara, who has known Zaak to withdraw into his moody silences or to leave one perplexed as to what one has done to annoy or slight him whenever he is in a fit of pique. She remembers him looking as sick as a dog suffering from diarrhea and taking shelter in ill humor. In contrast to him, Cambara is famously admired or feared for confronting problems head-on and immediately. Nor does she have difficulty admitting her failings, whatever these are. She is in her element only after she has sorted out a knotty situation; she is in an upbeat mood right after a fight, ready to work out a truce between her and the parties with whom she is warring. No backbiting for her and no slinking away or sinking into a brooding mood, while at the same time he bad-mouths others. She is eager to prove to Zaak and to the boy soldiers that her mettle is of a hardier stuff than all theirs put together. Bent on making things happen, she leads the way into the house, SilkHair following and the driver and the youths watching.

Once inside the house, the two of them alone, Cambara plucks the

courage to take SilkHair by the hand, and they walk up the stairway together, she with the resoluteness of someone with a purpose ahead, he
with the growing confidence of a youth putting his trust in someone
after what has proven to be an awful experience. Just then, she comes
to a sudden stop in front of the door to her rooms. She turns her back
on him, mouthing the words "Give me a moment," and then, with cir-
cumspective care, she replaces her hand slowly, rather tentatively
among the folds of her veil, eventually retrieving the key from where
she put it earlier, in her bra. Her forefinger and thumb rubbing and
chafing it, the key feels warmer from having snuggled near her breasts.

Again, she is indecisive, hesitating whether to take him downstairs
to Zaak's bathroom, where he should be having his shower, but, because she can't be bothered to inquire if Zaak might mind, Cambara
decides to go the easy way. She tells him, "Wait here." Then, moving
faster than she has done for a long time, she rushes into her room, as
if something is chasing her, and in a moment returns with a towel in
her right hand, her left engaged in pulling the door to her room and
closing it securely behind her.

She points him to where the bathroom is, into which he goes ahead
and waits a little warily, as if suddenly becoming conscious of crossing
a boundary. He keeps some distance as she turns the tap on at the same
time as she holds the towel in her left. Surprisingly, there is running
water. She fills a bucket, into which she dips her hand. Even though
there is a touch of chill in it, she thinks SilkHair is not likely to mind
having a cold shower. In fact, she thinks that he won't give a damn, at
least not as much as she does, she assumes, because he may not know
what it is to have it warm.

Face to face with him and a little closer, her heart goes out to him,
and she can't help wanting to touch him. On second thought, she feels
she is too forward and, as if covering her tracks, pulls back. She walks
over to the wobbly rack pushed into a corner and hardly used, and
places the towel on it. She tells him to have his shower and, before leaving the bathroom, adds, "You will find the change of clothes, which I
will leave for you outside this bathroom. I want you to put them on and
then to join us downstairs, clean and dressed."

In her room, she rummages in a suitcase marked "Dalmar's: For
Charities," and she selects two pairs of trousers, several underpants,

half a dozen T-shirts, and a portable CD player, which she tests, and having concluded that it is working, she brings along with her. She is confident that at least some of the clothes will fit SilkHair nicely. She leaves the pile for him outside the bathroom door before going down, dead set on shaking things up in Zaak's place in such a way as to make a difference when she is done.

Cambara tears down the stairway, as though on a warpath, and strides over to the toolshed in the backyard, which has been converted to the *qaat*-chewers' retreat. There, the driver and several youths are busy munching away, their cheeks bulging with the stuff, slurping very sweet tea and sipping Coca-Cola. From where she is eavesdropping on their conversation, barely a few meters from the door to the shed, she can hear them chatting lazily about cutthroat civil war politics and also debating about which warlord controls which of the most lucrative thoroughfares in the city and how much money he collects daily from his tax-levying ventures. Speculating, they move on to another related topic, mentioning the name of an upstart clansman of the same warlord, formerly a deputy to him, most likely to unseat said warlord with a view to laying his hands on the thriving business.

Having heard enough about warlords and their presumptive, empty jabbering, she decides it is time she barged in without announcing either her presence or motive. First, she takes her position in the doorway, blocking it—arms akimbo, her feet spread wide apart—and fuming at their conjectural politics and their slovenly behavior. Some of the men look appalled; others appear amused; yet others shake their heads in surprise, as they all unfailingly turn their heads in her direction and then toward each other. To a man, they stop whatever they have been doing, maybe because they were unprepared for her entry.

They are baffled, because it is unclear to them under whose authority she is acting, and because they have no idea where Zaak is on this or what part he is playing. One of them whispers to his mate that she is like a headmistress at a convent school who is disciplining her charges. His mate, in riposte, compares her to a parent waking his truant teenagers from a late lie-in, shaking them awake. When a couple of the others resume talking in their normal voices and some go back to their chewing or tea sipping, Cambara embarks on a more startling undertaking: She confiscates their *qaat*. The whisperer now says, "How incredibly fearless!" His mate remarks that it is not enough for her to barge in on them as if she owned the place; she must show us she is the boss. Another wonders where it will all end.

As if to prove the whisperer's mate right, she gathers the bundles of *qaat* that they have not so far consumed from in front of them—they are too gobsmacked to challenge her—and she dumps the sheaves in a waste bin crawling with noxious vermin. Turning and seeing the shock on their faces, she does not ease off. She shouts, "This is a sight worse than I've ever imagined. How can you stand living so close to the fetid odor coming from the waste bin, which none of you has bothered to empty for a very long time?" And before the driver or any of the youths has recovered from her relentless barrage, she tells them, "It is time to be up."

No one speaks. They are all eyes, fixed on her. After a brief pause, however, the driver gathers his things and joins her; several others do likewise. One might wonder why the driver or the youths act out of character and remain biddably unassertive when it is very common among the class of men to which the armed vigilantes and the driver belong to take recourse to the use of guns at the slightest provocation. Cambara puts their compliant mood down to the fact that her behavior has taken them by surprise and that many of the armed militiamen hardly know how to respond to the instructions of women.

She orders the driver to supervise the two youths who earlier had bullied SilkHair, whom she tells to wash the inside and outside of the truck, vacuum, and make sure they rid it of the execrable odor. When the driver retorts that he does not have a Hoover or any of the other sanitizers about which she is speaking, she suggests that they use a house disinfectant. Still, when each of them, except for the driver, picks up his gun—for they seem naked without one, now that they are upright, their hands uselessly hanging down—and they argue that they do not know where they can find any deodorizers, Cambara eyes them unkindly. Then she takes one of them by the hand, dragging him into the kitchen; she provides him with an assortment of these cleaning items from a stack of household goods, mostly for cleaning, which presumably Zaak bought and locked away in one of the cupboards. She returns with the youth bearing the stuff and breathing unevenly. She gets them down to work, on occasion swearing at them under her breath. On top of being amused, she watches them for a few minutes with keen interest. Good heavens, how clumsy they appear now that they are missing their weapons, which over the years have become extensions of themselves; they appear wretched without them. With their bodily movements uncoordinated, they are as ungainly as left-handers employing their right hands to lift something off the ground. For their part, the guns have an abandoned look about them, to all intents and purposes, just pieces of metal worked into pieces of wood and no more menacing than a child's toy.

When the driver and the other youths have washed the outside and the inside of the truck, she sets them to work in the living room: sweeping, dusting, and cleaning it. Watching them as they shift the settees and other furniture, she wonders if they have ever lifted anything heavier than their AK-47s. To while away the time pleasantly as they work, she puts on the CD player, and out comes blaring some Somali music, actually a song of her own composition, the CD cut privately in a back-alley studio in Toronto. The words and the voice-over are both hers, set to music by a Jamaican friend of Maimouna's. Maybe they recognize the voice, because they all stop working and stare at her in doe-eyed fascination. She becomes self-conscious, realizing that this is the first time she is listening to her own words and voice on a CD. In the context, she thinks that maybe she needs to do more work on it, tightening it here and there, strengthening the weaker parts, in short re-recording everything before releasing it. Thinking, "Not too bad, though," she lets them hear it several times.

In the song, a boy—the voice is that of Dalmar—says, "When is a man a man?"

A woman's voice, Cambara's, replies, "A man is a man when he can work like a man, hardy, dedicated, mindful that he uses his strength to serve the good of the community."

Eerily, her heart almost misses a beat, as she assumes that she has had a distinct glimpse of a boy wearing familiar clothes, a boy who reminds her of her son, and who is now standing in the entrance to the living room, dressed in *his* trousers and shirt. For an instant, Cambara feels dislocated from her surroundings, and then she remembers that she is the one who has presented SilkHair with the clothes, which fit him perfectly. When it dawns on her that she does not like the song anymore, she turns the CD off, then walks over to where SilkHair is and, beaming with delight, says to him, "Well done." Then things begin to take a bad turn.

Call it what you like: jealousy, because one of their number, the youngest, whom they could bully with impunity until earlier today, has been luckier than they, having charmed The Woman; call it in character or reverting to type, because you could not expect the youths to act as normally as others might. Whatever the case, one of the youths, bearing the nickname LongEars, who earlier bullied SilkHair, has found his tongue. He speaks loud enough for everyone to hear, now that the music is off, and everyone is invidiously focusing on Cambara hugging and welcoming SilkHair.

"We are not servants," LongEars announces. "We are Security." LongEars mispronounces the word, replacing the *c* in "Security" with a *g*. He continues, "We don't carry settees, we don't mop floors; we are Segurity. Not only that, we are men, and cleaning is a woman's job, and we won't do it."

In the uneasy silence that follows, Cambara and SilkHair stand apart, watching, warily waiting. She looks around, not knowing what to do and wondering whether to say something that will put things in perspective. She feels there is time yet for someone to calm things down. She also senses that if any of the other youths come forward and talk in support of LongEars, then you can be sure the mutineers will win the day. She prays that someone older and with more authority— she can mean only the driver, and she looks hopefully in his direction— might gamble on shoring up her plans, propping them with his own words of endorsement. But the driver remains not only silent but also noncommittal in his body language. She is about ready to take a walk away from it all when the driver clears his throat to attract attention and then enters the fray.

He addresses his words to LongEars, his voice level, calm, unafraid. The driver says, "I am older, and I remember the years when everybody had a job. I was a driver; someone was a cleaner; another was a clerk;

another was a head of department; whether he qualified for the job or not, there was a president of the country; and we had a government. Most important, we had peace. You have no memories of any of this; I do. You are not Security; you know it, and I know it. We are members of a nation of losers, of clans warring, of youths without schooling, of women continuously harangued. We are a people living in abnormal times."

In the silence, Cambara, her heart warmed, can now see the sun boldly shining through. SilkHair and almost all the other youths stand motionless, listening attentively to the driver's words with more attentiveness than they have ever imagined possible. LongEars seems alone, as lifeless as the tongue of a mute.

"If you think of it the way I do, this lady is a godsend," the driver goes on. "She has been with us for a couple of hours, and look at what she has achieved. In less than a day. Look at Agoon," he says, and they all turn to SilkHair, several of the youths nodding in agreement with the driver. "If she can bring about such positive change in the short time she has had with us, imagine what it will be like when she has been with us for much longer. My brothers, let's all resume working, for there is time yet for us to save ourselves. There is hope yet for us to regain peace."

A youth known to be an ally of LongEars has something to say. The driver encourages him to get it off his chest. "But this has always been a woman's job, cleaning, not a man's job."

The driver has an answer. "Because women are doing men's jobs. That is why. They are raising the young family and keeping the house and keeping it united, protected from hunger and death. And since women are doing our jobs, it follows that we must do theirs, doesn't it?"

She hears someone clapping and then sees the heads of several of the youths turning toward her, then away to the driver. LongEars storms out in anger. Cambara wonders if he may have gone to join forces with Zaak. Pray, what is Zaak up to?

To set an example, the driver is the first to get back on his knees, mopping, washing, and assisting another youth. She works together with SilkHair to remove the accumulated grit from a corner where two walls meet and where someone spilled a drink with high sugar content. It's just as well, she observes to herself, that they've dislodged a clan of ants that have set up their base of operation for several months. They all join in the general banter, teasing each other amicably. She takes the opportunity to remind them that even though they are half her age, they cannot haul the furniture back and forth without fuss or complaint. She challenges the remaining two bullies who were nasty to SilkHair to help her pick up the two two-seater settees. She discovers that neither has any idea how to lift his side of a settee off the floor without doing his back in. Then she tells them, "Forget it," and does it with SilkHair after explaining to him how to position his body.

All eyes swarm to her, as if she were a bee soon after the season's flowers have blossomed into pollen of welcome seeds. Thanks to the driver, she has stung every one of them, and they are besotted not so much with her as they are with the idea of her or the idea of what she can do for them. She hopes that the driver has helped them relax into what they are doing and into relishing the sweetness of their labor. Her skin bristling, her body serves her as a radar trap in which she catches their admiring eyes as they stray away from the work they are engaged in and zoom in on her. She is relieved that the driver has spoken, saving her from caving in under the pressure of making difficult choices. Now she has two allies, SilkHair and the driver: the one because she has stuck her neck out for him and then presented him with clothes; the other because he has gone out on a limb for her and set a precedent.

She believes that the youths have gotten to know her far better than they have Zaak, with whom they chew *qaat* and whom they see as a boss, because he never dirties his hands, never bothers about house cleaning or cooking. She reasons that since all her involvements with men have been on a one-to-one basis and since this has proven to be unsuccessful, it is her wish to build a bridge of some kind of rapport with so many men all at the same time, something that she hopes she is going to be good at, as an artist. There is no pleasure like the pleasure of watching audiences lapping up the heartfelt intimacies of an actor at her best, when the audience might confuse who she is in real life and what makes her tick, move, love, and hate with the character she is just portraying.

She thinks that SilkHair looks more grown-up than when he went into the bathroom. No longer in tatters, smelly, or dirty, he has become the envy of every youth who is there. Cambara assumes that in their eyes she deserves their high praise, especially after the driver has added his word to support her action. She hopes she will have become a person to befriend, not the new boss on the block. This nervy awareness puts a proud spring in her stride and a grin blemishing the corner of her mouth.

Someone asks, "Where is Zaak?"

Cambara couldn't care less where he is and does not want to talk about him. Instead, she wraps her arms around SilkHair, and together they walk to where the driver is giving the final touches to a spot he has just cleaned.

She asks, "What about lunch?"

"Chicken," SilkHair announces.

He strikes her as a poseur, and she is amused.

"A good idea," the driver comments.

A door in Cambara's head opens. She puts her hand in her slacks pockets, bringing out five U.S. dollars in singles, which she hands over to the driver, whom she asks to take two or three youths, including SilkHair, to the open-air market and to buy chicken and vegetables sufficient to feed everybody. SilkHair's eyes anchor their new cast in the bay of self-confidence.

The driver picks up the trace of worry entering Cambara's eyes when she notices that the kitchen is not clean enough to cook in. The driver takes three of the youths, whom she presumes to be closer to him, aside, and they speak in low voices. They volunteer to finish the job, mop the floor, clean out the cupboards and the surfaces, as Cambara goes up to have a shower.

Then the driver says, "Let's go get the food."

After yet another cold shower, for which she is better prepared, Cambara comes down to ready the kitchen in time for the youths' imminent return from the errand to the open-air market. In her effort to do so, she opens the lower and upper cupboards, the storeroom, the pantry, and every drawer with functioning runners and to her great dismay, finds the shelves not dusted as well as she might like. Moreover, she can see that although the youths have washed the cooking implements, they have not rinsed them in hot water, or properly. Not a single utensil or piece of crockery is of top quality. The wood of the cupboards is cracked, damaged, or warped; the soap too dry to be of use, or moldy. The more she gets to know of the state of disrepair of the kitchen and of the foul condition that it is in, despite the attempt on the part of the youths to clean it, the more she thinks of herself as a frontierswoman come to reclaim these men from their primitive condition. But she decides to keep her vow to the youths and cook for them in appreciation of their collaboration, certain that it will make a good impression on their thinking. She wants to leave the scene of their encounter in a more improved fettle than the one in which she has found it. Maybe then she may win over their hearts and minds—even if only briefly—to her triad of society: work, honest living, and peace. She is aware that in the views of someone like Zaak, she is being naive. So be it.

Like a rodent nosing an edible bit of food out of a spot difficult to access, she prises open the cupboards, the drawers, and the sideboards in order to ascertain what is in them. There is, overall, a basic lack: of cooking oil, of sharp knives or knife sharpeners, cutting boards, of butter that has not gone rancid, of sieves and swabs, of detergents, disinfectants, and serviceable sponges; of mops with enough pieces of string or cloth attached to the handle. Nor are there washing-up facilities, clean dishcloths, usable hand or paper towels, or wooden spoons and other implements necessary to provide a decent meal for a dozen persons. The pots are of the wrong shape or are of midget size, too small for her purposes. What there is in the way of cutlery points to the house's multiple occupancy through the years: comparable to the cutlery of variously married households, the plates not matching, the forks and the spoons likewise.

She tries to make do with what there is. She mixes soap powder with water, lathering it up, and eventually decides to use the facecloths as dishcloths. It takes her a long time to wash and then wipe the drain board, on which she plans to dry the pots and dishes.

Scarcely has she done that when she hears a sound, which, at first, she mistakes for a door with creaky hinges being forcibly opened. She is waiting for evidence of Zaak's presence nearby when she identifies the noise as being that of a chicken clucking. She cranes her head to have a glimpse of the scene before her and sees SilkHair carrying three live chickens, their heads down, their necks stretched and struggling, wings opening outward and wrestling, their legs tied together with string. Trailing behind him are a couple of the other youths, nerves strained. They are bearing baskets on their heads, their steps hesitant, slow, and exhausted.

She thinks disaster, remembering that she has never killed a chicken in all her years. Neither before she left the country, when there were servants who performed those chores, nor in Toronto, where she bought them ready to go into the oven. She wonders what she must do if the men are too untutored in the art of slaughtering chickens. After all, it does require some training or at least a type of guts to kill to eat. It will be no problem to boil their feathers off and then cook them, if someone hands them over, dead. Her mind is running fast through these and her other inadequacies when SilkHair joins her in the kitchen. He puts down the chickens in a corner on the floor and instructs the others to deposit their basket loads likewise. Just as the other youths make themselves scarce—returning, most likely, to their *qaat*-chewing—SilkHair crowns his sense of achievement by consulting a piece of paper, his tongue running off the price of potatoes, tomatoes, garlic, carrots, live chickens, washing-up liquid, metal brush, et cetera, first in Somali shillings, then in their dollar equivalent. Then he gives her wads of change in the local currency.

"Well done," she says. "I am impressed." Moved, she ruffles his silky hair, almost taking the liberty to hug him and then kiss him.

Expansive joy shines in his eyes. As he gazes into hers, her pupils are set ablaze with memories of her son. She turns her head away as though in obedience to a secret command that tells her not to weep but to rejoice.

Then something happens for which no one is ready. One of the birds kicks one leg free, and when SilkHair rushes to hold her, she kicks harder and harder until she releases her second leg and jumps out of his grasp, clucking, screeching, and crying, as chickens that know that their time has come, do. Cambara watches determined not to intervene or help him in any way, because she wants to know what stuff he is made of, how patient and resourceful he is, and whether he will tire easily and give up, throwing his hands up in the air.

He makes a wise move. He stands in the doorway, blocking the exit, then bends down, almost crouching, clucking over the bird's attempts to flee, admonishing her for embarrassing him, now snapping his fingers to go to him, now keeping his hands ahead of him, in readiness to accept her into his grasp, if not to pounce on her and take a good hold of her. He is silent; everything still, everything serious. Cambara watches as SilkHair waits, the sound he is making putting her in mind of the noise that some of the men who ply water in plastic jerry cans on the backs of donkeys utter in part to encourage their beasts of burden to move at a faster speed. No sooner has he turned round, seeking Cambara's approval, than the hen slips past his outstretched hands, out of the kitchen, and through his splayed legs.

Whereupon he chases the chicken into the living room and out, then past the kitchen, the bird half flying, half trotting, body atilt because of half-folded wings. Suddenly the chicken stops to look over a shoulder, eyes alert, and he pursues her into a corner to trap her. The chicken lifts her scrawny body up in time to fly above his head, mischievously clucking but only after securing safe escape.

The footloose chicken and the clamor in the kitchen in addition to the hubbub created by the youths who join SilkHair in the chase draw the driver out of the toolshed and bring Zaak out of his sulk, or is it sleep—Cambara cannot tell when she sees him.

"Have you gone mad?" Zaak asks her.

She runs past Zaak without bothering to answer his question. She tells herself that the youths stalking their lunch is, to her mind, more of a welcome relief than the thought of them running after their human victims to shoot or kill them. Excited by the chase, SilkHair is shouting loudly as he continues to pursue the chicken. Once the din reaches the back garden, LongEars comes out of the shed, cheeks swollen with his chewing and gun at the ready. Cambara has the calm to notice what LongEars wants to do, and she shouts to him, "Don't shoot."

The words have barely traveled the distance separating her from SilkHair and the chicken he is going after with fervor and is about to catch, having already bent down to do so, when she hears the gunshot, two bullets on the trot, the second one hitting its target and wounding it, feathers flying zigzag toward the ground. A hoarse cry emerges from the depth of SilkHair's viscera. Cambara has a tenuous comprehension of what it means to be powerless in the face of brute force. She stands stock still, feeling like someone opening her eyes to the engulfing darkness and coming to see an indescribable betrayal in the action of those around her. She goes over to where SilkHair is crouched, furiously weeping, as though mourning the death of a beloved pet. She lets him leave the chicken where it has fallen and walks past Zaak and the youths, who are all staring, into the kitchen—to prepare the other chickens.

Alone with SilkHair, she suggests that he swing each of the remaining birds as disc throwers do, making several full circles. Just when the first one has become disoriented and he is about to put it on the draining board in the kitchen, LongEars presents himself and offers to slaughter both birds, which he does with the efficiency of an assistant chef whose primary job it is to do so. One sudden swat, and the chicken is as good as dead and Cambara is ready to pour boiling water over it to help remove its feathers. She uses her Swiss penknife to quiet the thrashing of the second chicken, which is struggling animatedly. The rest proves to be as easy as one, two, three.

When she has prepared the meal and Zaak deigns to eat with them, Cambara requests that as soon as they have finished eating they ask the driver to take them in the truck so that Zaak can show her the family's expropriated property. To her great relief, he agrees to her demand.

EIGHT

Feeling like a different person with a brand-new selfhood, so to speak, Cambara comes out of Zaak's house the following morning, dressed in a head-to-foot veil in the all-occluding shape of a body tent. To top it off, she has worn a strip of muslin cloth, which she holds between her teeth, like a horse with a bit, to keep it firmly in place, covering her entire face. She is donning the all-hiding garment for the first and only time in her life in the hope of disguising her identity. She walks with the consciously cautious tread of an astronaut taking his very first steps in outer space. Her forward motion plodding, her every gait a pained shuffle, her pace is as slow moving as that of a camel with its feet tied together. From a distance, she looks like a miniature Somali nomad's *aqal* on wheels.

Cambara is on her way to her family's expropriated property, discreetly consulting a map she has drawn from memory; Zaak, along with the driver, took her to within a block of the house late yesterday afternoon. She is finding it cumbersome to do so or to look around, hampered by the all-obstructing veil. Her feet feel trapped, her chest choked and her motion hindered. She is hot; she is boiling under the collar like a traveler hauling heavy bags she does not know what to do with. She is angry with herself for not returning to Zaak and then changing into an easy-to-wear garment and supplementing this with a *niqab*, a mere face veil.

She slogs with the slowness of a van with terrible shock absorbers, leaning this way and then that in complete disharmony; she is in a great deal of discomfort, perspiring heavily inside her bothersome veil and hitching up her cotton drawers as though expecting that she might sense some air passing through. Notwithstanding all this, she lumbers on, convinced that she will tower above potential aggressors in the likeness of armed youths if they attack her from close range, thanks to her hidden weapon of choice, a knife tucked away in her pocket. Cambara has always seen herself as a potential member of a cloak-and-dagger sorority, and she thinks that a knife is handy when one is surprising an armed foe who is expecting one to be unarmed.

She walks tall and well built; she is very imposing, very impressive; she fearlessly hobbles along. She draws her eyebrows close together in concentration, her mind busily sorting out the thoughts coming at her in waves. She is thinking about the number of codes that she has broken both before coming here and since then. Even though she is officially married to Wardi, she is living alone in a house with Zaak, who is not her spouse. She has done this before under a different, albeit deceptive context. Of course, this is not Saudi Arabia. There, to enter a house, you use one of two entrances; a small, almost secret side door for the women and a bigger, more prominent one for the men. It amuses her to remember the number of times many a Somali living in those parts has committed a faux pas. Some of them have received fifty lashes for presenting themselves at the wrong door and scandalizing the household, with the women looking through the peephole, giggling, and then reporting to the harridan who chaperones the female brood. Harum-scarum and in terrific haste, the hag might ring the principal male householder, who might in turn phone the police to deal with the menace.

Only now does she wonder if she needs to go to the property in a disguise of sorts, considering that Gudcur, the warlord, has no idea who she is and does not know her genuine self. No doubt he or his family may suspect the motives of her visit, which is why, in spite of camouflage, Cambara has to think of plausible grounds that will enable her to gain entry between now and when she is ready to risk asking to be admitted. By then, she will have crossed and recrossed numerous boundaries and will have come upon the moment with which she will mark the action that will define her success or failure. She hopes that she will survive the perilous course on which she is moving, unafraid.

She has had warnings about the dangers that await any man or woman visiting or living in Mogadiscio, a city rampant with the ghosts of its innocent dead.

Her eyes are red like worry beads. She turns her thoughts away from herself for a moment and focuses her attention on the houses on either side of the road where she is walking. Nothing pretty to hold her interest; the streets have the destroyed countenance of a bombed tunnel that has fallen in on itself, and the houses boast the damaged look of a tin, now empty, crushed and lying abandoned by the roadside. She strides forth, sensing that she is separate from her surroundings not only because she is veiled but also because she is wary of running into youths who have more vigor than eunuchs do and who may try to force themselves on her, being presumably alone and unprotected.

Gray as her self-doubts, her sangfroid refuses to acquiesce to her fear; she taps her inner strength for wise guidance. Despite her ambivalence about wearing veils, she wishes someone had taken a photograph of her in the body tent. She assumes that she looks a perfect marvel, a whirl of wonder wrapped in the mysteriousness of a voluminous veil, as surefooted in the sharpness of her bodily responses to the dangers that may be posed as she is relaxed in her knowledge that she can defend herself. She pauses in her stride to observe two women wearing less elaborate veils passing. Farther up the road, coming her way, there is yet a third in a class of her own—she thinks of a dervish spinning a holy trail of dust raised in the act of Sufi worship-in-dance.

She resumes moving, commensurately conscious of the yet undetectable dangers lurking in every corner, up the road, down the drive, and in the alleys. Why? Of course, she is frightened. However, she works hard not to show her fear, her strides shortening like a fat-bellied mosquito climbing out of a deep crevice in the darkness of dawn, mindful not to allow doubts to overwhelm her. Neither does she want her worries to ride the cusp of her self-recrimination. On top of her fears, she is enraged when she thinks about Wardi's treachery, which led to Dalmar's death.

The weight of the knife in the pocket of the loose-fitting caftan she has on underneath the body tent reminds her of where she is and why. Then she remembers buying the veil in its soiled state from an outfit in Dearborn, Michigan, where there is a large and well-established

Yemeni community that came to this part of the United States in the thirties. The shop specializes in every imaginable outlandish wearable originating in an Islamic country. She drove over the border to Detroit and then to Dearborn. There is no better camouflage than a body tent, not merely because it looks so theatrical but because it allows a woman to walk with a strut and get away with it. Possibly, everyone will assume that the unevenness of the ground is affecting her gait adversely. She views the world from her vantage of knowing that so far, luck has taken a bit of a shine to her: Zaak meeting her at the airport and driving her home. That he has been wicked to her is all to the good too, as it has prompted her into quick action without relying on him. Then there is the boy soldier, SilkHair.

A rush of anxiety overpowers her as the other veil-wearer whom she saw earlier from a distance comes into view. Cambara is afraid that the other might work out that she is falsely hiding her identity; she knows that she does not belong to the same order as the women she passes by, women covered in a swathe of hand-me-downs, very unlike her own, which is of top drawer, devised in Afghanistan, as the Dearborn salesman explained, for the wife of a top Taliban dignitary to don on special ocaasions. Will it be obvious not only that she is from elsewhere but that she is not a local woman on an errand to a corner shop to buy a pound of sugar and a soda?

Here, at the junction, traffic is on the increase, the odd car rolling along, ramshackle metal rattling and issuing white smoke. Twice she senses the women's piercing stare, making her believe they see through her deceit, and she shudders in panic. She does not want to contemplate what will happen to her if someone discovers her disloyalty. She is so distraught at the thought of being found out that when three women stop and stare at her, one of them commenting that, judging from her gait, she is most likely "a foreigner" unaccustomed to wearing a veil, her knees weaken and she falters in her dodder. There is one advantage to putting on the veil though: No man focuses his predatory lust on a woman so dressed.

Cambara guesses that she is half a kilometer away from her destination, which has felt longer, because of her chameleonlike shuffle. The problem is that Zaak did not show her where the family house is in relation to his house. Vowing not to have anything to do with her madness, he distracted her from concentrating on mapping out a work-able, time-saving way of getting here. He kept harping on the fact that one must buy Gudcur's goodwill with a handsome payment, up front, in cash. Cambara does not want to hear of buying back her own house. She says, "I won't pay these murderers a cent. No way. My parents worked hard to own these properties."

For years, her father worked as a journalist until the tough going got tougher and it became difficult for him to practice his profession hon-orably. Then he set up a printing press, with Arda running the business part of it. The press specialized in printing visiting and wedding cards, and employed a staff of ten, excluding the cleaners, the menial work-ers, and several hangers-on who were the family's distant poor relations. He worked diligently, leaving very early in the morning to open up for business and coming home late, bone tired. However, even though he was good at making money, he had a huge failing: He was the prover-bial spendthrift and knew not how to save or how to invest wisely. It fell to Arda to do what was necessary. Astute, she was adept at making people and money do what she wanted them to—propagate phenom-enally as do plans and animals when the conditions are right. She man-aged the money side just as she managed the hearts of people, who gave their all to her and a lot more too. Before long, several embassies were signing lucrative contracts to print their invitation cards locally; some, like the Canadian Liaison Office, even requesting that she act as their local agent to deliver the cards by hand on its behalf.

Cambara's family owned two properties and, thanks to Arda's fore-sight and keen profit-making acumen, invested the surplus funds over-seas, in Canada, when it was not fashionable among Mogadiscians to do so. The family—her parents, herself, and Zaak—lived in the mod-est one, a bungalow with six rooms, two bathrooms, and a small out-building with its own toilet facilities, in which the family accommodated long-term guests. However, the property that she intends to repossess is the larger one, bought by her father on her mother's advice and de-scribed, in estate-agent terms, as a worthy investment. An upmarket property, it had pride of place with direct access to its own beach, not to speak of an immense garden, built to accommodate a large function. She remembers how—when she was young in Mogadiscio, when Somalis were then at peace with their own ideas about themselves and proud of their uniqueness as a nation—her parents raised a huge monthly income from renting the upmarket property to the Canadians, who used it as a guesthouse for their Kenya-based embassy officials during their brief visits to Somalia.

Her father's printing business helped settle almost all the family expenses, including Cambara's private schooling and Zaak's boarding school fees. The rent money from the property paid for the occasional trips abroad, and, to her mother's everlasting credit and management skill, the family put away the savings, which paid for Cambara's college education in Canada until she got a scholarship and then later helped buy an apartment for her to live in in Toronto. Sadly, Cambara did not return home in time before the collapse. However, her parents got out, flying first to Nairobi and then joining her in Toronto for a while as her guests. Half a year later, they relocated to Ottawa and bought their own place, a good-sized apartment in a housing complex in the eastern suburbs of Ottawa, close to Arda's Canadian friends in the diplomatic corps, with whom she had frequently dealt when they visited Somalia and whom she invited often to dinner whenever they were in Mogadiscio on some diplomatic business.

Nothing gave the newly relocated couple as much pleasure as seeing their daughter in her debut as an actor on the stage. There were rave notices in almost all the major papers, one of them singling her out as the best new talent to be revealed in Canada in years. These reviews—and the fact that her parents enjoyed the show—helped stir Cambara's blood so much that she believed she had an excellent chance of becoming a full-time actor. To supplement her income, she trained as a makeup artist, investing in it as a business, while she waited for a breakthrough.

Now she slows down considerably, almost coming to a halt, as the family house rears into view. Her heart racing, her brain on the boil working overtime, she has hardly decided what to do next when, nearing the gate to the property, she discovers it ajar, a large stone keeping it from closing. She sees evidence of life in the gate remaining half open, but there is no way she can determine who has left it that way and why. It was common enough for people to leave their doors open night and day when she lived in Mogadiscio and you could take peace for granted. Later, with kickbacks and other forms of corruption cre-

ating overnight millionaires, the city became flooded with the unemployed, the poor, and the migrants from the starving hinterland, and
fences went up faster than you could tally the changing death and
birth statistics. Sometime later, residents upgraded the fences, putting
broken glass, razor blades, and electric wire on top to deter robbers.
Imagine: an open gate. What can it mean?

As she waits, anxiety throws Cambara into an agitated state, with
the up-and-down convulsions of her chest resembling the suddenness
of an asthmatic attack invading at short notice, and she breaks out in
heavy perspiration. Then the actor in her takes over, and she calms herself down, wipes away the sweat from her forehead, and decides to act
the part, improvising, inventing. After all, she knows what she wants,
but the woman at the gate who is small and in advanced pregnancy has
no idea who Cambara is. It will be her ill fortune if Gudcur is at home
asleep, recovering from a long night of *qaat*-chewing orgy. She hopes
that there are more rewards in what she is doing than there are risks.

She takes one long, last look at the half-open gate, the sight of
which, fear and suspicion aside, makes sobering imagining. Cambara
nods as though agreeing with the rightness of the decision, and plucks
sufficient courage to move speedily toward the woman at the gate before questioning her own sanity.

Cambara leans against a wall, hidden from view, her heart pounding
terribly, the circulation of her blood going anxiously faster than is good
for her. The whole area, when she has had a moment to survey it,
strikes her as being more ruinous than she has expected: a run-down
rampart built to defend a soon-to-fall city. Tied up in knots churning
inside her guts, she takes her time looking around for anything or anyone that might pique her interest.

She is thinking long and not without despondency when, by a sin-
gular stroke of good fortune, the woman heavy with child waddles
wearily out, carrying out a bucket. The woman, in virtual rags, empties
the filthy contents of the bucket into an open sewer twenty or so meters to the left of the gate. Whatever words Cambara has meant to use,
words that she has rehearsed in her head endless times and with which
she might explain her business of being here, catch at her throat,

threatening to choke her and refusing to let go. Only after the actor in her reemerges and takes over, and she is able to breathe a little more freely, does she push aside the strip of muslin that has served as a face veil, the better to inhale or exhale normally. It is then that the woman becomes aware of Cambara's towering presence. Startled, the woman drops the bucket, cradling her head protectively with her hands and bracing herself for a blow, noisily breathing in and out, clearly in fright.

Cambara, her skin crawling with embarrassment, enunciates her speech. She says the one word "Water," likening it to the magical properties of a mirage and investing in the word everything paradisial that everlasting life has in store for one. The woman rubs her eyes with the heel of her soiled hands, then wipes her cheeks dry with the edge of her robe, exposing her advanced pregnancy and a larger-than-usual belly button.

When she is certain that she has the woman's full attention, Cambara speaks tentatively in her attempt to assure the woman that she has lost her way to the shopping complex and desperately needs some water to drink. She feigns a dry throat, and shortness of breath, from her thirst, and says "Water" repeatedly until the woman nods a couple of times, indicating that she has heard.

Cambara adds, "My hosts have told me that there is a small shopping complex in this neighborhood where I can get some bottled water. But I must have missed the right turn, have I?"

The woman looks up, her eyes filling with a fresh sense of welcome relief. "You've missed the turn. It is a couple of streets down this way," and she points, the ends of her fingernails charcoal-black with residual dirt, "then you turn left, and the small shopping block is there, you can't miss it," replies the woman.

"There is a general store?"

"There is a general store for foodstuffs, and a few stalls where you can get fresh vegetable produce, but you can't get meat there," the woman informs her. "But your hosts ought not to send you out on your own. It is not safe for a woman to be on her own in these parts of the city."

The woman retrieves the bucket before beckoning her to follow her and waddling ahead of Cambara into the house. A smile adorns the woman's lips. She keeps the pedestrian gate open, half curtsying, and

lets Cambara go past her. Cambara walks in warily and turns around a
little awkwardly, waiting for the woman to close the gate behind them.
Then she winces at the thought of harming this woman or her child
on impulse, in self-defense or in her desire to recover her family's property at a future point. She hopes to be on this woman's good side, at
least until she knows more about her relationship with the minor warlord. She resolves to shut out every moldering rot in the image she has
constructed in her head in order to take the woman into her trust.

"Let me get you some water," the woman says.

The woman gone, Cambara stands in the forecourt of the house,
with the carport, empty of vehicles, to her left and the large gate now
secured with a chain. She takes things in at a startling speed. She calculates the enormity of the ruin all around her and at a guess assumes
that it will require a great deal of funds to repair the damage done to
the property. She reckons that to make it rentable or habitable, nothing short of destroying everything and rebuilding it from scratch will
do. She sees irredeemable wreck everywhere she looks: the walls scal-
ing in large segments; the wood in the ceiling decomposing; the toilet
facing her with its door gaping open emitting rank evidence of misuse;
the windows emptied of glass panes; the carpets rolled up and stood
against the outside wall, in a corner. Cambara retches at the sight of
so much callousness; she places her hand in front of her mouth, as if
needing to vomit into it.

Cambara looks to her right and finds the woman extending a glass to
her, the color of the water mud-brown. She receives the proffered glass,
noticing smudges on the outside of it—maybe the result of the woman's
moist fingers—and murmurs a feeble thank-you. To earn the woman's
trust, Cambara puts the glass to her lips, and takes a lip-wetting sip.

The woman asks, "Would you like to sit down?"

"Yes, I would," says Cambara.

"Let me get you a decent chair, then."

The woman moves into the house with renewed enthusiasm, then
up a staircase, heaving forward ploddingly, like a dung beetle shifting
its ration up a steep gradient. Cambara now entertains herself with an
outrageously daring thought, on which she acts forthwith, no hesitation at all. Having seen the ruinous state of the outside of the house,
she wants to find out what the rooms are like, inside. Who lives in

them? What manner of furniture is there? But before taking her first step, she covers her face with the face veil, nervously biting the strip of muslin and sucking it in to the point of wetting it. Aware that nothing in her intuition or in her sense of general desperation can have prepared her for this derring-do, she enters the room facing her. Through the half-open door, she can see confirmation of the presence of children from the clothes that are strewn around the mattresses and the bunk bed. Cambara presumes that the children are not this woman's, so whose are they? How many families are sharing the house?

Yet she does not pause or draw back, as though answering to a stronger pull, for she has known the house inside and outside, played in it when it was under construction, and came to it when her mother, Arda, was showing it to the estate agent who would rent the property. Of course, she is well aware that embarking on such a dangerous mission is foolish, to say the least. All the same, she lunges forward at the same time as she reminds herself that she might not have abandoned herself to such a sudden impulse or behaved in this carefree way were it not for the fact that the property had been hers and she intended to repossess it. Could it be that her son's death, the fierce falling out with Wardi, and her beating him up have made her reckless, unafraid, indifferent to danger? What the hell, she thinks and pushes the door open, goes in, and then shuts it behind her.

With the curtains drawn, the room is very dim, until she removes her face veil. In addition, there is an oppressive odd mix of odors, principally of unwashed bodies. Her refusal to display fear helps her give the room an unhurried good scour until she sees the vague human forms, sleeping figures on the mats on the floor. Then she puzzles out the shapes of a couple of Kalashnikovs within reach of two of the men and a submachine gun close to one man, who is an island unto himself. The man, bare-chested and young, sits up in a startle, his sleep-squinted eyes finally focusing on Cambara. Befuddled, the man's dreamy look dwells on the tall, all-dark, motionless figure, and he is unclear in his head if he is conjuring her up or if she is there as real as he is staring at her. He is unable to decide what to make of her veiled presence; he shakes his head in disbelief, then listens to one of his mate's snoring rumpus and returns to his interrupted sleep.

Cambara waits long enough for his breathing to even up, her hand always on the Swiss knife. Eventually she slips out of the room, closing the door gently.

Once out of the room, Cambara is face to face with the woman, whose unfriendly bearing and bothered expression almost prompt Cambara to violent action. The woman asks, "What were you doing in the room?"

"I needed a toilet," Cambara says meekly.

"You should have waited for me," the woman says.

Cambara says, "I had no idea."

The woman's irritation lends her voice a harder edge. She says, "What do you really want?"

"A toilet, please," Cambara repeats.

"First water, then a toilet. What next?"

"It's urgent," Cambara says. "The toilet."

"Follow me, then, and stay with me, you hear."

The damp, rank odor hits her with a vengeance, and she cannot bring herself to close the toilet door, so penetrating the ferocity of its accumulated essences that Cambara almost brings out the vinegary intimations of her salad of a couple of days ago. She struggles to open the window, even if slightly, only it won't budge, no matter how hard she leans against it, pushing with all her might.

Cambara comes out of the toilet sick, like a cat unsure whether it is retching or coughing. From the look on the woman's face, Cambara concludes that she can guess what monstrosities she has seen: the accumulated brownielike concentrates floating in the toilet bowl to the top, almost welling out. On coming out, she takes in a fair dose of fresh air and then lights upon the woman's smile.

Her back to Cambara, the woman says, "They are worse than animals."

Cambara does not bother to ask the woman to elaborate. She thinks she knows whom the woman means. The upshot of it is that the woman's statement helps to break the ice.

Besides, exhaustion is ultimately having its toll on the woman, as evidenced by the many unfinished tasks still waiting for her: adult clothes soaking and in need of washing; children's school uniforms that have been washed, which need to be neatly folded, the creases ironed out; lunch to be cooked; the floor to be swept. How can a woman in her advanced pregnancy hope to finish these all on her own? Cambara thinks how, since her arrival, her own life has been taking a basic design in which she steps in to put other people's lives in some order. If there is anything positive about this, it is that she has less time to brood on her loss, to mourn, or to grieve and eat her heart out.

Cambara considers completely removing her face veil. After some hesitation, she takes off the body tent altogether, and with the exposure to the air, she feels lighter in her blood and bones. As she methodically folds the body tent into some shape easy to get into later, she gives the clothes she is now standing in a moment's scrutiny, no doubt wondering if it is wise to do away with her disguise, her guile. She shrugs her shoulders, what the hell, rolls up the sleeves of her caftan—only then becoming conscious of the weight of the knife in her pocket—and offers the woman a break. The woman is so worn out she is in no position to refuse. Scarcely has Cambara done a stroke of domestic work than she takes the measure of the woman's exhaustion.

She says, giving herself a false name, "My name is Xulbo. What's yours?"

The woman is silent for quite a while. She struggles to sit, now rubbing her back, now her hips, staring ahead of herself, her eyes rolling in amazement at what is happening here: a help at hand, what kindness! The woman is rigid in her appearance, preoccupied, busy worrying a blackhead, picking at it. Maybe she is deciding whether to accept Cambara's offer to help with the house chores; maybe the idea of telling her name to a total stranger does not sit easily with her or with the men sleeping off a night's *qaat*-chewing.

Finally she says, "My name is Jiijo."

Cambara knows that this is the short form of Khadija, a name common among the woman's Xamari community, the cosmopolitan residents of Mogadiscio, believed to have descended from Persians, Arabs, and Somali.

Cambara, the adored daughter of her parents, who never lifted a finger in this house in all the years that the family had owned it, now gets down to the serious business of washing the dishes and the clothes, and mopping the floor. It surprises her how much pleasure she is deriving from performing manual labor and how a few minutes' work has so far opened doors that might otherwise have remained closed to her. When she thinks she has done enough, she asks, "How many months?"

"Eight and a half."

"Your first baby?"

The woman nods feebly.

Cambara works her fingers to the bone, intent on completing as much of the job as possible before the return of the young children. She has seen evidence of clothes, boys' broken plastic toys, girls' dolls—when she surreptitiously entered the room with mattresses on the floor.

Cambara does the best she can under the rushed circumstances. She does not take leave of the woman or of the house before she gets a couch for Jiijo to lie on. In fact, she tiptoes out only after Jiijo has started to embark on an exhausted woman's snore.

NINE

Cambara makes a detour. She decides that instead of returning to Zaak's place directly she will walk to the shopping complex in the neighborhood in order to buy a few necessary items. This way she may gain some insight into the area, discover more of its features.

She sees the grocery shopping as part of her attempt at easing her way into the lives of those she has met so far: Jiijo, the armed youths, and Zaak's driver too, a hungry, needy lot worth cultivating for their loyalty. If they do terrible things to one another and to victims whom they do not know, it is because they are malcontents born into tragic times taking out their despair on other quarries who are just as unfortunate as they are.

She intends to buy locally bottled potable water to drink, a chopping board, a kitchen knife, and a couple of other items for Zaak's place. She also wants to get what there is in the way of vegetables, eggs, and sesame oil from the fresh-produce stalls nearby for the armed youths. While at it, she may purchase an item or two for Jiijo, as a token of appreciation. Even though she has no desire to raise her hopes only to dash them, Cambara will work on the assumption that she will get a taxi that will take her first to Hotel Shamac, from where she will go to Hotel Maanta, to link up with her friend's friend, Kiin.

It is getting into early afternoon. The sun is luxuriating in pursuit of its tropical routine, coming closer and closer by the second, its heat assuming a more vicious harshness as if taking vengeance on anyone who is not indoors to enjoy the cozy coolness of the siesta hour.

Cambara's eyes secrete a clear liquid and are itchy; she scratches them. She is all the more uncomfortable because of the body tent, which she has redonned. She considered just carrying it back but thought better of it, for the sake of consistency.

The sharp wind raises a sudden storm. The dust—clear, very fine, and powdery—whirls upward with such ferocity that a dervish of memories descends on Cambara. In one of these recollections, she is strong of heart and of mind, a beautiful young athlete, the most coveted, the most adored, the one who gets the highest grades in her class; in another, she is the darling of her fellow students, male and female, the one everyone pampers with affection. In her memories of recent times, she is not a mistress of her own fate; rather she is a woman in bondage. If her marriage to Zaak is written off as an aberration and that to Wardi as an anomaly, then how is one to describe her decision to come to Mogadiscio on impulse and then take on a warlord to recover the family property?

In the long time it takes to get to her destination, Cambara does not meet a soul or a vehicle on the road, not until she is within a hundred meters of the row of buildings facing the unpaved half-circle that the shopping complex comprises. She avoids looking into the staring eyes of a couple of chador-wearing women. Averting her face, she tells herself that she must do something about her elsewhere look, which is setting her apart from the other women, labeling her, in their eyes, as an alien in their midst. It is not the women who worry her so much as the men, who will zero in on her foreignness, which will produce, in and of itself, hostility. God knows, she can do without enmity, especially given the formidable hurdles that she must clear.

Just as she turns into the dusty road leading to the trading tenement, walking with the caution and care of a woman carrying the cosmos balanced on her head, an abrupt sorrow disheartens her. She thinks about the weather in this part of the world, which has been hostile for decades now: the drought without end, the soil and the environment degraded, the sea emptied of its fish. These conditions have been tough on humans and animals, driving the pastoralists, poor and needing food aid, to the urban areas. With no government to put these people's lives into some order. And no international help to come to their aid.

Then she notices several lean-to stalls covered with rush matting; these are set apart from the complex. Farther to the left, down in the direction where she is headed, there are low grotty tiny boxes that may have been put there erroneously in the first place, and then, as an afterthought, assembled by a one-eyed builder, because the geometry, the shapes, and the distance between them is so lopsided. As another whirlwind, bearing more dust and other debris, wafts at her boots with some fury, Cambara concludes that the nature of her circumstances have undergone some remarkable changes since she decided to make friendly gestures to the armed youths by catering to their stomachs and to Jiijo by, making a woman-to-woman contact. She is confident that both deeds will pay valuable dividends.

Unable to push her thoughts any further in any direction, she turns her face away from the shanty complex and stares into the glaring brightness of the afternoon sun, as if the solar omnipresence will provide her with an idea to pursue. Just then, as she is preparing to move again, the sudden noise made by a lizard crawling out of a clump of cacti gives her a startle. Then, fascinated, she watches the lizard doing push-ups, which reminds her of the fact that she has not been doing her routine exercises with regularity for quite some time now. Even so, she believes that she will have lost weight before long here, because of the unavailability of so many items.

Finally she goes forth, conscious of the reptiles and other small, unseen denizens of the low shrubs, their sudden, noisy appearances on the scene or at her feet bringing to the fore her nervy state, rattling her. At one point, she stops to focus on the movement she hears, and her eyes light on a pair of human feet, very dry and cracking at the heels. It takes her a long time to work out that the feet, clumsily wearing a pair of Chinese-made platform sandals as ugly as any footwear she has ever seen, belong to a man, most likely homeless, fully stretched out and asleep among the cluster of bushes. For all she knows, the man may be dead. Disturbed, she walks away faster and with more purpose.

Now that she has reached the edge of the shopping complex, she stops not so much to study the scene as to work out what to do next and where to go. In the event, she walks past the fresh-produce stall, giving it a cursory look and deciding that she will come back to it if there is need, and makes a straight move toward the general store, which promises, according to a board written in hand, that you can get "everything here." This being the second time she has been to a civil war Mogadiscio market, she finds it curious that the money changers, the armed youths, the women running the vegetable stalls, and those selling bundles of *qaat* all mix freely, as if amicably. One may be lulled into believing that everything is normal. Some people put forth the idea that economics is the spark plug that ignites the fuel that makes the civil war engine run. You buy, you sell, and everyone and everything is okay. Looking around, she thinks that everyone here is hard-core local, their accent rough on the edges and jarring on her ears and senses. In addition, Cambara observes that there are fewer veil-wearing women here. Maybe because everybody knows everyone, women feel safe among their own menfolk.

She pauses twenty meters or so before the general store. She is looking for telltale intimations of trouble in the shape of a gang of armed youths loitering at its entrance or in its vicinity. Finding none, she feels safe within her to go in.

The man running the general store stands tall and bearded on the other, the owner's, side of the counter. He smiles at her when she enters. The two youths who stand on either side of him help him run the business; they do not share a family resemblance with him. In fact, they strike Cambara as the kind that make an honest living during much of the time but may resort to illicit activities in their spare hours. When she looks back at the man, who has now instructed them to attend to other customers, the man turns to her; very businesslike he asks what he can do for her. Heartened, she removes her face veil to make it easier for her to engage his attention.

Then she notices his active eyes, taking the measure of every customer who walks in. For those he deems dangerous, perhaps he prepares to put his guns to use; for moneyed clients, he must display his charm. She suspects she belongs to the latter order. He has another classification for the mendicants touching him for alms, the good people who've fallen on hard times, and the bad people, with their bad smell and their bad habits.

Her shoulders slacken into a sense of relief as she concludes, with little evidence, that he has assigned her a category of her own; a woman apart. She stands motionless, hunched in the manner of someone turning serious thoughts over in her head. She beckons to him to come closer and, when he does, tells him that she has no local currency, only U.S. dollars in large denominations, and that she needs change before buying anything. He smiles, nods, and says, "No problem, no problem. Now, what would you like?"

A bad shopper, she is in the habit of going into supermarkets, even when in Toronto, to buy a couple of items only to end up forgetting the list, putting in her shopping basket or taking to the cash register a number of articles that do not match her original tally. With no transport at her disposal and not knowing when she may next find herself in a supermarket as well stocked as this, Cambara assembles the list in her head and allows herself time to improvise as she looks at what is available and on the shelves before speaking it aloud. The shopkeeper has a piece of paper and a pen handy, ready to write everything down. He says, "Take your time. I am here all day."

She relegates a couple of thoughts about general stores similar to this to a back burner. Only she can't help wondering who the wholesalers are that run the risks of importing these articles into the country and who their business partners overseas are. It is common knowledge that the civil war has been responsible for the destruction of Somalia's meager industrial base, the warlords profiting from the dismantling of its infrastructure, which they sold as scrap metal, Somali rumor mills in Toronto have it, to Abu Dhabi and China.

Now his tone urges her on; he says, "Waiting."

She understands this to mean that she has waited long enough, and straight away the provisional list that she will add to runs easily off her tongue: a kilo each of sugar, of flour, and of rice; a chopping board; a kitchen knife; two, three dishcloths; a packet of soap powder; some tea, preferably in bags; instant coffee; dried herbs, curry powder, and spices; tomato concentrate in tins; spaghetti; bottled water; several bottles of soda; paper plates and paper cups; plastic knives and forks; and napkins. A few packet of sweets, bars of chocolate, shampoo, soaps.

"Is that all?" he asks.

The shopkeeper's voice is of a comforting quality; it reminds her of many a friend of her parents whom as a young girl she unfailingly addressed as "Uncle." She finds his voice so soothing that she becomes wary of trusting him fully. Yet she contemplates easing the head-covering segment of the body tent a little when another woman wearing a veil and under it a curve-hugging frock comes into the shop to buy a bottle of soda. Cambara follows the woman with her eyes, remarking to herself that the woman is wearing the veil for the sake of form and feels at ease in who she is. Tomorrow, Cambara promises herself, she will wear a less heavy-duty veil of Yemeni origin, the fabric cotton, to let her skin breathe normally. Next time.

"Anything else?" the shopkeeper is asking her.

"You don't have vegetables, do you?" She is aware that he doesn't carry them, but she also knows that she can take advantage of the situation, place her order, and he will deal with it somehow. She bases her assumption that she will get her way and have his assistants fetch her all she needs on the fact that the man takes her for a respectable and well-to-do woman, just come from the Arab Emirates or Saudi Arabia, where women of high standing seldom mix with the rabble. No doubt, he will charge extra for the service.

"We can get you some, if you like," he offers.

She reels off the list. "In that case, a kilo of okra, one each of potatoes, carrots, half a kilo of onion, half of fresh tomato, three or four cloves of garlic, and some lemon or lime."

He sends out one of his boys to "bring nothing but the best of the best" and to "come back quick, quick," and asks the other to give "the lady" a chair. This done, every other shopper takes notice of her, and more than a dozen envious eyes turn on her. Cambara doesn't look bothered, reminding herself how often she has gloried in her role on the stage as an actor.

When the shopkeeper and his assistants have gathered everything, packed them professionally in shopping bags, and put them on the counter, some piled on top of each other, as if waiting for her to bag them in her own way, the man informs her that he has done his sums. Cambara makes yet another request that she assumes will exalt her in his esteem, marking her as belonging to a class apart.

"A taxi, please. Can you get me one?"

She sits back, her posture that of a woman accustomed to giving orders and used to them being obeyed.

The man nods ponderously, then whispers in the ears of one of the youths whom he sent out earlier to get the vegetables. Demurring to the shopkeeper, the youth goes through a back door so fast that Cambara feels that he will be back with a taxi in tow in less than a minute.

Cambara then produces a fifty-dollar bill folded over until it is as small as a postage stamp, unfolds it and lays it on her spread lap, then smooths it with her open palm before handing it to the youth, who in turn passes it to the shopkeeper.

The shopkeeper holds it discreetly to the light as he speaks, most likely studying the genuineness of its watermark and deciding whether it is counterfeit. He nods as if to himself, opens a drawer, lifts a tray within it, and then places the fifty-dollar note in a false bottom.

He turns to say to her, with every word dripping with the deference of the most irritating sort, "Our hearts sweeten when we see the likes of you visiting our city again." Her skin crawls with millipedes of hair, hearing the man's ill-expressed feeling. "This is proof, if anyone wants one, that our city is no longer as dangerous as before."

All of a sudden, Cambara wishes her mother were here to hear the shopkeeper say that. Now she remembers her last encounter with Arda and replays their conversation. Her mother, on the day, had a guest—a former Canadian diplomat thanks to whose facilitations and kind interventions her parents, Zaak, and Wardi were all able to go to Canada as landed immigrants. Arda, given to the habit of speaking about Cambara blamably and always in the third person, even when she is present, explains to Mr. Winthrop that her daughter's lack of humility, her inability to appreciate the simple aspects of living, worries her more than anything else. Arda adds, "Just imagine this. She is getting over the loss of her one and only son, my one and only grandchild, and before she is done with mourning, complicates things more. There is calm in acting humbly, in being simple. Not my daughter."

Mr. Winthrop feigns interest. "What's she up to?"

"She is off to Mogadiscio," Arda replies, as if going to Somalia is tantamount to committing a crime in a murder-free suburb in Ottawa. "She is off—to use her own words—to recover our family property. Do you remember the property, which you saw, loved, and then rented? She wants to wrest that property from the clutch of a warlord with lots of blood on his hands. No one is asking her to go in pursuit of trouble or of possible death. Not I. If she were to listen to my advice, I would suggest that she rid herself of her estranged husband, that she divorce him and not bother about the property. Alas, she will not hear of it. She just likes to complicate matters, maybe because the plainness of things wearies my daughter, drives her nuts. Up she must go to that wretched country and risk herself for nothing. Because I am sure that the property, which you and I know well and which brought us together, making us into the friends that we now are, is in ruins, unrecoverable. I keep asking, What is the use? I keep saying, What is the point?"

A sudden ruckus in the street brings Cambara back to the present, alerting her to the fact that not only is she in Mogadiscio, come on a reconnoitering walkabout, veiled, in disguise, she is now in a shop as part of her expedition and is bearing witness to two preteen boys locked in combat, kicking, punching, and tearing at each other's sarongs. A large woman in a wraparound *guntiino,* bearing a club the size and shape of an alpenhorn, comes out of one of the houses, walks past the crowd of onlookers now gathering, just watching. Silent and serious-looking, she puts her club down close to her feet, from where she can pick it up before grabbing one of the boys by his hair, pulling it. Throwing him back as if he were no bigger than a greasy dishcloth, she steps in between them, frighteningly huge. Then she stares down at one, then the other, not speaking but domineering.

The shopkeeper, with a touch of pride, says, "Here is further evidence if you need it."

"Evidence of what?"

"In former days," the man explains, "two boys of their age from different clans would have settled a small dispute by shooting at each other; not now. And they would not have allowed a woman to stop their fight; they would have killed her, point-blank. Now you can see them going their different ways, licking their wounds in humiliation and silence."

Cambara watches, mesmerized, as the amazon who a moment ago separated the two boys stands, elbows pointing outward, and waits for the crowd to disperse before returning to her house.

"Who is she to them?" she asks the shopkeeper.

"She is nothing to either of the boys," explains the shopkeeper. "Not their mother or aunt. Or even a distant relative."

"Where does she come into it, though?"

"She is a member of the Women for Peace network."

"Please tell me more," Cambara pleads.

The shopkeeper obliges. "In several of the city's districts, women have been organizing against gun violence. Gun violence has led to a high incidence of rape and the deaths of many. The failure of the country's political class to end the civil war has prompted the women to set up an NGO—Women for Peace—funded by the EU."

"How come you know all this?" she asks.

"Because my wife is on the steering committee."

Cambara realizes that he is looking at the back door, presumably through which he goes into his house, where his wife may be busy attending to some chore or other. She is about to ask if his wife is at home, when a young fellow enters the shop through the same back door to announce that he will take her to her waiting taxi.

The man does his sums for her benefit a second time, and Cambara collects her change in wads of Somali shillings, so bulky she does not know where to put it. The shopkeeper comes to her aid, giving her a handbag, almost new. When she hesitates, saying that she does not know when she will return it or how, he encourages her with the words "We're bound to see you again and will be happy to. Take it, and bring it back when you come again."

Thinking, "There goes my chance of asking the shopkeeper to give me his name or his wife's, or the source of the items on the shelves," she follows one of the assistants as he walks out through the front door, wheeling a barrel load of her purchases, covered in a toweling material. The young fellow turns a sharp right, then a sharp left. The taxi, an ancient Lada dating from the Cold War years, when the Soviets ran the show in Mogadiscio, boasts bald tires and is phenomenally rich in rust and paint loss, not to mention the number of things that she presumes will not work. She wonders if it is wise or safe to sit in it and be driven first to Hotel Shamac, where she can get to the business of tracking down Kiin, then perhaps to Hotel Maanta, and after that to Zaak's place.

"Where to?" asks the driver, as the youth puts her purchases in the car boot, the driver struggling first to open it, then to fit them in. She can see the glassless window open, she can feel the seat sagging, even before she goes in and sits, She can also see, from where she is, that the space where her feet will be when she enters is a gaping hole. If she derives any comfort from taking the taxi, it is that there is no one with a gun; even the driver seems unarmed. She is immensely relieved. Nonetheless, just to be sure, she asks, after he has closed the trunk, "No armed escort?"

"My taxi is so old it is safe," replies the driver, showing the cavities in his mouth as if she were a dentist requesting that he let her see his gums.

"Hotel Shamac, please."

"Please get in."

TEN

A small bother gains purchase in Cambara's mind. She wonders whether to settle on the invented identity of a veil-wearer or reestablish her own, now that she is driving away from the area in a taxi that is about to move. She finds the requirements of her veil-wearing identity not only too demanding but exhausting, burdensome, too hot to lug along, and too cumbersome to accommodate.

She remembers coming out of the shop, feeling elated and believing that she has achieved a feat far in excess of her own expectations. She recalls emerging into the glare of the afternoon hour, majestically wrapped in her tentlike garment, slow-moving and imposing in an eye-catching way, doing her utmost not to attract unnecessary attention to herself, yet this is what she has ended up doing. She could tell this from the way in which dozens of loiterers hanging outside the shop like paparazzi now fasten their stares on her, as if she were a celebrity. In preference to going in and sitting in the taxi, she decided to make sure the youth put all her shopping bags in before she turned her back on him.

To make matters worse, the youth who wheeled out the cart loaded with her purchases took his time off-loading it, transferring the items one by one into the many-holed trunk of the taxi. On occasion, he even rummaged in the shopping bags. She had no idea why and dared not ask him, lest she upset him—who knows what he may do, or whether he will react violently?

Now, the taxi engine running, Cambara keeps her wary eyes on the driver gawking at her, and the small crowd that has gathered staring. For his part, the driver has his foot on the brakes and the handbrake firmly in his right hand, maybe because he does not trust its efficacy.

When Cambara gives the youth who has helped off-load a tip in a wodge of shillings the real value of which she does not know, she gets in and says to the taxi driver, "Shall we go?"

The taxi is ill tempered, and its engine stalls as the driver engages it into a second gear to get moving, perhaps because the first is dysfunctional, she is not sure. He turns the key in the ignition two or three times before he cranks it and it catches. This reminds Cambara of her horrid experience in the truck, with Zaak. However, once she ceases to worry, the vehicle moves without stopping. Now she is unnecessarily preoccupied, not only because it is the first time she has put on a veil but also because it is the first time since her arrival in Mogadiscio that she is in a one-to-one situation, alone in a car with a male stranger. It is important that she settle on a choice of identity that makes her garb match her behavior. Can she measure up to the challenge as a pretender?

Two options are open to her. On the one hand, she can act as though finding herself alone in the company of a male stranger is frightening, wholly paralyzing, keep her face veil on for effect, and decline to exchange a single word with the driver during the entire journey. This, she knows, will necessitate staying out of his rearview mirror and his radius of vision. She doubts she can pull this off, with the seat in the back being so uncomfortable and her moving and readjusting to avoid the springs and the sagging inconvenience. Moreover, she has to ensure that at no time during the entire trip does her face wander into his discernment, or her eye make contact. She cannot act in a way he might construe remotely as coquettish. On the other hand, she can act true to form and don her God-given identity in place of the veil. Given the choice, she will opt for the identity in which she plays herself—a woman easygoing in the company of men. What to do with the trappings? Cambara resolves not to rush but to wait for the appropriate time.

He is saying, "Are you staying at Hotel Shamac?"

"Why do you ask?"

"Because I may up the price of the ride."

"Do you think that is fair?"

"I am afraid," he says, "the word 'fair' no longer forms part of the vocabulary here."

"I find that disconcerting."

"Do you know what that tells me about you?"

"What?"

"That you are from somewhere else."

"Because I've used the word 'fair'?"

"And also because of your veil."

"What about my veil?"

"It's obvious you are not accustomed to wearing one," he says, and manages a smile.

"How can you tell that?"

"In pre–civil war days, I used to head the transport unit of the Ministry of Foreign Affairs, assigned to chauffeur important dignitaries and ambassadors on missions to Somalia. I remember how often many of them would take off their ties, as if they were masks of disguise, the moment they were in the car and among their friends. How they would sigh, a large number of them, relieved."

She feels exposed, and fresh strong winds of self-doubt start battering her from all sides. Her bodily movements strenuous, she shifts, agitated, a part of her mind urging her to remove one of the disguises, the face veil; at least she will feel more comfortable. However, before she acts out her inner contradictions, she ponders whether caving in to the suggestion from a man unknown to her will undermine her objective and turn her into a quarry of his machination, whatever his motives. An uncanny memory, in which Wardi figures prominently, calls on her. She sits in the back of the vehicle as maudlin as a tanked-up drunk decidedly resisting surrendering to the groundswell of sorrows coming at her in sizzled waves.

She elects not to acquiesce to the easier of the options, her thoughts wandering away, her eyes likewise. She sees more ruin everywhere she looks, houses with no roofs, lampposts denuded of cables, windows lacking glass panes: a Mogadiscio raided and destroyed. Looking around from where she is, she sees women in cheap chadors, men in sarongs and flip-flops, their guns slung over their shoulders. She concludes that the city, from her encounter with it in the shape of most of its residents, appears to have been dispossessed of its cosmopolitan identity and in its place has begun to put on the clannish, throwaway habits of the vulgar, threadbare semi-pastoralists. Even though she cannot contain her despair, she does not wish to dwell on the conse-quences of the civil war and the destruction visited on the entirety of the society; she wants to talk about the positive side of things. Therefore, she decides to focus on the shopkeeper and his wife, who, according to her husband, is active in the Women for Peace network that Raxma had told her about.

"How long have you known the gentleman who runs the general store where you picked me up?" she asks.

"I've known him and his family for a long time."

"Tell me a little about them."

"What would you like to know?"

"His name, for a start," she says.

"Why are you interested in knowing about him?" the driver asks. From the expression on his face, she cannot decide if their conversa-tion is entertaining him or causing him worry.

"I've found him very friendly, a gentleman of the kind you rarely meet in a city said to belong to the self-serving warlords and their henchmen. It has been a pleasure doing business with him."

"What business are you in?"

Of course she does not want to tell him much about herself, but then how can she expect him to help her with her questions about a third party when she doesn't seem willing to talk about herself? She puts a different spin on a response to a question he did not ask at the same time as she tries to put him right.

"I am saying it has been a pleasure shopping at his store," she tells him. "Moreover, he has lent me a bag, and I want to return it to him as soon as I am done with it. It would be good if I knew his name. That is all."

"Everybody calls him by his nickname, Odeywaa," the driver tells her. "He is an unusual businessman with integrity. He is honest, he is fair, he is very forthright with everyone with whom he deals, including all the members in the atypical cooperative that he runs—the only co-operative of its kind."

"What is so unconventional about it?"

"He serves the community at large in a way no other cooperative does. Of the nearly two million Somalis in the diaspora, there are tens of thousands who find themselves in areas of the world from where they cannot make remittances to their needy relatives at home in convertible hard currencies, like the U.S. dollar, the euro, and the sterling. Odeywaa's aim in establishing the cooperative is to provide an outlet for the Somalis residing within the country who receive remittances in clothes and other goods, where they can sell them almost at cost price. It is a very rare thing he is doing, in this city where everyone is flocking to the warlords' homes, their heads bowed in fawning subservience to their authority, paying their respects and behaving as commoners do in the presence of their betters."

The driver goes quietly off on a woolgathering expedition, and from his face in the rearview mirror, she deduces that he is entertaining a private reverie; she lets him be, in silence, waiting.

He continues, "In this low intensity of the civil war, more of us are wising up to the fact that we have nothing but disdain for the warlords' doings, a kind of contempt equaled only by our scorn for the so-called clan elders, who sanction the recruitment of the youths into the fighting militia." He pauses long enough for Cambara to sit forward, eager to hear his words. "I see the warlords for what they are—men in drag, every one of them."

"Men in drag? That's a new one."

The driver goes on, "In fact, one of them—also known as The Butcher—fled the southern city of Kismayo, dressed as a woman, when he lost control of it."

"What do you think of the religious leaders?"

"Alas, they have shown their true colors too."

"What do you mean?"

"Nothing that they have done since the explosion of the civil war will endear us to the religious leaders, many of whom have lapsed into a state of despair, in which they have declared their loyalty not to Allah, the supreme, but to their birth communities, each to his own, as it were."

They drive in silence again, moving in a southwesterly direction, over potholes that insist on frequent, abrupt detours and occasional sudden halts, if only to avoid the roadside ditches or the piles of rubbish along them. They pass walls pocked with bullet holes and buildings teetering unsteadily away in the opposite direction from which they will eventually fall when they do collapse.

Cambara asks whether—now that the city is no longer divided into North and South, with two warlords running it, but has half a dozen less powerful *signori di guerra*, each ruling over his dysfunctional fiefdom—people are apprehensive, locked in a sense of insecurity, the Islamists may end up gaining the superior hand. These could appeal to the Somalis' sense of religious identity, in place of the clan one, which has proven unsatisfactory. The warlords are a spent force; the Islamists not yet.

As though on cue, young armed boys in fatigues, which have known better carers and cleaner wearers, emerge out of a building, and one of them raises his hand at their approach, stopping them. The grin that has been there for much of the trip—the grin of someone who knows something her interlocutor does not—descends toward her chin before disappearing completely. As the driver brakes with unprecedented abruptness, Cambara thinks ahead, imagining the vehicle collapsing, with the front and the back tires going their different ways and the rest of it landing on its belly and shuddering to a lifeless halt.

One of the boys goose-steps to the driver's side, his jaws busy chewing *qaat*. His hand extended out farther than his bleary eyes can focus, his tongue heavy, as if it were foam soaked in water, and his words running into one another competitively, he asks, "What have you got for us?"

"We meet again," says the driver.

A much taller youth who is standing behind the watery-eyed youth says, with sarcasm, "You were mean then. Now let me warn you that you and your passenger will pay dearly for it if you do not give generously this time."

The driver's eyes search in the depth of the rearview mirror for Cambara's, and because the grin that has been there all along has vanished, he takes it that she is afraid. His hand, foraging until then in the glove compartment, emerges with a large roll of cash, which he turns over to the youth standing closest to him. When the youth uses the wad as a fan, indicating his dissatisfaction, the driver throws in two bundles of *qaat*. "Now you are talking," the tallest of the youths, presumably their ringleader says, with a wave telling him to leave, which he does, as soon as he can.

Her elsewhere look is back, the driver notices with agreeable suddenness. She says, "If you work out, do not hesitate to add the armed youth's levy to my bill, and I will pay it gladly."

He recalls the days he served as head chauffeur driving visiting dignitaries on missions to the country, and he bows his head with deference, in thankful acknowledgment of her generosity. He says, "Yes, ma'am!"

A few hundred meters on, when they hear the distant hum of a huge generator, the driver informs her that they are less than half a kilometer away from their destination. For the first time since her arrival, Cambara is in awe of the enormity of her commitment: to come to Mogadiscio and help make the world that she finds a better place, in memory of her son, whose life has been cut short.

"Here we are," he says. "Hotel Shamac, ma'am!"

ELEVEN

They have barely come within view of the gate when an armed guard, in what she guesses to be the hotel uniform, comes out of a small lean-to recently assembled in haste from discarded zinc sheets when neither she nor the driver has prepared for it. The man is of medium height, has a wide face, prominent jaws, and a snub nose, his nostrils barely visible. SnubNose flags down the taxi, the tires of which screech to a halt, jerking her forward. Notwithstanding her edginess, Cambara affects total calm, even after another man appears on the scene. The second armed sentry has a long upper body and the tiny feet of a midget. TinyFeet orders the taxi driver to step out of the vehicle; he circles the vehicle several times, his finger on the trigger of his machine gun all the while and his attention focused on Cambara, maybe hoping that she will lower down her side of the window and show her face.

She sits back, with her face veil in place and eyes closed, as though trying to soothe herself into trusting that everything will be all right soon. Scarcely has she decided to explain to them that she intends to take a room in the hotel if there is a vacancy, when TinyFeet yanks the vehicle door open and instructs her to alight in order for her to be frisked.

A roaring row erupts between the taxi driver and SnubNose, when the driver shuts the door of the vehicle and encourages Cambara to stay put.

"Who are you to close the door when I've opened it?" TinyFeet challenges, furious and red-eyed. He pushes the driver away.

Cambara enjoins the driver, sotto voce, to desist from provoking the armed guards any further. The driver falls silent at her insistence, even though she can see that he is in a defiant mood, ready to rear up in further resistance and, if necessary, fight. Then, recalcitrant and fearless, he says to TinyFeet, "But can't you see, it is inappropriate for you to subject a woman to a body search? It is not done. A woman should be doing that kind of job, not men. At least not you." He adds, after a weighty pause, "Would you allow your wife or sister to be humiliated in this way by a man, whether armed or not?"

Now the altercation takes a more ominous twist, and SnubNose joins the shouting match, turning it into a threesome, two armed fools poised against her protector, who is unarmed—how unfair. Cambara listens, with a bilious discharge gathering in her gut, as she considers whether to step in. SnubNose speaks loudly and threateningly through his nose, but she cannot make sense of what he is saying, he is so enraged. Also, his accent is dyed-in-the-wool local, and his choice of words points to a speech pattern of a hard-edged sort and of a pastoral provenance that Cambara, who is city-born and has been away from the country, cannot follow.

TinyFeet involves himself and for her benefit interprets what his colleague has said. "Let us tell you something," he says. "We will shoot first at the tires of your taxi and then at the passenger if you do not go into reverse and leave immediately or if the woman does not alight. Make your choice and be quick about it too."

"Let us be sensible," the driver pleads.

"Are you accusing us of being women molesters?"

"I am doing no such thing," the driver insists.

"You are insulting us. I know what you are doing," says TinyFeet.

Cambara's pretense of composure is completely shattered; she cowers at the disturbing thought of her virtue being violated. But I'll be damned if I will allow them to touch me, she says to herself. She replaces her hand among the inner folds of her body tent, and only after she takes a good grip of the knife does she feel comforted.

In his desire to placate the armed guards, the driver lowers his voice. Speaking almost in a whisper, he implores TinyFeet. "Please, this is a very respectable lady, in a veil," he says. "I can vouch for her. She won't be any trouble if you allow her to go in without you frisking her. As it is, she intends to check out the hotel, because she wants to take a room. So why do we not escort her in? A woman at the reception can do the body search, inside, if there is need. I'll get back into the car and go in reverse and wait for her here. If not, then I suggest that you bring a woman out to where we are. Because it is not proper that you or any man touch her. She is a lady and must be treated as such."

When the goings-on jar on her nerves some more, she resolves to bring it all to a head—and suddenly. She alights from the taxi, laboring as she does so. Now that she is out of the car, her veiled persona imposing, she stretches her arms, straightens her back, massaging it, and repeatedly stamps her booted feet on the ground in the manner of an elephant frightening away its attackers. Besides getting the dust off her footwear, she hopes she will be able to cast a spell on the armed guards. If only she could forge bewitchments that will make them do her bidding. She looks stately; they seem enchanted, fascinated, their undivided attention fully focused on the enigmatic figure of a woman, veiled, standing a little over six feet, her hands ensconced among the wrappings of her tent, doing with them what only the Lord knows. Maybe because they are not used to women performing, Cambara's imperious presence unsettles them.

On the outside, she appears to know what she is doing; not so inside. She is terribly worried that she may not pull it off; her viscera keep churning overwhelming quantities of barf. But the actor in her takes absolute command of the situation.

"Since you won't let my taxi in," she says, "please let the driver bring out of the trunk of his taxi my oddment of purchases. You may inspect them. In fact, I would be grateful if one of you will give him a hand to bring them in, given that there are no page boys about."

She turns her back on them and walks away in an ungainly manner, every short shuffle a huge undertaking, conscious that no one can touch her for this out-and-out act. She has no way of knowing if they will shoot her in the back, but she doubts it. When she has taken a few paces, and they do not order her to stop unless she submits herself to being bodily searched, she looks back and sees them whispering to one another, nodding their heads; their acquiescent glances end in TinyFeet affecting a retreat and SnubNose following suit.

At TinyFeet's behest, the driver parks on the shoulder of the dusty road, then retrieves Cambara's shopping bags and follows her, grinning from cheek to cheek, his wandering eyes meeting the armed sentries' scowls. Neither offers to help carry the bags. In fact, SnubNose wags his finger menacingly at the driver. When he joins her at the reception, the driver, eager to return to his vehicle, puts the bags down and asks, "Do you want me to wait for you?"

"That won't be necessary," she says.

She removes her face veil and notices several men looking at her from different angles, not one of them making a move toward her. Curiously and rather irreverently, it strikes her as if, in the view of some of them, she is behaving like a stripper doing it on the cheap.

Self-conscious, she pulls out of her bag a handful of bills bundled into thousands with a rubber band. At a guess, she hands over to the driver several wads of the devalued currency. "Will this suffice?" she asks.

He weighs the wads, as if he can tell their value by weight alone, and then shakes them before his face, as if they're only good for use as fans. He seems pleased, though. "This will do," he says. "Thanks."

She gets closer to the reception desk, no longer enwrapped in the mystery that is of a piece with her veil, impressively tall, her head high. She takes her short steps with catwalk elegance difficult to reproduce, disregarding the half-dozen eyes that are trained on her every move. Wearing a triumphant expression, she struts with confidence.

One of the men behind the desk summons some of the page boys and asks them to stand by. They do so, with their hands behind their backs, waiting for instructions. Cambara feels certain they will handle their assignment with finesse; she imagines what it will be like to take a room in this four-star hotel, a world that is familiar to her from having stayed in many others of similar billing. Only this one in civil war Mogadiscio is visibly a bit run-down. All the same, it feels unreal to her after Zaak's place. She recovers her sangfroid the closer she is to the sign "Reception." She enjoys the feel of the place, the cleanness of it. She wonders if the management is aware of what is happening outside the gates. She can't tell if she will mention this to anyone.

From the near distance, she reads the sign "Deputy Manager," only the D in "Deputy" and the e in "Manager" are missing. For his part, he studies her with the knowing eyes of a familiar. Then he asks, "Can I help you?"

"I am sure you can," she says.

He looks away from her and at the computer screen, pressing buttons and taking sufficient time to consult before reporting the meaning of the entry he has just read. He clears his throat before begging her pardon. He surprises her by quizzing if, by any chance, her name is Cambara.

"Why do you ask?"

"Because we've received repeated phone calls and other inquiries from the manager of Maanta Hotel, who wants to know if we have a lady by that name as our guest. She has rung our hotel several times. Actually, she rang off less than five minutes ago."

Cambara's throat makes enough of a sound for the deputy manager to hear it. She is so pleased to receive this intelligence that she is at a loss for words; the thought and joy of knowing that she is about to talk to Kiin rasps her nerves.

The deputy manager senses her discomfort. He says, "Please forgive my forwardness. You see, Kiin's description of you fits you to a tee."

Her partisan belief that she has done the right thing coming here today hardens into an uncanny conviction, not only because of this extraordinary coincidence—that she has met someone who knows how to reach Kiin—but also because of the way the movement of the deputy manager's head reminds her of a marionette coming to life. The silence is broken now and again, whenever one of the page boys or the driver, who hangs about as if his services will be needed, makes unanticipated shifts.

"You are most welcome, then," he says effusively.

Her face tight with tension, she asks, "How might I contact Kiin?"

"I'll ring her right away."

"You are very kind," she says.

The deputy manager consults the computer screen a second time and jots a number down on hotel letterhead. Cambara has a comforting sensation in her solar plexus in anticipation of his next move and her response. He asks, "How else can I be of help in the meantime?"

"Do you have a restaurant?"

"One of the best in the city."

"May I leave these purchases in your care until I've had lunch?" she says, bending down to lift up one or two of the bags. This creates an immediate flutter of movement, with the page boys swarming around her, preparing to assist. When the page boys have stood back, affording her more space, she says, "I'll pick them up after lunch, if I may."

"By all means."

At the deputy manager's bidding, two of the page boys put her purchases in the luggage room, off to the right of the reception area. A third offers to escort her to the restaurant, on the fourth floor. As she follows the young page boy up the carpeted staircase, she can't help looking forward to the moment when she will take off the body tent, easing herself out of what has become hot, unmanageable, and more of a burden. She thinks she can afford to relax, because she feels as if she is among friends, and there is no need to continue pretending.

Soon she is in an air-conditioned room, and a waiter shows her to a table by the window farthest from the generator, which is on. Another waiter arrives, in white shirt and dark trousers, writing pad open, pen raised in midair, and informs her that the kitchen is closing. She tells him what she wants to eat: a tuna steak, well done, and rice, with a green salad on the side. Then she asks the waiter to point her to the washroom, which he does.

As she rises, she thinks, with a smile, that so far luck has favored her and wonders if it makes sense to take a dayroom in which to relax after a long and demanding day. Even before she reaches the door of the washroom, she knows that this is no option, for it will, in a big way, sabotage, complicate, or delay her eventual move to Kiin's Maanta Hotel.

She removes the constraint as soon as she is in the washroom, first taking off the veil and the colorful scarf with theatrical showmanship and then running her splayed fingers through her long hair as though recasting her features into new form. The mirror reflects an old self with which she is happy to get reacquainted. Energized, she hums one of her favorite tunes as she washes her face.

She tells herself that she has brought off something of a triumph, accomplished in half a day, fortunately without exposing herself to any danger and without receiving the slightest assistance from Zaak. She revels in the fact that she has visited her family property; gotten acquainted with Jiijo; found her way to the shopping complex in the neighborhood, where she has made all the necessary purchases; exchanged her dollars for Somali shillings; and then negotiated a taxi ride to Hotel Shamac. She will no doubt concede that she owes her linking up with Kiin to a coup of luck and good timing and less to cunning on her part. She counts it as a revelation that not all her worries or her mother's safety concerns are justified; that, in low-intensity civil wars, you might not come to harm if you take the required precautions and prepare yourself for the worst but that you might just as easily be spurring disaster, prompting and courting it through no fault of your own.

Up where she is, in the bathroom on the fourth floor, the sea breeze blows gently into her face and reactivates her memory, stimulating pleasant past associations in which she pays a return visit to her young days in Mogadiscio, when Somalis were at peace with their identities, happy with the shape of their world as it was then. The problem now is how to navigate the perilous paths, with mindless militiamen making everywhere unsafe; occupying other people's homes; vandalizing or removing and reusing the doors, garage gates, the motors and roofs of most of these properties.

She has never imagined she will see the day when she will appreciate the very thing she has always taken for granted—a clean washroom, the toilet system functioning, the bathroom floor immaculate, towels on the rails. She is comforted at the thought of being in an impeccable one for the first time since her arrival, and she is flushed with joy. It goes to show that only a corrupt society tolerates living in such filth, especially the men who put up with the muck they have made, as if dirt makes itself, reproduces itself. No woman with the means to do something about it will endure so much grunge. Her mother has always said that you are as clean as you make yourself.

In the restaurant, Cambara sits at her table with an exaggerated élan, eagerly waiting for her meal and a word from or about Kiin. A different waiter from the one who earlier showed her to the table helps take her body tent from her and places it on a clothes hanger. He introduces himself as the headwaiter and is in a white long-sleeved shirt, freshly ironed; well-tailored khaki trousers; and black lace-up shoes, recently polished to perfection. He brings her news from the deputy manager: Kiin is on her way and should get here shortly.

"Oh, but that's wonderful," she says, beaming.

"And the meal is on the house."

"Thank you."

She smiles with the effortless serenity of a woman who has just won the lottery. As he walks away, maybe to bring the starter, she remembers the awfulness of cooking in Zaak's kitchen, using what came to hand. She believes that she will never forget beheading their chickens with the dullest knife she has ever seen, tugging at the insides, gutting them, wiping off the blood of the birds she slaughtered for the armed youths, and cooking the chickens for their lunch.

The waiter returns bearing ice water, then a few seconds later a starter—a salad of tomato and mozzarella—and before leaving to get her second course, brings the olive oil bottle, the salt, and pepper closer to her. He is back soon enough, this time with her fish dish, browned to perfection and garnished with parsley and a slice of lemon.

Cambara tucks into her meal with an uncharacteristic joyous abandon, relishing every morsel. Just as she is debating whether to consider taking a room in the hotel for the sake of its kitchen and cleanness, her wandering gaze fastens upon a woman approaching with some urgency, her stride graceful. Cambara's heartbeat quickens, beating in anticipation of making Kiin's acquaintance, which she hopes will open many a door closed to her until now. To Cambara, the well-turned-out woman is walking with the dignity of one accustomed to carrying the world on her head and proud of doing so too. Eager as a preteen girl, Cambara prays that she and Kiin will share the sort of friendship only women are capable of forging. The Lord knows how badly a woman needs the friendship of other women in a civil war city repugnant with the trigger-happy degeneracy of its militiamen.

"I am Kiin," the woman in all-black chador and white bandanna says, "come to welcome you to Mogadiscio." Silence, then an exquisite smile attends Kiin's face, her eyes becoming wider with the brilliance of a gorgeous grin.

Wishing she were bold enough to hug Kiin in advance recognition of their becoming soul mates, Cambara pushes her chair back and has just about contented herself with the mere shaking of her hands, when

Kiin looks into her eyes, then embraces her chest to chest. Then Kiin plants a peck of a kiss on one cheek, then the other. An unbidden thought—that Kiin is a woman with formidable initiative, of strong character and profound conviction—coincides with a discordant idea as an eerie otherworldly feeling descends upon Cambara, in which she imagines herself as a discarded rag doll saved from the fire just in time and given a bit of dusting. Why have these colliding ideas—the one about a forsaken doll that has been abandoned by the child who has loved it and expects nothing short of continuous affection, the other about the redoubtable Kiin—come to her at the same time? Kiin's Emirate type of veil is of flimsy material, comforting to touch, with her breasts bulging downward in flattened acknowledgment of an early motherhood.

"Welcome," Kiin is saying. "Sit and eat."

Cambara's instant adoration of Kiin has the quality of an intense infatuation, the conditions for which are propitiously ripe. Prone to making sudden decisions, she decides to take a room in Kiin's hotel, certain that it will be to her liking and that using it as her local base and living in it will help their closeness, which will gain more strength with the passage of time. A relationship with like-minded people whose community of *jinn*, as Somalis say, are often in agreement with one another, can only achieve a great deal.

Kiin asks, "When did you come into the city? Why didn't you come to the hotel, to look for me? Raxma, my friend and cousin, has been ringing from Toronto twice a day, admonishing me for not having located you and given you a room in the hotel. She asks every time she phones if I've rung all the hotels, inquiring if you are putting up with them. I am glad that all our efforts have borne fruit and that I've found you safe and in good shape. I don't want to be indiscreet, and please no misunderstanding. Are you comfortable wherever you are? Most important, do you feel safe to go about your business, whatever it is? What sort of amenities does your place have? Does it have running water? Does it have electricity for much of the day, especially in the middle of the day when you need air-conditioning during siesta and at night for your safety and security?"

Cambara looks anew at Kiin, whom she finds to be very pleasant on the eye, a gorgeous woman imbued with practical understanding. In one instant, she is dizzy with delight, a child living in a world of light who has a command view of a much larger space than she has ever imagined possible. In the next instant, she is an adult with the memory of a child who has dwelled in a well-lit territory out of which a rogue of a man has expelled her. Her heart beating faster and faster, her anxiety rising in a déjà vu way, Cambara says, "I've been living in very primitive conditions, I'll be honest with you."

"Move into my hotel. We'll go get your things right away," Kiin suggests. "At Maanta, there is running water, the toilets are clean, the kitchen functions twenty-four hours a day, and we have power all day and all night. It is very secure too. We'll provide you with rides to and from any part of the city you require to get to; we'll do your shopping and your laundry; and we'll get you connected: e-mail, mobile, you name it."

"What I won't do for a clean room and a toilet!"

Kiin, moved, takes Cambara by the arm. She stares emotionally into her new friend's eyes and then says, "On your say-so and if you tell us where they are, I can send my driver and the staff in my car to get your stuff."

Cambara turns this over in her mind, in silence. Not too fast, she thinks, remembering how she rushed into loving and then marrying Wardi. Now look where she has ended up: in Mogadiscio, childless, bitter, risking her life in order to get the better of her loss.

Kiin reads her own meaning into Cambara's silence, and she asks if there is a problem.

"A problem?"

"If you'll permit an indiscretion," says Kiin.

"Please feel free."

"Is there a man hereabouts that you've come to see and from whom you do not wish to be separated? Put another way, do you have a man problem?" Kiin asks and, having done so, takes on a disarranged appearance, like a room that has been tossed and then left in haste.

"That is a very interesting way of putting it: a 'man problem.'" Cambara looks amused, nods her head, and repeats the phrase a couple of times, grinning.

Kiin says, "Tell me what you got yourself into and we can solve any man problem or any other difficulty, whatever its nature. I owe it to

Raxma; I owe it to you as a woman. We deal easily with men problems in civil war Mogadiscio."

Talk of holding the wrong end of a stick, which, considering Kiin's take on it, makes sense. Understandably, Kiin has misconstrued Cambara's story as told to her by Raxma and has played up the man problem, assuming Wardi to be the culprit. Unaware of the makeup of Cambara's hesitation to take up the offer of a clean room and toilet with immediate effect, Kiin has apparently shifted the scene, mistaking Toronto, where Cambara's man problem occurred, for Mogadiscio, where there is nothing of the kind.

"Tell you what?" Kiin soldiers on, determined to help. "Give me your list of needs, and I'll go shopping around and provide them the best I can."

Cambara is herself surprised the moment the words leave her lips, because she has not given serious thought to a shopping list in as clear a manner as she is now presenting it to Kiin. It is as if she is the medium for an elsewhere woman into whom she has lapsed for the present.

"I have jobs that require the services of an electrician, a carpenter, and a plumber," Cambara says. "I would like you to help me find these skilled workers and for them to start on the jobs I have in mind. There is no question about it. I will move into Maanta sooner than you think."

"Does that mean you've bought a property?"

"It does not mean that."

"Does it mean that you've recovered your family property, which ragged, qaat-chewing squatters have vandalized, reducing it to an inhabitable state? Are you living there now and want to move into Maanta while it is being renovated?" Kiin wonders.

"No, it does not mean that."

"What does it mean then? Why do you need a carpenter, a plumber, and an electrician?"

"It's all very complicated," replies Cambara.

"Will you kindly unpack the character of your difficulties, explaining what they are, so I am in a position to help?"

"Give me a day or two and I will," says Cambara.

Kiin behaves in a strange way. Her eyes, misting over, look away, to discourage Cambara from reading a meaning into her actions. Does

Kiin feel that she is cold-shouldering her? It seems as if her enthusiasm is collapsing like a balloon pricked with a sharp object and exploding, crumpling into lifelessness.

Kiin is the first to break the awkward silence and looks for a waiter, maybe to settle the bill and then go. It is obvious from the way she shifts in her seat that she is ending the conversation. She says to Cambara, "Do you have your own transport, or would you like me to organize a lift back to where you are staying?"

Cambara susses out that her silence has rubbed Kiin the suspicious way and tells herself that nothing she does or says will soften the hardness that has entered Kiin's voice or look. She realizes that she is to blame, not Kiin. It is too late, maybe, to revisit the topic. Anyhow, she needs the unrushed time to do the right thing, to get to know Kiin better. No more scrambling; she needs time and will insist on taking it.

"I would appreciate a lift, thank you."

"Where are you staying?"

"At my cousin's place."

"Where is his house?"

"Near the former cigarette factory."

Kiin catches the eye of the waiter, whom she sends out to call her driver up. The chauffeur, a very slim, handsome man in his early twenties, joins them and stands at an angle, half facing away, as he listens to Kiin, who tells him to take the staff of three—in Mogadiscio lingo, armed guards—and give a ride to Cambara, who is putting up in a house near the former cigarette factory.

"Am I to come back and pick you up from here?"

"No need," Kiin says. "This is my city."

Cambara asks politely, "Are you sure?"

"I'll borrow a car from this hotel."

As they part, Kiin hugging Cambara, and Cambara saying how much of a pleasure it has been to meet, she gives Cambara a piece of paper from an exercise book on which she has written all her coordinates. "You'll hear from me before the end of tomorrow," promises Kiin.

"I'll aim to see you soon," Cambara assures her.

TWELVE

Cambara, no longer wearing impediments of any form, comes down light-footed and fresh after a cold shower. She is carrying bagfuls of purchases from the shopping complex, which she puts down on the floor when she comes upon the ugliness that is Zaak. Bare-chested, he is standing wobbly in a sarong shakily tied round his waist, his forehead glowing with sweat. He is pacing the breadth and width of the living room. He stops moving when she is within a meter of him. He sniffs out a trace of the cologne she is wearing and for some reason is furious, like a jealous husband locating alien scents his partner has just brought in from the outside.

After a measured pause and with a mischievous grin embellishing his features, Zaak asks, "Have you been out and, if so, where?"

Nonplussed, she surrenders herself to the unbecoming mixed emotions knocking at the door of her brain. For, among other things, she wonders if it is worth her while to remind him that he has no right to put to her such a question in that tone of voice, which she finds intrusive, insensitive, offensive, and that she hopes that he withdraws it, since he can not expect her to answer it. She feels justified in ignoring him and remains unspeaking for a long time, making certain that she keeps her temper in check. What's his concern with where she goes? How dare he assume that he can ask her questions like that?

"Yes, I've been out," she says.

"Where have you been?"

Zaak's tone of voice belongs to a couple of unpleasant memories that she has often associated with the years following their separation as a couple when he showed his ugly colors.

"Here and there," she says.

His face, swollen from sleep deprivation, wears a porcine expression, and his throat issues something of a growl. He says, "Here and where?"

"Nowhere specific."

"And what did you do?"

"Nothing in particular."

Then he sounds unexpectedly friendlier than he feels, she thinks, as he asks, "You've been having the feel of the city, from which you've been away for a very long time, have you?"

"That's one way of putting it."

"Precisely where is here and where is there?"

Cambara looks into space, dejectedly pondering. After a few seconds, her thoughts take shape in bits and pieces, this resulting in enough angry words to crowd her windpipe, badgering her to speak them. She makes a considered attempt to put flesh on her ideas without giving in to her rage. To her surprise, because the jumbles of uncoordinated phrases catch at her throat, annoying her, she curses quietly in frustration. Several attempts later, she issues a sound that is neither a cringe nor a snicker but more like a naughty girl's attempt at fighting back a fit of giggles and failing. She continues swearing under her breath and still manages to control her anger, convinced that whatever she says now will seem inappropriate, even if she puts all she has into her rebuff in response to his mildly hostile rebuke, a reprimand cast in the guise of a question.

Perhaps it is time to change the subject, especially since she does not want to be bullied into lying, like a guilty spouse speaking small untruths to cover up the glaring huge gaps in his or her story. Nor does she feel rueful about doing what she has done; rather, she is terribly pleased with her achievements today, chuffed. Moreover, she wants to keep her affairs close to her chest. What's the point of sharing her joys with Zaak? She sees no benefit in his camaraderie and of course does not wish to be easily duped into believing that he will be of assistance to her, which he hasn't been to date. Now she remembers how her mother once compared her daughter's reticence,

when the mood demands, to a house capable of holding on to its secrets admirably. Cambara will move their conversation on in as natural a pace as a horse needing no encouragement from its rider to trot
faster.

She picks up her purchases. She is in the mood to cook, to feed
everyone who happens to be around. She thinks that it will do her spirits wonders. She asks, "What about supper?"

"Myself, I've eaten enough for the day."

That he is a spoiler is not lost on her. However, she tries to work out
how best to reap a benefit from having gone out of her way to buy the
utensils and food items for Zaak's house. Until now, she has been of
the view that her purchases will prove useful in the long run, will probably give her an advantage in influencing the thinking of the youths in
an unequivocal way, the better to cultivate their amity. She senses that
she can farm the untilled terrain of their brains only if she irrigates
them with kindnesses. What is she to do, chastise him in round terms,
or go directly to the youths through their stomachs, feeding them in
hope of winning them over to her side?

"What about the youths and the driver?" she says. "If I cook, maybe
they will want to eat? What do you think?"

He takes several short steps, removes himself ponderously from her,
as if she has requested that he give her a wide berth. He goes over to
his favorite chewing corner and rearranges his stuff, smoothing the
rug here and there, lifting the cushion and pushing the rug along with
the pillow against the wall, all the while humming a tune that she cannot make out.

He says, "What's with you and the armed youths?"

"How do you mean?"

"What are they to you, why are you bothering about them?"

Her face registers a passing fidget, and she thinks that it will be a
shame if she capitulates to Zaak's insinuations just because he has
proven resistant to making the necessary attitudinal changes toward the
youths. It will not surprise her in the least if he tries to thwart her
moves or opposes whatever it is she proposes, envious of the fact that
she is creating a new history in which she and the youths relate to each
other in an altered way, and he is being pushed out into the untamed
wilderness, isolated in his own home. She is no doubt aware that her

empathy with the youths will, at best, be fraught with all kinds of complications, especially if, exercising her powers of peaceful persuasion, she attempts to mold a working relationship with one or two of them. For what it is worth, she has made up her mind that nothing he does and no temper tantrums from any of the youths will make her refrain from pursuing her central idea: a truce of a sort with them as she strives to do all she can to recover the family property. It is well known that great opportunities are missed for lack of mastering the small mechanisms of a device, compelling one to abandon the use of it.

"I'll be more than pleased to cook for everybody," she volunteers.

"I don't give a toss about the youths and their food," he says tetchily. Readying to sit, he bends double, raising his bum, with his paunch tumescent, his hands supporting him, and he gropes for a comfortable way of first taking a crouch and then seating himself down. All the while perspiring, he is breathing heavily and with difficulty.

No point in telling him that she is self-serving when she feeds the youths. Not when it comes to attending to SilkHair, though; he is special. In any case, she doubts Zaak will understand.

Seated, his breathing even, he gloats, "I've already supplied them with their daily ration of fresh qaat, which they are now busy chewing; I doubt that cooked food will interest them. As for me, I am ready for a long, relaxed chew, and you are most welcome to join me."

The tone of her voice, being blatantly friendly, disaffirms the intent of what she says, half smiling. "Thank you, but no."

"Incidentally, what will you cook, since there is no food to speak of in the house and I did not bring in any?" he asks.

"I've bought some."

"You have?"

"In addition to the food," she says, surprising him, "I've also bought a couple of utensils for cooking and other items that will come in handy whenever I am in the kitchen."

Dusk, prematurely descending, enters Zaak's eyes, wherein it takes residence, the darkness of the moment making it difficult for Cambara to read his uncertain expression. She cannot tell if he is happy that she has gone on an errand and bought these items or if he is annoyed. Of one thing she is sure: that knowing no better and having not been truly informed of her movements and the contacts that she has made, he is not so much worried as offended. He confirms her suspicions when he speaks.

He says, "Tell me, have you, in your madness, launched yourself into one or the other of the city's dangerous territories in your insane attempt to visit the family property?"

"Dangerous or not, insane or not, as you can see I am still here and unhurt," she says. "Thanks for your help. I'll remember that."

He lifts his chin in anger. "What're you saying?"

"Nothing new for now."

"Are you threatening me in some way?"

Indignant, he rises, loses his bearing, at first not knowing where he is going or what he means to do; he moves around as if in search of an unrecoverable item. He is in a feral pique, angrier at himself than he is at Cambara. He stares at her fiercely, then looks away and has no idea what to do. Eventually, he calms his nerves, preparatory to making himself as comfortable as he can to have a good, sumptuous chew, his bundles of *qaat* spread about him. Because he drags his right leg behind him as he readies to sit, she is unsure if his foot has gone to sleep or if it has become incapacitated, in view of the fact that he never walks or exercises. He is so out of shape and so unhealthy, every physical activity or gesture pointing to his decrepitude, the infirmity, if you will, of his lowly ambition.

Cussing, he goes on all fours, kneels down, half crawls awkwardly, and supporting his clumsiness with both his hands, which shake, almost collapsing, he exerts a great deal of effort into making the hundred-eighty-degree turn before collapsing. The strain causes him to sweat. He is puffy, his shortness of breath worries him, he wheezes. Eventually, Zaak assumes a convenient squat position. Then he exhales, relieved.

When he has paused long enough and has regained his equanimity, he asks, "How did you go about getting there?"

"I walked."

"You walked everywhere?"

"I got a taxi on the way back."

"Where? Be specific."

She reflects upon the question and the command to be precise, sensing the presence of an invisible snare, like a speed trap, into which one goes unawares. There is no way of knowing if the driver or the youths have seen her in the taxi that took her from the shopping complex or from the hotel to the house. And since he has neither the charisma nor the guile to draw any information out of her, it is appropriate that she avoid the ambush.

She waffles. "You know I can walk for miles and miles if I put my mind to it? Remember how I used to jog ten miles every now and then without a break or a moment's rest?"

"No problems?"

"None whatsoever."

Zaak picks up a bundle of *qaat*, selects a couple of young shoots, snaps their tender ends off with the impulse of an executioner decapitating a criminal, and then stuffs them into his mouth. When his eyes tighten, Cambara assumes they do so at her inauspicious conduct—a madwoman courting danger by going it alone, walking, when he has offered her a lift in a truck, with a driver and an armed escort. That's what he will say, even if it is untrue.

"You are not okay in the head," he says.

"Maybe you're right."

"You're most peculiar in the way you behave."

She doesn't rise to his untoward comments but looks at her watch and studies its time-telling face, as a semi-literate might attempt to strain elusive sense from the sequence of the letters in front of her. She interprets his "You're not okay in the head" as meaning "You're not behaving like a woman." She remembers instances from her past in which men used similar words to put her down.

"You do find it all incredibly exciting, don't you? Courting danger," he sallies, his voice almost breaking, his gaze uncertain. Knowing him, Cambara imagines him to be more irritated with himself for appearing so helpless than with her for exhausting his graciousness and testing his patience.

"I won't deny that," Cambara responds.

"Wooing danger has some appeal?"

"To some people, it does."

"Does it to you?"

"I haven't thought of it that way."

Perhaps he sees her doings as the workings of a sex-starved woman mourning not the death of her only son but the loss of her husband. Is this why he retreats into the surrounds of his indulgent indecisiveness, one instant describing her as insane and wanting not to have anything to do with her rash behavior, the second displaying worry and warning her about going further? As for her, she turns a thought over and over in her head, and she analyzes it from every possible angle. Is it a tall order for her to want to leave every place better than she has found it? Is this why she has bought the food with the same ease with which she requested Kiin to get a plumber and an electrician? Maybe she needs to prepare Zaak for the changes that she plans to introduce. He is not likely to accept the changes without a struggle. After all, a pig is more comfortable wallowing in its squalor than lying on a bed with a mattress, bedspreads, and freshly laundered sheets.

"Why?" he asks, all of a sudden.

Then he holds his palms side by side in the gesture of someone praying Salaatul Khauf, performed in time of war when other prayers are difficult to recite for fear of the ongoing hostilities. Zaak stares at her, the expression on his face clouding. Cambara thinks he is annoyed in spite of himself; she suspects he thinks that she is raving mad, coming to Mogadiscio, as she has, and going it alone.

She does not bother to answer his question.

"Why?" he repeats, his palms opening and going toward each other in the gesture of one praying in preparation for a blessing.

"What do you mean, why?"

"Why are you doing this to me?"

"I am not doing anything to you."

"But you are," he says. "You know you are."

Zaak is in a sweat and is murmuring profanities. Cambara reckons she cannot relieve him of his sense of frustration, considering that she does not know the basis of it. Is he breaking in a kind of sudden high fever, because her uncontrolled impatience is destined to consign her to disaster? Or is it because he is disturbed that he cannot bend her to his will and that when she runs into ruin and he steps in to help, he will not be in a position to? There is no way he can avoid blame.

"I phoned your mother earlier today," he says.

A great unease descends on her mind. Her anger gives her a jolt and then suddenly rises toward her head, nearly blinding her.

She asks, "When did you call my mother?"

"I came back home unexpectedly just about noon and found you gone," he says, "no note from you, and no indication as to where you might have vanished. I was worried. As your host, cousin, and former partner, I kept thinking, 'What will I say to Arda if something happens to you?' That is when I rang her."

"Did you think she would know where I might be?"

"I thought she might fill me in."

"On what? Fill you in on what?"

"About things you do not tell me."

"I see," she says with knowing sarcasm.

"What do you see?"

"Bet you thought you were doing your duty by me?"

"How's that?"

"As a male cousin, you feel responsible."

"I won't deny that I do," he concedes.

"You keep your watchful male eyes on me and my doing, and you want to make sure that even though I may put my life in danger, because of an act of madness from which you will do all that is in your power to protect me, I must not bring dishonor to your name and the name of the family."

"I feel duty bound, that's right."

"Do you think we are in Saudi Arabia?" she asks.

"I have no idea what you are talking about."

She looks at him steadily in the eyes and lights upon his awkward expression, more surprised than shocked. Of course, he knows what she means: She is accusing him of behaving in an unenlightened way.

He takes a pretty long time to consider his response, and then he shakes his head, indicating his disapproval. Finally he says, "Don't be ridiculous."

Then he falls silent and furrows his forehead, maybe to add a rider to his admonition, and this results in a preoccupying thought darkening his face. When the shadow shrouding his appearance clears, he mouths the words "Don't be ridiculous" a second and a third time. It is then that Cambara happens upon his countenance, which reminds her of a quote from an author whose name she has forgotten that it's not the child but the boy that generally survives in the man.

"You're impossible!" he says.

She remembers his favorite descriptions of her behavior or general attitude when they were both young, and the word "impossible" was the key one, as in "You are impossible." Or he would use the word "incorrigible," as in "She is incorrigible." The former description was always directly addressed to her, the latter more often cast in the third person to third parties. In those days, his descriptions of her were made in an amicable tone of voice with not a trace of anger. He may have thought of her as too forward in the way she looked at him and in the teasing manner she threatened she would touch him, even though she never dared, fearing a reprimand from her mother. He was vulnerable when provoked and prone to giving in. She was wont to saying he was lying, and he wouldn't bother to tell her off, unless he felt embarrassed, which he often did in front of their peers. She remembers the shock on his face when she wore her first lipstick, her mother's, at the age of nine. There was an amused look of expression when he saw her putting on a bra, to cover the dark patches on her chest that passed for nipples.

Cambara is debating what to do or say when she discovers a change in the surroundings and then hears footsteps quiet enough to suggest the tread of someone tiptoeing, his or her intentions unknown. Turning, she sees a figure silhouetted against the fading light in the doorway and moving neither forward nor back. When she identifies the person as SilkHair, a smile of relief spreads itself all over her face.

She says to SilkHair, "Would you like to come and help me cook supper?"

He replies, "Yes, I would."

She tells SilkHair to go into the kitchen ahead of her and to start chopping the onions, tomatoes, and garlic on the new cutting board.

Then, just as she prepares to take her leave politely from Zaak, he speaks slowly, getting his words out sluggishly, maybe because the chewing has already affected the pattern of his speech. "Do you know why it does not augur well for outsiders who have no understanding of what is going on in Somalia and have no idea what has caused the civil war to erupt to meddle in it?"

She does not like the intent, the tone, or the implication of his question, but she realizes that she has no desire to engage him in further banter and cuts it to the quick. "Tell me?"

"Because when we Somalis are hemorrhaging one another, it is best that we sort out our differences without outside interference."

Cambara is impressed with the sensational progress SilkHair has made, his ability to get the hang of cooking improving at a phenomenal speed. She finds the onions chopped, the garlic crushed, the tomatoes cut into quarters, the potatoes and carrots washed, peeled, and then put to soak in water.

She assumes from his demeanor, his body language, and his speech mannerisms that in all probability he has a middle-class background—a ten-year-old boy fallen on tough civil war complications, maybe both parents dead and no living relation to look after him—but she chooses not to ask him questions, concerned that he might close her out. From his gradual opening to her, initiating the dialog himself and then terminating it, he puts her in mind both of a tortoise pulling in its head out of self-preservation and a lizard scuttling away at the slightest threat.

The vegetable curry and rice cooked, she asks him to take the food out to the youths in the outhouse, where they are camped. She makes him promise her that he will bring the containers back, wash them, put them on the drain board, and dispose of the paper plates and plastic knives. When she asks Zaak if he has changed his mind and will eat, he says, by way of dismissing her, "Good night."

She withdraws to her room to read and sleep.

THIRTEEN

Feeling young of heart, strong of body, questionable of judgment, and yet unbending in her doggedness to set things in motion, Cambara walks away from the gate to Zaak's house the following morning swathed in a baggy, custom-made all-gray veil with the sides zipped up for quick, easy removal in the event of a need to karate-kick an aggressor. The veil she has on today is easier and more pleasant to wear: less weighty, airier, and lighter in color. She ambles away from the entrance when she is certain that no one is shadowing her and after she has securely locked it. There is a determined spring in her stride that bespeaks of a secret urgency to which no one else is privy; there is much purpose to her gait. A casual observer might think of her as someone fleeing from a crime scene, edgy that she might get caught before escaping.

She draws her eyebrows together in concentration, frowning, her downcast look proof of her single-mindedness. She is carrying with her several items that she purchased yesterday from the general store and secretly stored in a corner of her room until this morning. She intends to offer as tokens of peace the boxes of sweets and a few bars of chocolate to Jiijo's charges; the body cream, lotion, shampoo, soaps, and other woman's things to Jiijo; and some rice. She would return the bag to the shopkeeper, if there is time. Faintly worried at the thought of staying longer than necessary, not knowing when the children get back from school, she hopes to present herself before Jiijo, get acquainted with the young ones, and complete her gentle questioning of Jiijo and leave before the minor warlord and his cohorts bestir themselves from their late lie-ins. Among other things, Cambara means to learn a few essential facts about her principal enemy, enough to know what to do and whether to share what information she gathers with Kiin and others who might give a hand in helping dislodge him. She needs all she can learn from today's conversation with Jiijo and her charges, anything that might lend her an advantage in furthering her plans. The expropriator of the house and his minions, from what she has worked out so far, appear to be totally lost to the real world, chewing *qaat* all their waking hours and sleeping it off until early afternoon. She prays they keep to this timetable and do not alter their habit.

As she moves forward with confidence, Cambara becomes aware that it may not be long before her repeat visits raise Jiijo's suspicions and she demands that Cambara explain her true motives. Cambara wonders how she can home in on who the various parties she will be up against are, what their relationships are to one another, and, more specifically, to the property: who stays where and how many of them sleep to a room, and where in this equation the children are. Friendly approaches and gift-giving can help deflect suspicions or can equally rouse someone's dormant mistrust. She herself does not know how resolute she will remain in the face of adversity; if her early attempts to get the information she is after produce no reliable results and the conditions become so inimical, she will have no choice left other than to try to stave off the unavoidable consequences that may lead to violence. Even though she has made inroads here and there and has discovered the presence of a soft center in the youths' outwardly hard attitude, as well as in Jiijo, Cambara is sure that it will be days before she makes a solid breakthrough.

If there is a concern that puts all her other worries in the shade, she thinks it wise to vary the routes she takes to get to the family property, detouring from the course of yesterday. This is because trouble comes with any territory that one passes through twice. One may go unnoticed the first time, but if one takes the same route a second time, then this presents someone with the opportunity to lay an ambush. The armed militiamen mount checkpoints in a matter of seconds, and they stop pedestrians and vehicles passing through, to harass, to impose a levy, to rob. That is how things are, she has been told more than a couple of times. Zaak has pointed out on more than one occasion that the vigilantes do not bother to differentiate between the goods on which a customs officer at a point of entry into a country may exact a tariff and a woman minding her business and walking through. But she dare not change the direction of her route too much for fear of losing her way to the property.

A minute into what she knows is going to be an arduous haul, Cambara walks straight into a localized rush of wind in full swing, tumultuously gusting. A dust storm is astir, impassionately working itself up into a high degree of turbulence and producing an impetuous whirlwind that whips, gathering its energy into an ungodly fury. The vortex of sand tosses her into a sidelong stumble, and she reels, staggers unsteadily, flounders forward, and has immense difficulty remaining upright and holding the shopping bags she intends to give to Jiijo and her charges. She dodders in her bid to see if there is anything to hold on to with her free hand, lest she fall into a ditch or totter into an open sewer, if there is one hereabouts. The wind-driven grit smacks straight into her eyes, hurting and blinding her. She ceases all movement, turns her back to the surge of sand, then, to regain her balance, moves blindly backward, her eyes shut.

During a brief breather, in which there is a near cessation of the gale, Cambara spots a hawk unperturbedly sitting on an electric pole from far off. Envying the bird the steadiness of its poise, she admires the hawk's agility, as it sways now a little forward, now a little backward. The hawk, in a dance of sorts, always manages to recover its equilibrium, the feathers of its wings slightly ruffled and opening outward, its claws clutching the wire tautly, its head tilted forward, as though in homage to a wind god. Cambara is at her most attentive and watching, when her foot encounters a pile of papers at which she kicks. She bends down to retrieve the thick pad of papers, deciding to examine them at her convenience later.

Soon after that she notices three figures rising mysteriously into her view. She is, however, unable to make out the figures in relation to the world the dust storm has thrown into utter confusion. She realizes too that she has to negotiate an obstacle course comprised of a disarray of zinc sheets that have come loose from the nails holding them to the roofs, and small and large pieces of plywood that have tumbled off in somersault urgency, going wherever the gust of dust has deposited them. She is wondering if the pad of papers she has just picked up and is now holding in her hands has anything to do with the figures that have materialized into recognizable human shapes. Unafraid because she has no idea why she should fear them, she puts down her bags and waits for the figures as they come closer. And as she does so, she places the pile of papers in one of the shopping bags and then transfers the weight to her left hand, the better to have a free hand in order to defend herself.

She rides her memory at a gallop, reminding herself that she is carrying a knife and that she has a good chance of winning a confrontation with any manner of youths; she reckons she has the element of surprise on her side. She has no idea who these young men are; for all she knows, they may have been on her heels ever since she left Zaak's place or have chosen to catch her in a snare, because they saw her walk the same way yesterday. She believes in her heart that ne'er-do-well rogues are weak-kneed, lily-livered, and incapable of standing up to a gutsy surprise-on-her-side, knife-in-her-hand woman who takes the fight to them, which she will do, you can be sure about it. Not that she has ever been mugged, or raped herself, except when acting. She has heard it said that raping women is the principal delight of Mogadiscio youth.

Then, as if on cue, more like a referee stopping a boxing match, a fresh sandstorm gets up so fiercely again that she cannot make them out anymore, and in fact she loses them in the wake of its rise. And when next she spots them, it feels as though they are stirring themselves into her sight, hurtling into view in a tumble of somersaults. At first they appear peripherally, then they come closer, assuming a physical prominence that she associates with imminent danger. Finally, they are there as an unwelcome menace to her existence.

She waits for them. At their approach, her discomfort empties her of all her courage and she feels weak where she has known herself to be strong: in her convictions. This is because she does not know the first thing about what they are after, or if the pad of papers that she picked up and put in her bag has anything to do with it. What can they want? Just to be sure, she stuffs the papers into the front of her veil, close to her chest, her heart beating abnormally fast. It has not been her intention to provoke anyone or attract attention to herself. However, if this is what has happened, she will have to deal with it; she will not fear them or run away from them, conscious that, like dogs, they will zero in on the slightest intimation of panic. They are now bearing down on her, as though they are a pride of lions cornering their pushover prey. She unzips the sides of her custom-made veil so she has more space in which to move about for self-defense.

Four youths, only one of them ostensibly armed, a second bearing a heavy club. She tells herself that she can take the armed one and the one with the club at a go, no question about it. She is worried about the two others, one of them a youth of indeterminate age, more like a dwarf, because of his size and his fully developed muscles, the other thin as a weed, barely a threat. Her knife in her left hand, hidden from view by a shopping bag, she moves away from them with the slowness of a huntress in a territory familiar to her, convincing herself that she is the one in pursuit of them, not they her. She stops all of a sudden and turns on them, the urge to strike at the gun-toting one so great in her mind that she struggles under the weight of her conscience, preoccupied that she might murder him and the one with the club too.

Then she speaks, her voice mean like a man's. She addresses her words to the tallest of them. She chooses him, because he is moving quickly toward her threateningly while the others stay back, as if deferring to the bodily boundary around a veiled woman, whom a man must not approach in an irreverent way.

"What's it you want?"

He puts a hard edge into his voice, and, throwing his club away to his right, he studies her expression, maybe with a view to finding out if she is afraid, before saying, "It's such a shame that you have to cover yourself. Why hide the beauty with which God has blessed you?"

The youth is an addict *qaat*-chewer, to judge from the rotten state of his teeth and his eyes red from sleeplessness. His demeanor is utterly disdainful once he gets going. He is in all likelihood a flasher too. She has seen his kind of sexual poise and lusty look in other men with equally sick minds. She will not let him frighten her into easy submission. Red-Eyed Randy cups his crotch with his hands and fondles the entire area, his stare trained on her.

"Don't you want it?" he asks.

To get the better of him, she takes a step back, creating a distance, as she weighs her options, considers what she must do in the face of such crass behavior, and tries to anticipate what his response might be. Of course, she is a novice when it comes to physical violence, this being the first time she has engaged a total stranger in this way. She reasons that it is one thing exchanging blows with Wardi, who in any case was no stranger, and another to take on the city's rogues. Her body temperature rises to the hotness of an airing cupboard; she is short of breath, her lungs empty of oxygen, feeling as though dried up. If she is not scared stiff, it is because she knows she can karate-kick him in the balls and for good measure boot him on his bum too.

Red-Eyed Randy is surprised that, unafraid, Cambara is fixing him through the veiled netting with a hateful smirk and treating him as if the two of them are duelists holding each in the other's steady stare, she looking the more amused and he appearing bothered, if a little shaken. This is the way she is playing her mental game: She wants to irritate him into acting prematurely. He has his own plan, however, and starts gesticulating as though masturbating. When she makes mockery of him, Red-Eyed Randy is flummoxed. He becomes more self-conscious the instant he imagines what impression his two mates, who are watching with great interest, will have of him.

In his attempt to gain the upper hand, Red-Eye appeals to his armed companion, maybe suggesting that he intervene. Cambara now concentrates her stonier stare on Red-Eye's mate, ArmedCompanion. The movements of her hand under her robe meet his worried expressions, and the armed youth takes a step backward. He stands apart from everyone else, vigilant, and even with his weapon poised, ready to shoot, he acts as though he is noncommittal. Cambara behaves as if none of this fazes her. She waits for one of the youths to make a move, and as she does, she bores her barely visible eyes into the soft center that she identifies in the youngest of the youths, who strikes her as very sweet and of a vulnerable age and perhaps background, even if susceptible to peer influence. She reckons that he has not the mad courage to challenge either Red-Eye or ArmedCompanion or to stop them from being a nuisance.

She says to him in an older woman's tone of voice, which sounds effortlessly shaky, "Have your friends no respect for a woman their mothers' age who is on her way to an ailing granddaughter who is as old as they are?"

MereBoy fidgets. He looks from Red-Eye to ArmedCompanion, then to his silent mate, and finally to Cambara, his expression marked with a huge indecision. The unreality of her current situation and MereBoy's pleading look prompt her to reach deep within her in an effort to tap her requisite sense of aplomb. She is aware that MereBoy is no challenge to them; she knows it and knows that they know it. Moreover, he does not have the words with which to set himself apart from them. And even though she discerns that he wishes he had the means to express his separateness, yet it is obvious that he is not bestowed with the physical strength or experience to fight off Red-Eye and ArmedCompanion successfully. It eases Cambara's anxiety a little that MereBoy is on her side. That leaves her to contend with the two who are picking a fight and a third who is silent all the time. Not knowing what he may do or if he will want to get involved, she prepares to practice her karate on anyone who makes the slightest threatening move.

When Cambara's hand moves in the direction of where her weapon and the pad of papers are tucked away, hidden, Red-Eye changes his mood as quickly as a traffic light turning amber. Cambara looks from Red-Eye to ArmedCompanion and to MereBoy.

"Give it here," he says.

Cambara looks from Red-Eyed Randy to ArmedCompanion and to MereBoy, and she acts with feigned fright. She achieves her aim.

MereBoy says to Red-Eye, "Why do you not let the lady be? Now look at what you have made her do. You are frightening her."

Cambara says to Red-Eye, "Give what here?"

Red-Eyed Randy stands close to ArmedCompanion, who has the unfazed expression of a professional boxer challenged to a fight by a drunken nightclub bouncer.

Meanwhile MereBoy is saying, "My mother walks to the market veiled. Please let's leave this woman alone. Can't you see? She is respectably veiled."

Red-Eyed Randy whispers in ArmedCompanion's ears before saying to MereBoy, "I'll kick you in the teeth if you don't shut your mouth. She is not like your mother or mine. She is a city-bred whore."

MereBoy says, "Whores do not cover themselves as this good woman does. So let her go about her business. Please."

Red-Eye says, impatiently, to MereBoy, "Ask her to take a couple of steps forward and a couple of steps back and you will see what I mean."

"What will I see?"

"Remember, you fool," he says to MereBoy, "that I was the one who spotted her yesterday and followed her for a long time. She does not walk like a respectable woman."

"Why does any of this matter?"

ArmedCompanion struts about pretending to be a model on a catwalk.

"She is not as beautiful as Iman."

"I bet she is. Underneath."

"Let us make her take off her veil," says Red-Eye.

"Will you find out what she is hiding in her bosom?"

"Let's." Moving in her direction, Red-Eye says to ArmedCompanion, "Cover me and I will." He stretches out his hand toward her.

She says, "Don't touch me."

"What if I do?"

"Be warned."

He turns to his companions. "She is threatening me."

"Show her you are man enough," says ArmedCompanion.

He says to Cambara, "Are you daring me?"

At his approaching, his hand ahead of him reaching to touch the material of her veil, Cambara smells his bad breath and is as repulsed as if he had requested that they have unwanted sex. She is most in-dignant at the thought of him defiling her, and she breaks rank with decorum and allows herself to become violent. She springs a surprise on them by grabbing RedEye by the hand and twisting his arm until she almost pulls it out of its socket. Then, in a move whose ferocity sur-prises even her, she acts as the mad version of a dog whose rabies shot is overdue, and, before ArmedCompanion knows what is happening, she aims a high kick with unexpected fury at ArmedCompanion, then at Red-Eye's crotch. ArmedCompanion loses his gun to her, and Red-Eye rolls on the ground, moaning and holding on to his wounded man-hood. She does not bother with MereBoy, who, wide-eyed with fear, bears witness to what has been done to his two tough-looking companions and looks from Cambara to Red-Eye and ArmedCompanion, who lie almost lifeless on the ground, the one holding his throat and groaning, the other clutching his crotch and crying with pain, and finally to their silent companion, who is probably deaf or dumb or something, Cambara thinks. For a moment, MereBoy is not certain whether to raise his hands in submissive surrender to her authority or reiterate his position that he has all along been of the opinion that they should let her be. Deciding to stay, MereBoy remarks not only that she has no need to behave in an animated way—she has made her point all right—but also that she is wearing handsome boots. Under her veil, which is no ordinary veil, because it unzips on the sides, allowing her kicking legs freedom of movement.

No sooner has she kicked the gun away from their reach than she hears a car approaching, then stopping, and men coming out. Cambara is clear in her mind that she will stand her ground and not run, no matter what. She reaches for her weapon in the event she may need to use it, at first to frighten them away and as a last resort to defend herself. The men, however, are taking their leisurely time, the ramrod-straight man walking toward her with the authority of one to whom the roads and everything and everyone on it belongs, the other, his hands hidden from her, assessing the situation with the professionalism of an army man. He bends down, never permitting his eyes to leave Red-Eye and ArmedCompanion, kicks the gun away as they do in films, and then nods at the ramrod-straight man.

The more she stares at the straight-backed man the more she feels drawn to him, convinced that her life will have changed immeasurably between the instant the two of them exchange a few words and the instant they part company. The mysterious man has the full features of a destiny offering itself to Cambara, and she is more than willing not only to acknowledge it but also to accept it with the powerlessness of a woman who has fallen victim to her fascination. The question is, is she ready to receive it?

The man with the ramrod back says to the military type, his voice deep and reassuring, "Are there any problems? Can we help?"

Cambara works herself up to a point of no fear. Moreover, she senses there are not many other courageous undertakings that are beyond her ability to handle. She is amused at her remembrance of an adage ascribed to a cowardly Mogadiscian that any man who can kill a rat with his bare hands and without fear is also able to slaughter a human.

Her voice belying the extent of her worry, she says, "There are no problems that I know of, unless you are bringing some yourself."

"We bring peace."

Misty-eyed, she looks from the man who introduces himself as Bile to the military type whom he presents to her as Dajaal. Bile is squinting at the sun as he does the presentations, whereas Dajaal is moving about as one does when securing a battle zone, making it safe for the victors currently occupying it. First off, he retrieves the firearm and the club before telling MereBoy to move away. Then he walks over to the car and brings out elastic cables with which he ties Red-Eye's and ArmedCompanion's hands to their backs.

Cambara asks Bile, "Why is he doing this?"

"To render them inactive until we leave."

Dajaal wonders aloud, "Where do we go from here?"

"Let's ask the lady," Bile suggests.

"A lift, please."

"Where do you live?" Dajaal says.

Cambara seizes up.

To assure Cambara of his good intentions, Bile says, "We'll take you where you want to go."

Dajaal does not seem to approve.

"Come anyway."

Eventually, as they leave, a general sense of triumph pervades the air. A feeling of relief etches itself on Cambara's face, as at Bile's insistence, Dajaal escorts her from "the scene of a virtuous woman's battle against the wicked forces that are besieging the city" to the vehicle, the tips of his fingers in discreet contact with the voluminous sleeve of her veil. Dajaal tells Red-Eye Randy and his mates to bugger off and gives them fierce kicks in their pants, promising them worse reprisals if he sees them in the neighborhood. Inspired hope rises before her as she sits in the back of the car behind Bile, who, when silent, strikes her as living in a world of his own.

Cambara acknowledges with caution that she must beware of surrendering to Bile's magic charm: a handsome man with a distinctively remote gaze not likely to come into close focus, despite Dajaal's gentle prompting. The only bodily exertion he engages in is to take off his glasses, breathe onto them, one at a time, and then wipe them with a clean handkerchief, which he then replaces in his trouser pocket. Then he rubs his eyes, permitting a smirk to spread across his features. Bile strikes her as if he is a child refusing to wake up from a deep sleep.

Dajaal asks, "Where to?"

He receives no response.

He says, "I've asked where you live."

She looks away from Dajaal to Bile, who, to the trained eye of a woman who takes pleasure in interpreting facial expressions, looks battle weary. Not that she can explain why it bothers her, but she cannot work out Bile and Dajaal's relationship: Dajaal takes the initiative, and Bile quietly and self-absorbedly sits in the back, hardly advancing an opinion. She notes that he is holding a book gingerly and using his index finger as a bookmark; he stares away impatiently as though he were eager to return to his interrupted reading. No matter how hard she tries, she is unable to make out the title of the book he has on his lap. Convinced that he is more interesting to get to know than Dajaal, Cambara wishes she could eavesdrop on his unspoken thoughts.

Restless, her drifting gaze meets Dajaal's, and she smiles. Although she does not wish to admit it, the truth is that she does not know the names of the streets they are in. Nor does she know how to lead him to the family property. After all, walking to a place is different from getting there in a car, driven by someone else.

"Shall I guide you to where I want to be taken?"

"Kindly do," says Dajaal.

He follows her instructions, making a conscious effort not to look at either her or Bile. He stares ahead of himself, turning left, veering right, and then going straight until they arrive at the shopping complex, where she requests that he stop, and he obliges. She gets out, thanking them both. She stands on the passenger side of the vehicle, close to where Bile is. He is writing phone numbers on a piece of paper, which he hands over to her without saying anything.

As she takes her first two steps away from the vehicle, she becomes mindful of the undeniable consciousness that her life in Mogadiscio and her destiny have both taken decisive turns. She hopes that her encounter with the two men, Bile above all, will prove to be propitious.

FOURTEEN

On her way to the family property with an escort, Cambara is delighted that the shopkeeper, to whom she returns the bag he loaned her, with thanks, has proven himself worthy of her confidence and admiration, because he has served her truly well. A pity she didn't remember to ask him about his wife, of whom, insofar as she could tell, there was no sign. Cambara has come away from the shopping complex laden with a motley collection of edibles, some of which she bought from him or some with his help; he has a friendly way of sending one of his assistants to get for her whatever she desires. At times, they go to other shops and on occasion to the stalls where you get fresh produce. Her purchases being too heavy for her to carry all by herself, the shopkeeper's nephew, a teenager, has volunteered to help her cart the stuff, the two of them walking level for much of the way, neither speaking. She wonders how she can dispense with his services just before she reaches her destination without arousing his suspicions or inconveniencing herself, considering the number of bags she has to haul all on her own. After all, she does not want him to know what she is up to, nor is she keen for him to meet Jiijo or any of the other objectionable characters. If luck is on her side, they will get to her target with no one near the gate to the property or its vicinity, or for that matter anywhere along the road. She thinks that she will stop two gates down or up the road from the property's, depending, tip him generously, and then dispose of him, saying, "Thanks, you've been most wonderful. I can cope now." When he has been gone for a couple of minutes, then, unescorted, she will knock on the gate.

As it happens, fortune has favored her yet again, she tells herself. As they near the house she informs him that they have come to her journey's end, thank you.

"My uncle . . ." he says.

"I know . . ." she interjects and falls silent.

"What will I tell him if I leave you here?"

"That you've seen me to my gate."

He hangs back, hesitating whether or not to obey her command and remains where he is as though waiting to hear a confirmation. He looks anxious, the way people with impaired hearing do when they are not sure if they have read someone's lips correctly. She hopes he won't continue hesitating to go. His body language indicates that he does not wish to leave her before she has gained a safe purchase on her point of call, possibly because the shopkeeper will expect him to report back. "Please be on your way," she says to him, her hands making shooing-away gestures. Unburdened of the load, the teenager stands awkwardly, looking a bit unbalanced, his eyes crossed with anxiety.

The teenager gives in to the curiosity of knowing what her next step might be, and he walks backward, pausing only after tripping awkwardly. He recovers his equilibrium quickly, and, turning around, grins from ear to ear. Then he takes his time and looks amusedly at the mound of earth that has halted his progress, showering curses on it. She waves good-bye to him the instant she senses a surge of excitement rising within her. Even if the source of her exhilaration is a mystery to her, she cannot help appreciating how fortunate she has been so far to get to where she has and achieve what little she has carried out without anyone taking hostile exception to her actions. It is to her good that she continues dealing amicably with the shopkeeper and his nephew if for no other reason than the expediency of seeking their assistance when she has settled on the means and the time to launch her plan and make her move to dislodge the minor warlord and his minions from the family house.

After a minute or so, when she is sure that she has got rid of her escort, she looks about herself with caution. Seeing nothing worth her worries, she lugs the shopping bags across to where she wants them, close to the gate of the family property, needing to return two, three times. She puts the bags down, breathing heavily, and plucks the courage to knock on the gate, first gently, repeatedly, then firmly. She waits, her heart pounding in her ears.

As she hangs fire, she feels out of sorts and asks herself if someone might accuse her quite rightly of being duplicitous, in that she has either misinformed people or withheld adequate intelligence from Zaak and everyone else she has so far met. She exculpates herself by reasoning that her objective is not so much to deceive anyone as it is to make it possible for her to get her way. Her ultimate aim, in the end, is to reacquire the family property in the least dangerous manner. She reckons that the less other people know of what she is doing, at least in the early block-building stages, the better her prospects of success. Above all, she wants Jiijo to relax into trusting her and eventually into looking upon her with approval.

Cambara senses that she is a different person from the self who, a little more than an hour earlier, karate-kicked the youths, forcing them to submit to the dictates of her physical as well as her mental willpower. Her current mind-set is at variance with her sundry way of thinking and is also at odds with that of the self who was in the same area on a reconnoitering mission only a couple of days ago. She has no doubt that she has achieved a great deal of good since then, thanks to her cool, commendable conviction in her amicable approaches to Jiijo. She has become more positive about her own ability to cope with the civil war conditions than she believed maintainable.

Her purchases strewn around the entrance, she stands to the side. Her anxiety is now much less prone to apprehension, even if she is overwhelmed with a sense of déjà vu, bizarrely because she is sure that she has known an instant similar to this in her past life when, denied access to what has belonged to her by right, she picked up the gauntlet, fought, and won the battle. It is as if she were a mere witness and not the main actor; it is as though whatever is to unfold is none of her concern. Then her heart starts to beat hurriedly against her now aching ribs, her lungs run short of breath, and she wonders if she has lost herself in a plot that someone else has authored. The light in her eyes turns to darkness.

She closes her eyes and stops short of celebrating her triumph when she hears someone's light footsteps coming and, without her tapping on it, the door opens with the slow cautiousness of a guest yawning in the presence of a hospitable host. Based on the half of the face that she can see, Cambara moves slightly to the right to place herself in Jiijo's eyeshot.

She says, "It is me, Jiijo. Please let me in."

Cambara stands stock still, recalling belatedly that in her attempt to privilege secretiveness and taciturnity, she had given Jiijo a false name, which, sadly, she cannot recollect now. She hopes that this mistake will not haunt her later or leave a serious blemish on the nature and character of their relationship.

Jiijo opens the gate. There is exhaustion in her eyes, the bags of which have distended toward her upper cheeks, to which there is hardly a shine now. Jiijo's bodily gestures reveal an overwhelming tiredness. As Jiijo straightens up, her features contorted into discomfiture, the two women stare at each other stupidly, neither moving or saying anything for a brief while.

"Go on in and take the weight off your feet," Cambara says to her gently. "I will bring in the stuff. Leave everything to me."

Jiijo lets go of the gate, wincing because of fresh thrusts of localized pain, and grabs her right flank, massaging it as she toddles forward into the courtyard, which is open to the sky. Cambara does not follow her immediately. She peers in, scanning the space before her, and waits to appraise the present situation, in cautious assessment of whether it is safe for her to go in. After all, it will not do to make the heady assumption that the minor warlord and his minions are sleeping it off after a night of chewing. When she is convinced that no one else is up and about and that the doors facing the courtyard are all closed, she goes in, helps Jiijo, who is still holding on to her side, rubbing it, into the very couch she led her before, then moves about to bring her purchases in and put them away.

"Can I get you something?" Cambara asks.

Even though unequivocal, Jiijo expresses her sense of relief inadequately, her demeanor giving countenance to her disregard. Then all of a sudden, the pained expression on her face prompts Jiijo to surrender herself totally to the reality as well as the memory of other pains, some of recent vintage.

As Cambara takes a good hold of herself, she debates whether to ease Jiijo's apparent physical unease by giving her a partial massage, a kind enough gesture to make in humble surrender to her own memory of being pregnant with Dalmar. She senses she is right in assuming that, like Wardi, Gudcur does not help Jiijo in her current state.

Cambara is distracted, however, the moment she feels the weight of the papers she salvaged from the youths. Briefly, her recall of her unpleasant encounter with them now preys on her mind, and she takes nervous account of the paper slipping downward, lodging inconveniently close to her belly button, irritably rendering Cambara's forepart itchy. But there is nothing she can do about it, and she wishes she were in a room all on her own where she might disrobe and then remove the papers before having a good scratch.

Disturbed that she cannot remember her alias, she now reminds herself that whereas she told nothing but distorted facts that are part of her disguise to Jiijo, she gave the truth to Dajaal and Bile. No doubt, she is understandably mistrustful of Jiijo; she cannot, however, articulate why she elected to be trusting of Dajaal and Bile, despite the fact that she knows neither of them. Whatever else happens, she must avoid letting her mind go walkabout, because that is where the pitfalls are.

Jiijo's labored breathing worries Cambara in that she is hopelessly unprepared for any eventuality that may compel her to look for outside help, someone to tell her where to get an ambulance or a doctor; she doesn't know what to do or who to turn to. She won't want to rely on Zaak and has no choice but to depend on strangers with whom she has made acquaintance only recently, namely Kiin, Dajaal, and Bile, or the shopkeeper, to give a hand. Now Cambara hears Jiijo saying something meekly and sounding uncertain, the words unnecessarily spaced, like computer-generated speech. After putting a lot of effort into deciphering Jiijo's statement, she decides that Jiijo is blaming herself for not remembering her name.

"Never mind what my name is," says Cambara, her voice firm, determinedly brave, despite the circumstances. For all she can tell, Jiijo may not be letting on that she has found out the truth about Cambara, whom she will eventually challenge. Careful not to stir into counterproductive action based on unproven suspicion, she says to Jiijo, "Tell me what is ailing you, where you hurt. I can fetch a taxi and then rush you to a hospital, if there is need."

Cambara's lump of worry, which has lodged itself for a short while in her throat, blocking it, melts. In its place, a sense of relief eases itself into her body, and she relaxes into the lengthening silence punctuated by Jiijo's strained breathing.

Jiijo sits up on the couch, in evident discomfort, her features pinched, her legs spread awkwardly, her skin showing signs of neglect, as dry as harmattan, flaky. It is possible that Jiijo's physical distress with her pregnancy began in her mind before it made its presence felt in the rest of her body.

Cambara asks, "Will you tell me what's ailing you so that I know what I need to do?"

"He beat me last night," says Jiijo weakly.

Cambara wagers her intuition that she can tell the man who beat her up. She remembers coming in on him lying prone and snoring, surrounded with half a dozen pillows and cushions, a man in a world separate from the others, as they had neither pillows nor cushions. Disgusted, she is tempted to give in to the temptation to walk into the bedroom, where she will find him and his *qaat*-chewing mates sleeping off an all-night session, and maul him, if for no other reason than to remember how she dealt with Wardi. Cambara hesitates to put to Jiijo the questions that are presenting themselves to her, as a trespass of her privacy. She wants to know what the man is to Jiijo, what the nature of their relationship is before electing her course of action. She has to take care not to add further humiliation to the infringement already meted out to Jiijo, lest she should seize up and refuse to talk altogether. In a moment, however, Cambara is studying Jiijo's situation from a perspective in which the two of them no longer dwell in distinctly autonomous spheres, marked off by their known differences in terms of class, provenance, and experience or by an invisible boundary of mistrust. She sees in this context that, as women, they share the communality of male violence, both having suffered in their different ways at the hands of their partners.

"Where is he?"

"He isn't here."

"What about his men?"

"They've all gone."

"Where?"

"They are all taking part in a skirmish over the control of a bridge-head near the town of Jowhar with access to Mogadiscio," Jiijo explains, drying her cheeks, now that she is no longer weeping.

"When do you expect them to be back?"

"No idea."

Cambara's quick thinking kicks in.

"Tell you what we will do."

Fear inserts itself into Jiijo's eyes and her voice too. She asks, "What do you want us to do?"

Cambara finds Jiijo's use of an inclusive "us" a little unsettling at first, then, after giving it some thought, becomes excited to the extent that she makes a slipshod patter. She says, "We'll fix you something to eat."

"I don't know if I can eat."

"In the meantime go and have a shower," Cambara says, convinced that she would persuade her to eat something. "We'll talk when you're done."

Jiijo obliges.

As paean to her attentiveness, Cambara calls on Jiijo every instant she is able to, now holding her hands away from herself, given that she is busy chopping onions or garlic, now washing them and touching the back of her hand to her forehead. On one occasion, the fever in Jiijo's gaze floats in the delirium of her high temperature, the pupils of her frenziedly restless look filmed with anxiety, her lips hardening as if encrusted with dried mud, her saliva flowing, much of her tongue out and motionless, like an alligator sunning.

Between cooking and attending to Jiijo's needs, Cambara avails herself of the opportunity to study the lay of the place. She surveys the condition the property is in, this being the first time she has had the run of it, free to go where she pleases. Overall, the house is in terrible disrepair, its shabbiness the consequence not only of the coarse indifference of its occupants, who before moving into it may never have set foot in a house similar to it, but also of having been vandalized, some of the rooms severely so. However, she is delighted with the immaculate state the hall, used for receptions and parties, is in. Otherwise, the house will require very detailed ministration, the kind of purposeful care an artwork in a bad state of repair requires.

The meal ready and her surveying done, Cambara brings two platefuls of food, one for her, the other for Jiijo. "Feed a fever," she says, encouraging her to eat, "and you will be on your feet in no time."

Jiijo tucks into her brunch but not before feasting her eyes, delighting in the attention that Cambara has so far lavished on her. When they have eaten and she has cleared the plates, Cambara returns and says to Jiijo, "Let's hear your story."

"Where to begin?" Jiijo says.

As she prepares to listen, Cambara assumes that Jiijo has the baptism blood of sacrifice running in her arteries. She remarks too that there is a big difference in her bearing today; the poor woman appears more broken than before, no longer a capable enough woman. When they first met, Jiijo struck her as a strong and purposefully alive woman, behaving in a manner befitting a woman of noble upbringing.

Her voice grave, she says, "I do not know who you are or why I am pouring out my heart to you. You could say that misfortune is my second name. If I am holding back nothing, it is because I know that nothing can hurt me more than I hurt already."

Then she pauses for a long while and, waiting for the story to develop in her head before she shares it with Cambara, her calloused right hand taking a good grip of her own thigh, which, like the rest of her body, appears lifelessly dry because of its exposure to the hostile elements. Cambara tells herself to remember to select a moisturizing cream from her own supply, certain that it will bring the shine of life back to Jiijo's skin. Jiijo massages her thigh up and down to ease the ache in her bones and help relieve her mental anguish at the same time.

"I am the daughter of a tailor," Jiijo introduces herself. "My father had a small tailoring business together with two of his younger brothers. We were okay, we had enough, there was always food on our tables, and we were happy with our lot. To make more money, my father ran a key-cutting service on the side, one of two such outfits in our part of the city. Because he and I were very close, I spent a lot of time with him in the tailoring business—something my uncles did not approve of—or helped him cut keys. From an early age, I felt wiser than my peers, many of whom I found to be shortsighted or immature. My father did not want to marry me off to one of my cousins, as we Xamaris tend to do, but allowed me to stay on in school. You could say that I am the only one among my cousins who has some kind of education. I was preparing to take my high school finals and then go to university when I became pregnant out of wedlock. There was no alternative but to marry, not the father of my baby but a cousin several times removed, who came from the richer side of my extended family. Then the collapse occurred."

Then silence, as if resisting the storm of fury in the form of the rage she feels inside of herself. The muscles of her face tighten, as though the mere thought of what happened causes her tremendous pain. Cambara, alert to her surroundings, lights upon the fact that Jiijo's plate, almost greedily cleaned up, is on the verge of falling off the table. She catches it in time and places it on the floor close to her feet.

Jiijo continues, "I have known gang rape as much as you can get to know someone on a first-name basis. Since the collapse, I have been a kept woman, living in a small room in a big house for much of the past few years, a small room with the lights off, which made me as frightened as a blind kitten. I suffered the daily humiliation of not knowing which of the many youths would come to the room and take me. It puzzles me that I did not go out of my mind totally or that I held on to the skirt of life the way a scared kitten clutches its mother's flank. My days of misery lasted until Gudcur came to claim me as his. As much as it is hard to accept it now, I admit to having seen him as my protector arriving on the scene to free me from further fear. Once it became apparent to everyone that I was his woman, I settled on relaxing into my condition, accepting it. My usual good-natured manner emerged when he showed how gentle he could be when he chose to."

Talking about her miserable past and touching on the terrible things that had befallen her seem to provide Jiijo with a provisional easing of her agonies. She manages to wear the grave aspect of a woman hurt at the same as she displays the strength of her personhood.

Her expression crestfallen, Jiijo goes on, "There are odd moments of satisfaction in my situation when you consider it. Being illiterate, the men come to me to assist them in managing their lives in a way that is strangely gratifying. I also read and write their letters, and cook all the meals. Until a year or two ago, when some of the schools reopened, I used to teach Gudcur's children."

Jiijo is something of a raconteur. As she speaks, she attends, bizarrely, to removing hair from her half-plucked armpits. Cambara looks upon Jiijo as another actor, raw, untrained. It is the way Jiijo talks, the way she lets go of her words with a baffling ease, telling as she does a tale, her own and the nation's. No doubt, the woman's life has been difficult. However, from the way she narrates her story, it is as though Jiijo is laying herself bare to Cambara, in the expansive attitude of one victim to another. Cambara strains her ears, listening for changes in the tone of her voice, miraculously managing to wish away all intimations of fear in the secure belief that no one will hurt Jiijo more than she has been already.

There is order too to Jiijo's narration of her story. There is also discipline in the choice of words with which she describes the current state of her mood. It occurs to Cambara that Jiijo, her countenance grim, is reveling in the telling of her tale; she is enthralling as she continues to improvise, letting go of a sentence at a time, an idea at a time. Captivated, she watches Jiijo reinvent herself right there and then. Cambara, through a combination of circumstances, senses that she has a glimpse of Jiijo's strong sense of personhood, striving hard and desisting from showing how startled she is when she hears Jiijo say, "What help is there for our doomed nation?"

Wanting to bring Jiijo back to her story, Cambara responds with a question. "What was it like being married not to the father of your baby but to another man, albeit a cousin, whom your parents chose for you, presumably to preserve the façade of family honor?" she asks.

Jiijo works in total concentration on a corn on the small toe of her right foot, peeling off dead skin and tossing it away. "I could not bring myself to deceive my new husband. Instead, I chose to deceive my family, for I went to a 'midnight nurse,' as they say in these parts, and aborted the baby without letting anyone know except a school friend. I took ill, terribly ill. My mother was the first to learn of the reason, and she persuaded my father, without letting him in on our secret, to postpone the marriage until I was well enough. It grieves me that he never got to know what I had done before he died in the second week of the civil war."

"Tell me about your husband."

Then Jiijo lunges forward into her speech with the assumed gravitas of what she means to convey.

"He was successful in business, and, strangely, we were happy with each other for a long while, he and I," she says. "He was a most gentle husband, wonderfully caring of me and all my requirements, granting me all my wishes and a lot more. However, I was unhappy in the marriage, because we were childless. After trying for several years and failing, he sent me off to Europe—no expense spared—to consult doctors, a number of whom I saw. The doctors did many tests, made me undergo numerous configurations, but to no avail. I wanted so much to bear a child, maybe out of regret for having aborted mine, or maybe out of guilt because he was such a nice man and I was a bad woman to whom something terrible would happen one day, I have no idea. I had the urge to take my body through a pregnancy, and I wanted him to share with me the experience, the tribulations and joys of motherhood. I thought this would bring us closer, would delight him and delight me too."

The story moves Cambara, who, remembering how much joy mothering gave her, appreciates the dilemma.

"I could not decide whether to make a clean breast of the fact that I had undergone an abortion," Jiijo continues, "but because I was not sure what good that might do, the doctors, who could read my body the way a blind person reads Braille, chose, for their own reasons, not to speak of my abortion to my husband."

Jiijo has worked herself up into a heightened state of disquiet, one moment speaking with brio, the next falling sorrowfully silent and sullen, and then talking with slothful abandonment, the tone of her voice moist with the unshed tears waiting to be let go.

"When I look back on how Gudcur has treated me, the man who has fathered my children, and I think about my condition of enslavement," Jiijo says, "I have difficulty reconciling his kindness to me, as his chosen woman, with the cruelty others associate with him. I will not deny having sensed his hard-heartedness. I've seen evidence of it when he plays mind games that are crueler than the physical pain the militiamen under his command mete out to their victims: beating, raping, looting, and plundering. And, of course, he beat me up last night. No denying that."

A mobile phone rings somewhere in the house, most likely in the room opposite where they are. Jiijo sits up, first wrinkling her face into a frown and then falling silent, in self-rebuke. The phone's ringing a few more times, with neither Jiijo nor Cambara answering it, coincides with the rapping on the pedestrian gate. On hearing the noisy arrival of her children's familiar voices, Jiijo requests that she let them in, and Cambara is happy to do so.

Worn out from talking, too tired from having told Cambara her story, and too exhausted to minister to their never-ending indigence, Jiijo seeks a quiet retreat from the children. She takes leave of the scene, fleeing surreptitiously, and then closing the door behind her.

Left alone with the four children just back from the Koranic school, ages ranging from six to twelve, begrimed, hungry, eager to get to know her, and competing for her attention, Cambara asks them questions about their day away without listening to their answers, feeds them, and then offers them sweets and chocolates, which they eat to their heart's content. Then she entertains them with an Indian fable, which she tells them from memory.

"Once upon a time, the pathways of kites and crows cross that of a wounded fox lying helpless under a tree. The kites and the crows concur among themselves that they will share the spoils in equal portions, with the upper half of the fox allotted to the crows and the lower part to the kites.

"The fox mocks at their options, and finding fault with the way its body parts have been apportioned, belabors the point that since, by the nature of things and in terms of creation, kites are superior to crows, it is baffled that its upper part has gone to the lowliest of scavengers, the crows. In the opinion of the fox, the head, the brain, and other delicate portions should go to the kites.

"Because they cannot agree among themselves, a war ensues between the kites and the crows, and a number of each group die as a result, the remaining handful fleeing the scene with difficulty. Meanwhile, the fox feasts for days on the dead kites and crows, leaving the place healthy, observing that the weak benefit from the disagreements of the powerful."

When the smallest of the children pleads with her to tell them another story, Cambara looks at her watch, realizing that she has been here for more than three hours. She calculates on the best way of handing the responsibility of caring for the children over to their mother, pinning her hopes on the youngest to rouse their mother so she can go away. Woken up, Jiijo joins them, looking revived albeit groggy-eyed. And Cambara withdraws into the bathroom to read the pages the storm had kicked up. These turn out to be pages torn from an American oil-drilling company's document detaling payments to one of Mogadiscio's notorious warlords. Alas, she forgets it there when she emerges.

Cambara takes leave of them, promising to Jiijo and the children that she will be back as soon as she can. She makes a dash for the door.

FIFTEEN

Cambara, following a civil war rule of thumb, takes a route different from the one she used earlier to the shopping complex, aiming to get a taxi to Maanta Hotel. She moves with the single-minded vigilance of a lizard, watchfully preparing to confront youths idling away their time on street corners or in front of their squats in wait for potential victims to walk past. Some people feel there is protection in numbers; not Cambara. She prefers doing her own thing her own way, believing that the key to success in her endeavors lies in acting alone.

She is an optimist by nature. Asked why she is embarking on this adventure, she might reply that she is trying her luck. Notwithstanding that, she is inclined to keep the various parties with whom she is dealing separate so that none of them is au courant of her plans, especially not when she makes sallies into another party's preserve. From the little she has seen of him, Bile strikes Cambara as a man with a noble spirit, and he keeps returning to her thoughts. Dajaal seems to act with a kind of authority and native ability that is formidable. It will be to her advantage to work in collusive partnership with Dajaal and to humor Bile while he, in turn, humors her. Kiin, a woman apart, has not capitulated to the strictures of living in the city, which is admirable, considering the potential danger. As for Jiijo, it is looking more and more likely that Cambara has already won her over. It saddens her, though, as a trace of gloom invades her own bearing at the thought of relying on Jiijo to betray Gudcur, who despite being a warlord and a brute, has fathered Jiijo's children. Cambara foresees incomparable complications ahead.

Cambara now puts more energy into her stride, springing faster and faster, her heart anxiously beating like that of a young girl on her way to a rendezvous with her first date ever. This is because she is overwhelmed by the desire to get together with Kiin, with whom she wishes to become better acquainted. She is more than conscious that she has not done a thing about one of her principal pursuits: to devote more time than she has so far toward the construction of "peace," so she may leave "the place" better than when she found it.

To advance her commitment to recruiting some of the youths and to promote the idea of peace, she hopes to give them a start in normal life. She will buy SilkHair, who is young enough to go to school, all the exercise and drawing books that he will need to register at one or another school as a remedial pupil. Then she trips up, losing her balance and catching herself in time before falling. As she tries to steady herself and regain her composure, her eyes fall on a clutch of men gathered at the bend in the dusty road just before the shopping complex. The men are staring; they have daggers for eyes, one of them managing to pierce through to the start of a weakening resolve. She stiffens her determination against the oncoming mugging, and the men seem to sense it, backing off as she approaches.

Odeywaa, the shopkeeper, finds her a taxi, which she takes not to Hotel Maanta, her destination, but—as a decoy—again to Hotel Shamac. There, the deputy manager receives her effusively, leads her to his air-conditioned office, and plies her with refreshments. He rings Kiin to alert her of Cambara's arrival, and learns that Kiin is expecting her.

The deputy manager says to Cambara, "My driver will take you to Hotel Maanta, where a message from Kiin is awaiting your arrival."

A few minutes later, the driver of the vehicle the deputy manager of Shamac has lent her is pressing the horn of the air-conditioned saloon car. Two sentries in blue uniform open the gate of Hotel Maanta, and, on making out the man at the wheel, they rise, as if in unison and in welcome recognition of him, greeting him with voluble chattiness. Cambara alights from the vehicle to find a thickset man in a white long-sleeved shirt, beige trousers, and black dress shoes moving in her direction, having taken the steps two at a time, nearly falling. He extends his hand, a smile spreading across his broad face, and comes toward her with the resolute intention of not permitting the guards to outdo him when it comes to receiving an honored client. Cambara surveys the scene ahead of her, favoring it with a cursory scrutiny, deciding that she likes what she has seen so far and is sure to fall in love with it the longer she is here. Moreover, she wants to be indebted to Kiin, to become friends with her, to receive good counsel from her; she wants Kiin to acquaint her with aspects of Mogadiscio that Cambara has not yet encountered. She looks forward to Kiin introducing her to the other women of whom Raxma has spoken, legions of women who are peace activists. Turning around, Cambara waves to the driver, who is maneuvering the vehicle out of a narrow space with consummate ease and leaving, while she mouths "Thanks" and he waves in acknowledgment.

Beaming from cheek to chin, the large man introduces himself. "My name is Mohammed. I am an assistant to Kiin, the manager, and I have a message for you."

"What's the message?"

Mohammed puts his hand in his trouser pockets only to bring it out empty and then study it as if it might reveal a mystery to him. Then he inserts it in the other pocket, rooting in it, with Cambara waiting for him all the while, thinking he may bring out a piece of paper with a message scribbled on it. She is anxious, patient. In a moment, despite her expectation, he is looking at a key and, for some reason that is unclear to her, appears first mystified, then despondent. He hangs his head to one side, like a boatswain whose vessel has mysteriously gone adrift. Mohammed offers the key to her, saying, "Here."

Cambara takes it with both hands, muttering her thanks, which to her sound a little fake, and averting her eyes, because there is something she does not understand. She stares at the key for a long while, amused. In her head, Cambara replaces the word "message" with "key," but this will not do. Rather than ask what to do with the key or to identify which room it is meant for, given that there is no number stamped on it and nothing to indicate what it may open, she asks, "And the message?"

Mohammed makes the laborious effort of someone struggling hard to mask a speech impediment. He speaks, pausing between every two or so words. Cambara strains to string the words together herself to make sense of them. "Kiin has said to give you a key to the room that she has reserved for you."

Cambara turns the proffered key this and that way. The wind in the trees, the sweetness of their shade, the fact that the air here is fresh and no cigarette odor is riding the breeze: these, she hopes, will help her spend a very pleasant time at the hotel and make her stay in it an abiding joy. Overwhelmed with a sense of elation, and, unnerved, because everything is working out beyond her expectation, she loses her focus for a moment and then her physical equilibrium. Her gaze unfocused, she looks farther into the undefined distance, and as she does so, places her left foot behind her right, with the big toe of her left foot pushing against the right heel until she feels excruciating pain; then steadies herself.

She asks Mohammed to lead her to her room and follows him not too closely as she conjures up images of her workaday situations during her stay at Hotel Maanta. After she ascends a flight of stairs down by the well to her left, her body cells register the proximity of water. The generator is on and providing electricity. She feels the earth under her feet tremble and prays that her room is farthest away from this ungodly din.

"Is the generator on all day and all night?"

"It's not on when we can tap into an ice factory in the proximity," replies Mohammed. "We turn it on whenever the owners of the factory are load shedding, and they do this without prior notice."

She remembers in the days when power was supplied by the municipality of the city and cost almost nothing, and no one ever heard of load shedding. Realizing that she is lagging a few paces behind Mohammed, she catches up with him, and they walk up another flight of stairs, down an asphalted lane, with trees and shrubs on either side of it, through a metal door, up the stairway to the first floor, and along the corridor.

Finally, Mohammed comes to a shuffling halt and points out the metal door with no number on it to her. She inserts the key in the lock somewhat tentatively and after several attempts, turns it with resolute thrust. She thanks him again and lets herself in, securing the door behind her with a bolt.

The two-room setup—neat, decent-sized, boasting two beds, both pushed against a wall—faces away from the two generators, one of which is on now, maybe because the minimal daytime supply of power provided by the privately run electricity company is off. That the air conditioner is on and that she can barely hear the noise of the generator assures her further that she will like it here.

Moving about the two rooms to explore the extent of their combined spaciousness, Cambara paces out the distance between the rooms and then the two beds, and then concentrates on measuring out their relative nearness to the bathroom. Like a spoiled child making a choice by going meeni-mano, now pointing at one bed and now at the other, she settles eventually on the bed on the right side in the belief that she will enjoy sleeping in it more. She stretches herself on it, testing how comfortable lying on it will be. Then she pulls open one cupboard after another until she discovers, discreetly worked into one wall, a safe, with instructions in Somali, Arabic, Italian, and English. Cambara is agreeably surprised to find, when she pulls the handle toward herself, intending to set the combination number of the safe to one she will remember, that her luck is favoring her with a good smile. This is because there is a Post-it note from Kiin informing Cambara that she has left a mobile phone under the mattress of the bed to the right-hand side of the room and asking her to "please ring her up" to let her know that all is well. She does as Kiin suggests, pressing the Menu button and speaking right away to her kind host. Then Kiin tells her that she has also arranged for a plumber to see Cambara in an hour or so and asks her to wait until he arrives, then take him and show him the jobs she wants done. Mohammed, on Cambara's say-so, will be only too glad to organize a vehicle and bodyguards for her.

Cambara rings off, her unbounded sense of exhilaration spreading to the point of affecting her so deeply that she is almost tearful. She decides no one can touch Kiin for out-and-out kindness shown without obvious ulterior impulse. Civil wars or not, there are people like Kiin who are by nature generous to a fault, well meaning, and excessively munificent. In contrast to the uncharitable Zaak, who is her cousin, her former "spouse," and her current host, Kiin has taken to seeing to all of Cambara's immediate needs despite the fact that they are not blood relations. Cambara thinks that this goes to prove that not every Somali is obsessed with the idea of clan affiliation and that many people behave normally even if the conditions in which they operate are themselves abnormal.

Cambara's display of marked, positive attitude toward Kiin's generosity is short lived when she starts to sorrow over the general state of decay in the compound opposite the hotels. The unsightly scene before her pulls her up for further grief. She stands directly behind the window, looking out and surveying a wasteland of heartbreaking ugliness: trees that have not grown to their natural height, scraps of wood and metal thrown any which way, children rifling in the arid waste all around, as though in search of something precious that they can sell. The fact that she sees adult men squatting and defecating in full view of the road, which is about fifty meters to their back, troubles her no end. Then her wandering gaze dwells for a few moments on a man wielding an ax and turning a huge metal pipe of industrial size into fragments, chopping it into cartable portions. She reckons that men giving themselves in to insatiable greed employed similar destructive methods first to dismantle the national monuments and then to break them up into bits before selling them off dirt-cheap in the one of the Gulf states.

It is when she turns away from the desolation outside and reenters the bathroom that she is impressed with how clean its floor is. She even forgets about all her other disconsolate impressions for a minute, and her eyes shine forth with radiance. Finally, she removes her boots and then takes off her clothes, item by item, dropping them on the floor and trampling on them, the way her son used to do whenever he was in a mood to try his father, Wardi's, patience. How Wardi would go berserk, ready to hit the boy for his obduracy. Cambara, in maternal circumspection for her son's well-being, would intervene, picking up the offending items herself from where her son dropped them and telling Wardi: "I want you to take it easy. And please let peace reign in this house." Remembering the turf wars fought over the raising of her only son, whom she failed, as she could not safeguard him from Wardi's filicidal tendencies, she is unable to keep her rage in check. She wishes that she had acted like a hen, clucking away in watchful frenzy over her chicks, shielding them from harm.

She is so full of rage that she takes a huge karate kick at the door. Fortunately, she doesn't break it in two. But that doesn't stop her from letting go a scream so ungodly that running feet come and someone taps gently on the door to ask after a decent interval if everything is okay with madam.

"Everything is fine, thank you," she says.

Then she sinks into a crouch, her fists balled into a fist, her teeth clenched, and her whole body in a tremor as if she is fortifying herself for a final showdown with her inner demons.

When her desperate attempt to calm her nerves leads her to mutter self-recriminations of the remonstrative kind, in which she blames Wardi for her own shortcomings, the activated part of her mind pulls itself back in the rational belief that this is self-destructive. Has she not come to Mogadiscio in hope of chancing upon a noble way of mourning her loss, not in anger but while recovering the family property to devote herself to the service of peace?

Then for the first time since her arrival in Mogadiscio, Cambara delights in walking barefoot in a bathroom, eyes closed, and her hands joyously caressing her naked body in the tactile appreciation of a blind bathing.

She considers taking a room at Maanta as a test of her commitment to making her own way toward her independence from Zaak. It is also to provide her with proof, if there be a need to show some, that, as a mistress of her actions, she is not beholden to someone else, not least of all to a man, be it Zaak or Wardi. She will most likely keep certain aspects of her life private and will treat the room as her hush-hush retreat, rather like the way one keeps an affair secret. It amuses her now that she never had the temptation to have a love affair in all the years that she was married sadly and miserably to Wardi.

Cambara comes out of her rooms after a hot shower, her first. She feels refreshed, with a younger spring in her step, as she bounces downstairs, past the cubicle that serves as the reception of the hotel wing, where the deputy manager of the hotel sits, reading. She assumes that Mohammed is reading a textbook, because he is underlining paragraphs of the text with a marker, very bright yellow. He is also mumbling something to himself the way semi-literates recite the letters of the alphabet when they have just mastered it. She nods her head to him in welcome acknowledgment of his warm grin.

Coming out into the sun, she goes up a couple of stone steps and, to avoid colliding with a small structure built around the well, which suddenly juts out, she turns a sharp left. Finally, she sees a woman at the farthest corner and then spots the woman's arms flailing in a manner suggestive more of someone drowning than of somebody waving. When she gets closer, she recognizes Kiin, who has a huge smile framing her face. Cambara moves speedily toward the restaurant-café, where Kiin is now at a table all on her own. The café part of the restaurant, which has a straw roof, is still under construction, supported by heavy beams on one side and metal scaffolding on the other.

Kiin is up on her feet by the time Cambara joins her table, her arms opening widely in an embrace. The two women hug and then kiss each other on both cheeks, like two childhood friends meeting for the first time in years, especially now that they are adult women, to share their fond memories of a long-forgotten era. Finally, Cambara sits in the chair diagonal to Kiin's, their knees touching, their emotionally charged closeness in so brief a time starting to worry Cambara. Even so, a tingling sensation in the entirety of her body makes Cambara recall her teens, when she first felt the ending of her innocent girlhood soon after becoming conscious of the evident changes in her and remarking on the fact that boys and men were looking purposefully at her. A memory of being alone in the bathroom, naked, and touching her budding breasts comes back to her. So do two other incidents: one about her first encounter with Zaak having an erection and the other about her own encounter with a peacock. She remembers how catching sight of the peacock aroused her sexually. She feels Kiin's closeness has nothing of a come-on to it. If anything, it is that of a woman who has lived a cloistered life showing her appreciation of an innocent friendship that will mean a great deal to her.

Kiin now takes hold of Cambara's hand and, kneading it and turning it this and that way, asks her, "How do you like your rooms?"

"I love them."

Cambara makes a conscious effort to avoid looking into Kiin's eyes, which are boring into hers at the same time as she tries to retrieve her hand, which is now lost to Kiin's tight grip.

"Lunch?" Kiin asks.

"I am starving."

"What would you like to have?"

"What's there to eat?"

Kiin summons the waiter, a short, very dark handsome man in his late twenties with thinning hair and a very beautiful smile. He approaches, and then, after being instructed to tell the honored guest what there is to have, the waiter recites the menu, deferentially addressing himself to Cambara, who, at first, has difficulty concentrating, because he is speaking very fast. After he has repeated itemizing the menu, Cambara places her order: salad, no first course, a dish of fish, sole, with a touch of garlic and plenty of lemon, fruit for dessert, coffee. When the waiter tells her that the espresso machine is not working, she asks for tea. Not sure whether Kiin has already put in her order of food and is waiting for it to arrive or whether she will eat elsewhere, Cambara looks from the waiter to Kiin, who nods to him, indicating that he is to go get Cambara her meal.

Cambara says, "Tell me your story, how you come to remain in a city many others have fled, and how you come to run a hotel."

As Kiin pauses to formulate her ideas, Cambara tries to requisition her hand in the gentle way a mother might reclaim her finger, without any untoward disturbance, from the clutches of a child now asleep.

"The city exploded into strife while I spent almost a month in the intensive care unit of the hospital under a doctor's supervision," Kiin says. "I had been married less than a year and was losing blood and had worries about my baby's state of health, fearing that I might suffer a miscarriage. Anyhow, I was in no condition physically or mentally to be discharged, what with the tubes and the drips that I was on. I was heavy, I was miserable in my self-loathing, I was sick—in short, I was everything I never wanted to be. Given my situation, it did not make sense to me or to my then husband to join those fleeing the fighting in the city."

At the mention of a then husband, Cambara takes note of a brief clouding of Kiin's features. Then she asks, "You had your baby, though, yes?"

"A baby girl, born premature."

"And surviving?"

"I have had another daughter since then."

"How old are they?"

"Ten and twelve."

"That's wonderful, that is wonderful."

"I would love you to meet them."

"Where are they?"

"Here with me," Kiin replies.

"Do they stay at the hotel?"

"No, at our home," Kiin says, her finger pointing to a hole in the wall, which Cambara eventually works out to be a door carved out of it. "In fact, it is the reason why I am not eating here. After I've kept you company, I will spend the afternoon with them, now that they are done with school for the day."

"Where do they school?"

The waiter brings the salad, which Cambara starts to dress, after receiving an indication that Kiin will not have any. Then Kiin explains that given the absence of a central government and the lack of a functioning school system in the country, many middle-class families residing in the city have organized themselves into schooling neighborhoods, pooling their financial resources and running home-schooling facilities for their children, with manageably smaller classes. To teach, the stay-in-the-city families, many of whom feel they belong here more than they do in Europe or North America as refugees or landed immigrants, have recruited the services of well-trained teachers—at times overqualified for primary-school teaching—from Tanzania, Uganda, and Kenya. Mostly single men out to make a windfall, considering the civil war conditions in which they operate, these foreign teachers receive higher pay than they might in their home countries, and in U.S. dollars.

"Are you satisfied with the education they are receiving?"

"Yes, we are, considering."

"What do poor families do to provide schooling for their children?"

"Sadly, because there is no state, the only other form of school is Koranic."

Kiin, in the meantime, displays some girlish behavior, giggling at the most unlikely places in their conversation. She also takes hold of Cambara's hand again, rubbing it, or just continuing to touch her, seeking and making bodily contact with her.

"You can tell me what you think of how, in your opinion, they are doing when you meet my two daughters, born and raised here," Kiin says. She falls silent when the waiter brings Cambara's well-done fish and a side dish of spinach.

"The father of the children?"

"We're still man and wife," Kiin says, "but we are separated. Like me, he has continued to live in this city, despite the civil war, in preference to leaving and relocating elsewhere as a refugee and then as a holder of the national papers of another country. We are happy here, never mind how others might describe us: as murderers of the clan families fleeing the city, as occupiers of their properties, as robbers, looters, plunderers of the city's wealth."

"You've been okay?"

"One gets used to all kinds of situations, however awful, to the extent that one will do what one can to survive minimally. If need be, one will become inventive, resourceful, and will find accommodating ways that are on occasion contradictory until one is doing relatively well even in the most terrible of conditions. We are doing well, as you can see. Meanwhile, I am raising my two daughters, and they are, thank God, growing up nicely."

Because the time does not seem right for Cambara to ask a leading question and Kiin has taken a pause, each of the two women remains absorbed in her silent thoughts.

Kiin says to Cambara, "You have been away from the country for a very long time, haven't you?"

Cambara feels that Kiin knows a lot more about her than she lets on, most likely because their mutual friend who alerted Kiin of Cambara's imminent arrival in the city will have filled her in on her life story. Their mutual friend will have described Cambara as a celebrated actor; as a woman whom a man betrayed; a mother grieving over the loss of her only son. A woman of good breeding, Kiin has not even alluded to any of this. There is time yet, though; there is time yet. The waiter retrieves Cambara's half-eaten meal and brings her half a mango, the size of a football, and cut into squares. Cambara is so sweetly impressed with her first mouthful that even Kiin's mouth waters, and she asks the waiter to bring her the other half. They eat scoops of it before Kiin dares to break the silence.

Then she continues, "Right now, Somali society is at its most disintegrated. There are so many fault lines that no two Somalis think alike, or are even likely to share a common concern for the nation's well-being. The men prefer starting wars to talking things over; they prefer going their different ways to coming together and sorting out their differences; they help provoke more fighting and begin shooting, despite the fact that their disagreements are about matters of little or no significance. Men are prone to escalating all minor differences until they become armed confrontations in which many lives are lost, every shoot-out boiling over into unstoppable battles and the battles exploding into wars. I would say my husband and I might not have upgraded our disagreements into a serious falling-out were it not for the uncivil conditions in which we find ourselves. We love each other, my husband and I, but we cannot see our way out of the positions we take. I am a woman and am for peace at all costs; my husband is not for peace at all costs. Living under such a stressful situation day in and day out for years has taken its toll on the way we relate."

Then, quite unexpectedly and without prior intimation or warning, Kiin remains unspeaking for a long time. She shakes her head, disturbed at the memory of her own and Cambara's broken home. Then suddenly she sniffs loudly and, with the abruptness of a storm raging, bursts into tears, her cheeks wet with the flood of emotions breaking their banks.

By way of explanation, following a pause, Kiin says, "It is times like these and stories like yours and the many tragedies of other women that are disheartening to listen to, the terrible things men have always done to women and gotten away with. It saddened me when I first learned of your tragic loss, and it breaks my heart now to remember how Wardi neglected your son."

Neither speaks; the waiter removes the plates.

Kiin says, "I am sorry that I have dropped the weight of my emotions on you in this way, tearfully linking your loss to mine and to all the other women that I know." She pauses, looking about, and then says, "Men are a dead loss to us, and they father wars, our miseries."

Uncomfortable in her silence and unable to think of what to say, Cambara shifts restlessly in her seat, her hand covering her mouth, unavoidably charged with a keg of emotion; she prays that she is capable of quashing them before they explode, like Kiin's. How delicate! And what a tempestuous woman!

Kiin says, "It is on behalf of the other community of women and because we have a mutual friend in Raxma that I am extending a hand
of friendship to you. Maybe we'll invite you to join us."

At first, Cambara knows neither how to react to what she has wit-
nessed nor how to respond to the proposal to join the community of
women working for peace.

"But of course," says Cambara finally.

"I am so pleased, so pleased," says Kiin, who, with disconcerting
jerkiness, rises and lifts Cambara, hugging and kissing her. She appears
pumped with the adrenaline that is of a piece with the joy of recruiting Cambara to the cause of women. She goes on, "We have our all-
women half-yearly party tomorrow evening, and I am hosting it here. I
am very, very happy that you can join us. You'll enjoy yourself: an all-
women party, good food, excellent music, lots and lots of dancing."

For her part, Cambara, now taking her seat and acting calmly, is
thinking how she has come to the end of her veil-wearing days, and
how, now that she can dispense with the need to be in disguise, she
will go to Zaak's and pick up a couple of her suitcases. She has in
mind the low-cut dress that she will put on for the party tomorrow
evening and is about to ask Kiin questions about the other women
when the gate opens and a man is shown in. Soon, Kiin is welcoming
the plumber who has come with his tools, and Kiin is organizing a car
and bodyguards.

"Be on your way with the plumber, take him where you want, and
show him the job you want done," Kiin says. "I trust you are carrying
the mobile, so call me if there is need. Or come to think of it, even if
there is no need, call to chat. In addition, I am sending along with you
a driver and the head of the hotel security, both of whom are family,
and they will treat you well and do what you ask of them. Let me know
if there is a problem. Meanwhile, I will go home and be with my daughters. Take care till we meet again at suppertime."

Cambara wonders if the world Kiin has entrusted to her will be a
better place when she has the time to give it a shape in which she will
be at ease.

SIXTEEN

Kiin lends her saloon car to Cambara, who, again in the veil she wore earlier, now sits in it waiting for the driver, for the youths assigned to the car as armed escorts, and for the plumber, who has been brought to her to give her an estimate, to finish praying. The escorts have stood their weapons against the wall they are facing, and the plumber has placed his tools close by, where he can keep an eye on them. To a man, they have left their shoes, which they took off before making their ablutions, behind them. They are almost halfway through praying, with the old man leading the prayer, reciting his verses excitedly, when a couple of the waiters, wearing their uniforms, join them, hastily prostrating in obeisance to the fast rhythm already set. As if not wanting to be left out, the chef of the restaurant, with his white paper toque still on, is the last to become a member of the praying party.

She remembers that when she was introduced to them one by one, their names recited as she shook their hands, Cambara found every one of them to be as carefree as a sailor on R&R, easygoing, blasé in the manner in which they engaged one another in amicable banter. The younger ones have the habit of yanking each other's chin or of challenging each other to a wrestling match. Young or old, Cambara is under the impression that they have been together for a long time, which may be so, and have shared life-and-death experiences. She feels certain too that they are prepared to stick their necks out for one another and that, in addition to delighting in the camaraderie of participating in the same battles, they are bound to one another by their commitments to the same blood family. On the strength of what she has seen so far, Cambara prefers their company to Zaak's lot, except for SilkHair, whom she is already missing. This is so, in part, because the Maanta management disallows any of its employees to chew *qaat* on the premises or while working. Buoyed by what she considers a healthier atmosphere and cheered to a large measure by the fretful chat with Kiin, her awareness of selfhood boosted, she feels invigorated. As a result, there is discernible pluck to her decisions and the actions arising from them.

The prayer inexplicably protracted, the old man leading it recites longer verses. She can only think that he is doing this because he believes the mission on which the armed escorts, the driver, the plumber, and Cambara are embarking is a dangerous one, and who can tell, maybe it is. For her part, Cambara prepares herself mentally for the return trip to Zaak's and then a visit to the property, the first in the company of anyone, most importantly armed escorts. She also primes her body for what she ranks to be her new station, in which she need not wear a veil if she is not of a mind to do so.

Now that she judges the veil to be a kind of entrapment, she removes the head scarf when no one is watching. When her eyes meet the driver's—his lips still astir with his recital of more Koranic verses—she smiles and then feels triumphant when he nods, presumably in approval of what she has done. She struggles to undo the knotted strings of her veil. She cranks down her side of the window, allowing the breeze to circulate more, and she revels in the waves of fresh wind fondling her cheeks and ears. Emboldened, she fiddles afresh with the knots of her head scarf, which now mysteriously slip off most easily. She exposes a bit of her hair, shifts in her seat, and sitting back, takes off the headwear altogether. Only the driver keeps a watchful eye on her doings; all the others, with their backs to her, are paying attention to the Koranic recitation. Her veil removed, she is, in her mind's eye, wearing a chemise, bought from a Pakistani outlet in Toronto, with a custom-made pair of baggy linen trousers.

Finally, the prayer ended, they all shake hands with the old man who led them through the worship, thanking him; he blesses the armed escorts, who retrieve their weapons and put on their shoes, and the plumber, who gathers his tools. He advises them to be careful. Then he bids farewell to the chef and the waiters, who go their own ways. The driver is the first to get into the car, and as each of the armed escorts finds his own cosy corner in the truck, the plumber is the last to enter, he places his tools at his feet, and slumps in the back. The driver opens the glove compartment and takes out the revolver, tucking it away in his top shirt pocket. Two of the armed escorts are badgering each other with personal questions neither has the desire to answer.

Cambara sits up front, eyes focused ahead of her, conscious of her closeness to the driver, whose hands keep colliding with hers whenever he changes the gears. She cannot tell if he is doing this to elicit some sort of response or if it is coincidental. Infused with self-doubts—she remembers him watching her with keen interest as she doffed her veil, then her headscarf. Maybe he thinks of her as modern, that is to say, game? She backs out, withdrawing into her silent thinking. She pictures finding Zaak or Gudcur in their respective houses, slouched and chewing their midday usual.

She reckons that convincing Zaak of her good intentions, if he happens to be home when she gets there today, with a plumber moving about the upstairs and downstairs bathrooms as well as the kitchen, will perhaps be easier with than coping with Gudcur's fury. She dares not imagine what he may do once he takes umbrage. After all, running into Gudcur, with a plumber, driver, and armed escorts in tow will bring her face to face with the stickiest of situations, the first of its perilous kind. It will be interesting to see how she holds up against the minor warlord, who, to find out what she is up to, will do his utmost to break down her resistance. Not having met the fellow in the flesh, awake, and not having gathered sufficient information about his character or weaknesses, Cambara can only conjure up the worst of scenarios: shootouts, deaths, and more blood. She imagines Gudcur's murderous fluids surging up within him, going to his head, spurting and squirting, boiling over and burning everything and everyone in sight. In all likelihood, the man, becoming angrier and therefore deadlier, will raise the stakes the moment he realizes that she has been coming repeatedly to the house, visiting Jiijo and his children, on whom she has been lavishing sweets. He will want her to explain her motives and the purpose of her visits; he will want to know her identity, why she is bringing his wife and children presents, why she is driving around with a plumber to *his* house, and why she has come with armed escorts from another clan. Gudcur will insist that Cambara tell him what her business with his family and *his* house are.

It takes the driver several attempts to reverse the vehicle out of a tight spot. He wheels the pre-power-steering model forward and then backward, his gear-changing polished, professional, and fast. However, when the two young escorts share a private joke, burst into laughter, and begin to roll in their seats in stitches, the driver loses his composure, braking just in time before crashing into a tree and then halting crudely before the front of the vehicle collides with the wall to his back. Unspeaking, the plumber is contemplative.

After the vehicle has exited and then eventually picked up moderate speed, heading north, and it hits one of the main subsidiary roads, Cambara prepares to give the driver several leads to help him get them to Zaak's place. Just then, she observes the driver's sudden loss of poise, which does not make sense to her until one of the armed escorts talks of his and the driver's last visit to the northern neighborhoods of the city. In his account, the young man tells her that the visit dates back to a decade ago when he and the driver participated in some of the fiercest skirmishes between former warlords StrongmanNorth and StrongmanSouth.

To keep panic from setting in, Cambara asks the driver questions, all the while struggling not to lose her sangfroid and doing her best to sound convincing and appear unruffled.

"On whose side did you and the driver fight?" she says and then looks away, almost trembling with judicious displeasure.

"We fought alongside StrongmanSouth's clansmen, who were allied with ours," replies one of the armed escorts in the back.

When her attempt to will herself into listening to the conversation without making comments proves unsuccessful and she settles on pandering to her curiosity, Cambara creases her features to display her displeasure with this stance. Then she sees herself as a woman with little knowledge of this thing everyone calls "the clan business," the unruliness of whose politics has brought the nation to ruin. That she is sharing the confined space of a vehicle with four men, three of whom have blood on their hands, makes her question the credentials of people like Kiin, who employ them. She wonders if she will rue her shortsightedness, if she will regret the fact that she has accepted Kiin's kind offer to lend her a car, a driver, and armed escort; call up a plumber, whom she uses herself; and help her to achieve her aims, whatever these are, since she has not insisted that Cambara tell her. But she thinks she doesn't want to go there, because in a civil war no one is innocent: men, women, youths, clerics, everyone is an accomplice in the killing and maiming of others, known and unknown. As the motorcar hurtles forward, she turns to the driver and asks him what his profession used to be before the country's collapse.

"I joined the National Army, now defunct, before taking my secondary-school finals and was sent away to the then Soviet Union on a scholarship to Odessa, where I trained as a tank engineer," he replies.

Cambara asks the driver, "Do you happen to remember where you were or rather what you were doing when Siyad Barre, the tyrant, fled the city in an army tank?"

"I was one of the few senior-ranking army officers who refused to join the militia that was out to take Mogadiscio, because it was there for the taking," the driver responds. "We learned soon enough, and especially after the dictator had fled and the presidential palace had fallen into the hands of the nativists, those of us fighting to live up to the ideals of the National Army formed a very small minority, but we were fighting a losing battle."

"So what did you do?"

"Together with a couple of like-minded military officers," the driver answers, "I set up a small unit numbering a dozen or so men and representing the clan spectrum of this country. We raised the unit with a view to protecting the members of the clan families of the 'chased-outs,' people whose properties had been rendered fair game—taken over, looted—and whose current occupants placed under constant menace, a scenario of 'You leave, or else the massacre!' Many departed against their will, becoming displaced or going to refugee camps in one or the other of the neighboring countries."

"What has become of your unit?"

"You are looking at the remnant of the unit."

The plumber speaks for the first time, saying, "Take seven, you have a mere three."

Cambara falls silent. In her vigorous attempt to concentrate, as though fearing that the hour of her failure is at hand, she furrows her forehead, her features a tangled affair. Of course she is sad to admit that a similar fate might be waiting to ambush her honorable intentions. Cambara will agree, if asked, that it is virtually impossible to live up to one's high ideals in these adverse conditions, but she prays that her effort will not falter or ultimately come to naught. For she plans to construct a counterlife dependent on a few individuals, namely Kiin, maybe Bile and Dajaal, whom she has cast in the likeness of reliable allies.

When the driver parks the vehicle in front of Zaak's house without needing further guidance, Cambara draws a breath, relaxing, and she looks as if someone has pulled her away from a disturbing view. Both of the armed escorts alight, one of them opening the gate, the other readying for any contingency, including a shootout. The driver looks this way and that before easing his foot off the brake and then engaging the gear. He stops under the shade of a tree, away from the prying eyes of prowlers who might casually spot the car.

Cambara leads the plumber into the house and shows him everything he needs to see: the kitchen, the toilets, the downstairs and the upstairs bathrooms. As he bones up on the overall situation, studying the source of the water, the pipes that have gone rusty, those that are in disrepair, and starts to scribble copious notes, she takes leave of him, suggesting they meet at the car.

Then she goes up to her room to pack two large suitcases. She fills one of them with several items of everyday clothing plus a couple of dresses for special occasions and five thousand U.S. dollars, a quarter of the money she has brought along, in cash. She stuffs the harder of the two large suitcases with books about puppetry, masks, and theater, several of them the size of coffee tables. She opens one, then takes a look at her sketches, her notes, and other relevant material that she has brought along to help her one day produce her play, a pet project at which she has been working on and off for several years, even if on the quiet. When she comes to making a choice of what to wear, she changes her mind several times and tries on different garments, mixing and matching styles before finally settling on a comfortably loose, cotton shirt and baggy trousers. She feels she can afford to do away with the veil and headwear altogether, and combs her hair, letting it down, as if reliving her young days in Mogadiscio. For effect, she wears a *garbasaar* shawl of the finest silk.

She decides not to ask any of the youths to help her bring down the suitcases to the vehicle and hauls it all on her own. The plumber, who is about to wrap up his note-taking and cross-checking, hears the footfalls of somebody shifting, half pulling, and half heaving a hefty suitcase with wheels down a staircase. It is only after he takes a second and a more concentrated look at the figure humping down the weighty object that he realizes that he is staring at Cambara, who has on a stylish outfit. Amazed at the mutation, he softens the impact on his mind by offering to cart it himself to the truck, only to discover that he cannot even lift it off the ground, let alone drag it the way she has been doing. Then, as if to prove a point, Cambara humps it all by herself all the way to the vehicle, while the plumber goes back into the house to retrieve his tools, measurements, and sketches. She takes notice of the armed escorts amusedly looking from her to the plumber and then calls to the driver to request that he open the boot for her, please.

On rejoining the group, the plumber, to cancel out his mates' jeers, asks Cambara what is in the suitcase. By way of reply, she points at an airline label with a picture of a porter rubbing a bent back that reads "Very Heavy." The plumber makes as if he will rephrase his question when the driver says to him, "It is rude to ask a lady what she is carrying in her suitcase."

Then Cambara looks from the driver to the armed escorts and finally at the plumber, wondering aloud if one of them will please come and give her a hand to bring down a second suitcase. The men exchange equivocal glances, none volunteering to go with her, because they all assume that the second suitcase might be bulkier than the first one. Not even her throwaway, singularly charged and defiantly delivered one word, "Men," her head raised, eyes audaciously expressive, moves any of the men to follow her.

When she rejoins them, swinging the suitcase, proving that it is much lighter than they have hypothesized, all four look embarrassed. No one, however, says anything for a long while. They get into the vehicle, the driver starts the engine, turns the radio on, maneuvering out of the gate, and then stops at the first intersection. He wants to know their destination. She instructs him where to go in a piecemeal fashion, telling him where to turn left just before they hit a bend, suggesting that he slow down prior to his veering right. Not one of the four men has the slightest idea that they are unwitting abettors, four men aiding a woman in her plot to achieve one of her aims. Nor have they the faintest inkling of their involvement in her dicey attempt to recover her family property.

They are well on their way to Cambara's family house when, the radio still on, a news item about a street-by-street turf war involving one Gudcur and his men against another militia group attracts everyone's attention. There is total silence inside as they listen to the latest wire dispatches filed by the Horn Afrique journalists close to the scene: Gudcur and his militiamen have lost several of their number, been pushed back a couple of streets, and have had to improvise the construction of a bunker on which they now rely as defense. According to eyewitness reports, Gudcur and his men's fighting prowess are under a great deal of strain, given the likelihood of another militia faction to their south, whom they dislodged a year earlier, joining forces with their opponents and attacking them from the rear.

When the news ends Cambara asks the driver, the volume of her twitchy voice drowning out the music, if he knows Gudcur.

The driver switches off the radio and says, "I don't know him personally, but I think that he is a thorough piece of work, objectionable in every possible way, and deserving of the punishment being dished out to him."

"Give me the background," she says, feigning total ignorance of the man and his past and current activities. "What's the fighting about and why now?"

The driver responds, "The fighting is for control of a checkpoint close to the main intersection to a bridge, which is seen as a lucrative means of exacting charges on the road users."

She knows it sounds naive even as she formulates the question, but she asks it all the same. She says, "Is it lucrative enough to meet his financial needs?"

"He wouldn't fight if it were not."

"How many checkpoints would a man like him control to make enough to feed his fighters and live in grand style?" she asks.

"He is a middle-ranking warlord," the driver explains, "subordinate to the high-ranking strongmen who have earned the right to occupy center stage in the country's politics and who are invited to every National Reconciliation conference held to provide our failed state with a central government. Gudcur is an ally of the current incumbent of StrongmanSouth's hub of operations."

Then one of the armed escorts joins in, throwing his words of contempt as if the object of his derision, Gudcur, were in the vehicle with them, sitting between Cambara and the driver. He says, "We are happy to hear that he is thrashing around, like a fish caught in a net."

The other armed escort nods his head vigorously in agreement with his mate. The plumber's closemouthed stance, however, bothers Cambara, because she has no idea what to make of his reticence, why he is tight-lipped. She assumes that it does not happen often that a professional residing in Mogadiscio does not confer empathy or loathing on the activities of a warlord, especially in a street-by-street battle for the taking of a checkpoint, the control of which allows him to impose a duty on every motor vehicle or good that comes through it.

Cambara says, "I hadn't realized."

"What? What hadn't you realized?"

Her heavy breathing is audible in the confines of the truck as she wears an impish grin on her forehead crossing swords with a tangle of fretfulness. This is because she is sick with worry, fearful that, unbeknownst to the four men, she is taking them to Gudcur's lair.

Scarcely has she prepared to intimate her deep involvement in Jiijo's life and her very complex connection to Gudcur than she realizes that they are almost there. Drawing comfort from the fact that she is not likely to meet Gudcur there, Cambara presses ahead and then tells the driver to stop opposite but not too close to the gate. Then she and the plumber alight, leaving the driver and the armed escorts to remain in the vehicle, covering them, in case of problems.

She knocks hard on the gate several times before anyone responds. She says, "It is me," to Jiijo's apprehensive "Who is it?"

Cambara is relieved that Jiijo is on her own.

When Cambara asks Jiijo where her husband and his fellow *qaat*-chewing mates are, Jiijo replies that they are out, attending to some important business without saying what this is. Cambara focuses her watchful eyes now on Jiijo in her vigilant attempt to puzzle out if she is telling the truth and now on the plumber to suss out if he knows about Jiijo being Gudcur's woman. Cambara infers from her cursory, hastily arrived supposition that neither is privy to other's secrets or identity.

Then she inquires where the children are, and Jiijo explains that someone has "come for them." Even though she notes that Jiijo does not elaborate, she does not put her on the spot, quiz her on who has "come for them," or if she, Jiijo, knows to which refuge the children have been spirited away for their own safety. And why has that "some-one" left her to fend for herself alone, in spite of her advanced state of pregnancy? Does it mean that insofar as Gudcur is concerned, she is dispensable? Cambara lets Jiijo's statement stand without comment or further questioning.

Then Jiijo asks, "Who is this man?" sizing up the plumber to de-termine whether he is friend or foe. "And why have you brought him here?"

Cambara's answer calms Jiijo's nerves. She says, "This gentleman is a plumber, and I've brought him along so that he will see to it that the plumbing problems in this house are dealt with before you have your baby. I will pay for his labor and all the alterations and expenses, just to make sure your baby is born in a house with clean water and healthy surrounds. He is here today to assess the conditions here and will give me figures and expenses. He will tell me what he needs to do."

The two women follow on the heels of the plumber into one room, then another and then another, enabling Cambara to see the entirety of the house for the second time, but more luxuriously and without needing to rush.

Half an hour later, everyone at Maanta offers Cambara a hand to help her lug her two suitcases to her rooms. It takes the determined effort of six men to cart them up the steps, past the mezzanine, where they pause for rest, and then eventually into her living quarters. The air con-ditioner on full blast, she takes a very, very long shower, which she en-joys immensely.

SEVENTEEN

Cambara draws herself up to her full height after an arduous workout in her rooms, the first serious exercise session since her arrival. When she thinks of it, breathing laboriously and perspiring profusely, she can't get over the fact that she has not been toning up her body to remain fit, in case she gets into a touch-and-go physical combat and has to karate-kick two or more armed thugs to stave them off—in short, to save her own life. Of late, some of the militiamen, having run out of victims with the wherewithal to pay them large sums of cash, have resorted either to becoming pirates on the high seas or to taking hostages on land and demanding huge ransoms while they keep their prey incommunicado. In such a situation, it is convenient if one is in good trim. She has seen enough of the militiamen to know they are not fighting fit. Even though she is pleased with the way things have gone up to now, she is possessed of understandable worries, many of them to do with her fear that she may not be able to withstand the pressures building up within and without her or may falter and then come apart at the seams at the wrong moment. She believes it prudent to train her mind and, for that matter, tone up her body for the day when she may crack up or when the luck that has sustained her may run out—and then what? She feels that she can be on top of things if, in addition to being strong of body and mind, she manages to impose some order on her activities.

In her effort to reimpose a healthy routine she sweats herself to exhaustion. Lacking a treadmill and the other sports facilities to which she is accustomed at home, and in view of the fact that she cannot imagine jogging down the dirt roads of the potholed city lest she become a shooting target of some gun-crazy youth, she stretches every muscle until she cannot stand the pain anymore. Moreover, to keep abreast of unfolding events, she has the radio on, anxiously expecting to hear the worst news: that Gudcur has prevailed in his campaign against his warring rivals. So far, all indications are that he will be triumphing over his opponents, who are in retreat, vacating territories they conquered and claiming this to be part of their strategic withdrawal.

She is in a sweat, preoccupied that she might be implicating an innocent man, the plumber, and inculpating Kiin's driver and security guards, who have so far shown her nothing but kindness. It worries her that she is getting Kiin, her newfound friend, involved in her dodgy affairs without leveling with her. A fresh panic sets in when, in a calm moment, she figures out what it will mean for all the parties concerned if in a day or two Gudcur triumphs over his competitors, who are also his clansmen and were at one time close allies, fighting hand in hand and living out of one another's thieving pockets. A decisive victory will no doubt result in raising Gudcur's self-confidence, thereby increasing his aplomb and, because of it, furthering his chances of conquering more territories and of extending his reign beyond his current domain. For Cambara, this can only spell insurmountable doom.

A grave shock, as disheartening as it must be debilitating, runs through her body the instant she realizes what Gudcur's victory implies. To fight off the sense of gloom that is about to engulf her and also to make sure that it doesn't weigh her down or get her worked up into a state of consternation, Cambara decides that it is best that she give Kiin a version of the events very close in general outline to the truth. Of course, she will do the best she can and, if need be, stretch the mode of telling it the way she knows best, adjusting the narration here and expanding on it there, especially where it is pliable, and naturally trimming it whenever the tale does not yield, because it lacks suppleness within its original material.

All the same, she perspires heavily, despite the cool air-conditioning in the room. Feeling tired, her sweatshirt sticking to her back, she paces to the extreme ends of the room on tiptoe. She looks at herself in the mirror on the back of the bathroom door; tall. She admires what she sees: a curvaceous body, shapely waist, breasts firm for a woman her age.

With her adrenaline in overdrive, she is thinking how sad it will make her if, untold because distrusted, Kiin not only does not buy into the version Cambara feeds her but also uncovers that she has misled her. Cambara, meanwhile, pictures herself trying to light-foot her way across a city peopled with misbegotten miscreants at the very time when whatever empathy Kiin has had for Cambara comes to an un-trusting end. Where will she go then? From whom will she seek help? Not from Zaak, who will most likely turn his back on her too; nor from Bile and Dajaal, two men she hardly knows. Her only hope is Kiin, with whom she thinks she shares a special empathy, even if this affinity re-mains undefined. Maybe it is this chemistry that each recognizes in the other. Cambara senses an onrush of unease when she imagines the woebegone scenario in which, having uncovered Cambara's untruths, Kiin shows her out: out of the hotel, out of her life, all contacts sev-ered. How weak the legs of untruths; how sturdy the legs of truth, how much faster they run than falsehood, which never gains on them. This projection results in her decision to confide in Kiin, to tell her what she is all about, why she is in the country, hiring plumbers, and so on. One woman counting on another, a woman yoked to another, a woman trusting another, a woman choosing to be truthful to another in the service of a higher ideal: of peace, of communal harmony.

What should she tell the plumber, who is much more likely than anyone else is, including her, to become a potential victim, if Gudcur, in a moment of ire, kills? What explanation should she give Zaak if he asks why, even though she is no longer putting up with him, she con-tinues meddling with his life? He will probably remind her of her changing his wardrobe and his dressing style, her making him wear clothes with a content higher in cotton than polyester. Before parting and divorcing, Zaak will complain that she made him exchange his austere living for a high-flying life of staying up till the small hours of the night, of mornings spent lying in, of behaving in a cavalier manner when it came to expenses, seldom worrying as if every day dawned bearing its special gift. If he takes this line with her, then she will re-mind him that she has ceased to be the woman he used to know from the instant she unloaded him and that in her reinvented self, she cares less about what he wears, more about her own problems.

Taking the plumber to her family's property without serious thought to the consequences of her action has made Cambara's commitment a more perilous concern. There is no running away from it, and there is no turning back either. She soaks up a few motionless seconds as she considers the matter. Meanwhile, she occupies her fidgety hands with an activity that she has been meaning to undertake: She bothers a blackhead, picking at it until she has almost removed it; then plucks at her armpit hair with the concentration of a woman applying eye pencil.

Someone starts the engine of a car, revving it, and then reverses it out through the gate, the harshness of the gear grating on her nerves. Cambara looks at her watch and, deciding it is time to choose what to wear for the evening, she pulls out the suitcase in which she has put her few changes of clothing. She has no difficulty choosing what to wear: a beautiful sleeveless up-and-down linen dress she received as a gift from her mother, who it bought it from a mainly African shopping mall in Toronto on her last visit before Cambara went away. She admires the dress, feeling it, her hand going against the grain, now along with it, and finally placing the top portion of it on the bed, studying the *denkyem,* the Ashanti symbol that the tailor sewed into it, the embroidery adding a natural balance and beauty to the material, its color close to her own.

She remembers the wisdom behind the Ashanti symbol; she remembers her mother telling her about the Ashanti proverb based on the system. According to her mother, the saying implies that even though the crocodile lives in water and has the enviable ability to stay on land too, the fact is it does breathe water; it breathes air. She interprets the symbol as meaning that like the crocodile, which lives in and off the bounty of water and the land surrounding it, she, Cambara, inhabits two contradictory states of mind: She dwells in peace even if the menacing closeness to the attrition that defines Somalia engulfs her. That is to say, she must adapt to the conditions that obtain in the city where she is and confront the situations that abound with uncomplaining hardiness, poised for worse scenarios, including death. She commends herself for reconciling herself to the continuously altering circumstances that are as formidably strenuous as they are dangerous. Ergo, she will put on the dress in deference to her acute sense of adaptability.

She has hardly had the time to shower when there is a gentle tap on the door. Cambara stays stock still, answering only when the person knocks several more times, every time meeker than before. She asks, "Who is it?"

"It is me," says a voice. "Kiin."

A spate of questions about where Cambara took Kiin's driver, bodyguards, and the plumber to whom she has introduced her invade Cambara's mind. These questions, coming as they do in the form of a deluge, each flowing from a tributary that brims over into an agitated river of self-doubts, fluster her. Praying that all is well with everyone who went in that vehicle with her, and her voice almost breaking, Cambara says, "Just give me a moment, please."

"No need to open the door," says Kiin. "I've come to find out how you are doing and to tell you that it is teatime and that I am at the café. So come and join me whenever you are ready."

Cambara opens the door, dressed in her linen outfit with the *denkyem* symbol embroidered into it.

On letting Kiin enter, Cambara observes, as if for the first time, that her rooms are host to the inevitable mess travelers create, with a bevy of plans they do not follow through on for one reason or another, when there are more suitcases and little in the way of a sense of how best to unpack and when. Strewn around on the floors in both rooms and on the beds therein are books of coffee-table dimensions and other paraphernalia that indicate the current occupant's abiding passion for masks and theater, including a couple of miniature masks of wood. Kiin takes keen interest in the books, opening an illustrated one designed to help bring such a play to the stage before moving away and focusing first on the masks, which she picks up and fingers, her fervor evident, and then a flimsy book, the size of a pamphlet, titled *The Eagle and the Chickens.*

From the expression on her face—open as though with a vista of possibilities—Kiin is apparently enthused about puppet theater and all of Cambara's material. "I wonder if you will tell me about all of this— if you have plans that I should know about and can help you with, that

we, the Women's Network, can help you with. Perhaps you would consider putting on a play? The network could fund it. Would you? For
peace? About peace? For women?"

"Nothing will give me more pleasure," Cambara says, "given the opportunity and provided that we succeed in achieving our aims."

Kiin does the high five, saying, "That's great."

Chuffed, Cambara says breatlessly, "Thanks." This is her dream
project.

In the silence, Cambara puckers her forehead, the wrinkles calling
Kiin's attention to the unwashed sweat resulting from Cambara's strenuous workout a few minutes earlier.

"So tell me all," says Kiin in an exhausted afternoon-without-
siesta voice. "Where have you been to? And have you achieved your
purpose?"

Cambara replies with sangfroid, never letting on that she has rehearsed her responses to the possible questions that Kiin might put to
her at the first opportunity. She tells her everything with the judicious
shrewdness of a culprit placing herself at a remove from a misdeed
without insisting on the primacy of her innocence.

"Who is Jiijo to you?"

Cambara grows restive before asking Kiin, "Do you know Jiijo?"

Kiin's reply that she does not know her makes Cambara puzzle over
her meaning. Neither speaks for a long time.

"Your escorts have chatted to her."

Not that Cambara is aware that they and Jiijo have exchanged a single word. Perhaps they sneaked in and had a word with her when she
was showing the plumber the toilets and the bathrooms upstairs.

"What has she told them?"

With the prospect of receiving an answer to her question coming to
nought, Cambara realizes that Kiin is probably showing her that she too
can hold back as much valuable information as Cambara has withheld
from her. Is this a token of the challenging times, when no one trusts
another enough to share a bit of news that is essential to both?

"What about Gudcur?" Kiin asks.

"What about him?"

Kiin says, "Tell me why you are interested in the property that he
has occupied for a very long time and that he uses as his 'family' home.
Apart from the fact that it is yours. That goes without saying."

Then she trains her inhospitable look on Cambara, into whose eyes she stares, drilling deep into an area no one has ever reached. Kiin's otherworldly glare puts the fear of the devil into her. This, together with the expectant silence and her restlessness, startles Cambara. When Kiin prods her with more questions, formulating them differently but essentially keeping to the same format, Cambara sits up as if a sharp metal object has pricked her; she wears the pained expression of someone who has no idea what is happening to her.

Then she tells Kiin everything, beginning with her son's death, the irreconcilable fissure between her and Wardi. Cambara informs how the rift led her to leave and come to Mogadiscio, in the belief that mourning her loss will make a clement sense only if she involves herself at the same time in repairing her relationship with the country, to whose well-being she has never contributed in any direct way.

"How do you intend to go about mending the rapport?" Kiin asks.

Cambara responds that there are two sides to her endeavor, both personal. Even though she hopes that she can achieve the recovery of her family's property, which she has planned to do all on her own without involving others directly, the truth is she has dragged others into it.

"Remind me something, please do," Kiin requests, and she hitches up her head scarf, tucking back in a lock of hair that has come undone. "How advanced is Jiijo's pregnancy?"

"Eight months plus."

"Let me get this right," Kiin goes on. "You say that the children have been sent away for their safety and that she, Jiijo, is alone in the house, as we speak, because Gudcur is engaged in the street-by-street battle to recover the territory he has lost?"

"So far as I am aware of the situation, yes."

She watches, with eagerness, as Kiin turns an idea over in her head, silent. Cambara suspects Kiin of entertaining a daring thought, and wonders if or when her newfound friend might share her conclusions once she has drawn them.

"What's on your mind?" Cambara asks.

Kiin looks away and up at the ceiling, as if the boards might reveal some secret message to her. Then, nodding in the gesture of someone who has finally unraveled a mystery, she pulls out her mobile, punches in a number, and waits for a long time. When the phone is answered,

Kiin asks of the person with the shrill voice, "Where are you, Farxia dear, and how busy are you?"

Kiin has put the phone on a speaker system, allowing Cambara to listen in. She explains, in a whispered aside, that she is talking to Farxia, a medical doctor at a clinic who is closing for the day. Farxia asks Kiin if there is an emergency and if her presence at the hotel is of immediate necessity. In reply, Kiin says that everything is okay with her, with Cambara too. At first, Kiin is hesitant, as if she has changed her mind about sharing whatever it is that has been bothering her and then tries lamely to assure Farxia that "things are all right, actually."

Farxia, her voice more high-pitched than before, says, "I doubt if whatever has made you call me on the emergency line can wait, even though things are all right, actually."

"I'll talk to you tomorrow evening," Kiin says.

"I urge you not to postpone talking to me until tomorrow," Farxia says. "So talk and talk now."

At Farxia's insistence, Kiin, who thinks aloud, most likely for Cambara's benefit, wonders whether the esteemed doctor will accommodate a daring thought. Kiin takes a long time to discuss what is on her mind, even though Cambara believes that, whatever it is, no one will suspect Kiin of taking leave of her senses.

"Don't play hard to get, Kiin."

"I am not."

"Then come clean, and fast," commands Farxia.

Kiin obliges, saying, "Do you or one of your junior colleagues at the clinic have time to make a home visit?"

"Right away?"

"Better still," Kiin says, the tone of her voice suggesting someone thinking on her feet, quick, capable of improving on ideas that are even more daring. "Do you have an ambulance and staff to help fetch a heavily pregnant woman and take her to your clinic?"

"Where is the pregnant woman?"

Kiin then suggests that Farxia wait at the clinic for her driver to come with a note from her, giving the pregnant woman's name and details. The driver will lead the ambulance to the house where the said woman is.

"Will do," Farxia says.

Cambara cannot help being impressed with how fast Kiin has sunk the future of her entire life and business by taking the single most daring step: emptying the family house of the only remaining proof of Gudcur's occupancy. When she thinks how she is beholden to Kiin for doing what she has done, she is at a loss for words. Nor will the damp stains silhouetted against the ceiling and from which Kiin received inspiration earlier give her counsel, telling her what to do.

"One dealt with," Kiin says, "another to go."

Something sets Cambara off, and, thinking ahead, she starts to wonder how sad she will be if things go wrong. After all, that means that she has endangered Kiin's and her daughters' lives, not to mention her hotel business, the lady doctor, whom she has not met, and her colleagues, staff, and clinic. She shakes, feeling as light as a leaf blowing in the sea breeze, with the tremor that has its beginning in worry.

"My second effort has to do with women, the theater, and an abiding commitment to peace," Cambara says. "Let me affirm that I feel certain that with your assistance, I will not have any difficulty achieving the things I've set my mind to."

"Be specific," Kiin says. "How can I be of help?"

Cambara settles in to the agreeable feeling of Kiin sorting out all her problems. She addresses herself to difficulties that she is likely to encounter when she starts to get down to the business of putting on a play in a country no longer familiar with this mode of entertainment. She goes on, "In fact, this is why I've wanted to meet a carpenter so I can construct a stage and help make the masks I've designed for it. I need an especially talented carpenter who can double as a joiner and who is bold in his or her interpretation of my sketches."

Kiin strikes a charming pose, visibly pleased. "I know such a person," she says.

"Here in this city?"

"He is Irish and I know him well."

"Does he live in Mogadiscio?"

"He's lived here for a number of years, has adopted Somalia as his own and, what is more, survived it."

"What's an Irishman doing here?"

"That's a long story."

"What is his name?"

"Seamus."

EIGHTEEN

Early the next morning, at eight o'clock, Cambara sits alone at a table in the hotel restaurant with her large writing pad open before her, studying her scribblings and then revising them, now adding and now deleting. She does this in the halfhearted way a professor not interested in what she is reading peruses a student's text. She turns the pages of the pad, which boast of chicken scratches only she can decipher, among them a sketch, in the form of a diagram for a play that she has worked on more off than on for several years; she thinks it will be ideal to produce the play here. She hopes that agreeing to put on a puppet theater will not only improve her chances of artistic success but also release her from her feel-bad factor, in terms of never having pulled off staging her own work.

She wishes she could work out what has prompted Kiin to talk readily, knowingly, and convincingly about Cambara's passion in producing a play for peace in Mogadiscio. She guesses that Raxma, their mutual friend, has most likely been in touch, intimating Cambara's keenness, which, as Arda has put it, "is generated by an obsession to make a name for herself at the same time as an actor and a playwright." To date, she has kept her dream alive but has little to show for it, apart from some amateur efforts of which she can't be proud. Not to worry about anything in connection with her artistic pursuit, though, for that can wait until she has scored successes on other fronts; then, she feels certain, agreeing to produce a play is going to be a sinecure, no sweat.

She can only imagine how much pleasure it will be if Gudcur comes back from the fighting wounded or is fatally injured and dies; then she will be in a much better position. As is her wont, she starts to count her chicks before her eggs hatch and thinks ahead to the day when she may use the family property's banquet hall as her rehearsal site. With Gudcur gone, his fighters no longer posing a threat to her plans, and Jiijo out of the way and having her baby in hospital—in view of the arrangements that are afoot, thanks to Kiin and Farxia—Cambara is convinced she will make headway fast. She interprets her dream at dawn, in which she saw several hawks overpowering the hyenas whom they were battling, as meaning that she will outsmart her opponents, whoever they are and achieve her aim, whatever that turns out to be.

She reminds herself that, according to one of the Horn Afrique radio correspondents who filed his dispatch at seven in the morning, Gudcur's men have been sent packing, are on the retreat, having been hustled out of several more checkpoints. Moreover, unconfirmed more up-to-date bulletins attributed to other news agencies allude to the heavy toll of dead and injured among his men. However, in view of the fact that no reporter mentions seeing Gudcur in person, the hearsay that he is dead or at least badly hurt is gaining credibility, fueled by the rumor that his deputy is acting as if he is unmistakably in charge. At one point during the interview, Gudcur's second-in-command let it slip that he is leading the campaign, now faltering, because of a faulty command structure. She sees the stand-in questioning Gudcur's authority not so much as evidence of a humiliating rout but as indisputable proof of his powerlessness.

Fretful, she sits up, smiling in genuine welcome as the waiter arrives with an item of her breakfast: two slices of mango prepared the way Mogadiscians like them. Her mouth watering, she admires the sweet golden fruit that is cut in equal halves, the flat, rounded stone removed, the fleshy portion segmented, with a knife, into sections, ready for her to eat. When the waiter does not move, as though expecting her to say something, Cambara tells him not to bother bringing her the second dish, one of liver, to be eaten with *canjeero*-pancake, a favorite among middle-class Mogadiscians. In response to his gentle attempt to persuade her against her decision—"It is our specialty, liver and pancake," he says—she explains that she doubts if she has the stomach for it. "Not this morning," she adds.

Nodding, the waiter departs. Then just as she takes her first spoon-
ful, an unheralded carnival of voices, as erratic as they are mercurial,
unsettle her. A horde of young men are frenziedly carrying items of furniture, lifting and heaving them in the clumsy way untrained bearers
pick up and hoist heavy, many-legged movables. She recognizes one or
two of the young men, and she begins to worry that they may hurt their
backs on top of disfiguring or breaking the odd table, chair, or sofa,
which will no doubt set Kiin back a bit. She watches them with a mix
of anxiety and amusement as they haltingly struggle to bring a table that
by her reckoning seats ten through a door that is too narrow for it.
What is more, these youths' maladroitness—raising the table above
their heads with the likelihood of breaking one of its legs instead of tilt-
ing it to the side or bringing it out a leg at time—fills her with such unease she wonders if they will be good enough to participate in her play.
In fact, she finds that her fearful worries have been realized: The table's
two front legs are wobbly, and the young men are drenched with sweat
and panting. They go past the well to their left, then stumble, ungainly,
up a stone stairway to her right, in the direction of the outhouse with
the thatched roof and the windows that open outward at awkward
angles.

Following them with her eyes, her gaze finally falls on the outhouse,
which has an added-on aspect to it, an afterthought resulting from a
need not only for more space but for something like a hall. She understands that that is where the hotel holds parties overflowing with
revelers. In her mind, Cambara thinks of a future when peace is
supreme and when Kiin's preteen children may employ it as a bache-
lor pad. How curious that she realizes, only after watching the youths
putting themselves out, hoisting and hauling, that the outhouse has an
upstairs hall and a downstairs eat-in, the latter boasting a dozen or so
tables and chairs dressed in colorful cloths and arranged as though for
a formal function. Cambara has high aspirations that she will enjoy herself at the women-only party to which Kiin has invited her and will try
to muster one or two of the women to help her with her plans, thank
Farxia for what she has done and maybe at last meet the shopkeeper
Odeywaa's wife.

She looks up startled, with doubts starting to gnaw at her insides.
Then again, she is consumed by an overwhelming uncertainty the mo-

ment she considers the furious tempo at which the new developments
have unfolded, with Kiin becoming the plinth upon which the pillars
of Cambara's causes rest, and Zaak and Wardi virtually out of her sight
and out of her mind. She persists, against reason, to rely wholly on Kiin,
even though she feels that she must cultivate the friendship of other
people to whom she can turn; otherwise, Kiin will be the only one on
whom she will depend, however well appointed she has been or will be.
Sadly, whenever she has had a good reason to celebrate a moment of
triumph, Cambara is given to suffering an attack of anxiety, fearing the
consequences of future failures instead of gathering the robe of success around her. *Basta,* enough!

SilkHair. What are her intentions toward him in the event that she
commits herself more and more to his welfare? Will the time ever come
when she may adopt him legally? This is one of her concerns. The idea
of taking SilkHair in, even though it is not necessarily in the cards, does
have its appeal, as it will give her more purchase when she decides to
return to Toronto. She imagines saying, in response to her friends, who
may ask why she is back so soon after leaving, "But you know,
Mogadiscio is no place in which to raise an intelligent, ambitious child,
as there are no schools, in fact nothing to recommend it." Of course,
there is no way of knowing how things will pan out, or whether SilkHair
will prove to be a willing partner in her project, bearing in mind that
he is the kind of boy who has clear ideas about what he wants to do
with his life—for a boy of his age and background. More important, is
she a good enough mother for a boy of his social circumstances. Is her
hardiness comparable to Seamus's, whom Kiin says has adopted the entire country and survived it?

She puckers her lips into wrinkled annoyance, disturbed at the re-
current thought that by inviting others into her life, she will bring into
it complications without which she can do very well. Why does she
keep doing that? Is it because she is perennially lonely, needing the
company of others in the very same way some people have pets or married couples who are having difficulties invite third or fourth parties,
because they cannot face each other alone? Why—even before she is
certain of a favorable outcome about SilkHair—is she thinking about
Bile? Maybe she believes that, in his own way, Bile not only will have
supplemented and in the end completed her new self, but will have en-

riched it too. Like it or not, the question that comes to her mind now is whether or not she is exchanging Wardi, the estranged husband whom she has shed off, for Bile, and whether admitting SilkHair into the parameters of her newly reconstructed self will have given it a firmer format.

Her face brightens with a smile at the thought of not only meeting this Seamus but also placing the sketches of her plans before him and requesting that he carve the masks and, if feasible, build the stage and set too. Happy at the prospect of achieving her aim, Cambara takes a slow sip from her bottle of mineral water.

She takes a mouthful of the mango. She thinks, What a beauty, what a mango! Then she muses what shape this new self will take if allowed to develop to its full potential. To make things work, she will have to find out what kind of homeschooling Kiin has organized for her daughters and find out what chances there are for SilkHair. The question is how best to organize the life of a young boy in these difficult times and in such a way that it is manageable. Will she survive journeying into yet another new "thing" whenever the old "thing," to which she gave her concentrated attention for many days, many weeks, many months, or many years, no longer fills her heart with excitement and emotion?

Suddenly, she hears a female voice that is at once familiar and full of animated vigor, giving instructions and shouting at several people at the same time. The part of Kiin's voice that is familiar is imbued with an irresistible charm; the unfamiliar strain of it is raised, hastily spoken, stressed to the point of sounding plagued—the voice of a woman who is harried, hassled, and perfunctory too. Eventually, she catches sight of Kiin as she comes into view, riding the waves of her elegant stride. Deeply moved, excitement catches at Cambara's throat, and she manages only to wave and wave. Eventually, Kiin acknowledges her beckoning motions and indicates, with a gesture of her hand, that she will be with her shortly.

Kiin joins her, even though it is clear that she is fretting, maybe because she has not much time to chat, what with the number of things that she must attend to before the evening party. The two friends hug, touching cheeks, kissing, each asking how the other is, and then answering, in unison, "Fine, very fine," and finding this humorous and giggling.

When they have stood apart for a few seconds, Kiin says, "Have you heard from him? He's promised that he will call you."

It does not do Cambara's heart any good to hear a generic allusion to a "he" and to remember that she has forgotten the mobile phone in the room—not knowing what manner of tidings this "he" will bring and whether they are good or bad. Who is supposed to have called her? Bless the fellow—Bile? Curse the fellow—Zaak? God forbid—Gudcur?

"From whom am I supposed to have heard?"

"Seamus."

"How stupid of me," Cambara says.

"What makes you say that?"

"Because I've left the phone in the room."

"Seamus has rung me."

"What does he say?"

"That he'll be here shortly."

Cambara pushes her breakfast things away and, as soon as she does, grows restless, looking from the plates to Kiin and then finally at her sketch pad, which is to the right of her, and is filled with scrawls and patterns that make a fascinating viewing, at least from where Kiin is standing.

Kiin, meanwhile, instructs the waiter to go to the kitchen and place an order of double espresso and breakfast—liver, underdone, and *canjeero*-pancakes—for Seamus, and to bring it to Cambara's table.

When the waiter has gone and they are alone, Kiin says, "I would like you to join us for lunch, my daughters and me."

"Be glad to," Cambara says.

"Lunch at one-thirty for two."

Cambara half rises, readying to thank Kiin for everything and at the very same moment thinking of her, rather enviously, as a woman in charge of her life.

Kiin is off, saying, "See you then."

The first intimation, insofar as Cambara is concerned, that something unusual is taking place comes in the shape of an eerie quietness when one of the sentries switches off a radio. From that instant on, Cambara takes interest in the inexorable, if unorthodox, movements of several of the junior unarmed security guards who amuse themselves as they have a peek, one at a time, through the peephole of the pedestrian gate. Then they exchange quizzical looks as they consult one another and then debate among themselves what action to take if any, before sheepishly glancing in the direction of a man who looks as though he is dead to their world, maybe sleeping.

A perfunctory appraisal confirms her suspicions: that the man sleeping in the chair, with his arms hugging his chest, his feet forward, and whom the junior unarmed sentries at the gate have not dared to disturb is, indeed, the man who led yesterday's afternoon prayer. He is, apparently, the head of security, and now she remembers him directing the show in the car. Kiin has told her how much she relies on him.

Eventually he wakes of his own accord, maybe because, with the radio no longer on, the uncanny soundlessness alerts him to the changes of which he takes notice. He opens his eyes with the slowness of a cock squawking an exhausted crow from the depth of its drowsiness and then stretches his arms into the full extent of a yawn before doddering to his tallness. He rubs the weariness out of his eyes, leans against the wall for support, and asks what is happening. Receiving no answer from the others, who can only stare at him, he places his eye to the spy hole. He sees an ungainly white man with the hangdog expression of someone who has no business being there, a man with a beer paunch pulling at his bearded face and nervously feeding chunks of the graying hair into his mouth, chewing at it ceaselessly.

The head of security gives what he can see of the white man a once-over and then barks instructions at one of the youths to "let the gentleman in."

It is then that Seamus steps in, his hands fisted, his features breaking into a friendly grin, his stride even, his demeanor unafraid and unworried. However, because of the thickness of his facial hair and the distance separating her from him, Cambara cannot determine the nature of his amity or to whom he is addressing it or if it is turning into a snicker. Even so, Cambara says, "Terra firma," to herself, as she studies him, thinking "What a great presence," from the vantage point of seeing him and guessing who he is before he has laid his eyes on her. To welcome him, she gets to her feet, almost daring to call out to him by his first name. She takes a good hold of herself and then sits down, fussily smoothing her hair with her hands and touching them to her face in callous disregard of what anyone else watching her might think.

Seamus goes round shaking hands, taking the hand of everyone in his vicinity in his own. He starts with the head of security and then holds the hands of the other man in his for a few moments, eventually shuffling in her direction, his steps short, paunch more prominent than he likes it to be, and his right hand ahead of him, as if he might make a present of it to her. Seamus, she thinks, has the look of an exhausted beast of burden that is carrying more than twice its weight and rises to its diminished height, knees burdensomely bent and aching, gaze wary, and mouth pouting, as if annoyed. Look at him wanting to shake everyone's hand; watch him hitching his belt up every so often and, while doing so, subtly touching his private parts as if making sure they are still there. Pray, how does he get around? What means of transport does he have, if any?

"I am Bile's friend," Seamus says loud enough for the benefit of all those overhearing him, this way defining a kind of kinship that he hopes will make sense to the armed and unarmed youths: a mascot for Bile, for friendship. She makes a knowing effort not to return the goggle-eyed stare of the youths, who, in her view, are merely highlighting their curiosity, it being the first time for them, perhaps, to see a Somali woman not in a veil welcoming a European man in view of so many of them. In broad daylight. Without a chaperone.

She says, "Seamus, I presume," shaking his hand with the warmth of one who might even go as far as hugging him but stopping just short of that.

"Welcome to our city, Cambara," he says, pronouncing faultlessly the guttural c with which her name begins. "Bile says hi and so does Dajaal, both having had the pleasure to make your acquaintance under unfavorable conditions. It seems to me I am the lucky one, in that I meet you when you look rested, relaxed, and ready to host me at your hotel."

"The pleasure of meeting you in this friendlier situation is all mine, Seamus," she says, mouthing his disyllabic name as if taking more of an ownership than she has meant to.

When the waiter arrives, carrying a double espresso for him, Cambara points Seamus to a chair, which he takes, his back to the youths who are presently undressing both of them with their leering. Seamus says, "Thanks," instinctively, addressing his word neither to her nor to the waiter. He gives the waiter sufficient time to move away, shifting in his seat, then has his first long, pensive sip of the coffee but stops short of telling Cambara whether it is to his taste or not.

He pulls at the bristles on his chin, now and then rooting out a loose hair snuggling in the bend of his fat, thick fingers with the thoughtfulness of a farmer picking weeds in the underbrush. Something about the way he is sitting tells her that Seamus has grown into his Somaliness in the same way alien vegetation adapts to take root eventually in the soil in which it has been planted.

"Tell me," Seamus says conversationally.

"Where does one begin?" she says. She sounds evidently charmed, her cheerfulness as spontaneous as a baby's first grin.

"Begin anywhere," he smiles encouragingly. "Anywhere will do."

"I am sure you are familiar with John Coltrane?"

"Not as much as you are, I presume."

"My favorite Coltrane is 'A Love Supreme.'"

"And is that where you want to begin?"

"I may equally begin it with a moment of on-the-level sadness, when one discovers one's partner is glorying in one's debasement, luxuriating in it?" She looks away, as though embarrassed, maybe because she is uncertain if he is following her meaning.

Her hand moves toward the upper part of her cheek—a woman who hasn't decided whether she is wiping away tears or removing a bit of kohl with a Kleenex. She recalls not putting on eyeliner for several months now—she, who has trained as a makeup artist—not since losing her dear, darling son.

"My son died," she says. "Drowned."

"I am very sorry," Seamus says, looking away.

"In my husband's lover's pool."

He mouths the word "Sorry," but issues not a sound. Again, he looks away and then at his fingernails, which, Cambara notices, either have been chewed down to the flesh or are long and dirty.

"You could say that I've come here to grieve."

Seamus swallows as if he had a fish bone in his throat, which he clears. He is the image of a man who wants to help but does not know how, who wants to say something but has no idea what words will express what is on his mind.

Then after a long silence, when Cambara is at a loss for words, he says, "And while grieving, while mourning . . ."

"I've vowed to recover our family property."

"Kiin has made no mention of that."

"What has she spoken to you about?"

"Mourning, peace, and masks," he says, brief in his choice of words, as if tapping out his thinking in Morse.

"I hope to be of some service to the community of women among whom I find myself," Cambara explains. "I am thrilled Kiin has asked me to make my contribution in that regard."

Seamus behaves as if he is ill prepared for what he is about to say, and so he frets, his beady eyes dwelling on his nails, which, biting, he has cut close to the flesh and are bleeding a little. In the disquiet that is of a piece with his absentmindedness, he puts his finger in his mouth and, tasting blood, frowns.

He says, "Put plainly, you need our help."

"That's right."

As the waiter returns, this time with Seamus's order of liver-and-pancake breakfast, Seamus smiles distractedly, then she sees his right hand going up and waving with enthusiasm to someone, she presumes. Cambara wants to know whom he is greeting, notwithstanding, and spots Kiin gesticulating and finally touching her open palm to her lips in a quick dispatch of kisses to both of them before moving away from the balcony of the upstairs of the outhouse.

Cambara asks Seamus, "How is Bile?"

Seamus replies, "He is a little unwell."

"What's ailing him? Is he depressed?"

"That's one way of putting it," agrees Seamus.

Then he beckons to the waiter who is standing close by, against the wall. In accented Somali he says he would like another espresso, no sugar, please.

"Tell me in plain language what it is you need help with," Seamus says to Cambara, "and I will see what I can do and tell you whether or not I can."

She speaks plainly and to the point, starting from the beginning, now that she is no longer nervous in his presence and need not try to impress him. She talks animatedly about her plans: how she will be grateful for any assistance he can offer her, especially in the carving of masks. Then she explains that she has already sketched everything herself and shares with him the pencil drawings she has done on her sketch pad.

"What about the text?" he says.

Cambara gives him a synopsis of the story on which she plans to base the play. She goes on, "The version of the play I have in mind to produce is inspired by an oral parable from Ghana, first committed to paper by one Kwegyir Aggrey, famously known as Aggrey of Africa."

Seamus falls in love with the idea, promising to lend a hand, rally round, and help all he can. But he shakes his head, adding, "I do not know if I am the right person or, more appropriately, if I am capable of carving masks, having never had any training in the art or in theater for that matter."

"I have brought the very thing you need: sketches upon sketches, models, and how-to books for beginners interested in learning the art of puppet theater."

"Then we are in business," he says, and, half rising, he stretches his hand out to her, his bare beer paunch and its hirsute features distracting Cambara for a second, and they shake hands on it.

"We will have a great deal of fun doing it," he says when his rounded bottom hits his seat, "and it will be instructive to all concerned if we manage to stage it."

She hands the sketches across to Seamus, who takes the pad and, studying them, turns the pages after he has looked at each of them, nodding with approval. Then they hear the gentle sound of a klaxon. Seamus looks away and then at the gate and watches one of the unarmed sentries putting his eye to the peephole. The sentry opens the gate, and a vehicle is driven in. Seamus recognizes the car, and, about to end his conversation, looks at his watch and nods as though his timing has worked to perfection. It is Cambara's turn to recognize the driver, Dajaal, who comes out of the car and exchanges greetings with the armed and unarmed sentries staffing the gates, calling each of them by name.

Dajaal joins Cambara and Seamus, bows his head in acknowledgment of her warm greeting but stands apart, his body stiffening, a little too formal for her liking, distant. All the same, she points him to a chair, offers him his choice of tea, some coffee, a glass of water, perhaps, anything. Dajaal declines and taps on his wristwatch, indicating he has no time. He eyes Seamus with a knowing grin, and when the Irishman does not get up to go with him, Dajaal says to Seamus, in Italian, "Bile is waiting."

Still, Seamus does not move.

"We must be on our way," Dajaal says.

Cambara says to Seamus, "Take the sketch pad with you, and let's meet and talk further in a couple of days, by which time I will have prepared a photocopy of the text of the play."

"So long," Seamus says.

Dajaal urges Seamus, taking hold of his elbow, as if helping him to get to his feet. Although he does not like what Dajaal is insinuating, Seamus humors him by not saying anything. She cannot for the life of her determine what it is about these three men, each of them charming and very likable in his own way, that makes similar movie personages come to mind when she thinks of them. Walter Matthau and his cohorts in the comedies, including Jack Lemmon and another whose name she cannot recall; and of course there are Frank Sinatra, Dean Martin, and Sammy Davis, Jr. You think of one, you think of the others.

Cambara says, "Greetings to Bile."

She feels that the charmed part of her is going with them as they get into the car, which Dajaal starts energetically. She wishes she could join them. In fact, she is tempted to wave to Dajaal, shout to him to stop the vehicle, go back to her rooms, put together an overnight bag in which to carry her basics, this time including a makeup kit, and then hop in at the back for no other reason perhaps than to see Bile. Yet she can't define the source of this keenness or point her finger precisely at the fount of this longing, having met the man only the one time and not under ideal circumstances.

Just then—what a spoiler—her memory brings up a horrid scene

from one of her ugly encounters with Zaak on the first day of her arrival. Trust her to remember his admonition, spoken in his inimitably
cruel tone of voice, saying "Woman, grow up." No longer waving or
grinning, her hand goes down with the speed of a punctured tire.

Cursing the day she met Zaak, she withdraws into herself, reaching
deep down to where she knows she is strong; she retreats into the purposeful pensive mood of a woman determined to pull herself together.
And even though she goes into her rooms to put on a touch of makeup
before joining Kiin and her daughters for lunch, she is so restless that
she cannot bear the thought of being alone in her rooms.

She sits in the café with a book in her hand, the mobile phone in her
lap eerily silent. She watches the goings-on near the gate where the
armed and unarmed guards have gathered, engaging in some friendly
banter. Wandering, her thoughts lead her back to the conversation she
has had with Seamus, to whom she has revealed more of her sad side
than she imagined she would. Maybe it has been her intention to dis-
pel any glamour-girl status that Bile may have; who better to leak this
to than a third party, in this case Seamus, who is bound to share it with
him. Why, Seamus too has let it slip that Bile is a depressive.

All is well when all is revealed early!

NINETEEN

No sooner has Cambara sat in the shade and located the page where she left off in her thriller than she sees the driver waving to her in greeting. She is about to acknowledge it when, turning, she spots a young boy who draws her attention away from everyone and everything else. She wonders to herself if she is hallucinating or seeing apparitions, because a boy, until then nameless and definitely not known to her and yet seemingly familiar as he reminds her of her own son, Dalmar, is suddenly there. It is as though he has materialized out of nowhere, with the air around him thickening with mystery the longer she looks at him.

The waiter has by chance returned to the café to wipe the tables with a wet cloth and then lay them for the lunch seating. She calls him over and asks him, "Do you happen to know the boy or what his name is?"

"Gacal is his name."

"Whose son is he?"

"He is no one's son," replies the waiter.

"No one's son?"

"That's right. He is nobody's son." The waiter speaks with the straight face of someone who does not quite realize the pithy quality of his remarks. He is not even remotely aware how fired up Cambara is as she repeats his utterance to herself, relishing its inspired nature.

"He is no one's son," he says again.

Now that is a new one, she thinks. She finds the observation most becoming, out of the ordinary: a boy, not quite ten by her reckoning, who displays a developed-enough personality and qualifies as no one's son. More like a mythical persona: no parents like Adam; no known biological father like Jesus. Will this Gacal accomplish heroic feats like Krishna's? Is there a shadow side to him, and if so what is it? Does Gacal share any of the traits of Sundiata, who, in Mandingo myth, was born not through a woman's vagina, because of its associations with all manner of discharges, but through a finger, undefiled?

Apparently, the boy has come much closer, self-conscious of the rags he has on. It is as though he is on a performance trip, the way he poses; maybe, in a younger life, he was used to being photographed with alarming frequency, a loving mother cuddling him and his dad near and adoring. Look at how he blinks his eyes. Is he remembering the flash of the camera blinding him, the sun in his eyes dimmed? What manner of a poseur is he? Gacal has the sort of flair you associate with the well-born. He carries himself with élan. It does not require much imagination to sense that he is of a different class, physically aware of where he is in relation to where others are. Not only does he surround himself with much space, but he is also mindful not to encroach on yours. Does his behavior point to a middle-class upbringing in his past? Nor does he have shoes on. What's more, she observes, he has the habit of raising himself on the tip of his toes, craning his neck, as if standing in a crowd between people taller than he is, watching a street revue.

Now that he is here, what is she to do? How is she to deal with the boy's presence or just cope with things, preoccupied as she is with the family house and what will have become of it, if it is empty of Jiijo? Is she to welcome him, *dolce far niente,* without any need of explanation or justification?

Grinning, Gacal stands at a little distance to her right, quiet, his hands seemingly deferential in that they are clasped behind his back, his face grimy, and his rags grubby. His mouth curves upward, as if in a smile, at the same time as he smirks impishly, defiantly waiting for Cambara to read his bearing, interpret it any way she likes. Cambara gives herself time enough to weigh her options, contrasting the possible advantages of not committing herself one way or the other to taking the indulgent position of a mother figure. She assumes that Gacal has not been in the company of either of his parents or that of a caring adult for a long while. What is his story? The question she dares not ask is whether he knows SilkHair, and, if he does, whether the two of them been in communication with each other about this soft woman, whom anyone can touch and who will come up with gestures of kindness no child in Mogadiscio has ever known. Beware of the sense of paranoia taking over your thinking, Cambara tells herself, and then takes a fresh interest in Gacal.

He has been in a brawl. That much is obvious. In fact, there is enough evidence to warrant the supposition that he has been in a very savage fight: the blood on his forehead and lower lip that is now dry; a few chin-bound, down-facing abrasions crossing others that are upward-bound, one of them ending close to the right eye; lacerations on his arms and neck; gashes on his chest. Moreover, he has lost the sleeve of the shirt, the zipper on his trousers is ripped off, and his skin is liberally grazed here and there. In addition, he looks hungry, and she feels sure that he has not slept a wink for the last twenty-four hours and that, by the look of it, eating and having a lie down may bring his color back to his cheeks and put a smile on his parched lips. Maybe it is not the time to badger him with questions. That can wait until she has had him fed and has organized a place for him to lie down.

Cambara beckons to the waiter, into whose ear she whispers her request: that, in view of the lateness of the hour, might he marshal a meal, a clean towel, a shower, and a mat-under-a-tree to lie down on for Gacal. When he nods his head, she says, "I will pay the charge."

As the waiter tiptoes away purposefully, the scene puts her in mind of a questionable collusion between her and Wardi in their early days when, notwithstanding her misgivings about the rightness of getting involved with him, the woman in her could not resist giving in to the dictates of her heart. Wardi took advantage of her, cashing in on her naiveté, in the end making a substantial killing. Look at where he is now: in Toronto, comfortable. Look at where she is now: in Mogadiscio and putting some kind of a life together. Look at the brittle mischief in Gacal's eyes, a sign that her interference is more likely than not to lead to a similar situation. There are two possible ways to deal with Gacal: have him follow the waiter, eat, sleep his exhaustion off, and then meet; or engage him in a desultory dialog right away and then finis! In any event, she invites him over. He makes as if to launch into an explanation, but she won't have it.

She raises her hand, silencing him. After a pause, she says to him, "Go after the waiter, and he will give you something to eat, a clean towel, and will show you where you can have a bucket shower." But she does not tell him that, meanwhile, she will look for a pair of trousers and a T-shirt for him, since his are as soiled as the hind legs of a hyena or as torn as the gouged eye of a matador.

Gacal does as she tells him, turning away as petulant as a cat whose advances have not gotten her a place on her mistress's lap. As for Cambara, she goes forthwith to her rooms, not sure if she has the right to be pleased with the way she has handled him and wondering if Gacal will have learned where the boundaries of her tolerance will end and what the framework of their relationship is. Of course, she looks forward to having a long chat with him later.

For now, she rummages in the suitcase for clothes that once belonged to her son, Dalmar, trying to find a pair of cotton trousers and a T-shirt for Gacal. Finally, she lays her nervous hands on clothes that she hopes will be a perfect fit for him. Then she rings the reception, asking that one of the youths please collect the items she's chosen and give them to Gacal. She explains that the waiter will know where to find him.

It dawns belatedly that she is behaving like a fawner: a childless woman doing her utmost to pamper a parentless boy with affection to make him take a liking to her. By the time the waiter assigned to do her bidding turns up to fetch the clothes and hand them over to the boy after a shower, Cambara knows that she wants to bring *Pinocchio*, the videocassette, and Gacal along to Kiin's place for lunch.

Three-quarters of an hour later, Cambara is at her desk in the workroom. She has got down to serious work, studying the notes on her scratch pad and admiring the easy-to-carry miniature wooden masks that she hopes the boy playing the role of the eagle in the fable on which she has based her play will be wearing on his head. The one she is holding in her hand is a replica of the original sculptured for her on commission by an Igbo living in Toronto.

The mask in her clutch is beige, of soft wood, inspired by a nineteenth-century piece in ivory that can be traced to the Kingdom of Benin in Nigeria, a cola-nut vessel in the shape of an antelope's head, the horns scored with designs in darker hues and engraved with motifs, used for ceremonial purposes. Around the ears, to be precise, just below the right side of the head of the antelope, there is a fish bone, the fish eye bold in its prominence. She returns to her notes and thumbs though the photocopies she has made of the original sculpture. The beauty of the piece is so staggering that it astounds Cambara for a moment.

She runs her eyes over several other copies of some of the other masks that she intends Seamus to sculpt for her play. Among these, one piece stands out: a twentieth-century Senufo headdress carved out of a rectangular board and worn as a mask. This arrests her attention, for on it there are very abstract figures of animals that stand in two-dimensional profiles in four wide openings. In addition to the animal figures, several other difficult-to-identify forms are organized according to a systemic concept, with round contours of figures in the front and back of the board foregrounding the mask. There is a female figure in front of the head of the antelope, dominating it, and in the back or, rather, above the antelope head, there is a bird in the likeness of an eaglet, more abstract than the other figures in the front.

She consults her file further and comes across yet another piece of breathtaking artistry said to have been found among Leo Frobenius's collection, bought in 1904 in what is now the Democratic Republic of the Congo. This is either a nineteenth- or an early-twentieth-century comb carved out of wood in the abstract shape of a human. Dominating the design are a protruding nose and a crested headdress, shapes that are worked with impressive artistry into the comb, its projection forming part of the small head. High-ranking men and young men participating in the festivities at the end of their initiation ceremony wore these combs as hair ornaments. Cambara hopes that Seamus will be able to sculpt pieces in the likeness of rods that the actors playing the characters and speaking their roles can easily manipulate.

Just then, she hears a tap at the door and gets to her feet with the speed of someone expecting a visitor. As she does so, she collides with the desk, knocking her thigh against its edge, the pain instant and atrocious, and her veins smarting. She limps to the door, wincing, and because she pulls the door open without asking who is there, wonders if she is being injudicious. After all, the knocker could be anyone: Gudcur or one of his militiamen come with the premeditation and motive to harm her; Zaak, arriving to vent his spleen, as malodorous as it is ill humored; or any other gun-toting youth, deranged enough to shoot without a care in the world.

"There you are," she says to Gacal, who is standing there. She sounds genuinely happy, chuffed that he looks more elegant than she has imagined possible in the outfit she has sent down to him.

"I am here," he says, his tone of voice that of a wooer manqué, come without a hat to tip to the woman he is courting. His thumb and index are poised, as if to raise a hat.

Cambara takes his measure, training her eyes on him, feeling more confident than ever in her choice and judging him right for the role she wants him to play. Pleased that he will serve her purposes, and content too that he is meeting her quick appraisal with a chutzpah in the form of a twinkle of a smile, she watches with amusement as he rubs his flat open palm over the creases in the trousers, smoothing them. She gives him an A-plus mark; he nods his head, maybe confirming her thoughts. She is debating whether to invite him into her room when she realizes that he is barefoot and remembers why even after she donated shoes to the Salvation Army in Toronto she felt the need to apologize to the officer receiving them. Dalmar would describe his feet as "funny," because of the differences in their size, his left foot being the larger by nearly three sizes, a deformity that Wardi blamed her for, at one point ascribing it to what he called Cambara's degeneracy. She would order her son's footwear from a U.K.-based outfit, Sole Mates, which specializes in supplying people like Dalmar with shoes matching the varying sizes of their feet. She broods over the matter of shoes a little more and then invites Gacal into the room. She takes him by the hand before giving his feet a cursory assessment and deciding that for the time being he can use her open leather sandals, which she reckons are merely one size too big.

When she returns her gaze to concentrate on Gacal, she finds that he is focusing his full attention on the replica of a wooden mask that has been cut out of cardboard and painted a dark color. She is equally enthralled, watching him, spellbound. She is moved, her transport of joy knowing no limits. Elated, she walks back into the room, picking up the object of his fascination, and says, "Try it on."

Gacal steps forward to receive the mask in the respectful self-possession of someone collecting a prize from royalty—reverentially and with both his hands. He behaves self-consciously, turning it this way and that admiringly. One might think that he has always known its great import, even though, from the awestruck way he is now holding it, Cambara is not sure if he has any idea what it is for.

To spare him blushes, she decides to help him out. She says, "See if it will fit your head." When he stares back at her hesitantly, obviously confused and not knowing what to do, she says, "Here," and she snatches it back from him, her manner gentle, her grin gushy. Then she places it on his head in much the same rigorous ritualism as a commoner chosen to put a crown on the head of a noble person, honoring him or her. That done, she moves back to confirm her decision to cast Gacal in the role of the eagle in the play as soon as she laid her eyes on him. She says, "There."

Gacal's hands flail blindly but very cautiously above his head, not daring to touch the mask lest he upset its balance or upend it. It is then that she leads him by the hand to the full-length mirror in the bathroom. To afford both of them the possibility of concentration, she stands apart from him and out of the mirror's frame. She describes the scene before her as an instant of breathtaking beauty. "No doubt about it, no doubt about it," she repeats several times.

When he makes as if to ask what it is for, she reclaims the mask, holds it at the range of a trombone, and says, "The clothes I've given you may not be a perfect fit and I may not have got you a pair of shoes, but this suits you wonderfully."

A masterpiece of unequalled handsomeness; she feels almost content with the world and fills her eyes with Dalmar's look-alike.

Her mobile rings. She answers it, her eyes brightening as the voice of the woman at the other end gives her very good news. Then she listens some more and asks, "Are you sure, Kiin dear, that you do not mind if I bring my young guest to lunch? Also to bring along *Pinocchio*, so that he and your two daughters, whom I am so looking forward to meeting, can watch it while we chat in uninterrupted peace?"

"But of course." Cambara picks up a trace of annoyance in Kiin's voice, suspecting that there is something bothering her, even if she is not telling her what it is. This gets Cambara's back up, but she lets it be in the hope that she will eventually hear of what is bugging Kiin. Understandably, Kiin may not be very keen on having a boy unknown to her play with her daughters alone, well aware that he is a different make from them. You never know what mischief an urchin with no known beginnings might conjure up if such an opportunity were to present itself. It is just as well that she will be close by, keeping her eyes and ears alert for any possible misadventure. Will Gacal, who may have a troubled history, interrupt the placidity that Kiin has created for herself and her daughters?

"Let's go," she says. "It's lunchtime."

Gacal looks ecstatic. Cambara imagines him to be comfortable in who he is becoming: a clean, well-fed lad who has on clothes as good as new, plus a pair of leather sandals—never mind that it is no easy matter to scuttle speedily in them—his hand in the grip of a woman fostering him to high ambitions. What more can he want?

To get to Kiin's place on foot, Cambara, leading Gacal by the hand, walks through a door set clandestinely into the wall separating the hotel grounds from Kiin's residence. Paned green and wrapped in vines grown purposely to disguise it, the door is visible only to those who know of its existence. It is to the rear of a spot where the sentries have provisionally mounted a guard to the right of the main entrance. Cambara uses the door that is Kiin's family preserve, relieved to be spared a little of the bother of leaving the hotel and stepping into the main dirt road, walking a hundred or so meters and then turning left into Kiin's gate.

Serenity steals over all her taut nerves, helping her to relax the moment she and Gacal enter the grounds of Kiin's residence. Her heart leaps with joy at the sight of such an idyllic scene: a sunlit place of peace and harmony in the midst of so much darkness. Cambara lets go of Gacal's hand, in part because his are sweaty, hers dry, and because she wants him to carry *Pinocchio*. She guesses that his ear-to-ear grin can only point to the attainment of a dream: a parent figure to entrust him with an important assignment. There is confidence in his stride, his forward-leaning pose suggesting an eagerness to prove his worth.

They light upon a man who is supine on a straw mat in the shade of a large, fruiting mango tree. She assumes he is the gardener, taking a lunch break close to the shed. Scattered all around him, as if by design, are his tools: a wheelbarrow, rakes, a hoe, and other implements. Farther on, beyond the blooming orchids, two beautiful girls run after each other and around a tree, excited, their voices full of life and their chases alive with the equanimity of the fearless giggles. There are the swings and the seesaw that form the center of the playground; close to these, Cambara spots a tree house having a ladder with a missing rung up near the top end. Along the way, Cambara is tempted to pick up a couple of dolls and a few toys that look as if a child has flung them, a leg up, the head twisted, toys abandoned in the middle of play.

Kiin may be living in a city that has not known peace for ten years and more, which is all the more reason why the legion of comforts that she has created are remarkable in themselves, amenities that are on the one hand pure pleasure and on the other startling when you come upon them. Cambara cannot help drawing a conclusion: that only someone blessed with abundant self-confidence and the joys of living in the coziness of a snug life, fitting in the protected nature of its refuge, can be as giving and magnanimous as Kiin has been to her and, presumably, to many others.

No matter what she thinks of it, Cambara again is sad that she is pinning all her hopes of success on Kiin, whom she hardly knows. What will she do, on whom will she depend, whose assistance will she seek if something terrible happens to the one basket into which she has put all her eggs? It is a pity, she thinks, that Zaak, on whom her mother had hoped she should rely, has proven to be slothful and unworthy of her respect. You can see the differences between Kiin's and Zaak's characters in the homes they have created and the lives they lead. Kiin's life is orderly, an oasis with a spring of plenitude in which countless edibles, flowers, and shady trees flourish and blossom into a Shangri-La of incomparable potential.

At Cambara and Gacal's approach, the girls fall silent, the younger one running away after a pause and the older one waiting bashfully and smiling. She has a fetching way of carrying herself, her entire spare

frame, tall for her age, Cambara presumes, supporting itself on the tiptoe of her right foot in the style of a ballet dancer: kittenish, teasingly
coquettish, eyes rolling, her messages mixed. Gacal raises his gaze at
Cambara, as if seeking her counsel.

The girl, sounding tuckered out, says to Cambara, "My mum says
that she will be late but that you and your guest are to go ahead and
our housekeeper will serve you drinks until she joins you."

Cambara introduces herself as her mother's friend and then changes
her mind just in time before presenting Gacal, not certain how this will
play out. She goes closer to the girl, asking, "Tell me, sweet, what's
yours?"

"My name is Sumaya, my sister's name is Nuura," the girl replies,
indicating to Cambara, from the way she carries herself, that she is
older than her chronological age. Her eyes say, "I know a lot more than
you think I do."

Because of this "eye-speak," Cambara locates Kiin's worry, assuming that as a mother to a knockout girl brought up in such a protective
environment, you will not want to bring along a Gacal who might take
advantage of her. Since there is no going back, she decides to play it
as safe as possible.

"Why don't you show us the way?" Cambara suggests.

Sumaya leads them to the veranda, where she shows them to the
seats facing the garden. Then, before vanishing into a wing of the
house to Cambara's back, she calls to the housekeeper to let her know
that the guests have arrived.

Gacal says, "Nice."

Cambara is not sure what Gacal intends to say, and hopes that he
wants simply to point out that Sumaya is nice in the sense that she is
pleasant on the eye and that the whole setup, of which she is a significant part, perhaps the center, is delightful. She prays he will leave it
at that and not lust after her nor permit his sexual urges—not that there
is any evidence of such so far—to exercise total control over his rapport with Sumaya or her younger sister, because that may upset the
mother in Kiin and by extension will disturb the friend in her.

She wishes she had had enough time to get to know what Gacal is
made of. What manner of boy is he in the presence of "nice" girls with
"nice" little tits who grow up in "nice" homes, girls who come at him

showily, as if courting someone who is different from them turns them on? She is aware that it is too late to undo what she has done or to wish that she had not rushed in her desire to spend several hours with him by inviting him to Kiin's lunch for her. It is typical of her to complicate matters unnecessarily. Why must she always take a not-thought-through plunge, abandoning herself to the dictates of her emotions and committing herself in haste to positions or to persons when what she needs is to take stock of her alternatives, reflect on what is possible and wise and what is foolish and needing revision? Yet she hates to backtrack and is highly reluctant to admit a sense of remorse, insisting that the notion of regret is alien to her. It distresses her too that she has imposed on Kiin, forcing her to agree to Gacal's presence when it has been obvious that she does not want Gacal to watch *Pinocchio* with the girls. Maybe Kiin prefers making other arrangements; alas, Kiin hasn't had much of a chance to propose another option to Cambara's suggestion.

"You will behave, won't you?" she says to Gacal.

"I will," he says, with a glint in his eye and grinning knowingly.

Cambara stops in her tracks, as if considering her course of action. Wising to what is happening, Gacal reaches for her hand, and he takes it in his. He says, "See you later."

TWENTY

Cambara is deeply worried, searching for the right words, when Sumaya impatiently grabs at the videocassette, taking it from her, and then tells Nuura and Gacal to follow her to the video room. The two girls and Gacal dash off eagerly, with Sumaya promising Gacal that she will show him their rooms, the toys they have there, and the reception room where they will watch *Pinocchio*. Kiin's older daughter says, "You can't imagine how we've always wanted to see this film, Nuura and me."

There is impishness lighting Gacal's eyes. Full of mischief, he turns to Cambara and for effect elongates his vowels. "See you laaaater, Aligaaator," he says.

She is about to tell him off, at least remind him to behave, when Nuura drags him away, pulling him by the hand. Just before they disappear around a wall and then into the corridor, she follows them for a bit, then watches them, in silence, unable to decide whether to go after them and call him back or to let him be and wait for another opportunity. She settles on pleading with them and says, "Wait, wait, let me tell you what I think," but they slink off speedily, and one of the girls closes the door from inside.

Turning, alone in the corridor, the two girls gone with Gacal in tow, Cambara finds herself overwhelmed by a sense of desperation, whereon she replays her first and so far only potential contretemps with Kiin, who was hesitant to allow Gacal to join them for lunch at her house and then watch *Pinocchio* with her daughters. It was in connection with this that Cambara had a judicious rethink, almost calling off her original idea that Gacal come with her or that he watch the film with her daughters. Now she attributes her earlier disquiet to the fact that she didn't follow through with the suggestion that she take him back to the hotel for his lunch, not necessarily at the restaurant but maybe at the kitchen, like the other employees. After all, Sumaya, too eager and too quick, made a grab for the videocassette, snatching it away from him, and ran off with it, the others pursuing her as excited children often do. Maybe she was too slow in finding the appropriate words in which to divulge her revised agenda, which apparently presented itself as a new trajectory, by far wiser and less harmful to all concerned. Meanwhile, Sumaya, fast moving in her eagerness to watch the film, is off, half running, the others chasing and paying no heed to Cambara's repeated appeals to wait and listen, as her only chance to present her new plan slips away.

She wonders if Gacal is a Lucignolo, similar in outlook and behavior to the character in *Pinocchio*—Lucignolo in the original Italian, Lampwick in the English translation—who is a Bad Bad Boy. She reminds herself that the book is about the misadventures of a handful of boys, some of whom are Good Bad Boys and some just too bad to be put back on the straight and narrow. Lucignolo is such a boy—bad, very bad. By her reckoning, Pinocchio, even though he is gullible, is at heart a Good Bad Boy. A pity she had not heard Gacal's story or anything much about his beginnings, who his parents were and why he is where he is at present. If one is to assume that Gacal resembles Pinocchio in terms of personality and makeup more than SilkHair does, primarily because he strikes her as having had a middle-class background, then perhaps SilkHair, also unknown to her, is more like Lucignolo, given his current situation. It would be fun not only to get to know them better but also eventually to get them together. Of the two boys, which of them will be Lucifer, for that is presumably from where the name Lucignolo is derived, and which the star pupil, no longer a puppet whose strings are in the hands of someone who controls their actions.

Cambara's immediate worry is of a different nature, though. It is about whether, left alone with the girls, Gacal may become a possible source of misbegotten schemes and likely to lead Sumaya and Nuura, who, insofar as it is conceivable to imagine, have up to now led highly protected lives, down a garden path. It is about whether she has compromised her prospective friendship with Kiin in such a way as to put it at some risk, endangering its potential growth to great heights. Maybe Kiin is more conscious of what is involved. This is understandable, given the circumstances.

Cambara recalls reading *Pinocchio* in the original as a child and enjoying it, even then getting a great deal out of it. More recently, she has had the opportunity to reacquaint herself with it, this time reading it in English to and/or with Dalmar. The book struck her then as a precursor of much of the literature about a hick from the sticks coming to the city and being duped by a slick con man. In her recent rereading and viewing of the Disney video, the thought occurred to her that *Pinocchio* is perhaps about small boys—the majority of them parentless and innocent—hoodwinked into joining armed militias as fighters and made to commit crimes in the name of ideals they do not fully comprehend or support. Boys having fun, even when killing.

As she walks back into the living room, rueful that she has not gone with her first instinct and dreading to think what Sumaya and Nuura, seeing the video in the company of Gacal, will make of it, she is of two minds whether to join them, if only to mediate a more enlightened interpretation to help them understand the story from her own perspective. In the end, however, she decides to wait for Kiin and see what her friend says.

Kiin breezes in, as fast as a whirlwind that has just sprung up and is rising. Cambara observes Kiin pausing, her right foot ahead of her left, her body tense and bent at the knees; she has the elegant poise of an athlete on her marks, a runner listening for "Ready," then "Steady," "Go," and then finally the shot before sprinting off. Maybe she is going to take off her shoes first and then her various layers of clothing? For Kiin is wearing a *khimaar*, which covers her face, head, and hair, and a *shukka*, a button-down overcoat, neither of which Cambara remembers seeing her wearing on the previous occasions when the two of them have met. Cambara thinks that neither the face veil nor the *shukka* reflects Kiin's character or her own idea of an athlete poised to take part in an athletic meet. What reason could there be for Kiin wearing these?

It is then that Kiin removes her *khimaar* and her *shukka* in a flash, as if on impulse, peeling off one, then the other, consciously ridding herself of an encumberance keeping her from accessing a more intimate aspect of her self. Maybe Kiin wants to believe that she is returning to the person she has been for much of her life: a Muslim woman and a Somali one at that. After all, her own kind have not been given, until recently, to the habit of putting on *khimaar* and *shukka*. Perhaps Kiin needs to deliver up the mode of dressing just to be comfortable outside; that's all. Meanwhile, Cambara cannot help staring, following Kiin with her eyes, silently gawking, as if provoked into doing so. She ogles, enraptured. And Kiin, as if to make a point, is all there, standing tall and imposing in a see-through dress, no bra, her underclothing visible in all its bright patterns, the expanding girth of her abundance in a display of sorts, challenging Cambara to check her out. A simpler explanation is worth considering: that Kiin has come home after a hard day at work and is chilling out at home in a light skirt with a designer bodice. Nothing is wrong with that. Now she turns to Kiin, who is asking her a question.

"How have things been?"

"You have a beautiful home here," Cambara says.

"The accursed veils," Kiin mumbles in fury, as she gathers them from the couch, where she threw them earlier, and then folding them neatly and putting them out of her way as she decides whether to sit or remain standing. Cambara can hear Kiin uttering obscenities, concluding, "How annoying," and she looks at the pile as if for the last time. "How cumbersome these veils are!"

Cambara empathizes with her friend's sentiment, remembering how she has resorted to putting on the veil not only because it would draw away the unwanted attention of the armed youths but also because the idea of camouflaging oneself has its built-in attraction. She can't remember where she has read or heard that Islam makes sex so exciting: all the veiling, all the hiding, all the seeking and searching for a momentary peek of that which is concealed; the gaze of the covered woman coy; her behavior come-hither coquettish. That you are discouraged from meeting a woman alone in a room unless she is your spouse or your sister—these things, while some people may think of them as impediments, reify the idea of sex, turning it into something hard to get and therefore worth pursuing. Cambara is about to put a question to Kiin when her friend speaks.

"You've met my daughters, haven't you?" Kiin asks. She holds her body upright, her hand busy removing the fluffs and then smoothing the front of her overcoat with fastidious care. She adds after a very thoughtful pause. "Tell me, what are your first impressions?"

"We've had the pleasure of talking only to Sumaya, the younger one having shown no interest in chatting with us at all," Cambara explains. Then she goes on, "Children, I find, have their own way of relating to adults; there is no running away from that. You ask what my impression is. I would say that Sumaya is very much her own girl."

"Can you imagine Sumaya in a veil, though?"

She looks from Kiin to the ceiling, and before deciding what to say and whether to react to a query of a rhetorical nature, Cambara wonders how much of Kiin there is in the way Sumaya behaves. Better still, if one takes Kiin's just-ended performance as one's measure, then surely one might ascribe her daughter's earlier deportment to playacting, a preteen girl emulating her mother and having nothing to do with sexual charge. But because there is little for Cambara to go on, she opts to remain silent on the subject, suspecting that she might hurt the feelings of her new friend and host. Cambara finds it difficult to imagine Somali women in veils and has forebodings about it as much as she dreads the idea of a little girl being infibulated.

Then she sees Gacal and so does Kiin.

"Hello, what're you doing here?" Cambara asks.

"I am here," Gacal says cheekily.

Kiin says, with a touch of surprise in her voice, "Where have you just come from, young fellow?" She is friendly but firm, insisting that he give an immediate response. When he doesn't, she goes on, "I am asking what a charming and happy-looking fellow is doing in the family part of our house? I hope you have an explanation," she says, her sweeping gaze taking in Cambara, at whom she closes her right eye briefly, as if in a signal.

Neither Cambara nor Gacal knows how to interpret the wink. Is it accidental, or is she doing it in jest? Alternatively, is she communicating something that is eluding both? Moreover, Gacal is discomfited; he fidgets, eyes shifty, mouth opening and closing, like a baby feeding. Not speaking, he allows the smirk to spread, then takes his time before attempting to do something about removing it. Cambara, assuming that Kiin, in all likelihood, has forgotten that she has spoken of the boy whom she will bring to lunch, makes as if she will intervene.

Kiin says, "He can speak for himself. He has a tongue, and a sharp one, I bet."

Gacal says nothing, does nothing.

"What's your answer?

"What's the question?"

"Where have you been?"

"I've been here and there."

"Where is here and where is there?" Kiin is crotchety, the surfeit of her ill humor overflowing.

Neither Cambara nor Gacal moves; they listen.

Kiin continues, "Myself, I have had the displeasure to put on a *khimaar* and a *shukka* today to appease a posse of men in saintly robes: my father-in-law and his cronies, who deigned to command me to present myself before them. Do you know the topic of our discussion? The custody of my two daughters. In other words, am I fit enough to mother them in the way tradition demands? I wore the *khimaar* and the *shukka* not because I like doing so but because I hadn't the guts to displease them. Who are they to question my ability to raise my daughters? You might as well ask. And if I am found to be unfit, then they will award the custody of my children to their stepmother, my estranged husband's older sister, a barren woman. Now, why am I telling you this? I am doing so because I want you to get used to doing things from which you may not derive the slightest pleasure but which will help you get some purchase on what you most need: a place you call home, food to eat, a school, clothes, and someone's affections. We are charitable to you now, but to remain in our good graces, you have to work at it, on occasion doing things that bore you, that annoy you."

Kiin, looking as though drained of energy, speaking; Cambara, a little clouded in the eyes, listening for the silences between the unsaid words. Gacal doesn't appear affected one way or the other. Attentive like a theater enthusiast watching a play, he keeps his eyes focused on Kiin, his ears intently pricked.

Kiin asks him, "How old are you?"

"I am old," he replies.

"How old is old?"

"I am as old as you want me to be."

Cambara steps in and explains who Gacal is. "Remember, he is the boy I said I would bring to have lunch and, if possible, watch *Pinocchio* with Sumaya and Nuura," she says. Then she turns to him, "Why have you come away from watching the movie?"

"Because I've seen it endless times," he says.

"Where?"

"In our house."

Cambara takes note of this fact, reminding herself that Gacal is piling up mystery upon mystery. Kiin asks, "When?"

"A lifetime ago," replies Gacal.

Kiin appears troubled and tired-looking, with a prominent "I can't be bothered" expression. It strikes Cambara that she is a woman uncertain of what she wants to see, what she wants to hear, or what subject to discuss. As for Gacal, Cambara interprets his countenance as being crowded with contradictory messages. It puts her in mind of a weed-infested rose bed. Where do you start? Where do you end?

Cambara decides to end the conversation, which is going nowhere, if only to allow Kiin and her enough time to have lunch and talk. She says to Kiin, "Please, can we have him fed? I am sure he won't mind eating in the kitchen."

Kiin rings a bell, and she and Cambara wait.

Gacal bows a gentle bow, expectantly silent.

A very long silence follows, into which a young woman—maybe house help to judge from the shabbiness of her clothes—appears, and an eerie quiet takes hold. All eyes turn to the new arrival, Kiin and Cambara watching her steady shuffle as she makes slow progress, chameleonlike.

Something about the house help irritates Kiin, who sounds irked. "If you are here about our lunch, then get a move on and hurry. Take away this young fellow and have him fed. In the kitchen. My friend and I will eat in the veranda. Bring everything on trays. Remember to bring us cloth napkins. No paper napkins, please. I do not like paper napkins, and I hate those who serve them to my guests or me. As I've said, get a move on. Hurry. I have a guest to entertain and an evening party to organize too at the restaurant. So get a move on. Be quick."

The house help coaxes a quickening of pace from the potential that must have always been there, tapping into it. Likewise Gacal, who, enlivened, bestirs himself and stands up with the speed of somebody a black ant has stung on his posterior. He scampers hurriedly after the young girl, presumably to the kitchen.

Kiin leading and Cambara following, they walk down a corridor, past the room where Sumaya and Nuura are watching *Pinocchio*. The loud volume puts her in mind of cheap motels where long-term-residence clients play video all day to kill time. The spacious veranda, which is handsomely prepared in all aspects, opens onto the garden in the back, its walls grown with ivy, the couches in colorful Baidoa material.

The drinks come in less time than it has taken Kiin and Cambara to exchange a glance and a few words. Served by no other than Gacal, who is now wearing an apron, the chilled *lassi* tastes divine to Cambara. A few minutes later, their lunches are on trays, and the cloth napkins folded the way they do at fancy restaurants.

Having a long, drawn-out lunch is of the essence when you want to relax, and since the idea is for them to talk, undisturbed, Kiin speaking and Cambara mostly listening, while Sumaya and Nuura watch *Pinocchio* and Gacal eats in the kitchen, probably all on his own. Cambara and Kiin are perhaps looking forward to having their siesta in their respective rooms later. Kiin is the kind of friend, Cambara thinks, who has more time for others than for her own worries. Until now she has never even alluded to what must be bothering her—the likelihood of losing custody of her two daughters.

At first, what Kiin is saying about who has said what to whom does not make sense, but she perseveres, listening. Cambara knows two of the names that occur in their conversation, and Raxma's figures among them. Apparently, Arda, Cambara's mother, rang Raxma, in some understandable panic, to request that she kindly find out from Kiin what Cambara's story is and please to phone her back with the news as soon as possible. From what Kiin has gleaned, Zaak telephoned Arda to alert her to the fact that he has not set eyes on her, or spoken to anyone who has, or received a note or message from her daughter for a few days now, and that she may have been kidnapped or come to some harm, but he cannot be sure. The upshot of Zaak's rant is this: things being what they are in Mogadiscio—what with people thought to be rich being taken hostage and their families in Europe and America made to pay a huge ransom—he wants no one to blame him if she is hurt.

"What have you told Raxma?" asks Cambara.

Smarting, Cambara is disturbed by Kiin's long silence, which brings out her worst apprehensions, her sorrow obvious, her heart sinking, her anger, not at Zaak but at herself, rising, and her whole body trembling.

Kiin replies, "I haven't told her anything."

"Why not?" she asks.

Cambara's fingers hold the fork as if menacingly in midair, like a fencer dueling with her internal demons, not with her challenger.

"Because I want you to talk to her yourself."

Her gaze remote, Cambara looks away at the sky, her eyes settling on the clouds that have blocked the sun. No matter, her biliousness swirls upward and pours into the back of her throat. She tastes the brine of a memory gone sour.

"You can call both Raxma and your mother from here," Kiin says. "It will be the right time to call when we are done with our lunch."

The image of her mother pacing back and forth in the living room of her apartment, fulminating against the foolishness of both her charges, her bad leg catching up with her good one, her body wrapped in the Day-Glo of her rage, her eyes as full of stir as fireflies in the darkness of the moment. Revenge resulting from rage is on her mind, not the anodyne desire to make amends and to let peace prevail, and meanwhile for the lunch to continue as if nothing consequential has occurred. The truth is, however, a phone call is in order, but how can she explain everything that has taken place up to now? What aspects of the story so far must she suppress? And emphasize?

"It is naive of me to trust another man who has let me down," Cambara says. "When will I learn? More to the point, will I ever learn?"

From what she says, it is clear that Kiin has already moved on and is ready to change the topic in order to give her counsel about the crisis. "In life," Kiin says, "you gain some, you lose some."

Rankled, with a raw rage crawling insectlike all over the invisible parts of her body, Cambara breaks out in spots of outrage. "I cannot think of any gains I've made, only losses."

When Kiin's dogged attempt at lightening Cambara's mood and tempering it with a sense of moderate expectation doesn't work, she decides to change her approach.

Kiin says, "Here is some other news."

"How I could do with good tidings."

"News about Jiijo, from Farxia, her doctor."

"Tell me."

"Jiijo has given birth to a baby boy."

Cambara knows that Kiin has rendered much assistance without expecting any returns and that helping her has not been free of risks. Moreover, moving Jiijo from the family property in an ambulance and transporting her to a private clinic does not come cheap. She is indebted to Kiin, owes whatever successes she has made in this regard to Kiin's ingenuity. Even though she will ask for it, Cambara doubts if the gynecologist will bother to submit Jiijo's hospital bill to settle, which she is willing to pay. At worst, Kiin or her network of women friends will foot it. She must insist on meeting the expenses, because she is the one who stands to gain from the charitable intervention.

"How are they, mother and baby?"

"They're doing super. Both are."

"How long does Farxia plan to keep her at the clinic?" asks Cambara.

Kiin replies, "There are not a lot of options to consider. Jiijo will have to go hush-hush, preferably before the evening. The problem is where we must take her to, once discharged. We do not want her to go back to your house, having emptied her of it. Neither does Farxia want her to spend an hour longer at her clinic. Remember, Farxia removed her from your property without a paper trail. Now how can she explain it away? And how or from whom did she, Farxia, learn of Jiijo's condition before deciding to send an ambulance to fetch her to the clinic? Dicey questions with no easy answers."

"Does anyone know where Gudcur is?"

"We do not."

"What does it mean that no one mentions having seen or talked to him and that no radio station refers to the fighting anymore?" Cambara asks, her expression worried.

"It can mean both nothing and everything."

"A daunting prospect," says Cambara.

"Some of the members of the network have been through situations a lot worse than this," Kiin assures her. "Don't worry. In the end, the network always wins."

"What a lot of trouble I've been to you and to the other women in your network, to whom I am grateful, every one of them," says Cambara. "I cannot help wishing I had consulted you before embarking on this."

"We're pleased to be of help, as fellow women."

Cambara resumes eating. She sits awkwardly forward, her plate almost falling over. Kiin watches over her friend's food, and although she is not saying anything, you can see that she is ready to step in and take charge. Cambara, meanwhile, is floundering about in the sudden impulse of finding the right words with which to express her worried delight, worried, because she thinks Jiijo is laden with the inconvenience and the tragic responsibility of rearing the son of a man she hates. Perhaps this is the lot of many a woman: raising the offspring of men whom they cannot stand and at times without whom they can barely exist. How can she help? How can anyone be of assistance to women like Jiijo, who are in such a terrible bind? Treated worse than chattels, beaten daily, and tortured too, yet as the mothers to the offspring of these monsters, their consanguinity is in no doubt; it is all there for everyone to see. Ideally, one must make sure that Jiijo and her baby are in a safe home, out of harm's way and beyond Gudcur's reach.

Cambara wonders aloud, her face blank. "Suppose we fly her out of the country, once she is discharged?" And no sooner has Cambara formulated the question in her mind and then spoken it than she realizes that she is being a twit.

Kiin has the kindness of heart and the indulgence to make as if the freshness of Cambara's proposition is worth giving serious thought to before nipping off its new shoots.

"Put her on a plane, straight to Nairobi?"

"Maybe that won't work," Cambara submits.

Kiin does not give up the chase so easily. She says, "It would work if Jiijo were in a condition that warranted her being taken there—to save her life or her baby's—but as it is, they are both well and thriving. And at the risk of being found out, we can shelve the idea, use it if the other plans that we've set into motion fail."

"What are these plans?"

"We are discussing plans that rely wholly on the members of the network for success," Kiin explains. "No one else will get to know or hear about the plans until executed. We've done similar jobs before for women in trouble. We've perfected our methods."

"Tell me more about the plan."

"We spirit away women from the men posing the gravest danger to them or their children. In the interim, we deal with the men concerned. On one occasion, we have had to poison his food—end of the nuisance."

For an instant, Cambara tries to come up with an alternative, one that is more practicable and likelier to work. Alas, her mind is blank, with not a thought presenting itself. Turning the pressing worries over in her brain, she concludes that she has perhaps now become home to a proverbial despair, the angst resulting from the problems running riot inside her head.

"Your house is at your disposal, you know that? We've had the locks changed, and have serviced the back entrance, away from the prying eyes of the neighbors and the curious, to make it operational," Kiin says.

"So much work in such a short time," says Cambara. She is clearly impressed and is on the verge of getting emotional, the well of her eyes close to filling up with tears of joy.

Kiin continues, "In addition, we've engaged an armed security outfit with the aim of closely monitoring the movements in the entire neighborhood and setting up checkpoints manned by a freelance youth-for-peace brigade that is run, no less, by Dajaal's nephew Qasiir. Before long, we will know what has become of Gudcur and try to find out if there is any chance of him or his men returning. If he survives, then we will factor in the possibility of a fierce confrontation with him. We are preparing for the worst scenario. And we are confident that we will be able to hold on to the property."

"You won't want Jiijo to live in it?"

"Why complicate matters?" Kiin says.

"I see what you mean."

"If I understand correctly, you want to turn the ballroom into your rehearsal space, once you are ready to start working on your play, yes?" Kiin asks, eyes widening, voice rising a little irritably and head shaking. "Isn't that what you had in mind all along, to repossess it and use it?"

"That's right."

"Remember why you are here?"

A scintilla of Cambara's memory of her anger at Wardi, which spurred her into action, is now stirring in the bottom of her eyes, and prompting her to look away. Her recollection touches off a precipitate return of the many terrible things that men have done to her: Wardi causing Dalmar's death; Zaak crossing her, and so on.

Sumaya's soft tread awakens Cambara from her reverie just before startling Kiin from a similar woolgathering. Such is the sweetness of the little one's contagious smile that both Cambara and Kiin invite her, her mother saying "Come and give me a hug, darling," and Cambara blowing her a kiss and saying "Come, my cutie." Sumaya goes to her mother, who wraps her generous body around her.

Kiin's antennae are alert to an abrupt change in Cambara's mood and, attributing this to the fact that she is reliving the sad death of her Dalmar, decides to perk up her spirits.

"Why not?"

Cambara hauls herself up and then focuses her gaze on Kiin and Sumaya. Even so, the thoughts that call on her preclude her gaining solid purchase on a toehold in her scuffle with her demons.

"Please let someone walk Gacal back to the hotel when he is done in the kitchen," Cambara says, preparing to take leave. "Meanwhile, keep the film for your daughters."

"Gladly," Kiin says.

"And if I may impose on you . . ." Cambara begins and then trails off.

"Yes?"

"It is about Gacal's accommodation."

"What about it?"

"Can you organize a place for him to sleep," Cambara says, "perhaps with the other youths until we find a more agreeable solution for him?"

"No problem."

"Thanks a lot."

"See you at the party, if not before."

"Pleasure."

TWENTY-ONE

Waiting for Gacal, having already spoken on the phone to the deputy manager, who confirmed that Kiin called him and that he has set in place the arrangements for accommodating and feeding Gacal, Cambara sprawls on her bed, her eyes closed, her thoughts far away in pursuit of some memories that are eluding her. She is relaxed. The air conditioner is on, the noise of the generator a distant hum, even if the voices of some of the daytime sentries sound a little bit too close for comfort.

She is in a loose-fitting outfit into which she changed soon after returning from lunch with Kiin. In place of a pillow, her hands are under her head; she is reviewing the events of the past few days. She sits up after these few intense moments to remind herself that she knows less about Gacal than she needs to if they are to share a rapport solid enough to serve as a workable foundation.

Yet how strange that her expression turns unexpectedly so sour all of a sudden, making her think that it might curdle into milk that has gone bad. She feels bitter that she has rushed into committing herself to Gacal against her current, that is to say, better judgment before finding out much about his background. No wonder Arda has tended to describe Cambara's discernments as not being of top-drawer quality. "Your gut feeling reigns supreme," Arda said to her once, "and you pledge your affections fast, not on the basis of what you know but on the strength of your passion at that moment."

Cambara removes her hands from under her head, and she closes and opens her fist to bring her fingers, which have gone to sleep, back to life. She contemplates the ceiling, convinced that she is set on a course that will bear fruit, thanks to Kiin, who has jump-started her varied plans, some of which have stalled to the point of inaction, others forging forward. She feels justified in safeguarding the gains she has made, yields that may provide her with a rock-steady anchor in the city's realities. In some measure, she considers herself lucky, in that she has become a key factor in the lives of several people whose paths have crossed hers. It falls to her to take care, wary that a single misstep can give rise to irreversible results.

Now she hears a gentle knocking on the door, assuming it to be no other than Gacal's. But she waits and listens for a second tapping before she attends to it, for she wants him to identify himself, as if hearing him speak his name might help her form an opinion, assist her in settling on how to proceed, eventually, with their talk. However, when he keeps knocking without confirming his identity, she takes the initiative at the fourth rapping. She asks, "Who is it?"

"You've said to come, and I am here," Gacal says.

She moves toward the door, relatively sanguine about the rightness of her initial visceral reaction to Gacal, now that she is about to meet him. This is because she finds his choice of evasive answer—saying that she said to come and that he is here instead of giving his name, as asked—winsome, circuitous, challenging, original. Whatever else she may think after they have spoken, Cambara is positive that Gacal is brimful with a mix of self-confidence and bravura. She does not remember ever encountering these qualities in any boy his age, except perhaps in Dalmar. Or in SilkHair to a smaller extent.

Finally, the door open, she meets his smug smile, presumably because he too is playing his own game in which he scores high marks. Moreover, he has his hand outstretched. Is he daring Cambara to ignore it or to shake it and then hug him? Looking at Cambara, you might agree that he has won this round.

She doesn't take his hand, nor does she embrace him. Instead, as if to prove a point to herself, she turns her back on him and says, "Come on in."

He enters, no longer in smug satisfaction. He closes the door gingerly behind him, his sense of gaminess tapering off a little. He tiptoes farther into the room and waits anxiously, his whole body tense; it is as though he is preparing for her reprimand.

"Tell me," she says.

Readying to answer her command, he does his best to replace what someone might describe as ragamuffin behavior with a kind of deportment that can win someone like Cambara over. He sits down, unbidden.

"Who are you?" she asks.

"Depends."

Cambara flinches from the hostile thought that has presented itself to her, a not-so-friendly go-hang-yourself catchphrase, the kind of braggadocio his answer deserves. On second thought, she does nothing of the sort, in part because he reminds her of Dalmar, who kept the motif of dialog in vibrant relief long after the exchange had lost its flair. She relives the fury with which Wardi often greeted Dalmar's back-talk bravado and how he threatened him with violence if the boy did not stop provoking him. She recalls advising Wardi to desist from browbeating Dalmar into becoming a different child and saying "You might as well instruct a bird not to sing as tell Dalmar not to back talk."

Another reason why she indulges Gacal's boldness is related to the fact that he is clearly as capable of resisting adult pressure, especially when someone bludgeons him into toeing the line, as he is of accommodating himself to an acquiescent mood, if he puts his mind to it.

Her smile as thin as a new run in an old pair of stockings, she decides to break his resistance by giving him the bare bones of her own story, with special emphasis on her loss of a son more or less his age, whose death she is now mourning. When she is done with the telling, a very sad memory darkens Gacal's expression. He is silent for a long time, looking grave. Then he speaks.

Gacal speaks with an elegiac touch to express the unimaginable tragedy that has been his young life. He tells of an equally great loss: the murder of his father, with whom he came to Mogadiscio two years earlier. Killed by the militiamen who had abducted the two of them, kept them apart and incommunicado, his father was shot in the head and robbed of his cash before they let Gacal go. As he talks, Cambara gapes at him in shock, observing how adult he sounds as he pauses occasionally for a phrase that is eluding him or searches for the words with which to describe his grief. She notices too that he has the habit of turning his face away slightly either to the left or right in the manner of somebody striking a pose. He sits, pricking up his ears, as though listening for danger in one menacing form or other to walk in and at one single move end the world that he has known. His story is very difficult to put together, since much of it does not make sense. A man leaves America and brings along his son to expose him to the language and culture of his people on the advice of his wife, the boy's mother, who wants them away so she can finish some project. Armed militiamen seize the two soon after they have landed at one of the city's warlord-run airports and entered a vehicle marked "Taxi." That much is believable. It is when Gacal tells the other part of his story in America that Cambara starts to wonder if this is truth or fiction.

Gacal says, "I was born in Duluth to Somali parents who were granted resettlement rights in the United States after having lived in refugee camps in Kenya for several years. After their first stop in San Diego, they relocated to Minnesota."

Cambara takes note of his adult register: the tone of voice, choice of words, and body language too. The only part of him that matches his chronological age is his nose, wet like a kitten's. Because his eyes keep straying impishly, she can't date them with precision. "I've been able to unravel the mess that my life has become only lately," he continues in an adult voice of a more philosophical register, "almost two years since I got here with my father."

"Where is your mother?"

"Back in the States."

"In Duluth?"

"I have no idea."

"You've called her, haven't you?"

"Our home phone number has been disconnected."

She can't bring herself to envisage being in his position, without imagining as though his horror were hers. She senses this is beyond her, because she doesn't know enough about him. She is aware that civil wars have separated many families from one another, husbands from wives, children from their parents. In the case of Somalia, she knows about the efforts of the International Red Cross to help unite some of the separated families and about the BBC Somali Service's "Missing Persons" program, broadcast almost daily, with people giving the names of their missing ones, when and where they were last seen, and providing their own whereabouts and telephone numbers in the hope of hearing from them. Maybe she can get him into the program?

"Have you tried your friends at school or relatives, if you can remember their phone numbers?" She feels foolish the moment the words have left her lips. How can he phone if he doesn't know a soul and doesn't have the wherewithal to make the call?

"I have."

A lump in Cambara's throat prevents her from speaking and asking an indiscreet question, which for a long while lays siege to her tongue too. Despite this, she puts it to him. "How did you get the money to pay for the call?"

"You don't want to know."

"I do. Otherwise I wouldn't ask."

"Frisked the pockets of a corpse and stole it."

His answer so unsettles her that the jolt brings her back to the civil war realities. But despite that rude awakening, Cambara asks, "Were you successful in tracking down anyone?"

"All my attempts to do so have failed."

Silent, he narrows his eyes, as if concentrating on an as-yet-unformed thought in the far distance. For all Cambara can tell, he is revisiting a scene from the past and perhaps thinking about how his present predicament is forcing him to bare himself before a strange woman in Mogadiscio.

She wants to know but dares not ask why he and his father have done away with the woman who bore him, because a son his age without a mother in the wings is unheard-of, an anomaly. She fidgets in her seat, preparing to speak. She can't imagine the woman being written off, as if redundant. She thinks that parents need to be needed, mothers above all. She starts to say, "Your mother . . . !" and then trails off.

Gacal says, "We weren't supposed to come here."

Cambara feels the sort of helplessness that people feel when they are confronted with a problem about which they can do nothing. When she looks in his direction, he seems impervious to her twinge. It is as if he is saying "No pitying please."

"Where is your mother in your story?"

Cambara interprets what Gacal tells her in an adult language Gacal is incapable of improvising. She understands that his father came to Nairobi as a private consultant, hired to set up IT companies in East Africa and to make them profitable. The two of them being inseparable, he brought along his son, as their visit coincided with the long summer holidays. It was his mother's idea that Gacal benefit from living in a place safer than Mogadiscio and far more citylike than any other metropolis on the Somali peninsula, so he could learn Somali. While her husband and son were gone, the mother intended to lock herself away in order to complete some requirement or other from a university in another state where she must have been registered for an advanced degree.

"Did they quarrel often, your parents?"

"They were too busy for that, both working and happy in their jobs," he says. "I was their only child, and they were pleased. They said that often, to me, or to others within my hearing."

"Your father traveled a lot?"

"He did, and she looked after me."

"Did he let her know you were coming here?"

"I doubt that he did."

"What makes you say that?"

"He meant us to come for four days during a long weekend," Gacal said. "I kept pestering him, asking him what this place from which the two of them came and where they grew up and married was like, having never known it. I kept saying I wished I could come and see it and maybe live here. One day, we upped and, without booking a flight in advance, went to some out-of-the-way airport and flew in a small plane carrying *qaat*. The plan was for us to spend the long weekend; that is all. He was that kind of man, my dad."

Hard to imagine . . . the tragedy of it. One day, Gacal is a middle-class boy, connected to a world that treats him with protective care; the following day, the only world he knows has vanished, and he is adrift in a man-eat-dog city. Unmoored.

"What's your father's full name?"

Gacal gives it; she does not know it.

"Your mother's?"

Gacal tells it; she does not know it either.

The next logical step in traditional Somali society is to ask for other pointers, like his father's and mother's respective clans, to help her identify them. She is sure that someone or other either here in Mogadiscio or somewhere in North America would know. If only she can bring herself to ask him for their clan identities. Somalis with so-called progressive thinking do not instill the clan ethos in their children's frame of mind; some do not even allow the names of these clans to pass their lips. Maybe she will assign the job of delving into this aspect of the problem to someone like the old man at the gate; he won't mind helping her. By now, it is possible that he and everyone else knows Gacal's clan identity. In her own case, she made sure she didn't encourage Dalmar to bother about his own or hers. Many city- or foreign-born Somalis do not necessarily know theirs.

There are many questions to which she would like answers, but she is finding it difficult to put them to him. How did he cope alone the first few days, months, or years after his father's death? How did he mourn the loss? How did he spend the first few days between coming here and learning his altered circumstances?

"Do you remember the name of the company your dad worked for in Duluth?" she asks.

"He was self-employed."

"What about the name of the firm in Nairobi or any of the people with whom your father worked? Do you remember the names of any of them, because then we could call information?" she asks.

"It is so long ago I cannot remember anything."

"Do you remember your mother's friends' names?"

"Only by their first names."

"To what school did you go, in Duluth?"

Gacal gives her a name, which she writes down. Once Gacal is gone and she is alone, she will ring up Raxma and ask her to look into it. Most probably Raxma will make direct inquiries right away, if only to ascertain the truth or otherwise. Raxma will come back with suggestions about what is and what is not possible, after seeking Maimouna's legal advice. But when Cambara calls her mother, she won't make any mention of Gacal, her latest infatuation.

Cambara rises to her feet and, opening the door, smiles sweetly at Gacal, who stands to his full height and joins her, ready to exit. He grins, bows, and then says, "See you."

Scarcely has she closed the door when she remembers seeing

Deliverance, a 1970s film of a harrowing account of a disastrous canoe trip of four men down a river in Georgia, not that the film's and Gacal's story lines are identical or even similar. Maybe the traumatic nature of such sudden changes in Gacal's life has put her in mind of the distress the men go through, lives as horror-ridden as they are impossible to imagine.

Heavyhearted, she consults her watch and, deciding that it is a decent hour to telephone America, rings the reception and requests that she be given an outside line. She dials Raxma's number from memory. Raxma answers it on the third ring and says, "Cambo dearest, Kiin has been in touch and has been sharing with me the good news."

Cambara cannot decide how to respond, and she remains silent. A couple of seconds later, when Raxma asks her if she is still there, she asks, "What good news has she been sharing with you?"

"That they are in the process of negotiating with you about your staging a play, which the Women's Network will fund and you will mount, the first of its kind in Mogadiscio. For peace. That, to this end, they are providing you with free accommodation and lodging for as long as you want and hiring an Irishman living in Mogadiscio to carve wood masks based on your own designs and, per your instructions, some carpenters to build the stage, and, if I'm right, electricians and other technicians, all of whom are to be paid by the Women's Network. I am so pleased for you, my sweet. I also hear that Kiin and her coterie of friends are helping you recover the property. If that is not good news, I don't know what is, Cambo dearest."

This is the first Cambara has heard of any of this in such clear terms. This is also the first time that someone, most importantly a community of women, has gloried in her artistic output. Pinch, pinch. Am I dreaming? She thinks.

"What other news? Good, I hope. Tell it quick."

Cambara draws a deep breath, hesitant to talk. It's only at Raxma's insistence—"I am off to work, my sweet, so get on with it"—that she fills Raxma in on her other doings so far without leaving out anything of importance. How ironic; what could be more pivotal than Raxma's confirmation of what has been afoot? Anyhow, she speaks of Kiin's invitation to lunch at her place and of meeting her two lovely daughters; Jiijo and where she is; SilkHair, what he is like and her involvement in his life; Seamus and his willingness to design the masks; and finally the Women's Network, whose numbers she will soon meet at a party. Then she provides Raxma with the basic details of Gacal's story.

Raxma asks, "You want me to inquire into this boy's story and to come back to you with my findings? Leave it to me. I'll ring you up in a day or two. Okay? I must get off if I am to beat the rush hour."

"You are a darling."

Then she telephones Arda, and they talk shop for a few minutes before Cambara gives the old woman a watered-down version of her activities, no mention of Kiin's commissioning of her play and none of Gacal's and SilkHair's stories. She staves off all possible contentious issues that might produce a heated debate between the two of them.

Her telephone call to Raxma makes her restless, her adrenaline pumping faster. Although she is itching to move, at first she doesn't know how best to utilize the energy that her enthrallment is producing until she gives it a focus. She tells herself then that it is time for her to collect the remainder of her stuff from Zaak's, time to think seriously of relegating him to the position of a pariah, no barge poles please! Or maybe she will keep the line of communication open, but without ever activating it. You never know with civil wars; she might need him to give her a hand, so why cut him off totally.

All the same, she can't help thinking of him as a despicable character, a host who takes pleasure in spreading malicious gossip about his guest. It means he has no self-respect. She might attribute the measure of his small-mindedness to his being a hick from the sticks and a born loser. Never mind that Arda has always taken great pains to make him into someone other than the person he is. Having put up with him without ever speaking out, there is no knowing now with whom she should be short: her mother, herself, or the foolish man. His behavior is as unwarranted as it is undeserving of a response.

Rather than let Zaak spurn her, she is happy that she has moved out and that without any help from him, has managed to tap her available talents in a resourceful manner. Before long, she will have drawn profitably on the benevolence of the friends she has made and benefited from this creative exercise and to hell with Zaak. Now she sits at the desk to write down the names of those she expects will offer help or she will recruit in one capacity or another for her efforts: Kiin, the jewel of her finds; Farxia, the medical doctor who spirited Jiijo away; Seamus, the anonymous, the genius; Dajaal, a tactful man who will be useful in providing the overall security; Bile, man behind the scenes, prompting Dajaal and Seamus to assist; the shopkeeper Odeywaa, and his wife, not yet the head of security at Hotel Maanta; and of course Raxma. Where would she be without Raxma? Under a separate column, she jots down the names Gacal, SilkHair, and Jiijo, underlining each of them and putting a question mark against the last.

An overwhelming anxiety rushes in on her, inundating her with a mix of contriteness and helplessness: contrite, because she knows that she has never been truthful with Jiijo; helpless, because now that things have been set in motion, there is no further room for maneuver, none whatsoever. Nor is there anything she can do for Jiijo until Gudcur's situation becomes clear. If he is dead and the property is entirely at her disposal, then she is not averse to having Jiijo move into the property as a caretaker of sorts. But if Gudcur is alive and constitutes a threat, then surely it will not be wise to have anything to do with her. Not that she wants to count her chickens before her eggs hatch, but she is certain that with the property back in her hands, she will delight in rehearsing the play in the ballroom. Ideally, she will want the kitchen, which will feed everyone, to be run, and who better than Jiijo, with a bit of help from Kiin's chef, to do so.

To achieve her daring plan and make the production of her play a success, she will need more than a ballroom and a posse of untrained but willing boys eager to accommodate her wishes. Her spirits sagging as though in mild despair, she falls prey to her worry of finding someone to furnish her with as much intellectual input as she needs. Of the people whom she has met up to now, she can name only four who might supply her with the cerebral companionship essential to her in her present situation: Kiin, Bile, Seamus, and, in his own way, Gacal. Every one of these four individuals is indispensable. Seamus will provide much needed succor, especially in matters of a technical nature such as carving the masks, not to mention some of her other requirements: carpentry, stage design, lighting. She will expect a lot of goodwill from Kiin, Bile, and Gacal, to each of whom she will assign a task. A friendship with Bile is worth cultivating. This is why she must call on him at the first opportunity.

Cambara feels as though she has only just now come to recognize that many a watershed moment since her arrival has passed without her becoming aware of its passage and without her making full use of it. She senses, too, that her coming here and hitting it off with Kiin has been replete with turning points, each one of them as important as the milestone that has preceded it, and as significant in her doings as the benchmark that came after it. Now she is in a catching-up mood, ringing Raxma and retrieving the remainder of her stuff. She is scampering about in her haste to make up for lost time in much the same way as someone running after her future before it has become part of the present or the past.

Her sudden worry about the time she has so far wasted and the opportunities she has missed starts to make her so restless that she behaves as though a black ant has pricked her. Stung into action, she pulls out her mobile phone and rings Bile's number.

Dajaal answers and then transfers her not to Bile but to Seamus, who tells her that Bile is indisposed at present and that he will give him her warm wishes when he speaks to him. He also tells her how happy he is that she has called, because in fact he has been meaning to do just that. "I have something to show you," he says. "When and where can we meet?"

"Meet you at yours tomorrow a.m.?" she asks.

"At ten, if that is okay."

"Ten it is."

"Okey-dokey. See you then."

She says, "Remember me to Bile, please."

"Will do," he says.

She is tempted to offer to call on Bile right away, but she keeps her enthusiasm in check, fearing that Seamus might think of her as very forward. How she would like to wrap her body around Bile! She is convinced this would ease her own heartache at the same time as it would relieve Bile's pain.

Then she remembers the suitcases that are waiting to be picked up from Zaak's. So she phones Kiin as part of her effort to speed things up. She stops just in time before letting it slip about her telephone conversation with Raxma because Kiin thinks it unwise to involve anyone else.

"A favor please," she says.

"Ask and it'll be done," Kiin says.

Can Kiin spare the four-wheel-drive truck and several of her armed youths, because she intends to retrieve the remainder of her possessions from Zaak's place? Again, she holds out on Kiin. She does not tell her of her plans to bring SilkHair, whom Cambara wants to entice away from Zaak's team. What use will SilkHair, a gun-toting teenager, serve? Potential playmate and companion to Gacal?

With Gacal's name sweetening her present assignment to retrieve her stuff and possibly running into Zaak, she hopes that she will stay the course, brave in her desire to muscle back into his house. She will not hem and haw if he provokes her; she might even take delight in rubbing it in and inform him that she is doing very well without him on all fronts, thank you very much.

When Kiin rings to confirm that the truck is fueled and ready to go, with its armed escorts mounted and waiting by the gate, Cambara says, "Thanks. Be down in a minute."

As she hands her keys over to the receptionist, Cambara hears a cold diesel engine starting, and then the head of hotel security calling to the youths and instructing them to get a move on. "Quick, quick. Madam is on her way."

As she arrives on the scene, she stops a meter or so from the truck when she sees the driver standing by the door, keeping it open, and bowing his head. This puts Cambara in mind of a man pleased with the manner in which he is acquitting himself.

She mumbles her thanks as she climbs into the truck, then nods and again murmurs something when he closes the door after her. What a ritual, she thinks. You can be sure that Kiin has instructed every one of them to do Cambara's bidding and to be very polite and accommodating to her at all times. The head of the security detail sits up front, next to the driver in the cabin from where he is admonishing the five youths, three of them heavily armed, two only lightly. The youths have been standing idly by, and he is now telling them to mount the roof of the vehicle, presto, and they do. She owes it all to Kiin for smoothing her way around all manner of difficulties so she may go about her business without any hitches.

Cambara asks the head of security if he remembers how to get to Zaak's place; he was with her in the same truck the first time. He nods, and she sits back, preparatory to the truck moving, ready, in her mind, for all eventualities. It is just when she is relaxed and satisfied enough with the agreeable way that things have gone that her mind is visited by the presentiment that something terrible might happen, not only to her but to Kiin's men and truck too. She prays that Zaak's armed bodyguards and Kiin's will not trigger off a battle in which lives are lost and properties destroyed. How tragic it would be if a fierce gunfight were to ensue as a consequence of her desire to retrieve her belongings, among them a suitcase containing a dress for the party in the evening!

She braces her fearlessness, her inner strength, her faith, and the rightness of her actions against the cowardly behavior of a handful of Gudcurs who have taken the entire country hostage. Nothing causes her as much worry as coming face to face with Gudcur or his kind in a time and setting of their choosing. That will no doubt have the detrimental effect of immediately endangering and compromising her life. Imagine her delight, her surprise when Kiin and her associates have taken upon themselves to facilitate handing the property over to her, despite the risk to their lives or businesses. And here she is all agitated, because she has no idea how to explain away her absence to Zaak or why she hasn't been in touch with him or whether she will apologize to him for her failure to do so. When, if truth be told, she cannot wait to sever all relations with him forthwith.

She feels reassured when, her hand in the pocket of her caftan, she finds the Swiss knife and key, which she plans to use to let herself and the men with her in if Zaak is not there. She will empty her rooms of all her belongings. She may not bother to leave a note for him. But what if he has changed the locks on the gate, the front door, or those to her rooms? Cambara doubts that he will have gotten round to doing that, knowing how lethargic his *qaat*-chewing, go-slow temperament is, forever insouciantly unmotivated.

She feels disheartened as the truck hurtles northward, the light of the day weakening, the heat of the sun diminishing, the head of secu-

rity chatting away with the driver, and the armed youths on the roof becoming rowdier. The door in her mind opens, letting in a streak of
anger: and she remembers her fight with Wardi. She thinks that there
are two kinds of anger: the kind that will endure, outliving one, a rage
that presses in on her brain, choking her—the way she would describe
her anger at Wardi. The other type of anger—the one that she feels now
that she is on her way to Zaak's place—is deep and likely to be short-
lived. It is not a murderous rage but a mere disappointment. She thinks
that while she has to allow the two angers to run along side by side for
part of the way, she must make sure that they do not ever run into each
other and are not mistaken for each other. If need be, they can be made
to complement one another on occasion, but at no point should she
permit these rages to mix seamlessly into a cocktail, for that would be
much too explosive, and she could end up a victim of her own making.

As is to be expected, she will run out of luck one day, but she has
no idea when. In the event, she can only pray that it will be without
detriment to Kiin or any other person who has given her a hand in
achieving her aims. Not that she minds facing the consequences of her
actions herself, but she would feel terrible if something were to happen to any of her well-wishers. But why does she reckon that her fortune will desert her, especially now that everything is starting to fall into
place and some of her plans are bearing fruit? Does she imagine that
calling on Zaak will not only earn her his displeasure but will also chase
away the luck that is smiling on her? It is as if visiting Zaak will start
her on an ill-starred legion of contagions that will set her back immeasurably and lead eventually to disaster.

Cambara pulls herself out of the trance, because the truck has
slowed down to a near halt and the head of security is turning to ask
her in a voice that is a little uncertain if they should follow the second
or the third fork in the road to their right. It is no easy matter for
Cambara to tell him what to do, at first appearing as if she has no
inkling where she might be or who the man talking to her is. Then she
gathers her wits, looks out of the window, and recognizes where they
are. Then, in two shakes, she takes over and tells the driver where to
go. The truck moves, and she sits up, her hand going to her hair,
smoothing it.

She wishes she could take a quick look in the rearview mirror, given that she did not bring one herself. No woman, after all, wants her former companion to see her not looking her best. She curses her gutlessness, and tells herself, "That's enough!"

Zaak comes to the gate in a state of semiundress to answer it, the klaxon that the driver has sounded a touch too often having, in all probability, driven him to the edge. He is barefoot, his jaws active, his lips traced with the green spit of someone chewing mouthful after mouthful of *qaat* for the best part of a day. Unseeing, he moves about on tiptoe. He is in a pair of threadbare pants, donned in haste and crookedly and which, in consequence, cannot accommodate his paunch's overspill. As he comes into view, she envies the unembarrassed ugliness of him, she, who earlier kept smoothing her hair with her hands, because she didn't want to see a single hair out of place. She takes a moment to study the expressions of everyone else: shocked, some snickering, others exchanging looks. When he gets his bead on the armed youths alighting from the roof of the truck, he panics, ceasing all movement and striking an awkward pose in the attitude of a frightened man who does not know whether to raise his hands in surrender or fall on his knees and beg for mercy.

"Zaak, it is me, Cambara," she shouts repeatedly above the din that has risen, like dust, between the two of them.

When he recognizes her at last, he looks first at the armed youths, the driver, and the head of security; studies their faces, scrutinizing their bodily gestures for signs of danger; and, finding nothing to worry him, turns on Cambara and fixes her with a stare imbued not so much with anger as with sarcasm. From the way he is swaying to the sides, she is unsure if he is drunk. His heavy tongue, his muck green complexion, his speech pattern, and the elongation of his vowels confirm that he is inebriated.

He says, "I am tickled to see you arrive here in the unenviable company of armed witnesses. Why have you found it necessary to do so? You could have come on your own. Or are you a hostage and expecting me to pay a ransom for your release, in which case I haven't the cash."

She makes light of his remarks—the words of a drunk—and pretends that his verbal rebuff does not hurt her. Smiling, she braves out of the car, takes a decisive step toward him, and stretches her hand to him as a token of their amity. But he snubs her offer to shake hands and stands apart with his arm akimbo. He is now all there, solidly unafraid, his feet firmly where he wants them.

"I've come to retrieve my stuff," she says, almost choking on her anger.

"Have I ever stopped you from taking away your stuff? Why have you needed to come in a borrowed truck with an armed escort?"

"A friend has lent me the truck."

"Why have you needed to come armed?" he asks.

"What's the point? You don't understand."

"I know a pea-brained idea when I hear one," he says and blocks her way with his bulkiness, unspeaking and sizing her up as one dueler might appraise another.

Remembering her fight with Wardi, where the story of her coming has it origins, she says, "You put a finger anywhere on my body and you will regret it."

Then she turns to the head of security and tells him that he and three other unarmed youths should follow her; she will go ahead. Meanwhile, the driver is to park the vehicle in the shade of the tree and the armed youths are to stay with him, guarding the truck.

She walks too close to Zack for comfort, and as she prepares to go past him into the house, with the security man and the youths trailing her, she halts, because she hears his labored breathing and cannot help assuming that his is a faltering heart and that he may be on his way out. Perhaps he is not worth her rage, nor the energy she is expending on him.

Amid the confusion resulting from her inability to decide whether to defy him and go in or to talk to him and make amends there is the noise of another truck bearing down on the gate, followed by the sound of tires on the gravel driveway scattering pebbles and raising a storm of sand. The first to recognize Cambara, SilkHair alights from the second truck and is down on the ground, running in her direction and calling her "Auntie, Auntie," auntie being a form of deference the young bestow on an older woman. Then all the youths in Zaak's employ take turns, forming a line to pay their admiring respect to her. The last to shake her hand is the driver, and he says to her, "We've missed you. I hope you are well wherever you are."

Then everyone, save Zaak, lends a hand to load the truck with her stuff. With the world around him active and in continuous motion, he does what he knows best: he caters to a huge huff and is clearly subdued, his arms around his paunch, his eyes following the comings and the goings of those hauling suitcases or helping to make sure there is space for everything. The youths that serve as armed security on his truck lean their guns against the tree, close to where Zaak's truck is parked, whereas the ones who have come with Cambara pile their weapons up front in the cabin of the truck. Meanwhile, the two lots of youths celebrate their camaraderie by swapping humorous repartee. For her part, Cambara is circumspect in her exchanges with all of them, surreptitiously mindful that an inconsequential put-down from one youth to another can spark off a firefight.

When Cambara is all packed and ready to go, Zaak shows unmatched eagerness to make amends to her before the truck leaves; but she can't be bothered. She says "Let's go" to the driver, then calls to Zaak's youths, among whom she distributes wads of local currency as *baksheesh,* and heads in the direction of the truck. Someone is keeping a door open, hand extended ready to help if need be.

Then she turns round to have a quiet word with SilkHair, who is standing close by. She hugs him to herself and then looks into his eyes, their noses almost touching. Her voice low so no one can hear it, she asks, "What about you, SilkHair?"

"What about me?" he says.

"Would you like to come with me, in the truck?"

When, to her delightful surprise, SilkHair announces publicly that he would like to try his luck with her, she is at a loss for words, even though this is what she has been wanting all along. She hugs him and, taking hold of his thin wrist, urges him to get into the truck ahead of her, which he does.

She says to Zaak, "I'll see you around."

TWENTY-TWO

They arrive back at the hotel without incident in the gathering dusk, and Kiin, of whom she is even fonder, based on what Raxma told her earlier, is among the small crowd that throngs the truck, many giving a hand at Kiin's insistence. Every time Cambara tries to lift something, Kiin or someone else discourages her from doing so. "Leave these to us," the head of security says. "We are born to perform this sort of task, not you. Just relax." In the end, she stands back, watching as the youths, under his supervision, bring out the heavier of the cases and then the lighter one, then carrying them unsteadily up the steps. One or the other of the youths queries, "What are in these; they are so bulky."

SilkHair is beside himself with excitement, like a puppy that is in the company of its kind and wants to play. He quips to no one in particular, "She is too clever to be carrying stones."

Gacal, for his part, is drawn to SilkHair the minute he lays his eyes on him; maybe because, in addition to being his only peer, he is more or less of the same height and of a similar build, and he is wearing clothes comparable in style and cut to his. Or maybe because he recognizes some of the boyish traits that are in evidence: a young boy out of place and trying hard to fit in with the grown-ups. SilkHair seems more on the level of the other youths though, in that, from the way he moves about, he feels as if he has already been admitted into the gun-carrying coterie. Observing him, Cambara is worried and wonders if SilkHair is more likely to feel the strong pull toward the armed militiamen, who are his kindred spirits, than he is to become close to Gacal as a playmate and companion. She knows that her work is cut out for her. She looks ahead to the exciting times and to the intimations of botheration as well as joy that are of a piece with being a parent, in her case a surrogate one. Early on in the exercise, Cambara assigns to the two of them the responsibility of remaining in the rooms and keeping count of things.

When the off-loading has concluded and she is sufficiently relaxed to look around, she is mildly shocked to discover that Gacal has remained in the rooms, as if he has more right than SilkHair to be guarding her property, and has sent SilkHair out to inform her that, in Gacal's words, the unloading is complete and she can now return to her rooms to take over. And just as she heads for her rooms, SilkHair, instead of joining her, goes in the opposite direction, to where the armed sentries are gathered, their weapons leaning in a pile of disorder, exchanging crude repartee of the kind that might make a lady cringe. Cambara looks back over her shoulder, because curiosity stops her dead in her tracks. She is not at all surprised that the boy is in his element, participating in the ribald humor, and that he is one of a kind when in the company of the armed youths, not in hers or Gacal's. Maybe she ought to have a rethink; maybe she ought not to try to impose her will on him.

Crestfallen, she leaves SilkHair to his choice for the moment and walks up the flight of stairs toward her rooms, deep in thought and eager to be reunited with Gacal. Finding the door shut, she calls out Gacal's name as she gives it a judicious push, gentle at first and then a little firmer in her determination to open it. She tries to turn the handle but to no avail. After several unsuccessful attempts at pushing it open and unsure of what is happening or rather of what Gacal is up to, desperation begins to set in. What can he be doing, locking the room from inside? She can't be certain in what state she has left the suitcases containing her cash or if he has had all the time in the world to help himself to everything: her passport, her notes, her sketch pads? Why is he not answering? She dreads what Arda will say when she learns how naive Cambara has been to trust a boy with no known history. Serves you right, she will say. The seeds of her suspicion are beginning to multiply to such an extent that she is about to take the drastic action of summoning Kiin and having the door broken, when her ears pick out the sound of room keys in the pockets of her caftan and she retrieves them in haste and uses them.

She lets herself in quietly. She tiptoes in, her despair mounting by the second. Topmost in her mind is his future as she has imagined it, a boy set to rights, given a life with a future. When he is not in the first room, and there is no sound from the inner room, which serves as her bedroom, she wonders if she will be staring the first signs of misfortune in the eye, if her luck is running out at last, if all that she has constructed with so much help from so many people will have come to nought. She is not sure how she might control her rage if she catches him fiddling, thieving. Wild with impatience, she moves forward speedily into her private sanctum, the refuge where she does her thinking, her writing, and sketching, only to come upon Gacal asleep, a pile of heavy books substituting for a pillow. He is lying on his back, his feet resting on a suitcase, his face partially hidden from view, his hands held together close to his chin and as though in *namaste* greeting and suggesting someone in worship. To his right flank but on the floor, a thin book titled *Fly, Eagle, Fly* lies open on page seven. Delighted to presume that he has been leafing through the text on which she is planning to base her play, she is, however, disturbed that he has read it, if that is what he has done, without her express permission.

Exhausted, she collapses on the bed a foot away.

A few minutes later, Kiin joins Cambara in her rooms, admittedly to find out not only how Cambara is coping with the fresh inrush of baggage but also how cramped or how accommodating the rooms look. Getting into the front room, she has had to watch her step, with suitcases everywhere, some open and their contents spread outside of them in piles, others pushed into the corner and heaped any which way on top of one another. Before proceeding any farther, Kiin can't help assuming that Cambara is either searching for a specific item of clothing, which she has not found yet, or reorganizing her paraphernalia, what with the notepads, markers, makeup kits, eye pencils, and bottles of coloring stuff that Kiin cannot identify, into heaps before repacking them or is simply airing them.

Kiin holds the door handle as if she is prepared to pull it shut. On second thought, she stops where she is and says, "Since you are in the middle of sorting things out and I do not want to distract you, maybe I will come and see you another time. Then we'll talk."

Cambara, in a rush to welcome her, if only, among other things, to have Kiin enlighten her about her plans, misses her footing, almost falling over. She pauses to catch her breath and, as she speaks, stumbles over her words. "All this can wait. Please come in." She pushes two of the suitcases that tripped her out of the way, creating more space for Kiin to enter.

Kiin now proceeds into the front room with ease, but when she is invited into Cambara's inner sanctum and sees a young figure sleeping, she halts in much the same way as she might had she come upon a couple kissing. Cambara urges her to enter, explaining, "He fell asleep, poor thing!" Kiin does so hesitantly, with the care of someone not wanting to disturb; her knees might buckle, she is so cautious. Then she takes the chair that Cambara indicates, turns around, and speaks slowly. She asks, "First things first. How was it with Zaak?" Sprawled on Kiin's features is a smile charged with warmth as well as concern. In the meantime, her eyes, curious, anxious, search for signs of worry in Cambara's. She is curious about the boy sleeping on the door. Who he is to Cambara, who has just committed herself to looking after another boy nicknamed SilkHair? And she wonders whether he can hear their conversation. Cambara registers the antsy expression on Kiin's face, even if she can't identify its source.

"Glad you're rid of Zaak?"

"Zaak and his hick mentality," responds Cambara.

"What are you saying?"

"It is the look of defeat in his eyes all the time we were there," Cambara explains. "The fellow was disagreeably in his drawers, chewing *qaat,* his look distant, lethargic, his hands on his hips." Then she changes tack, and, as though usurping Kiin's part in the dialog, she takes the plunge and offers what she thinks of as an appropriate way to define a generation of Somali men, lines more appropriate coming from Kiin's mouth than from hers. Even so, Cambara says, "Zaak is a top-of-the-range loser, typical among the men to whom we've entrusted the fate of this nation for far too long. Brainless, the lot of them."

"From what I hear you've handled him superbly."

"The honest truth is that I derived no pleasure from doing so," she says, her voice weakening, as if she is suddenly lacking in conviction. Then, after a considerable pause, with the consistency of her voice thickening like quality sauce, she adds, "I find it shocking that he was *my* husband once. Never mind that the marriage was not consummated and that it was only on paper to facilitate his emigration to Canada."

"I'll presume that your entire luggage is here."

"That's right."

Kiin's tone of voice picks itself up, thanks to a surge in her adrenaline, and she says, "I see that you've upgraded the new acquaintance to a higher status, as if he were your own child, or at least he has promoted himself thus. Admirably asleep. Handsome to boot and angelic-looking at that."

It is not in Cambara's nature to admit that at times she is a slow thinker. It's been an exhausting day, hasn't it? And because of this, she thinks she might not do adequate justice to the question, which, anyhow, she does not much like, considering the insinuation of the phrase "upgrading the new acquaintance to a higher status" and knowing too—although Kiin has no idea that Cambara does, thanks to Raxma—that she, Kiin, or, if you please, the Women's Network, is footing the bill. Cambara turns all these facts over in her mind not in an attempt to answer the unasked question but to figure out if, in the meantime, Raxma has been in touch to divulge the details of Cambara's latest assignment: to trace Gacal's parents.

This is why Cambara asks, lending their dialogue the illusion that a number of unspoken-of matters flow from this very question, "What do you mean 'upgrading the new acquaintance to a higher status'?"

Next thing she knows, Kiin is trying to defuse the tension. Kiin, smiling, says, "One more mouth to feed won't present us with a problem. You can be sure of that."

In her obtuseness, the result, perhaps, of having taken on too much and been on the go ever since her arrival, Cambara looks blankly about herself. Not that she bothers to ask herself if the correct response might be there in view and for the taking, if only she were to search for it. And instead of concentrating on the job at hand, she is so anxious she is at a loss as to what to do or say. She repeats the phrase "one more mouth . . ." then falls silent. "I am prepared to foot the bill. With a lot of thanks."

To ease the challenge with which Cambara is failing to cope, Kiin gets to her full height and says, "I can see that you've had a long day, and I know that an even much longer night is upon us. So I suggest that you be less demanding of yourself and that you take a break, perhaps even a short nap, then a very hot shower to recharge. Don't bother yourself about the young fellow you've named SilkHair; I'll see to it that he has all that he requires in the way of something to eat and a place to sleep. At the party then."

Cambara limps forward toward the bed, eyes unfocused, nostrils broadening, as her jaws open and she cannot help yawning. Suddenly overwhelmed by a memory related to labor pains, she feels as though she is inhaling methyl, and her knees begin to wobble, her eyes smart, her tongue becomes heavy and highly uncooperative, and the floor appears to move from under her feet, because of its unevenness. Her memory of the epidural jab combined with her son's subsequent death brings on a knockout exhaustion, which, in turn, leads to drowsiness.

Then, before she has figured out what to do, Kiin is gone, and she is alone in her rooms, the door shut, the curtains drawn, and she is sprawled on her bed, ready to crawl into a deep well of sleep. But then she sits up, awake to the presence of someone else breathing close by and sleeping in the same room as she for the first time in months, ever since Dalmar's death, when she moved out of the bedroom she shared with Wardi. It has been a long day replete with exigencies, some of them more demanding than others, and there is of course Gacal and the difficult choice she has had to make: whether to wake him up and boot him out or accommodate him, given his age and her fondness for him. She listens to his small snore, similar to a pipe being gently blown, the hole partially covered. Cambara debates whether to let Gacal continue his sleep undisturbed, in the end deciding that she wants to have her inner sanctum to herself, with no one else around. She calls his name. He stirs, then suddenly starts, rubbing his eyes sore. Fully alert, he apologizes.

"I'm sorry. I'm sorry. I didn't mean to."

"That's okay. You were tired."

"See you later." He is off, his head downcast.

No regrets though. For there is time yet to know Gacal after Raxma
has gotten back to her. Until then, she will act as if she has Arda by
her side, preparing to pounce on her for her recklessness, chastising
her for her weaknesses, and reminding her, as always, of her failings.

It takes Cambara a long time to fall asleep.

A couple of hours later, Cambara wakes up all atwitter. It is after nine
in the evening by her watch, time she has showered and then changed
into something of a dress, not necessarily fancy. She is eager to join the
evening revel as soon as she can manage it; she is already late. A pity
she hadn't the calmness of mind to ask reception for a wake-up call before sleep overcame her. Now she must step out quickly.

Looking for something to wear, she lights upon a plain caftan, which
she puts on in haste. Her hair combed back, head uncovered, she wraps
her shoulders in a *garbasaar* shawl of Indonesian make that boasts an
elaborate pattern: peacocks in pursuit of peahens, the one in full display and eager to get done, the others acting coy and delighting in the
long-drawn-out courtship. A pair of drop earrings for her ears. For
shoes, she has leather sandals, bought in Rome a couple of years ago.
She isn't carrying a handbag, which she thinks of as an ecumbrance,
and her hands swing freely as she takes her long strides. Finally, she
does an odd thing: She admires her neatly varnished nails, colored gentle purple.

She applies a very light makeup, a balm to her current state of unease for not being one of the first to arrive. So far, she has been able
to pay little attention to her body. She is happy to have made inroads
into other areas of interest, namely the recovery of the family property.
She feels certain that a fruitful expedition into her imaginative side
when she starts to block and rehearse the play will prompt the serious
healing she needs. She prays that the evening will provide her with inspiration that will give her a fix on the very qualities that set her apart
from the other women at the party, many of whom, she presumes, have
their bases here and are deeply involved in the politics of the city.

She walks down the steps, past reception, which has no staff and
thus no one to answer the two telephones that are squealing. She
strides with the perturbation of someone who is heavy of heart, disturbed of mind, because of a gap in her memory as to what caused her

blackout—exhaustion? In her distraction, she nearly collides with two women, young of voice but of indeterminate age, who are giggling as they share a bit of gossip about one of their number caught in bed with her bodyguard, whom she accused of raping her at gunpoint. "When it's clear it's been voluntary," adds one of them and, chuckling, takes her friend's hand, pulling it toward her, the two of them doubling over in rip-roaring laughter. Cambara does not see what is amusing in the rape story she has just overheard. What kind of women are these?

She slows down her pace, pretending that she is listening to the loud Somali music blaring out of the upstairs hall where the party is taking place, when she is actually avoiding making eye contact with Gacal and SilkHair, who are sitting on the floor and playing cards under the light. She goes around a pillar and then seats herself on a chair in the café. She looks up at the clear, starry, beautiful evening. Again, her memory fails, because she cannot remember where in the sky she might look if she is to spot the camel-in-the-heavens constellation.

As she resumes walking, she tries to identify the Somali song coming from the hall. Alas, she fails to do so and reminds herself that Kiin will be presenting her to a handful of her friends, among whom, she hopes, will be the gynecologist who helped not only to deliver Jiijo's baby boy but also to organize for her a safe home away from Gudcur's reach. But will Cambara remember these women if she meets them somewhere else, or will their names have dropped into a black hole, irredeemably lost, like what happened a couple of hours earlier. Maybe she has nothing to worry about. Maybe she just had a simple fainting spell, not that she has ever had one before. Anyhow, there is no reason to give way to unwarranted anxieties. This is no way to proceed; she might as well pack up and leave. The question, however, is this: Is departing an option? She has already committed herself to cutting off her relationship with Zaak. Does it now make sense to alienate Kiin and all the other people who have put their lives on the line? It is time that Cambara relax, time that she prepare to enjoy herself at the party.

As she ambles forward, taking her time, she recalls the countless instances of newly arrived Somali women living in Toronto inviting her to one ceremony or another: a daughter graduating from university; a son, a nephew, or a niece getting married; a young woman or man being honored for her or his achievement in business or sports. It is no

wonder that Cambara, who attended only a few of the numerous occasions to which she was unfailingly invited, is now dragging her feet,
no longer eager to get to this party.

Now she finds herself standing as two women in all-black chador
who are chattering away and gossiping about a man pass her. The
women speak loudly and do not seem at all bothered by who might hear
them. Stepping aside, Cambara is curious that although veiled to a tee
they are in stiletto heels, which click away with echoing intensity, irritating Cambara. Moreover, when both lift their veils off the ground to
make sure they don't get dirty or do not trip on them, Cambara is certain she can see the bright pink undergarments of one of them. She can
hear the two women talking ceaselessly and coarsely until they go up
the stone steps that will lead into the dance hall.

Patience is of the essence, she tells herself. It gives her a moment's
comfort to think that this is the first time that she has seen Somali
women behave uninhibitedly, remembering of course that outside the
hotel grounds, it is bandit country where women may not step out of
line. Or else!

The party is in full swing, and Cambara's entry attracts long gawking
from several women near the entrance to the hall. Not wanting to interfere with the flow of human traffic going in and out, and behaving
excitedly, she reins in her enthusiasm, and stands to the left of the doorway, watching. She leans against the wall, close to a coat rack on which
the women have hung lengths of dark material, presumably their veils,
now that they are among women only, indoors, and no longer required
to wear them.

There are many women on the floor, animatedly dancing, even if
their arrhythmic bodily gyrations are at variance with their intentions.
Several of those near her are hip heavy, and they can barely move in
keeping with the fast beat of the music, a few of them giving up and
then being encouraged by those in the same circle to adapt their pace
to the pulse, to measure their movements against theirs. Alas to no
avail, for they fail in their efforts to achieve the required tempo. When
Cambara surveys the scene from her vantage point, taking in the extent of the dancing qua dining hall, she sees a sea of beautiful richness

in varicolored vibrancy, reminiscent of Soviet- and Chinese-style displays that used to be mounted often to celebrate special national occasions with the pomp and ceremony of the so-called socialist states. Tens of thousands of children, trained in acrobatics and in the art of sycophancy, would be coached in constructing color-coordinated collages representing all the good things that the state had accomplished in the name of its valiant people. Looking at the scene before her from close range, she does not find much that appeals to her aesthetic, not with so many mistiming, and their missteps now and then causing the dancers to fall over one another.

Then Kiin comes on the scene. She hugs Cambara, kissing now one cheek, now the other, and, speaking endearments, adds, as if for good measure, a tribute, "How good that you are here at last."

Cambara feels certain that she is well advised not to entertain any worries. All is well with Kiin and her. Whatever has made her think otherwise?

Kiin takes Cambara by the hand, almost dragging her, and says, "Come, my dear, come." And she presents her cursorily to a number of women before offering her a paper cup with a bright yellow drink of which Cambara takes a cautious sip, her expression guarded, so as not to give it away. Finding the proffered drink too sweet for her liking, she puts it on a windowsill at the first opportunity, ostensibly to shake the extended hand of a woman to whom Kiin has just introduced her, and then walks away from it.

"You know who I would like to meet?"

"Who?"

"The wife of the shopkeeper in the neighborhood of the family property," Cambara says. "I feel I know her. Just to say hello. That's all."

"She's out of town, I am afraid."

"Gone out of the country or something?"

"As a matter of fact, she has," Kiin replies. "She is in Nairobi at the National Reconciliation Conference as a delegate, representing our branch of the Women's Network."

"Another time, maybe."

"Let's go."

Then Kiin and Cambara embark on a walkabout, with one or the other of them engaging in inconsequential talk with women whose names she is not likely ever to remember. But she enjoys the tactile nature of their camaraderie, the fellow feeling with women whose names won't matter to her, because she hasn't caught them, given the loudness of the music, and won't remember, because she can't think of a reason why she should. From what she can gather, Kiin, who is leading her by the hand the way a sighted person might guide a blind one, is looking to spot someone, her neck craned, her eyes peeled. Yet they move on, at times with the faint acknowledgment of two young women in jeans who are registering everything on a video camera.

She and Kiin separate when Cambara knocks into one of the chairs placed against the wall. She hurts her right knee, stops, and then nurses the bump, rubbing it. Then she lights upon two young women who are different from many of the others not only in their approach to dancing but also in what they are wearing. One of them is standing in a pair of bloomers, with nothing covering her upper torso, not even a brassiere, her breasts firm and her body equally so. She is belly dancing and doing it well, almost like a professional. The other is in a very tight dress, her long, jet-black hair down, her frontal and posterior bulges prominently distended. Not that Cambara, fascinated, falls under their spell, but she finds it curious that no one else has. Every woman is doing her own thing.

Cambara finds her hand in the good warm grip of someone else's. Turning, she is face to face with Kiin's eager eyes, which put her in mind of the troubled muddy waters of a river working itself up to an overflowing point before finally bursting at the banks in a rainy season. Cambara puts a lot of effort into hiding her feeling and smiles reproachfully, because she has no idea why she senses a disturbing stir in the hollow of her stomach. Nothing that Kiin has done or said to her so far accounts for her behavior.

Kiin says, "Come with me."

Kiin holds out her hand to her and grabs it, taking a very tight grip of it. Cambara has the eerie sensation of a minor tremor running through them, only she is not certain which of them is responsible for the quiver.

"Where are we headed?"

"Come and you'll find out."

In the café downstairs, Kiin introduces her to Farxia, the medical doctor at whose clinic Jiijo delivered her baby boy and who has been looking after her since then and providing the "fugitive" mother with a temporary safe house. Farxia is holding a mug and sipping from it. (In a number of Muslim countries, someone drinking alcohol may disguise it this way. Cambara is not sure if this is so, in Farxia's case.)

Farxia, austerely dressed in a shirt and khaki trousers, is sitting in a dimly lit corner from which she can watch all the comings and goings. She has three strings around her neck, two for mobile phones and a third for her computer's memory stick. From what Cambara can see in the little light provided, she wears no makeup at all and no jewelry either. Farxia, whom Cambara guesses to be in her late thirties or early forties, is a slender, soft-spoken woman of medium height, with a stern expression and a slight squint.

She has a firm handshake, however. Once introduced, she nods to acknowledge Cambara's presence but does not say anything. There is a brief intense look in the eyes, nothing else. Barely have Cambara and Kiin seated themselves when a young woman arrives with platters of finger food: chicken wings lightly sautéed in honey, lemon, and garlic; baby carrots and a few sticks of almost-dry celery; a variety of dips and a choice of baguette and *nan*-like *sabaayo*; and a spread of salad for the three of them.

Farxia dispenses with all formalities and serves herself a very small portion of the food, at which she nibbles. As she does so, she looks down and studies her trimmed nails and her well-scrubbed, many-times-washed hands; she might be consulting them, she is so focused, her lips astir. Then she says to no one in particular, "Jiijo and her baby are both fine."

Farxia frets; she is a little on edge, probably thinking not so much of what she has so far done for Jiijo as of the commitments she will have made to keeping the woman and her baby safe. And she keeps peering around in the softly lit darkness with which they are all surrounded, as if she is expecting an attacker to materialize. However, there is no fear in Farxia's eyes. Cambara thinks she can read the unbending determination of a woman pursuing an ideal.

Farxia continues, "We're lucky the delivery went smoothly and happy that to date there have been no complications of any sort."

Cambara speaks despite the fact that she sounds highly unprepared to let go of the words, as if parting with them might cause offense. "Where are they, mother and baby?"

Farxia hesitates, clearly not wanting to divulge a secret pact. She looks at Cambara, then at Kiin before replying, "I have had them moved from the clinic to a private home. To a place where they are safe. And I have assigned a nurse to attend to them. I am in constant contact with the nurse, a trustworthy woman who used to work with Bile, whom I understand you've already met. I look in on them twice daily: just before dawn and late at night."

At the mention of Bile's name, Cambara fidgets self-consciously. She is reassured that neither woman takes notice of her squirm. Maybe as a decoy to put Farxia off, Kiin, in an audible tone of voice as confident as it is welcome, says in the manner of someone anticipating the relevant question that is to come, "Our network delivers them food and all their other needs."

"I've been meaning to ask."

"Yes?" from Farxia.

Cambara speaks slowly. "In what way can I pay for your consultation as a doctor at the clinic, not to speak of the ambulance that transported Jiijo from the property and the expenses incurred in housing her, feeding her, and mounting an armed security?"

"My dear, you'll have to talk to Kiin."

And Kiin cuts in, "Everything in due course."

"These are huge expenses, and I am willing to settle it right away, in cash, in U.S. dollars, since that is all I have," Cambara says, feeling foolish as the words pass her tremulous lips.

Kiin and Farxia exchange brief looks, then their eyes focus on Cambara a little too long, neither speaking. It's obvious they are not going to share their thoughts with her. Kiin says, "We'll talk about expenses in due course."

Cambara senses a surge of apprehension rising within her from the lower pit of her stomach at the thought of how much she is costing these women, how much her meddling in the affairs of others must be affecting their lives.

It is in keeping with the Cambara who is given to complicating matters at the very moment when everything is running smoothly that she ask, "Can I visit Jiijo and her baby?"

"Why do you want to do that?" Farxia challenges.

If Cambara cannot bring herself to give flesh to the thought that crosses her mind, it is because she is aware that saying she might benefit from a touchy-feely reunion with Jiijo and her baby won't do. If she has not shared her introspection with anyone, it is because Farxia has stared hostilely away, thus reducing Cambara to bashful silence.

Again, Kiin rescues Cambara from embarrassment. She says, "Even though it may not be advisable to call on Jiijo and her baby at their hideout, I'll tell you where you can go without fear or worry."

"Where?"

"Your family property."

Cambara feels that before she admits to knowing of it, the good tidings—that at least she can go to her family property without fear or worry, thanks to Kiin and her friends in the network—will have wrought a keen sense of self-fulfillment.

"Anyone holding the fort?" she asks.

"Dajaal, his nephew, and their men."

Cambara thinks that as much as she owes Kiin fealty, the fact is that she is also grateful to other well-wishers, including Bile, who has probably encouraged Dajaal to get involved, help in the recovery of her family property. Who knows, Bile may have been instrumental in making Seamus commit himself to giving her a hand. For her part, Cambara will have been responsible for everything that is detrimental to the well-being of the community: endangering Kiin, Farxia, and all these other women; exposing Dajaal, Qasiir, his nephew, and their sidekicks to possible peril. She prays only that nothing terrible will happen to all these good people.

Cambara asks Farxia, "How is Bile, do you know?"

"He has been heavy of heart, ever since Raasta departed," Farxia says. "Lonely in his melancholy, he falls deeper and frequently into a sense of depression, refusing to come to terms with how things are."

Cambara sinks into a slouch, exhausted, silent.

TWENTY-THREE

Cambara wakes up early the following morning to a noise already familiar to her from a dream just before dawn, a dream in which the clamor of several people eating is the predominant din. Now, after rising from another brief nap, she can hear the clamor of knives and forks clashing, the raucous cacophony of crockery, and, in the background, the clanging plates against saucers and other tableware being washed and stacked together in a chaotic manner.

In her dream, Cambara has prepared a special dinner: prawn cocktails; a fish platter composed of freshwater cockles, eaten with lemon and chili sauce; calamari fried in butter and smothered in garlic and herbs; and a dish of lemon sole with rice and veggies. There are three other people: Wardi, who occupies one head of the table, which is big enough to seat twenty; Dalmar, who sits very close to her, their bodies touching; and Arda, who is at the other head of the table. There is not much in the way of conversation, and what there is does not flow at all, with Dalmar and Arda trying to keep it going, if only because they cannot stand the weighty silence. Wardi delights in making poisonous remarks meant not so much to annoy her as to insult all three of them. His look in Cambara's direction has in it only contempt; that in Arda's, a mere challenge; that in Dalmar's, a mix of betrayal and disparagement. Clearly annoyed, she can't wait for this travesty of a family dinner to end. All the while, she shows Wardi her clenched fist, vowing to hit him as soon as Arda is gone, Dalmar is asleep in his room, and the two of them are alone.

Not only does Cambara refuse to put a good face on the matter and engage her mother or son in pointless talk, but she also does not touch her favorite food, the first time she remembers doing so. In contrast, Wardi is garrulously jittery, brazenly telling an improper joke about half a dozen Italians from a hick town in Sicily who, sharing a house in the suburbs of Milan, hire the services of a whore. Arda appeals to his sense of decorum, but Wardi does not heed her pleas, and just as he is about to launch into telling yet another gag, Arda says, the tone of her voice firm and uncouth, "That's enough. No more of this in the presence of Dalmar."

Wardi turns on his mother-in-law and makes as if he will challenge her. No sooner has he uttered the first syllable of a long word than his lips move soundlessly like that of a fish biting bait, his eyes dilate to the point of popping out of their sockets, his jaw drops, and he foams at the mouth. Apparently, Wardi is having a seizure, the fit of an epileptic. He ceases breathing altogether and his muscles stiffen, hard as the back of the chair he is sitting on. Arda looks from him to Cambara, who just nods. Whereupon, with a huge, knowing smile brightening his face, Dalmar makes the V sign. Then he says to Cambara, "You know, Mummy, I love you, love you, no matter what."

"I love you too, my sweet darling."

It is when Dalmar gets up to hug his mother, pulling her toward him, and then his grandmother, snuffling loudly preparatory to a crying fit, which is theatrical to the point of having been rehearsed, that Wardi falls off his chair. No one moves; no one speaks for a long time, the silence contagiously spreading so that even Dalmar hasn't the boldness to break it. The first to stir, Dalmar changes his position with the quietness of someone aware of other presences to which he defers.

Dalmar says, "What do we do now?"

Cambara takes his hand, as if consoling him.

Arda asks Cambara, "How do you explain?"

"Allergy."

Cambara takes large mouthfuls of her food for the first time and encourages her son and her mother to resume eating theirs.

"No idea he was allergic to fish," from Arda.

Cambara does not accord him even a single look in his direction now that he lies on the floor, rigor mortis ruling—she hates him so. "He's died not knowing that he is allergic to fish, the fool."

"How did you come to know of it?" Arda asks.

"I've my ways of knowing."

The dogged sense of remorse makes Dalmar so restless that he rises from his chair and crouches by Wardi, checking his pulse and reporting, "No beating. Mummy, he's gone cold. And look at his body: bloodless yellow. What do we do with him?"

"Dalmar is right. What do we do now?" Arda asks.

Cambara, her held-in grin making her lips seem smaller and her whole face stiff, pulls out her mobile phone and dials a number. To the woman at the other end, she says, "Susannah, do come and pick up your Wardi. He is on the floor, having a fit of the fatal kind, and we do not know what to do."

The voice says, "I'll be with you in a minute."

Cambara says to Arda and Dalmar, "There. Done."

Dalmar walks over to where Wardi's corpse lies coiled on the floor, and he kicks him, not once but two, three times in quick succession. Furious at him, Cambara gives him a dressing down, saying, "You must treat his dead body with respect. He is your father."

He retorts, "But he used to hit me. Remember?"

Cambara gets a telling-off from Arda, who says, "It's your fault. Everything. Dalmar's ill-mannered behavior. Wardi's ill will toward us all."

The doorbell rings. As she gets up, steadies herself, and goes toward the door, she announces, "It's Susannah come to pick up her darling dead."

The door opens, the sun in her eyes. Susannah not there, she turns to say something to Dalmar and Arda, neither of whom is there.

Cambara blinks the dream away.

She wakes up in her room at Hotel Maanta in Mogadiscio in an apparent sweat over what she has done: killed in hate, out of revenge. Disturbed, she takes a deep breath, looks about the room, and, dropping into a state of bleary-eyed conundrum, wonders if a dream such as the one she has just had will have redeemed her from her desire to commit murder.

Half an hour later, her commitment to creating a family to replace the dysfunctional one she did away with in the dream strengthens with the sudden coming into view of Gacal and SilkHair, who are deep in amicable discussion. She watches them from her vantage point in the café, where she is consuming her first order of breakfast: two slices of mango and a pot of coffee. With her free hand, she is leafing through the text of her play, of which she intends to give a copy later to Gacal. She doesn't know enough about SilkHair, who hasn't yet told her his story. There is time, time to hear from Raxma, who is at her investigative best, probing, digging. No need to rush. All the same, she reckons that SilkHair is not much of a reader; possibly, he has never been to a school in the proper sense of the term. "We'll see," she says to herself aloud.

As she looks shortsightedly at them, almost missing a heartbeat, her breathing labored, she sits up, too eager to welcome them. She stops short of calling out to them by name and waits, half rising from her seat, with her coffee mug held up and close to her chin but tilted a little forward, nearly tipping. She thinks of SilkHair and Gacal as forming the nub of her alternative family, with which she might yet succeed in replacing the one that died with Dalmar. Tears of emotion flood her eyes at the memory of the wonderful times spent in loving, raising, teaching, mothering Dalmar. In her current reassessment, she will admit that she learned from her Dalmar as much as she taught him. More to the present point, she is getting to know a lot about herself, because of her dealings with Gacal and SilkHair, who are assisting her in her effort to reassess her self-worth as a grieving mother.

Cambara's spirits soar on the winds of optimism, gliding with a sense of elation at imagining how she might ultimately accomplish one of her main aims: to repair several of the wrongs to which the societies of men have subjected women through the ages—in her case, Wardi— thanks to the intervention of the Women's Network, with Kiin at its head, decidedly steering it to actionable success. She doubts if her goodwill and inner strength could stir compunction in the heart of a Wardi as she might in those of the Dajaals, Seamuses, and Biles of this world. These strike her as having stopped fibbing or faffing about and have started to fine-tune their act. Is it because they are reconstructed men, able to express their humanness in a way that is beneficial to all? Not Wardi; no humanness in him, none whatsoever.

The first to see her, SilkHair gives a nudge to Gacal and, pointing at Cambara with the barely visible movement of his head, comes toward her with the rough-hewn attitude of someone not given to restraining his impulses. Gacal, for his part, is content to remain where he is and to wave in salutation. Cambara asks herself if he is waiting to be invited or if he is upset, because he felt affronted by the manner in which she booted him out of her room yesterday evening. There is nothing standoffish about Gacal's staying behind, she concludes, from where she is, she can sense the tremor of a smile forming.

Meanwhile, she turns her attention to SilkHair, who is lobbing his body forward with the speed of a tennis player eager to get on with the game. He is at her side before she has settled on what to say to him. But what is she to do, what is she to say? Open her arms for a quick hug? Ask him what he has done with his time since their last encounter? He steps back, his Adam's apple busy making swallowing noises and his gaze focusing on her breakfast, so she invites him to order something to eat. With SilkHair seated and helping himself to one of her mangoes, she summons Gacal to join them. Gacal inserts himself in the space left untaken between her and SilkHair and leans forward as if he might receive a peck. Cambara gives his thigh a gentle pat and then pushes her remaining slice of mango toward him. He behaves as a well-bred boy of his age who has just eaten and who is not worried about his next meal.

He says, "Thanks. We've had breakfast."

His cheeks mango-stained and his chin dripping with the mature yellow juice of the fruit, SilkHair eventually gives in to his gluttony. He pulls the remaining slice toward him without Cambara saying that he might and pounces on it with equal enthusiasm.

She says to Gacal, "What did you have?"

Gacal replies, "Porridge."

"What was it like?"

"Filling," he says.

"How has it been then, your first night?"

Gacal and SilkHair talk in tandem, their choice of words pointing her to their different dispositions, Gacal pronouncing it as "passable," in contrast to SilkHair, who describes his experience thus: "So far it has been wonderful." Cambara thinks that it is too early in the day to ar-

rive at a conclusion about their character, but she stores these obser-
vations in her memory for future consideration.

She snaps her fingers, and the waiter takes his time coming, his un-
willingness, perhaps to serve the two boys, discernible in his body language. He smiles at her, bowing his head slightly. But when he turns
his face to speak to them, his expression assumes a hostility that has
not been there before; his eyes harden; his choice of idiom rough
and ready.

Obviously offended, Gacal looks from the waiter to Cambara, if
only to indicate that, to his credit, he is sharing his frustrations with
her in submissive silence, not rising to it. Not that SilkHair is unaware
of what is happening, but he hurries to empty his face of an expression
that might allow anyone to interpret it in any way before placing his
order of breakfast: a large glass of orange juice, liver, and pancake. He
is the kind of boy—"another mouth to feed"—who has known what it
is like to kill for his meals. Gacal wants "Nothing for the moment," and
he might as well have added the phrase "from that waiter."

"What did you do last night?" she asks them.

SilkHair puts his index finger close to his lips in the attitude of
someone embarrassed to speak about something; he also avoids making eye contact with her. Cambara cannot help assuming that the boys
went somewhere or did something of which SilkHair is not proud in
the light of day. When she tries to decode its meaning, that is not the
impression she gets from training her gaze on Gacal. Gacal is defiant,
in that he stares back at her as though he is daring her to turn her attention to him.

"Did you go somewhere last night?"

"We went to see a movie," Gacal says.

"What sort of movie? Where?"

Gacal explains that they went to a building that once belonged to
the defunct state, namely the former Ministry of Foreign Affairs, where
there is a hall with two ends, each with a video screen. SilkHair saw a
Hindi movie dubbed into Somali at one end, then a Korean kung fu
film whose soundtrack had also been rendered into Somali, never mind
that it was done very badly, hastily, and cheaply too. He goes on,
"Myself, I watched a different sort of movie in the end of the hall."

"And you enjoyed it?"

"Very much."

"What was it called, the film you saw?"

"I don't recall the name."

"What was it about?"

SilkHair strikes her as someone easier in his mind as soon as the waiter put his breakfast in front of him. He tucks into it promptly, she thinks, not because he is hungry, but in great part because he is not accustomed to having this kind of food. Unlike Gacal, he does not cut a bashful figure in her presence. Which leads her to conclude that Gacal knows more than he is letting on.

"I am waiting," she eggs Gacal on.

Gacal decoys her curiosity, baiting and turning it subtly away from the question for which he has not provided an answer to his disgust and disapproval of the slurping, smacking, and loud munching noises SilkHair has the habit of making whenever he takes a mouthful, but she won't fall for it.

She says, "Tell me what you saw. I'm waiting."

Gacal says nothing, eyes evasive.

In between two mouthfuls, each as noisy as ever, SilkHair volunteers with dash, saying, "Since he won't tell, I will. He watched a sex film."

Cambara stares at SilkHair with disapproval, as if she might charge him with stealing the thunder that is Gacal's by right. As an actor, Cambara is a sucker for someone with a penchant for pace when developing or telling a story. Gacal has it to perfection; she has enjoyed listening to him, watching him perform. She always hated it when, in the process of narrating a tale, Wardi interposed himself into her telling of it, in effect killing it.

She asks Gacal, "Did you enjoy it?"

"I did."

Silent, Cambara's face tightens, as she asks herself what her reaction might have been if her son Dalmar had sneaked away after dark, seen a blue film, and told her without batting an eye that he had enjoyed it. No matter, she thinks. She knows what Wardi would have done. He would have beaten him to a pulp and then would have blamed what he often called her permissiveness, which, in his view, is no way to raise a Somali child in North America. Will Gacal's penchant for blue films, developed perhaps since getting here, judging by his cool attitude, eventually affect their own relationship? Too difficult to predict; she will have to wait and see.

Then a part of her tingles with renewed excitement. She shifts in her seat, precipitously itching to discover if he might read and enjoy the text of her play. She will do so at the appropriate time, alone, in her room, without SilkHair's presence. SilkHair strikes her as competitive, capable of the fury with which he tops his unjustified jealousy. Is she premature in thinking that her gamble to get to know Gacal and see if he has what it takes to be in her play has paid off?

She thinks it best to act very cautiously from now on, considering the traces of tension between the two boys, traceable most definitely to the fact that they are aware of their contemporariness in her interest. That neither is of her own flesh and blood complicates matters, each being of the view, perhaps, that he can outdo the other in earning her trust, her affection. Moreover, she has to keep this fact in mind, knowing that it is one thing when dealing with one's own offspring, to whom one might speak any way one pleases, confident that there is a fund of forgiveness there for the parent and offspring to share between them, and altogether something else when one is confronted by youngsters not one's own, youths who have come with their own baggage and attendant history. She remembers umpteen occasions when she and Dalmar had fierce quarrels; still, they stayed together. It won't be so with these two. Of this, she is certain.

Just before the waiter returns to retrieve the breakfast cutlery, Cambara calls up Kiin to ask for yet another favor, this time for someone to escort "one of my boys" who has no shoes and to help him buy a pair of flip-flops. A minute of so later, as it happens, the waiter arrives to inform her that Kiin has instructed him to take along the money and "one of her boys" to the main market for a pair of slip-ons.

"How much does a pair cost?"

The waiter mentions a sum in the thousands. Cambara does not bother to know how much this is in greenbacks, assuming that it can't be more than two or three dollars. She borrows a pen from the waiter, and she addresses a note to the deputy manager of the hotel authorizing him to hand over the said amount plus a couple more thousands, just to be on the safe side, to the bearer.

The waiter tells SilkHair to wait for him near the exit; excited,

SilkHair does so most willingly. Alone with Gacal, she is nervous. Why this is so, she can't decide. Is it because she is holding out on him, not telling him that she is showing her sweet side while, behind his back, she is having Raxma delve into how he is where he is, what his story is, who his parents might be—questions that may take a while to resolve?

To make up with him, she takes him to her room.

Then she provides him with a soft drink from her small fridge, a variant of Coca-Cola bottled in Arabia and imported into Mogadiscio at some cost. This variety is apparently much sweeter and said to give the drinker more of a kick than its American prototype. She is sure that when he gets back from shopping for a pair of flip-flops, SilkHair will want one too, if he hears about it.

Not sweet-toothed, she sips at her mineral-water bottle, making it last longer. She sits on the floor on a rug, and seeing him look at her as a young man might eye a woman he is fancying, she keeps her physical remove, remembering his talk earlier about enjoying watching a blue film. There is no telling what he might do; she has to be careful, that's all. To put distance between them, she points him to the settee. Neither speaks until both are seemingly cozy.

She asks, "Incidentally, did you read the thin book that you had beside you when you fell asleep? You know the one I mean?"

"It was called *Fly, Eagle, Fly*, wasn't it?"

"That's right."

"I did," he says. "I read it."

"What did you make of it?"

He says, "Liked it. Read it twice and was reading it for the third time, in fact was halfway through it when I must have fallen asleep."

The temptation to give Gacal her entire text based on her reading of *Fly, Eagle, Fly*, and let him get on with it, read it by himself, and then come back to her with his comments is appealing; yet Cambara feels a little uncomfortable, if equally doubtful that it would be wise to do so. She is not certain whether the boy has the gumption to make as gainful a reading alone and without help as he might with her there, beside him, offering guidance. Of course, even though she knows that he can't have seen a play since coming to Mogadiscio, where the gun is glorified and culture enjoys no kudos at all, she assumes that he may have watched or acted in a play in Duluth. It is safe to assume that he is familiar with the basics, from having presumably seen films of one kind or another—American before getting here; Indian, Korean, or Egyptian since arriving in Mogadiscio—films in which some dialog occurs. She should simply give him the damn text and study his reaction. Be done with this dillydallying, woman!

"Here," she says, giving him the parallel text, in English and Somali, printed in double space and elegantly bound.

"What's this?" he asks, weighing it, as if to determine its value that way.

"Open and see."

He does so and reads the title in Somali, first to himself with the vigilance of someone being examined who does not want to make a hasty error. He reads the title for the second time, enunciating each word separately and with formidable panache, maybe because he has realized the nature of the text with which he is dealing: *Gallayrro iyo Dooro* (Eagles Among the Chickens). Once he turns the page, he appears charmed, as if meeting a person whom he likes; she assumes that he is encountering the text on its own terms, he is so engaged. An instant later, he is so taken with the reading of it that he absentmindedly kicks the Coca-Cola bottle, spilling its contents. Apologizing, he gets up to help mop up the mess, but she says she will wipe it with an ancient rag she finds among her castaways. When she hunkers down on the rug on the floor, she watches as his concentration becomes him: seemingly older than his years, his focus centered wholly on what he is reading, and not a muscle of his moving, despite his strained breathing.

Cambara compares what she imagines to be the earthiness of Gacal's strength of character to clay: compact when wet and yet malleable; soft and yet susceptible to becoming hard, if left to itself. There is of course the question of what he will make of the text when he has read it. If he likes it, what does he like about it? She has reason to feel optimistic about Gacal, who, since his father's murder, has lived the life of a mouse in a cage. And what a life it has been, one in which violence has figured frequently and in which he has had to do with the meanness of other people, many of them unknown and unrelated to him.

Has he the willpower to set himself free, with a lot of help from her, of course? She can only be impressed, suspecting what he is capable of and seeing him act grown, mature . . . and responsible.

Does she know what kind of relationship she envisages for the two of them? She must not rush in and must not take on more than she can cope with. She reasons that Arda, her mother, will accuse her of engaging in a "trade-off," her mother's provocative statement that her daughter "bought" the unsuitable Wardi: bartered his affections for Canadian papers as well as paid college retraining fees so that he could obtain employment in exchange for his love. Her past follies, these—she need try to be more cautious this time around.

Turning, she watches Gacal reading and turning the pages with rapt attentiveness. He reminds her of Dalmar, whom she hoped to raise to become a keen reader, to learn many languages and life's skills, a child diametrically opposite Wardi, who often boasted that he had not opened another book since taking his re-sit to graduate from a community college. The idiot described reading a four-page brief for a case as tiresome, when he was incapable of changing a bulb, hammering in a nail, or fixing the flushing mechanism of a toilet—Wardi the nincompoop. Gacal is doing fine, she decides, for a child hamstrung by the unfortunate situation in which she has found himself.

"Done," he says.

"Have you enjoyed it as much as you enjoyed the film you saw last night?" Cambara asks.

"I enjoyed this much more."

"Tell me more."

He asks, "What is it for, anyway?"

"What do you think it is for?"

"Would you like me to act in it? I would like you to be one of the eagles," he says.

"Which one?"

"The younger one," he says. "It will be great fun, like making a film. I would love to be in the play, as an actor. I can do it. Easy."

Before she reacts to Gacal's outpouring of emotions, the phone rings, and the deputy manager of the hotel informs her that a man would like to speak to her.

"The man's name?"

"Dajaal."

"Please put him on."

"This is Dajaal," the deep voice of a man comes on the line. "I am at the reception, and if you have a moment, I would like you to come down."

She waits for him to explain why or to inform her that he has brought along Seamus or Bile, but he does nothing of the sort; he just hangs up.

For some reason, Cambara takes Dajaal's behavior in a surprisingly positive light. She thinks that a man who is as economical with his words as Dajaal deserves nothing short of her respect. She gets to her feet in haste, ready to go down and meet with him. She tells Gacal to hurry up too, and they are at reception in a moment.

"Let's go," Dajaal says.

"Where?"

He doesn't answer immediately.

"Where Dajaal?"

"We go first to your family property," he says.

"Why go there?"

"There has been a change of plan."

"What do you mean change of plan?"

"Seamus is at your family property, with a couple of carpenters, an electrician, and several others. He's asked me to bring you to him. I am just the messenger, doing what he has asked me to."

She remembers agreeing to meet up with Seamus so that the two might spend time together and talk over the carving of the masks that she has designed. Now he has turned his attention to her family property, helping fix it, make it habitable. Cambara refrains from asking Dajaal any of the questions that come to mind, including one about paying for his service and that of the others and one about determining how safe the place is. It's not the time.

Instead, she says, "Can I bring along somebody?"

"Do you mean this young fellow?" Dajaal points his fingers teasingly at Gacal.

"What about me?"

Turning, she is surprised to see SilkHair, come back from shopping and wearing a pair of bright pink flip-flops, interpose himself between Dajaal and Cambara, invidiously pushing Gacal out of the way.

"So you're back," she says, sounding pleased.

"See," he points at his pink flip-flops. "Don't you like them?"

Gacal says, "How can you bear to wear these?"

"Can he come too?" she asks Dajaal.

"Who am I to say no if you say yes?" he says.

There is something lighthearted about Dajaal, who delights in join-ing the raillery all around, an avuncular man playing the role of a peacemaker between Gacal and SilkHair. He goes ahead of them to-ward the vehicle, Cambara following closely. She wonders if things are shaping up better than she has ever imagined they would: two boys, an avuncular Dajaal, and at last the family property back in her hands. Maybe calling on Bile will be the bonus of the day.

"How is Bile?" she asks him.

"Would you like to see him?"

"Is he out of his dark mood?"

Not speaking, Dajaal stares into the distance. Maybe he just does not want to commit himself either way. Meanwhile, he opens the front passenger door and tells the man sitting there to go into the back with the boys. Dajaal does not bother to introduce Cambara. That the man is brandishing a revolver and that he will be sharing the backseat with Gacal and SilkHair does not agree with the plans she has in mind for them—a life in which they are not made vulnerable to gun appeal—but then who is she to quibble over the matter of a small handgun when SilkHair has handled AK-47s and machine guns?

Dajaal goes around to where she is standing, and he places his hand discreetly on the shoulder closer to him, as if assuring her that there is nothing to worry about and that everything will be fine; she will see.

"I hope so," she says. And she gets in beside him.

TWENTY-FOUR

Dajaal drives out of the hotel gates, turns left onto a sandy road, and then takes the bend fast in the petulant attitude of a man to whom someone has shown an undeserved mean-spiritedness. The vehicle veers out of control and comes close to colliding with a boulder on the wrong side of the road. He slows down, however, and holds the steering wheel firm in his hands until the tires get a solid purchase on the ground and the car has regained its balance.

Gacal and SilkHair chat nonstop, though, teasing each other, pulling each other's leg, each putting riddles to the other to solve. The man in the back, fiercely alert to his surroundings, is unsmiling, unspeaking—poised, gun ready, as if he can discern some danger only he is able to see. In addition, it seems to her as if Dajaal is ill at ease with her; he has a sour face for the first time since they first met. Has she done something to offend him? Or said something that has upset him? Or is she being oversensitive, as usual?

"Is everything okay, Dajaal?" she asks.

He nods without looking at her but says nothing.

Cambara resists asking the man in the back if he is expecting an attack on their vehicle; not only because she is not sure if his mood has something to do with Dajaal's but also because she remembers how often she has run into Somalis who are in the habit of trespassing on her generous disposition when she inquires how they have fared in the civil war, many of whom have spoken of war-related trauma. Many point out how lucky she has been not to have experienced it firsthand.

She has read enough about these men and women and met a sufficient number of these veterans to know that some of them tell the tales of their woes as though they were medals they wear to a gathering of fellow sufferers; they revel in excluding those, like her, who have not endured the physical and mental pain of the strife.

The man's childish pout and his physical posture, no longer as refined as when he was younger and serving in the army, equal a body language with which she has become familiar since meeting Zaak and Wardi. She has known of other Somalis who have come out of Mogadiscio following the disintegration and whose moods are high one moment, full of jovial talk and amity, and then in the next instant, when you think that all is going well with their world, something goes out of sync, and all of a sudden they behave out of character. Doleful, she has often seen Wardi going down, down, down, drooling, a man devoid of life's energy. His life, or what there was of it when dejected, would fall apart right before her, literally as she watched him, disintegrating. How tragic! The sad part was that he blamed only her for his muddle, even when she had no hand in it. An individual under so much civil war pressure is bound to succumb to the strain of madness that passes for clan politics, even though most Somalis tell you that what keeps the fire of the strife going is the economic base on which the civil war rests. She has known Wardi to waver between his loyalty to the principles of justice and his allegiance to his immediate blood community. You can bet that anyone who has lived through the worst years of Somalia's strife will have a god-awful countenance like the man sitting in the back. Wardi has no equal when it comes to his unjustified sense of paranoia. Maybe this man too? Not so Dajaal; she must ask him why.

She thinks that whatever else she doesn't know about Dajaal, she imagines that his character has benefited from his associations with Bile and Seamus, an alliance that has kept a potentially disheveled state of being in constant check. Anyone in their company would rein in their impulsiveness. A side glance at Dajaal strengthens her faith, vicariously, in the burgeoning closeness that she imagines is taking shape between herself and Bile through her relationships with Dajaal and Seamus.

In the darkroom of her imagining, she develops the picture of a woman who bears a visage similar to hers and who shares with her several significant particulars. As it happens, this woman is sitting in the passenger seat, next to a man who answers to the name of Dajaal; she has a hangdog expression and is trying to work out how fast she can wipe it off and replace it with a seemingly agreeable grin. Is she up to the challenge though, not only of erasing the shamefacedness of her features but also of engaging in small talk? After all, Dajaal has been very accommodating of her, and has taken one of the most daring challenges in that he has secured her family property, to which he is now driving her.

She asks him, "Has Bile had a hand in the recovery of the property? How much have you involved him?"

His voice inscrutable, he says, "In what way?"

She goes on, the timbre of her voice low, almost a whisper, "Has he talked you into stepping in or did the idea to do so originate with you? Likewise, have you coerced your grandson to help organize the mounting of roadblocks and the setting up of security?"

Answering neither of her questions, Dajaal changes gears, preparatory to coming to a halt, hand brake up, hazard lights on. He sits very still after stopping, his ears erect, listening for alien sounds that might require his attention or that of the man sitting in the back, weapon poised. Gacal and SilkHair fall silent, the former turning around, curious; the latter about to duck, flattening himself on the floor of the vehicle the instant there is an exchange of fire.

When she looks at him, wanting an explanation, he says, "We are here, madam, at one of the access points to your family property, the first of three checkpoints mounted to control the movements into and out of the streets leading there. We are barely two minutes' drive from it. Listen."

She notices a formidable change in the air that makes her insides tense, and the silence more haunting. Now she hears the distant hum of a medium-sized generator, something unusual in this part of the city at this time of day. Then her eyes fall, as if accidentally, on an unmanned boom fifty meters or so farther down the dirt road and just before it a sign that says "JoOgSo," scribbled most likely in the hand of a dyslexic, and under it the word "sToP."

She looks around and realizes where they are. Down one city block, then right, and you will be facing the gate. Will it make sense to move her main base to the property? No doubt, it will be less costly than running up hotel bills, but will the place be sufficiently safe for her to pursue her theater work? Moreover, if it is the sound of a generator she has just heard and if it is coming from the house, then whose is it? Then she becomes aware, gradually, of purposeful movements both inside the vehicle and outside of it. The man in the back of the car she is in steps out with the gentleness of a grandmother quitting the room in which her daughter who has just delivered a baby has fallen asleep and closes the door firmly and speedily. Gacal and SilkHair, for their part, show signs of fear, and they both fret, not knowing what to do. Cambara tells them to sit tight, and they do.

Meanwhile, Dajaal puts his hand into the glove compartment and brings out a firearm, which he keeps hidden from view. He watches with studied caution as three young men crawl out of a camouflage of leafage, at first wary, then very friendly and enthusiastically waving. No older than Gacal or SilkHair, some of them are affecting the air of taking part in a skirmish between two armed militia groups, their tread measured, eyes darting in this or that direction, their weapons pointed, and their fingers restless. To her, it is all part of a theater of some absurd war, whose militiamen will fight without knowing when it will stop once it has started.

As the young boy who is clad in a baggy pair of trousers, which he hitches up every now and then, and carrying a compact machine gun whose weight jars with that of his own long-legged, skinny body approaches, he lowers his weapon out of deference to Dajaal, whom he salutes in imitation of the U.S. Marines he has probably seen in movies.

"Where is my nephew?" Dajaal asks the boy.

As if on cue, Cambara claps her eyes on him, a short youth with a god-awful stride, swaggering as if preparing for the second take in a rehearsal on a set for a movie in which he is playing opposite Clint Eastwood. He says, his accent as seasoned as it is put on to impress her, "Here I am. We are okay on all fronts, Uncle. How about you, are you okay?"

"This is Qasiir, my nephew," Dajaal says.

Qasiir performs his stand-up routine with a New York Yankees cap and a white T-shirt with the words "Iraq Hawks Down" stenciled in black. Under the writing is an eagle with no wings and empty sockets for eyes, scarily unsightly. Qasiir is self-consciously posing, and when he realizes he is not making any impression on Cambara, he puts on a mortified expression and chews nervously on the end of the matchstick sticking out of the left side of his mouth à la Jean-Paul Belmondo.

"Any more questions?" he says, clearly hurt.

Dajaal asks, "All is well on all fronts?"

"As far as I know, all is well on all fronts."

"That's good," Dajaal says.

"*Hasta la vista,*" Qasiir says, and off he trots, almost colliding with one of his mates, as he scuttles on his platform shoes, in the direction of a tree under which there is a canvas chair, resembling that of a movie director, only this one has an arm missing.

When they finally get to her family's gate, she notices the remarkable transformation under way. She senses the variety of activities going on inside and tries her best to sort them out in her mind, in the hope of identifying them. She succeeds in doing so, notwithstanding the hubbub that is one with a house in the process of renovation and which is being gutted. She strains to hear through the loud noise of a working heavy-duty generator. Dajaal toots the horn, in code, and before she is able to say "sesame," the gate—the rust on it that took years to form removed, its hinges repaired, and a first lick of paint applied—opens.

Two youths come into view, both bowing theatrically and curtsying as clowns might. They urge Dajaal to drive in, and, as he does so, they wave to her in delightful consciousness, grinning. She can see a man, maybe an electrician, going up the rungs of a ladder placed against the wall with the slowness of a cripple coming out of a deep well. Lying in the courtyard that is open to the sky, there are a couple of cisterns, both new, if a little dusty, and other bathroom and toilet wares waiting to be installed. In short, a world, to the construction of which she has contributed little, is now being reinvented, thanks to these charitable souls. But as she looks farther to the right of the house and spots Seamus emerging from a truck parked there, she starts to wonder if she has the right to see herself as a catalyst for such remarkable revamping. She alights from the car, waiting beside it, as he moves, smiling, toward her. She believes that Seamus, Kiin, and Dajaal have the license to be pleased with the ways things are going. All the same, she wonders if she has the wherewithal to maintain the property and keep it in this style, taking into account how much it has cost to put the process of repossessing it into motion.

Dajaal gets back into the car, waves very enthusiastically to Seamus, to whom he speaks in kitchen Somali, spiced with a couple of infinitives in Italian, and then says to Cambara, "I'll come back for you in an hour, to take you to Bile, if that is what you want."

"That's what I want. Thank you."

Then he reverses the vehicle, making as much ruckus as the mason drilling into the wall does. Seamus clenches his teeth irritably and waits until Dajaal is safely out of the gate and out of his hearing before he says to Cambara, "How terrible, terrible, terrible." Not sure she has heard his comment right, she grins.

After a relative pause in which he weighs matters in his head, Seamus speaks to her in English, even though for some reason he is inclined to lapse into Italian today. She has no idea why she expects him to put a cigar or a pipe into his mouth and light it up. She imagines that the hair on his face or head will benefit from becoming more wreathed in ashes of a riotous sort, salt-and-pepper attractive, curls the shape of garlic from the Mezzogiorno, like those of a don at some elite Jesuit college somewhere, where they drink good wine, eat terrible food of the boiled variety, and address one another by their surnames, no titles.

He says, "Welcome to this neck of the woods, my dear girl," and he approaches her with care.

She says, "Good to see you wherever, whenever."

As she chums up to him to give him a peck on the cheeks thrice, she catches a whiff of his sweat; she assumes that he may have had only a birdbath since yesterday, as the house is not yet connected to the city's aqueduct or to an alternative system. She can't help comparing his odor to Zaak's and deciding that this does not disturb her in the least, because Seamus has been hard at work in honest slog, whereas Zaak is a lazy dullard. It's under the pain of being tickled that she has kissed him; she has had to show restraint, despite the temptation of letting go of a chortle, or is she being too girlish for that? She decides to ask the first fully formed question that comes to her.

"How is Bile?" she says.

"At times, he can't tell the difference between day and night," Seamus says.

"How long has he been like that?"

"Off and on for two days now."

"That bad?" she wonders aloud.

"It could be worse," Seamus says. "I hope we can do something about his deteriorating state."

"We? Who is we?" she asks.

"You and I and everybody around him."

Not wanting to catch his eyes, she looks away.

"Especially Dajaal," Seamus adds.

Then he apologizes for rescheduling their meeting. "In one way, I felt things were so barmy I sought solace in work. Came here, where I dossed down in one of the rooms on a mat. I couldn't bear the thought of returning to the apartment. Anyway, it was almost one o'clock in the morning when I was ready to take a break."

"A formidable commitment, indeed," she says.

Her eyes encounter his, and she looks into them from close range, the brownness of his dark pupils, which are in the process of withdrawing from being seen, startles her. Here is a man, she thinks, who might use his shamanic powers to good effect, if he were to choose to.

"There's a lot to be done," he assures her.

She takes in her surroundings, agrees with him, and then adds, "But now that you've laid the foundation of the work, which is the most demanding aspect of any job, I'm certain that the remainder will be a lot easier."

A man, most likely a plumber, walks by, his young assistant following, and they pick up a cistern each and then disappear into the bowels of the house without exchanging a word with either of them.

Seamus says, his eyebrows raised, "Espresso?"

Before responding to his offer, she commits a few moments to discovering where her two charges have ended up and what they have been doing. She locates them easily enough, because they are close by: SilkHair mixing chattily with the armed militiamen operating the gates; Gacal standing at the foot of the ladder, having attached himself to the electrician, busy passing him his tools and sharing a joke with another man removing coils of electric wire from their casings.

"I would love an espresso, thank you," she says.

Then he says, "Sorry," to Cambara and goes straight to where two of the militiamen have turned over a china washbasin to sit on, as they chat away with obvious excitement to SilkHair. Cambara hears him give the command *Kac*—Somali for "Stand up"—his pronunciation of the guttural *c* in *kac* perfect. The young men rise at his behest all right but, in typical Somali fashion, admit no wrong and argue in self-justification. According to them, their body weights together are so light they cannot break the washbasin by sitting on it. Seamus wags his finger at them and, before leaving them, speaks his last salvo. *"Maya, maya,"* he repeats. "No, no."

He beckons her to follow him to the hall, which he has turned into a workshop. He goes behind a worktable, on which there are papers scattered where he may have scribbled his notes. When he sits down, his tools and some of the masks that he has carved since their last encounter are within easy reach. And to the right of the unoccupied surface of the worktable is a flask and beside it two demitasses. In a corner behind the worktable is an espresso machine and next to it several large bottles of mineral water; to the back of Seamus is a small fridge.

"Such heels, these militiamen," he says.

Brooding and silent, he makes the espresso. She is taken with the beauty, the moment she sees them, of the lifelike face and head masks that Seamus has carved for her play in the likeness of eagles and chickens. The masks have become the object of her new enhancement; she is so captivated that she dares not turn her gaze away. No one looks happier than a touchy-feely Cambara who now lifts a full-bodied mask hewed out of fine wood in the semblance of a young eagle, almost bringing it close enough to her face to kiss its gorgeousness, then another, this time one sculpted in the semblance of a mother eagle, then one of a young chicken nervously cackling.

"What do you take with your espresso?"

"A glass of water, please," she says, and she sits down and then turns around and extends both her hands to receive the espresso he has just made for her in one hand and then the water in the other.

Again, she focuses on the masks.

"They are gorgeous beyond belief," she says.

"I'm not done with them."

"I love what I see."

"You are very sweet."

She tells herself that a lot has indeed taken place since her first unannounced call at this house, in a body tent, making her acquaintance of Jiijo and then setting about worming her way into her confidence before moving in on her for the kill, so to speak. It has been a worthwhile effort.

Now she says to Seamus, "Tell me about Dajaal."

"What do you wish to know?"

"What's bothering him?"

Seamus pulls at his liberally grown beard at the same time as he begins to insinuate a couple of the strands of hair close to the right side of his mouth into it.

"There is a lot that he keeps close to his chest. Dajaal has been in a snit ever since he completed his assignment, which, among other things, involved the repossessing of your property. When I pressed him, he admitted to his unhappiness; he is very upset that I've carved masks in the likeness of eagles and chickens," Seamus says. "He does not approve of what we are doing."

"To what do you ascribe this?" Cambara asks.

"I have never known him to reveal his religious leaning to this extent; I've never thought of him as gung-ho devout," Seamus says.

Cambara scowls, then says, "I want to know what has unsettled Dajaal: seeing you carve the masks, or is he just raising a storm about other matters? I am not clear what exactly is forbidden in Islam and what is not."

"It is forbidden to create a likeness of Allah's living creation," replies Seamus. "You will know that the Arabic *sawara*, used for 'creation of likenesses,' is the same word that is used nowadays for photography."

She pauses to reflect on his remarks, and then looks at him as if intending to challenge his certainity, asking, "Don't tell me that photography is forbidden?"

Seamus, grinning, reads from his notes, and, cautious like a septuagenarian treading on slippery ground, replies, "According to the late Sheikh Muhammad Bakheet, a former Mufti of Egypt, photography is not forbidden, because, he says, 'this art is no more than captivating a shade or a reflection by special technique, similar to what we see in mirrors.' What is not allowed is to 'create a likeness which has no previous existence,' a likeness that might be construed as competing with Allah's creation. Statues, sculptures—these are forbidden. Unless they are meant to serve as toys."

She gives serious thought to what he has just said, and then asks, "What are we to make of Dajaal's response?"

"He's organized a posse of men to stab Gudcur, who is a clansman of his and Bile's," Seamus replies. "Why he has chosen to act in this contradictory way when it comes to the masks is beyond me."

"We need Dajaal on our side," Cambara says.

"If you want to know, Dajaal's hostility to the idea of my carving the eagles and chickens has, in part, precipitated my moving here from the apartment I share with Bile last night. And that is saying something."

"Will talking to Dajaal be of any use?" she asks. "Has Dajaal bothered to quote an authority on the basis of which a Muslim is forbidden to carve, say, a mask in the likeness of an eagle or a chicken?"

"I doubt that he knows any authority to quote," says Seamus.

"He does not even pray with any regularity."

She takes a sip of her espresso, cold and bitter.

Seamus goes on, "I've never seen him say his devotions even once in all the time we've spent together, and we've spent many a sunup and many a sundown together. I've known him to be disciplined enough to keep his opinions about many matters to himself. He is so private, Bile and I do not know what he does after work." A despairing look spreads itself on his face as he says, "Now this!"

"Just a thought."

He looks for a long while at his fingers, stained, most likely with Superglue and other adhesives. He applies a clear liquid with an odor reminiscent of linseed oil, and then he rubs his hands together.

"I owe him thanks for all this," she says, her hands gesticulating. "It can't have been easy to achieve what Dajaal has done. Such a strategist, especially if he has had a hand in staging the attack on Gudcur's redoubt, that drew him out of the property."

"Now that I think of it," Seamus says, his face lighting up with the flames of memory, "I remember Dajaal being in a state a few days ago after he and Bile had a long talk, in camera, so to speak. In all the years I've known the two of them and I've known them for donkey's years, neither of them wanted me in on their discussion. Then I didn't see Dajaal for a whole day, and when next he turned up, he was not alone. He had Kaahin, a former fellow officer in the now defunct National Army, in tow. Another in-camera huddle. I knew then that some sort of secret operation that would require renting one or two battlewagons and as many as a dozen highly trained fighters was being mounted. Later, I learned how much it would cost to pull it off. I only know of all this because I was the one who went to our money changer to pay off the men, none of whom I had ever seen."

"Where did the funds come from?"

"Some benefactor from abroad. Otherwise, it is all hush-hush. Kiin is in the picture somewhere. It's all unclear to me."

Cambara suspects that Arda, with help from Raxma, is up to her old tricks, funneling the funds in through an intermediary. Her head pounds with pain, as if the drilling coming from another room were boring into her, reducing her to someone with a brain needing to be overhauled.

"It distresses me that it has come to this."

"Let's not despair. Talk to Bile. About Dajaal."

"Let's find a way of somehow involving Dajaal in the production."

"Talk to Bile; he'll know what to suggest better than I."

"Do you think that having Bile talk to him may persuade him to come to our side of the fence? Or if he were to read the text, he would like it?"

"No idea."

They fall silent, neither able to find anything to say. Gacal comes in to announce that Dajaal is waiting in the car for Cambara to join him, and when she does, she discovers that the engine is on, idling. She gets in, puts on her seat belt, and he reverses, then drives off speedily without a single word.

TWENTY-FIVE

No sooner has Cambara fastened her seat belt and readied to start engaging Dajaal in a conversation about the masks in the play than he whips out his mobile phone and, calling some man by name, tells him that he and a guest are on their way and that he should meet the vehicle at the usual entrance; he won't have time to go to the apartment himself.

It is then that her itinerant eyes fall on two items with religious significance: a rosary and the word "Allah," in Arabic, both hanging down prominently behind the rearview mirror. She stares at them, as though in a hypnotic state. At first she looks alternately bemused and baffled, and then she reasons with calmness that she is being facile in inferring Dajaal's religious inclination or lack thereof from two artifacts that may have come with the car whenever it was imported as a reconditioned vehicle from the Arabian Gulf, as many of the cars plying the roads in Mogadiscio are. Nor does she need reminding that she too has donned a body tent, the type of veil associated in the minds of Muslims with the most devout women, something she is not, yet she has worn it anyway.

It won't do her or her cause any good if she broaches the subject head-on when he appears not to be well disposed toward her. Who knows if he may relent in a day or so, perhaps after he has had a chance to read the text. She will have a word with Bile, who may agree to intercede with him. Moreover, is it not possible that Seamus may have got the wrong end of the stick? It is feasible to interpret Dajaal's posi-

tion as that of making a theological point to an Irishman, something
he does not need to do when speaking with her, a fellow Muslim, albeit secular leaning. In any case, she must try her utmost and without
prejudice to get on the right side of Dajaal's goodwill. To bring this
about, it is unwise to discuss the subject with him now, much less pick
a quarrel with him over his objections to her use of the masks later.
Dajaal deserves a heartfelt thank-you from her.

As she embarks on speaking his praises, she realizes how much
pluck it will take to find the words with which to express not only her
genuine intentions but also her ambiguities. Her mixed emotions stiffen
her features, and she senses that whatever she has to say will not pass
muster and that whatever phrases she lights on will sound either in-
adequate or too formal. Silence being no alternative, she settles on
speaking and does so only after her attempt to make eye contact with
him has failed.

She says, "I've meant to thank you for all your help, Dajaal. You've
put your life and the lives of others on the line. Thank you."

He is as brief in his response as he is self-contained in his reticence. "My pleasure."

Silent, he gives his full attention to his driving, and he looks straight
ahead, conscious, nonetheless, of her stare. If she is daring him to
meet her gaze, then maybe the slight grin that forms and then disap-
pears momentarily is his way of responding to it.

"You've set things in motion, with admirable results, managing
something not short of a miracle: organizing the repossession of my
family property without shedding a drop of blood. Thank you."

"My pleasure." Then silence.

She falls despondently quiet, the faint echo of her voice replaying
in her head. She feels as if she is in a free fall, the string attaching her
to the parachute becoming so entangled that there is no chance of it
opening. The intensity of her vulnerability, the unpredictable nature of
her volatility surprises her as much as it shocks her.

The first to break the silence, Dajaal says, "I fear that Seamus may
have misinformed you or worried you rather unnecessarily."

"Please explain what you mean," she says.

He obliges. "Maybe Seamus has misunderstood me."

Cambara says nothing; waits.

"I have no objections to the use you are making of masks in *your* play," he continues. "All I've said to him is that Islamic Courts folks might object to the use of carved images in theater and that if that were to happen we would run into trouble. Insurmountable trouble."

"Have you ever seen any puppet theater yourself?"

"I have."

"Not in this country?"

"No. In the former Soviet Union," he says, adding, "when I was a student there, training as a military officer. A theater troupe from Ukraine came to perform for us. We also had the Guinean Ballet troupe perform, as they did here in Mogadiscio too, several years later. Both here and in Odessa—I am speaking of the ballet now—the audiences were shocked when the women performing in it bared their breasts in the final act. In Odessa, they gawked and asked for an encore. Here, in Mogadiscio, the audiences applauded. But then the courts were not much of a threat. Siyad Barre was in power then and he wouldn't have countenanced their objections. Things are different now. The Islamists have terrific clout and an armed militia, and cinema owners and TV producers do their bidding when they forbid the showing of a program or the airing of a broadcast."

Cambara recalls that for generations, women in Africa have employed the baring of breasts not so much as art, as the Guinean Ballet is known to have done, but as a political forum, used in opposition to the male order of society, which is corrupt, inefficient, retrograde. But that is not where she wants their talk to go; so she brings it back into line, saying "Do you know anyone who might raise objections to my use of the wooden masks? Personally?"

"I haven't discussed the topic with anyone other than Seamus," he says, "but I know the way things are here. All you need is one hardline Islamist quoting a verse from the Koran on so-called religious grounds, and you will find holier-than-thou crowds with placards gathering in front of the theater, picketing, and stoning the building or anyone entering it. Some self-described Muslim leader is bound to pass a fatwa on the head of the author, and a Mogadiscio businessman, eager to gain popularity and fame, will promise a sum of money in hundreds of U.S. dollars to anyone who will carry out the death sentence. In the meantime, the BBC Somali Service will interview the Muslim leader, the businessman in question, and the author of the puppet theater on their Friday program."

Recalling her conversation with Seamus, she asks what he would do *if,* for whatever reason, someone were to object to the props as being graven. "In other words, on which side of the fence will you be if and when my life is under threat or if the hall in which I produce the play is firebombed?"

He acts as though he is impervious to her stare, which she has now trained on him. It's obvious not only that he is not oblivious to it but also that he is bothered, a little shaken.

"I'll have to give that some serious thought."

"Fair enough."

Neither speaks for a long time.

"You wouldn't say the images are un-Islamic?"

"Some people would," he says.

"*You* wouldn't, would you?"

When he doesn't wish to commit himself to a position, a sudden sense of apprehension quietly seeps like an oil slick into unreachable and therefore uncleanable areas of her awareness, she feels disaffected. Why has she never considered that it may come to this? Which would she rather walk away from: her art or the family property, which is as good as recovered, as good as restored, and therefore all her own? She notices that Dajaal is slowing down, driving at funeral speed and looking now in the rearview mirror, now ahead, as if trying to spot someone.

Her voice meek, she says, "What a stark choice to make!"

Dajaal says, "I am aware of it, yes."

Then both of them catch sight of an elderly man emerging from a huge, dilapidated building, moving in haste toward the vehicle, with his hands flailing excitedly. When the man gets closer, a smile of recognition spreads its wings on the old man's wrinkled face. Dajaal eases off, changing gears and braking, but he does not switch the engine off.

He says to the old man, "Please take this woman to Bile," and to Cambara he says, "Ring me on my mobile when you want to be picked up, and I will do so. Pronto."

He reverses without waving, and off he goes.

A little antsy, Cambara steps out of the vehicle affording herself the time to wave and then address her words of thanks in Dajaal's direction, although she is aware he won't hear them. Maybe she is doing it for the sake of form, given the presence of the old man, of whom she is now in pursuit.

Catching up with him, they walk in parallel past a metal gate and a desolate space, down a stairway into a cool, damp, and dark basement. She wonders where they are, maybe in a sort of cave with flaky walls and an otherworldly echo. Afraid, she stays close to him, as they pass puddles of water, provenance unclear. They walk toward human voices—women chattering noisily, children in playful pursuit of one another—but she cannot tell from where they are emanating, from up above or from another basement below. The old man is hell-bent on getting her to Bile's and she on not being left behind in this place, which is as damp as the bottom of a grave recently dug close to a swamp and emitting a god-awful smell, like Zaak's mouth soon after he has awoken.

The old man, perforce, takes it easy when they come to a slippery staircase, holding on to the side railing, which is rusty and wettish. She too is cautious, moderating her pace to match his, her shoed feet meeting a perilous clamminess. The old man says, "Careful," when she trips, and sighs heavily when she stands on the tips of her toes, flapping about, until she grabs hold of the side railing in time before falling. It is a mystery to her how the old man can figure out where to go or what is happening to her without looking over his shoulders; it is as though he has eyes on his back.

She feels relieved when they emerge into an open space, a former parking lot with no cars now. They climb up a short stairway, past a courtyard with a row of potted flowers and walls covered with creepers, dark, green, and young: the leaves of passion fruit in full splendor.

They stop in front of a metal door, the old man hesitating to press the bell. As for Cambara, she is reading a verse on a plaque nailed to the lintel: "Deliver me from blood guiltiness, O God." Scarcely has she had the time to decide from which holy scripture it was taken than the old man pushes the door open and leaves as fast as someone running away from a crime scene does.

As soon as she walks, unescorted, into the apartment, a telling odor, ominous in its fierceness and rather irrepressible, hits Cambara in the face, overwhelming her senses. The smell takes her back to a memory in her distant past, and which she thinks of no reason to relive: a baby making a terrible mess, soiling its clothes with its own waste, and she, the mother of the child, cleaning it all up.

Feeling protective toward Bile, as soon as she has worked out the source of the odor before taking even one step further. She decides not to allow anyone else, including or rather especially the old man, to be privy to any of this, she closes the door behind her. When she tries to figure out what to do or how to attend to the smell, a recalcitrant thought, disturbing in its meaning, crosses her mind.

Then she approaches Bile, his eyes glazed over, soiled, the dominating image that comes to her one of a strong workhorse with weak knees. He is lying on his side, dissipated, with no more energy to expend on getting up, his left hand under his head, the right hand balled into a fist and stretched forward; both the back and the front of his trousers brown, most probably with his waste; one of his slippers off and the other half on. His right cheek is plastered with the thick deposit of dried yellow detritus probably stained with some partly digested food that the rest of his body, not agreeing with it, has rejected. It is obvious from his misted-over gaze that Bile does not even recognize her, but, as if needing to exonerate him of blame, she remembers that when they met, she was in an "elsewhere veil." Now she is in a caftan, hair uncovered; he is in his apartment and is in an otherworldly state of mind, hardly capable of determining how come he has ended up adorning his clothes with his bodily discharges.

She does what she has done many times before as a mother. First she helps him to a half crouch, allowing him all the time in the world to stay on his knees, then assisting him to lean forward and against her before pulling him, very slowly, and gradually up and up and up into a sitting position on the couch. She minds neither the awfulness of the stench nor the fact that his vomit- and waste-stained cheek and his smudged trousers are rubbing against her body. After she has let him catch his constrained breath, she makes him lie on the couch on his back.

The sun entering the apartment falls on Bile's eyes, but they do not reflect light, only darkness, like that of a night of terrible sorrow. Even so, a distant smile traces his face.

No time to spare, Cambara moves speedily about the apartment and soon enough she finds the bathroom, where she notices an unusual mess: the sink blocked with debris, the toilet and the seat of the bidet edged with slurry, the paper off its holder, unfurled and lying on its side. She goes to the kitchen, fills a kettle with water, and turns the flame on. While the water is boiling, she goes back to the bathroom and runs the taps, discovering that there is hot water for a shower. A minute or so later, she comes out carrying a huge bath towel, a flannel bathrobe, and a bucket full of hot water. All this while, Bile is lost to the world. When she comes to do the preliminary cleansing before leading him into the bathroom for his eventual shower, he does not collaborate or show any resistance, nor does he open his eyes as she wipes his face clean with a flannel. She moves him to this side and then that side until she places the huge bath towel under him. Then she covers him with the bathrobe. She undoes his belt; he stirs, alerting her to his conscious state. But even though he does not push her away, she leaves the room to answer the kettle's singing, and make a pot of tea. She finds a tray and some honey.

She helps him sit up, the bathrobe covering his front, with the huge towel below him needing to be readjusted. If she doesn't solicit his opinion as to what she must do next or does not ask how he is, it is because she believes that he is in no condition to describe what is happening to him. She also knows that for a man of his age, he looks very trim, but there is no knowing what the question "How are you?" might produce and whether, trained as a doctor, he will be too scientific in his litany of complaints. Has he vomited because of an intestinal obstruction or because of a disorder in his inner ear? Has he struck his head against something, injuring it, and then, having lost consciousness, vomited, let go of his poo, as an infant might? His liver may have failed; he might be developing gout, the way a baobab tree might grow a calloused fungus. In a man his age, anything can happen; in one's second babyhood, anything can occur.

She makes the tea strong. Then she finds the sugar, two spoons of which end up in the cup, and stirs it with determined energy. As she places the cup in his hands, after adding honey into the brew, she encourages him to take a sip. She says, "Good for you," in the same way a mother might address an ailing child whom she is encouraging to drink a bowl of broth. "Good for you."

She waits until he puts the rim of the cup to his lower lip to take his first slow swallow. Then she imagines Bile bringing gravitas, more than anyone else she has ever known, to the idea of sadness, nearly ennobling it. Clean of face, because she has already wiped it, less disconsolate of expression, because maybe he now feels energized by her presence, Cambara assumes that she sees intimations of normalcy in his behavior as well as in his body language, optimistically concluding that she is wrong about his being unwell, which now strikes her as no more than a moment's aberration. nothing very serious. She ascribes the swelling of his face to the sudden gaining of much weight due to the indisposition of diarrheal complications. A day's bed rest with lots of TLC thrown in will do him wonders. As a student of living theater, which she hasn't had much time to practice or perfect, she sees him as a man acting out an imagined life at the same time as he is living it, in the end, crowning it all with the finest of details.

Bile extends his hand to her, and she takes it. Pulling him toward her, she is tempted to give him a kiss on the cheek, convinced that this innocuous act might touch him wherever it is that he is hurting and cure him. That this is the first time in a long while that she has found herself in a situation that has so moved her, making her want to give him a kiss on the cheek, must mean something. In Canada, she might not hesitate to give a peck to a man leaving a party soon after being introduced to him but not here, where things are different, especially after the civil war. Some people might look askance at a woman doing what she has done. Not only has she stayed at Zaak's house as a guest, but she has come into Bile's apartment with no chaperone. And now look at what she has been up to: She has disrobed him and is now waiting to give him a shower. No way will such an insular society permit her to employ her theater props of the kind a mufti won't approve.

He won't let go of her hand, no matter how gently she makes her intimations clear: that she wants it back to keep his bathrobe in place. He holds it as a child might a teddy bear in his sleep: hogging, hugging, squeezing it. Her naive hope that the tea will revive him does not materialize, at least not instantly. Now and then he winces as if in pain, then in less than the blink of an eye, his expressions worry her when she tries to give him a shower. His eyes do not seem right, not at all. Maybe so much suffering of whatever nature does not necessarily up-lift one. He is restless, so jumpy, that his eyes are opening and closing with the speed of a worried stutterer's tongue. His eyes are totally vac-uous, a sad, sad emptiness caused, most likely, by the kicking in of a delayed reaction to antidepressants taken ill advisedly.

He talks a fever talk. At first, he is inaudible. Then what he says does not make sense, until she asks him to repeat it two or three times.

"Tell me," he says, "what is gold to someone who does not under-stand its value? What's a mansion to someone who won't live in it? What manner of a man trains as a doctor and helps to cure others but can't apply what he has learned to his own illness?"

Cambara decides she is bearing witness to the birth of a terrible ug-liness, the start of a gradual falling apart of a giant man who is other-wise famous, from what she has heard, for his inner strength. The swelling of his face puts her in mind of Marlon Brando in *Apocalypse Now,* playing the role of Kurtz, a highly disturbed former military offi-cer gone madder and madder with insatiable greed who builds, neu-rotically, a castle of bones out of the brutal massacres of humans. She thinks Bile is caving in, his nihilistic self-assessments confronting the evil manifestations of the darker side of the Somali character in these troubled times. Now silent, he gives the impression of being self-contained, a noble man refusing to share his internal torments with a woman barely known to him. Why pretend to be the willing host of this wretchedness?

Why hasn't he consulted a doctor? Why hasn't he left the country if he is of the view that there are no other doctors good enough to di-agnose his condition? Unless he assumes there is a way of tapping a mysterious underlife in the darkness in which he has dwelled? Maybe something worse than she can ever know is the matter with him. In any case, what can she do? Can she help him come out of the land closed off in a faraway country of profound depression?

There are huge lacks in both of them, she decides. A pity she does not know him well, does not know if he has contemplated suicide. Based on a bottle of pills she is not quite sure she remembers seeing somewhere in one of the rooms, she has her suspicions that this is what he has tried to do. Her mother will tell her, perhaps rightly, that she must not take on someone else's problems. Why must she fall for problem men? But Bile is not a problem man; he is a solution man. To discourage her, her mother will remind her of how Zaak and Wardi battened on her until she was no longer of use to them. See how ungrateful they proved themselves to be; see how they struck out on their own without a care in the world for her feelings. Won't Bile do the same? What guarantees do you have that he will not?

He mumbles something as she finally frees her hand from his clasp. "Are you okay?" she asks, when he chokes on his words.

Grinning, his eyes alight, he says, "It is like blaming your feather mattress for your bedsores." Then he looks at her cockily, staring at her in a way that surprises her. "Like blaming your feather mattress for your bedsores. Can you imagine?"

A premonition, overwhelming in its intensity, comes suddenly in the form of an inner warning voice that advises her not to think of him as an insane man speaking wisdom but as a man gradually recovering his senses. The voice suggests that she must not shun him but remain on her guard.

He sits up and, bringing to bear a lighthearted feeling on his bodily movements, wills himself first to look at Cambara in as friendly a way as he can muster, and then grins. For her. After which, he puts a great deal of purpose into placing the book he has been trying to read aside, managing this simple act with the slowness of a person with Down's syndrome attempting to speak a complicated thought. Bile's eyes dim after a moment, his features darken with dissonant intimations, and his lips move with the terrible exertion of someone emerging out of an ungodly grouse. With his brooding mood seemingly rawer than when she arrived, Cambara fears that he will take her along with him into a world of despair. He rises to his feet and tries a step, hesitates, half tumbles over, then straightens his body, not quite as straight as a bow. His expression is wooden, his eyes as heavy as lead. He finally gives up and lowers his body back into the couch. He sighs. The eerie quality of his unspeaking stare causes her much worry.

He says, "Blame your bedsores on the mattress."

"What are you saying?" she asks.

But he does not answer. There is something disturbingly haunting about the diffuseness of his eyes, as if they are wrestling with an unidentified host of negative forces of unknown origin. At this point, she asks herself if Dajaal, who may have known of Bile's state of physical and mental deterioration, has set her up. But why? Is he throwing her a challenge? See how you fare—you who have a liking for difficult tasks, stray boys with no parents, and armed youths with no future. Or is Dajaal intimating, in his own way, that she is somehow the cause of Bile's torment and that it is time she dealt with it?

"Come," she says.

"Where?"

"A shower will do you a lot of good."

He takes his time to wrap himself with the bathrobe, and, discouraging her from treating him like an invalid anymore, he stands up, first swaying a little and eventually standing upright before doddering toward the bathroom.

"Do you need any help?" she says to his back.

He stops walking and, nodding, mumbles a phrase that sounds to Cambara like "Yes, please." She hears him not with her ears but with her heart.

"The trousers," he says, pronouncing the word as if it has more consonants. "My legs are too weak," he adds. "My hands too."

It takes several clumsy efforts for her to help him remove his trousers, at one point the two of them nearly falling into a heap. Then, despite the pervasive odor, she remains with him until she runs the water and he has had a douche. Then she finds and then passes him a clean towel, a pair of slip-ons, a T-shirt, and a sarong.

She leads him by the hand to his bedroom. The bed looks slept in, the room stuffy. She opens the windows to let in air. After she has tucked him in, she returns to the bathroom to soak his soiled clothes. In the kitchen, she clears space and finds enough ingredients to prepare a vegetable consommé. When she hears him mumbling a few words, maybe calling to her, she finds a bowl and goes to feed him. Again she says, "Good for you," giving him spoonfuls of it. On her way out of the room, she takes interest in the photographs decorating the walls: of two girls, one of them pretty and ordinary looking, the other a Down's syndrome, and of an older woman, who shares family resemblance with Bile. Then back to the bathroom to soap his dirty clothes, pouring on them water close to boiling, almost burning herself when she first puts her hand in.

It bothers her that she cannot decide what to do next. There is no shortage of people to ring up: Dajaal, Seamus, Kiin, Farxia—the only medical doctor, albeit a gynecologist, only she doesn't recall taking her mobile number.

Back in the bedroom, she watches him eat his soup. The smell of the sick; the clothes worn night and day; pairs of socks dropped on the floor and not picked up—these convince her to take charge, the urge turning into a commitment. Now she remembers Seamus or Dajaal saying that Bile has good and bad days.

She isn't certain if she is imagining it or if Seamus has said that when Bile's days are bad, they are so bad, like the darkness of winter descending on the soil of Bile's mind, that nothing will grow on such a soil. If good, the days are bright; the sun shines and shines all the time. If this is his bad, bad day, will she get to see his good day?

"I've been meaning to ask?" he says.

"Please," she encourages him.

"Doesn't it feel lonely?"

How bizarre: a man speaking in non sequiturs.

"Doesn't what feel lonely?"

"Doesn't a veil make the wearer feel lonely?"

Cambara can't think of an answer.

Again a question. "You know what?" he says.

"Tell me," she encourages him.

"Every virtue is its own reward."

Then silence, as total as that of a classroom in which matriculants are writing their finals. Cambara wonders if grave changes are in store for her, and she is nervous, like a teenager in love for the first time. She is in a twitter, because she has met Bile on his home ground and has proven herself worthy of his trust. She hopes to deal with his and her problems with the subtlety of a highly professional puppeteer controlling her marionettes with the help of invisible wires.

Then she phones Dajaal. "Please pick me up in about an hour and a half."

"How is Bile?"

"He is okay."

TWENTY-SIX

Bile's secret, which is how Cambara wants to think of his indisposition, will be safe with her, for she has no wish to speak of it to anyone, neither to Seamus nor to Dajaal. She assumes that given Bile's sense of discretion—why does she always tend to believe in her heart that she knows him when she doesn't—he may not approve of her broadcasting his bodily aberrations to his close friends and sundry acquaintances. At least, from the time she spent with him, she got the impression that he is a discreet man.

When she thinks that Dajaal has left to pick her up, she rings Seamus to ask him what the two boys, her charges, are up to and when he, Seamus, is likely to return to the apartment. When Seamus says that he won't be there until early evening, if not much later, and that, in any case, he will bring along a takeaway and that she needn't worry herself about Gacal and SilkHair, for they are being kept purposefully busy, she gets down to the business of ridding the apartment and herself of the rank odor. She strives to work as quietly as possible so Bile might find shelter in the sleep of his embarrassment. She even considers disconnecting her mobile and the landline to make sure that no ringing phones disturb him. On second thought, she abandons the idea as being too drastic a measure.

She scrubs the floors of the bathroom and then has a long, very hot shower herself before changing into the first outfit she lays her hands on, an ill-fitting pair of baggies and a matching top—she hopes they are Bile's—before washing her own clothes to get rid of the intrusive smell. The stench is so pervasive that not only has it stuck to her body, escorting her everywhere, but it has also started to reside in her nostrils, as if permanently glued to the hair growing there. She washes her own clothes, then she bolts the bathroom door from the inside and loads the wet clothes into the drying machine, praying that Bile does not wake up, need the bathroom, since this appears to be the only one, and find her in his pajamas, dressed like a dog's dinner. Moreover, part of her is fearful that he may have misunderstood her honorable right-minded actions. But what are they, these respectable intentions? What are her designs, since she must have some?

As she listens to the thudding, rhythmic sound of the drying machine, she returns, in memory, to the first few days spent at Zaak's as a guest, and she cannot help comparing her disapproval then, exposed as she was to Zaak's malodorous condition, to her attitude today, which, on the face of it, appears more tolerant. She wonders if she has found Zaak's evil-smelling mouth disturbing because it did not connect her in any way to one of her former states: that of mother to a sweet young boy and that of daughter to a bedridden father so sick the last few months of his life that he would occasionally wet his bed and soil his clothes. That in her mind she prefers referring to the mishap involving Bile as a bodily aberration and seems not to be highly disturbed by it can only indicate that she is inclined to suffer it without it getting under her skin the way Zaak did. Anyhow, how does it happen that in less than a fortnight she has had the fortune or misfortune to meet two men, one of them with a God-almighty BO that you can't help avoiding, the other smeared with his waste, like some tribal dancer painted with dung?

Apropos of this, she quotes to herself the Somali wisdom that if feces were wealth, everybody would call it by a different name. She reasons that she is in all likelihood more charitable toward Bile because of his kindness to her. If she is intolerant of Zaak and cannot endure his smelly presence, it is simply because he has been uncompromising and been beastly toward her.

She sits on the toilet, with the lid down, as much for the comfort of resting her exhausted bones as for the fact that it might afford her a pause to make sure that she does not overreach herself. Then she resolves to hold herself in check and not to lament the sad truth that she has not been alone with her thoughts since getting to Mogadiscio, what with the constant interferences and external forces that have seldom allowed her to concentrate her mind wholly on herself. Rushing here, rushing there, a light makeup before an all-woman's party, run, and run, bone tired. Granted, where in Toronto, she might entertain an idea for its own sake, indulge herself to her heart's content, and, if she is of a mind, unplug her phone, take a break from it all, and lie fallow like the land of a farm resting, here it has not been possible for her to lead a private existence. Always in some car, being ferried there and back; constantly in the sight of a gun, never mind if it is friendly; always under someone's constant supervision purportedly for her safety; sentries at the gate, either granting or denying her entry; armed youths out to ensnare her. How annoying that her movements in this city are restricted.

Home is Mogadiscio, home from Toronto, but the question is: Is she the homing pigeon among the cats, or has the cat been put among the pigeons to flutter their dovecotes? No doubt, her presence has brought a number of situations to a head and has somehow stimulated sufficient interest in a handful of persons who have made a number of changes, many of them for the better. The way Cambara sees it, she has prompted Kiin to set things in motion with the help of the Women's Network, Zaak having to all intents and purposes shown her that he wouldn't give her a hand. Bile has few equals, in that he has stepped in, prodding Dajaal into action, without her ever soliciting his intervention. And Dajaal has delivered: He helped to repossess the property but not before Kiin and Farxia conspired to rid it of Jiijo, every one of them risking their lives. In the meantime, Seamus too has joined in, most likely at Bile's suggestion. What more can she want?

She gets to her feet, pulls the door of the drying machine open to determine if her clothes are now sufficiently dry for her to wear them. They are. Scarcely has she taken them out when another of her knee-jerk reminiscences deposits her at the door to yet another memory: that of her cooking for Zaak's militiamen. She stops in midmotion, telling herself that feeding is one of the most ancient strategies women have employed to cope with the restlessness caused by men's overabundance of testosterone; feeding them is one way of disempowering them, even if for a period of brief duration. Women have fallen back repeatedly on making men ingest the foods they have cooked and "bewitched" them, in this way pacifying their conjugal cohorts' agitated nerves. It is not surprising how, in many languages—Somali included—the notion of eating is interchangeable with lovemaking.

She dwells in an animated suspension, neither managing to start putting on her clothes, which although not completely dry are wearable, nor to embark on another activity. One thought leads to another, and she is telling herself that there is no doubt in her mind that if fighting off the militiamen on the day she met Dajaal and Bile is seen as the first time fortune smiled in her favor so as to make things work to her advantage, then cooking for Zaak's militiamen when she did, mollifying and therefore moderating their behavior, was the second most important step. Moreover, she will never forget the youths' initial shock of discovering that chopping off a chicken's head with the intention of lunching on it, pulling its viscera out in one go, and plucking its feathers after boiling it are no easier matter than putting your finger on the trigger of an AK-47 and killing a human being.

Not sure that she has heard a tapping on the door, she listens for it a second time, but nothing happens. Then she hears the sound of the key turning in the apartment door, and she ceases all movement, waiting for the person who is now indoors to identify himself before coming out of the bathroom and making her appearance.

"It is me, Seamus," the voice says.

"I am in the bathroom," she lets him know.

Then she takes off the borrowed clothes she has been wearing and puts on her own, even if a bit damp in the armpits or the nether regions in which some moisture has gathered. She comes out, her hands busy smoothing the creases.

Maybe there is no basis for her supposition that Dajaal is trying to avoid her and has, instead, persuaded Seamus to replace her. To ascertain if this is the case, she says, "I rang Dajaal to come get me."

"There has been a small security problem," Seamus explains. "Dajaal has dropped me off and gone back to deal with it urgently. Something to do with a kinsman of Gudcur's who's turned up armed at one of the checkpoints leading to your family property. One of Qasiir's boys shot the kinsman dead point-blank. Dajaal is organizing both the removal of the corpse and the burial before nightfall."

In her mind, she pushes all that has to do with skirmishes and gunfights aside, because she sees these armed combats as belonging to a realm different from her domain. And now that she is calmer and feels less compelled to deal with emergencies resulting from Bile's affliction, cleaning up the mess after him and coping with his needs, she takes fresh notice of things. How well-appointed the apartment is; what a refined handiwork, presumably Seamus's, from what Kiin has informed her.

"When will this insecurity end?"

"Not for a good while yet," Seamus says.

"You seem unfazed. How do you manage?"

"Haven't I told you that I am from Belfast?"

"Even so, this is Mogadiscio. Remember that."

"So. What if it is?"

There is an awkward silence.

"Tea?"

"Yes, please."

Seamus goes into the kitchen to make it. She joins him there just about. She stands facing him, her back leaning against the doorjamb, her legs splayed. She finds the kitchen pleasantly kitted with all the gadgets you need to produce a decent meal. She deems it slightly impolite to ask, but she suspects that Seamus is the factotum running this ménage, the efficient handyman with the practical know-how, the cook, the repairman when the generator packs up. Typical of a Somali to be the beneficiary of "Euro largesse." The sad truth is that when death comes baying at the gates in the form of perennial famines, the Somali appeals to the Euro sense of humanity and asks to be fed. However, in defense of Bile, again from what Kiin has told her, he led a very active life before he became indisposed. A doctor in charge of a refuge. Not many of them about.

"Tea with biscuits in the living room?"

Changing scene, she brings the tea tray; he, coming after her and humming what she imagines to be a Somali song of the nationalistic variety, is already opening the wrappings of the crackling biscuits. Her gaze, wandering, rests for a few moments on a runic writing: "The sun shall be turned into darkness, and the moon into blood."

Whatever does that mean, she thinks. He offers her a biscuit; she pours out the tea. No sugar—she drinks her tea white; he drinks his as it comes, black.

A very long silence.

"About Bile," he says, broaching the subject, with the compunction of someone to whom has fallen the unenviable task of looking after an ailing person.

Seamus tries his damnedest not to appear unnecessarily intrusive. Cambara waits for him to continue, convinced that he is about to launch into an explanation of what, in his view, is the matter. But he doesn't, his eyes furtively focusing first on his watch and then on a spot to the right of her, maybe on a stain at the bottom of her dress that she has failed to clean up. Cambara supposes that he has picked up a faint sound coming from Bile's room, the way a mother does when her baby is sleeping somewhere close, and, jumpy, he gets up and, without saying anything to her, paces back and forth, muttering something to himself, looking in the direction of Bile's room, door closed, maybe waiting for confirmation of whether he has heard something or not.

His next move takes him to the sideboard, where he sets about laying a table in record time: three places, three plates, three table mats, crockery, water tumblers each with ice cubes and slices of lemon in them, and a large bottle of mineral water.

"Can I help?" she says timidly

"Just in case Bile wakes up."

"What would you like me to do?"

"When he does wake up, I will want him to eat something, because I've assumed from having been in the kitchen while making tea that he hasn't cooked and you haven't prepared a meal for him." Then, like a caregiver remarking on the habits of his ward, "That he is fretful in his sleep means that he is having a bad, bad day."

Seamus walks into the kitchen, washes his hands, puts on an apron, fumbles about in the pantry, brings out and opens several tins containing soup and green peas, empties the contents into microwave containers, and, using gloves, sticks them in the microwave. He turns the cooker on; brings out onions, chopping and frying them in olive oil; opens a tin of tomatoes; turns and pulls out pans, spices, garlic; and voilà, an easy-to-make sauce in quick time. He lowers the flames so nothing burns, then joins her, takes a sip of his cold tea, frowns, and asks aloud if she might like a fresh pot. She offers to make it; he shrugs a don't-bother shoulder shrug, and sits down, one part of him listening for a sound from Bile's room, a second timing the oven and the sauce on the cooker, and a third attending to her. She finds herself remembering Dalmar as a baby and her early days as a mother.

"In what state did you find him?" Seamus asks.

"Lying amid his waste."

"But he won't listen."

She won't allow herself to ask the question "To what won't he listen?" no matter how often she wants to; she is unable to voice her sentiments: "But you don't ask someone in his state what to do, you just do it." What's more, she remembers her vow not to talk about what she saw to a living soul. She knows she has no choice but to leave the job of what to do, from now on, to those who have been close to him for much longer. She raises her head and, when she encounters Seamus's expectant look, she turns away, evasive.

"It breaks my heart for you to have seen Bile in this sort of sorry state," Seamus says. "I've known him for much longer, from when we were both in our early twenties, and he was a live wire then, bright, fun to be with. We spent the wonder that is youth together, in Padua. We were a threesome, Bile, Jeebleh, and me. Jeebleh came to visit us a couple of years ago, a visit that set off a tremor that became an earthquake. Death called, and Bile's half-brother answered; then Raasta, Bile's niece, and her Down's-syndrome companion and playmate, Makka, to whom he was attached, left the country for schooling in Dublin, as did Shanta, Bile's younger sister, and her husband, Faahiye. From then on, his emotional fix, especially since Raasta's departure, has been one of sadness, marked by inactivity. He doesn't want to practice medicine, his thinking has slowed down to a frightening pace, he has disturbed sleep, and the smallest things upset him. Much of this is set off by a childhood trauma, linked to his half-brother Caloosha killing his, Bile's, father."

Seamus falls silent, and, hearing no sound emanating from Bile's room, he gathers the tea things and returns to the kitchen to do what's necessary. He puts the food that is ready in bowls and comes back. "Sorry," he says.

"Why are you sorry this time?"

He doesn't speak directly, because he goes to the kitchen, fetches the food, and lays it out on the table, maybe waiting for Bile to emerge. In her imagining, Seamus is apologetic because he has probably entertained the vision of Bile and Cambara talking and getting to know each other. Maybe he thinks that she is good for him, that he likes her enough to share Bile with her as a friend. Maybe Seamus believes that she might inspire Bile sufficiently to brighten his dark days, liven up his lethargic hours, and banish his pessimism. Maybe he had hoped that Bile would benefit from her company until he became too exhausted to stay up. Or perhaps he finds his own prying into their private conversation invasive. He comes back and he sits.

"Sorry I was not around when you got here."

"What matters is that you are here now."

Seamus's eyes are dimming, Cambara supposes, from the strenuous effort of concentrating on several things at the same time. Also, something is disturbing him, for he is looking around as if someone has changed the position of the furniture in the apartment, his gaze traveling from one item to another, his nose seemingly active, busy trying to identify the foreign odor. Earlier, she remembers him focusing on a stain at the bottom of her caftan; now he is zeroing in on a blotch on the top end of the chair farthest from him, his nose twitching in the disturbed attitude of a house-proud person discovering a blemish where there oughtn't to be any. He gets up quickly, as if driven by the anxiety to isolate the culprit chair, quarantining it in its own corner to be dealt with later, but he makes a point of not looking in her direction, lest she assume that he is blaming her for it.

"Had I known?" he says, as he takes his seat.

She looks deep into his eyes, as she says, "You were doing more useful jobs in our family house than I could ever dream of undertaking. I am most indebted to you."

"Did you see him take any pills?"

"No. What pills does he take?"

"He is irregular about the antidepressants he ingests," Seamus explains. "He takes a combination of drug therapy: some when he is in a dejected mood, others when he suffers from an abrupt onset, yet others when he is working on a quick-recovery plan. When he is regular, he eats fluoxetine. I know that Dajaal rang him to inform him of your visit, and although I have nothing to go on, I am guessing that to pre-pare himself for it, he took imipramine, administering the intramus-cular injection himself. This may have resulted in his body's excessive reaction to the drug. He has a large store of medication. I've known him to take enuretic tablets—you know, they are for bed-wetters—saved from the days when he ran the clinic at The Refuge."

"He belongs in a hospital," she says.

"Not here. A hospital in Europe or America."

"I agree with you."

"I've proposed to fly him to Nairobi, for a start, and from there somewhere else. He won't hear of it."

"A great pity. Such a waste."

Seamus says, "He has been having a terrible time of late and won't even hear of us hiring a twenty-four-hour nurse or of considering con-sulting doctors outside the country. Up in the early part of the day, functioning reasonably well; in the latter part, down in the depth of a well as dark as it is damp and worrying. Clinical depression of the worst sort."

All she can say is "I had no idea."

"It will be said of him—if something is to happen to him, God forbid—that he has made a deliberate effort to mess up his life, like a man willing his own slow death."

"Is he in a position to know?"

"Why does he avoid taking his pills for the longest time possible and then eat them by the fistful, dozens and dozens of them, well beyond the normal dose?" Seamus says.

"A death wish."

"I attribute this to the well of his bottomless sorrow, which the years have dug in and around him, and which no words can describe, it is so deep," Seamus says. "In addition to the childhood trauma of his half-brother murdering his dad, I trace his indisposition—here comes my psychobabble, if you can bear it—to his decades-long detention in in-humane conditions, the worst of it caused by his being kept in total iso-lation. You may not know that he spent years in isolation after being given a life sentence for opposing the tyrannical regime, whose misrule led to the civil war. It was no accident that the prison gates were opened, this coinciding with the flight of the then dictator in an army tank, a tactic encouraged by armed militiamen at the command of a certain general, who just happened to be a clansman of Bile's and who eventually became a warlord with his own fiefdom in the divided city, the southern part of which went to him and the north to another warlord. Anyhow, the tyrant's fall happened to coincide with Bile gaining his freedom, the birth of Raasta, his niece, and the collapse of the state. To all intents and purposes, it appeared as if he had pulled through, put his memories of his worst years behind him, once he set up The Refuge and ran it with incredible devotion. This act of supreme ingenuity served to hold several of his sides together, enabling him to be close to his niece and her playmate, Makka, and his sister, each of them contributing to the rationale behind The Refuge and Bile's well-being. You would have appreciated it if you had come in its heyday or even just before the idea of its irrelevance began to become clear, soon after Jeebleh's visit."

Cambara raises her eyebrows, asking a number of unspoken questions about Jeebleh: Who? What? Why?

Seamus's moment of hesitation prolongs itself into a minute of stillness, his mouth slightly ajar but not issuing a sound.

Seamus goes on, "You see, it was a couple of years after he set up The Refuge that Bile and I linked up and, together, made things work and pretty well, I would say. We created our own paradise in a country that had gone to hell, a country with little hope of ever recovering from a state of total reliance on handouts from the international community. We did what we could then to assist in providing a rationale to disarm the militias through training them at a younger age and weaning them from glorifying the gun. But there was—there is—need for more universal commitments; no do-gooders can do as much as it will take to reconstruct the country's infrastructure, reorient the people of this nation so they might find their proper bearing and help them to reestablish the state on a viable footing. Boring rhetoric, boring politics, yes, but the truth is that the political class has failed this country. Nor can you speak intelligently about Somalia or for that matter about Bile or Jeebleh or Dajaal without the wholesale condemnation of the cowardly intellectual class too."

Silent, Cambara thinks that not many people have eyes like Seamus's, which are like a falcon's: alert to an impending peril, darting in several directions in the time it takes you to blink just once. Now she watches him stare straight ahead, his mind elsewhere and mulling over things. Cambara wonders if she is correct in interpreting his expression as rueful or as just plain hangdog, in that he has been lacking in humility, having stressed his contribution to his friend's wellness more than he likes.

"Lately, however, since your arrival, actually his ups have been mightily high and his downs terribly down, highs and lows, which have brought us closer to despair."

Cambara is surprised to hear that she plays such a role—though perhaps not too surprised, given the prominent role Bile has played in her imagination, and especially now that she is convinced without evidence to go on that Bile has been involved with reclaiming her property. "How do they manifest, these changes?"

"He has spoken of his dreams, in which he wakes up dressed in a stranger's clothes or dining with persons totally unknown to him," Seamus says.

"Does he enjoy the meals?"

"Toward the end of these eat-until-you-can't-eat-any-more occasions, he feels that they are cause for celebration, especially when he has a glimpse of you, better still when he meets you. Only you invariably arrive as he is about to depart, or you are seated in a place he cannot get to, because the path to you is inaccessible."

"How does he respond?"

"In the dream, his anxiety goes haywire," explains Seamus. "His highs and lows keep vacillating, his moods continue to seesaw. One moment he behaves normally, even if he finds himself in a stranger's clothes and among people whom he does not know, and in the next instant he becomes unpredictable, he is irritable and gets into fights."

"Very odd and worrying."

"Bile strikes me as an adolescent falling in love for the first time. This, in a sense, is the case, considering that before he met you that one time, in the car, he never seemed capable of love. He is not a man to display his emotions. When he was younger, he was so self-controlled that he could choose not to show his affections toward a woman, say, and operate clandestinely instead, having affairs on the quiet. But they were never affairs of the heart—maybe brief relationships for companionship or just for the heck of it. I have known him for more than half his life; I know the man well, better than most."

"Does anyone beside you know of any of this?"

"Dajaal does."

"And what is Dajaal's take?"

"When I've encouraged Bile to pursue the dictates of his heart, suggesting that he search you out, look you up, ring you up, fix an appointment with you, do something, do anything, Dajaal has opposed it."

"On what basis?" She can hear the suspicion in her voice, and regrets it.

"Not on the basis of the clan business."

"I wouldn't have thought so."

"Dajaal argues that this is no way for a man of Bile's age to act, fall in love at first sight," Seamus says. "You'll know it more than I do, but Dajaal's reaction is no different from the reactions of many a Somali, typical. They do not expect a man of Bile's background and age to do certain things, even if he is sick with love."

Cambara is tempted to tell Seamus that what she feels for Bile is not so very different, even though, because she is a woman, she might use different terms to describe her emotions, but she stops herself just before the words make their way out of their secret place, where she has hidden them ever since meeting Bile.

"There is another way of explaining Dajaal."

"What's that?" she asks.

Seamus says, "He is worried about the changes that your presence in Bile's life will bring into their relationship and is afraid he will lose out, because you might decide to take him away to Canada. With you. You can imagine how much that would devastate him."

It is at that instant that two things happen almost simultaneously: The phone rings, and Seamus answers it quickly, in an undertone, not wanting its squealing to wake Bile up. But then, just as suddenly, Bile comes into Cambara's line of vision, leaning against the doorjamb, tall, very thin, his gaze conspiratorial, as if reminding her not to divulge their secret.

Seamus, unaware of Bile's whereabouts, says to Cambara, "Dajaal is downstairs in the parking lot and is waiting to take you to your hotel, if that is where you want to go."

Nodding, Cambara rises to her feet and then points her chin in Bile's direction to alert Seamus of the new development. She takes long strides toward Bile, hugs him long and lovingly, and whispers a few private words in his ear.

She lets go and holds him at some distance, her lips trembling with the words that she struggles to flesh them out with sound. They look each other in the eye for a long while, neither moving nor saying anything, Cambara's hands on Bile's elbow. Then she turns away from him and waves to Seamus, thanking him for everything, promising to look him up. Then, with her head in a muddle, her legs almost failing to carry her away from the apartment, because she does not want to go, she hopes that she will find the parking lot, where Dajaal is waiting for her in the car.

"Don't bother. I'll see myself out," she says, leaving.

TWENTY-SEVEN

Going down with no one to guide her out of the building, Cambara runs into a blind cat soon after bouncing down the stairway, two steps at a time. She comes almost to a superstitious impasse, and is tempted to go back, pick up the cat, and knock on the apartment door to make Bile and Seamus aware of its presence. She decides not to, and continues on her way down, determined to get to Dajaal fast.

She seems most herself when she thinks that she can adequately describe her own current mental state as turbulent, because she is at a crossroads where anything may happen: She could lose almost every major gain she has made at one single go or just as easily hold on to what she has won and procure more. This is the arbitrary character of civil war: wanton in its injustice, casual in the randomness of its violence. No law protects you; everything is in disorder. In great part, it is Dajaal who decides. In one manner or the other, all depends on him. He is now playing a role as significant as the one Zaak did in her first couple of days, as Kiin did for a while, Kiin who assisted her in planting her feet on terra firma. How is she to continue from here on?

She is reflecting on the nature of her agitation and whether she can do something about the inopportunity of Bile's and her affections—as Dajaal seems to see it—when she not only loses her way in the labyrinth of her conflicting emotions but also follows the wrong fork in the footway leading down. She steps straight into the passageway ahead of her, having been misled by the unseasonable brightness of the sun at this hour, her mood so low that it is imposing a sinking feeling on her thinking. It occurs to her, after a short while, that she is actually walking away from the light into a narrow corridor that is darkening the farther she proceeds. She doubts if this pathway will eventually conduct her to the parking lot. Lo and behold, she has ended up in a basement.

Disoriented, as if she has walked into a cul-de-sac when she expected a throughway, she decides that the basement does not appear to have even a tenuous link to the upper portion of the building from where she has just come. Nothing makes sense to Cambara anymore. She knows that going forward, when she has no idea where she might end up, is no option worth pursuing, but then backtracking in hope of retracing her steps and finding Bile and Seamus's apartment does not sound appealing either. She feels she is at the center of a storm of her own making, she, the unseeing eye.

Her head fills with childhood memories, above all her intimate conversations with the echoing darkness late at night in a house faintly ringing with the depth of a predawn silence. Now that she is much older, grieving for her dead son and trying to build an alternative to the life she shared with Wardi, not to speak of the false life her mother had imposed on her, she does what she used to do as a child to fend off the oncoming feeling of fear. She improvises a song of her own composition and hums a half-remembered tune. After which, she repeats to herself some of her favorite lyrics, "Hello, darkness, my old friend." The phrase caresses her lips, stirring and activating them with pleasant remembrances. Her heart beats frenziedly fast, her mind active in its effort to freeze-frame the memory into an image: that of a child in tacit dialogue with daytime darkness, reminiscent of an eclipse suddenly descending on the cosmos with Stygian blackness. But where is she? And what manner of basement is this? Will someone kindly lend her the wick of a candle?

Cambara wonders what impression she will make on Arda, on Zaak, on Dajaal, on Kiin, above all on Bile, if they hear of it: the first time Bile and Seamus acquiesce to her request that she see herself out and they oblige, she loses her way. In a basement of all places. To the best of her memory, no one has ever spoken of shadowed forests hereabouts, definitely not in the center of an ancient city that has been under civil war siege for some ten-plus years. But where has she gotten to? Might it be that she is conjuring it all up out of an eagerness to be with Bile? She is no doubt anxious about the sightless cat too, a good enough ruse to excuse her knocking on Bile and Seamus's apartment door and say-ing, "Isn't it funny I can't seem to go away from you? Fancy finding an eyeless cat going down and then losing my way in a forest, most likely, of my own manufacture. Here, do let's feed her. A saucer for her milk, please. And I will need a mattress on the floor to crash on." Then she'll stay. But how much further will such tactics take her?

In her attempt to get a good hold of herself, Cambara reminds her-self how, in a number of children's stories, among them *Pinocchio,* children who do not follow the set paths and knowingly or even mis-chievously stray away from them often meet with terrible conse-quences: *Alice in Wonderland,* in which the principal character goes down a rabbit hole; and C. S. Lewis's *Chronicles of Narnia,* in which Lucy and then the others pass through an open-ended wardrobe and, as their story progresses, try to grow the necessary will and strength to overcome impossible difficulties. Is her own adventure one that is to equal theirs? Does it mean that something awful, something disagree-able is about to happen to her for being naughty, and, if so, what form will this take? What has she done to deserve this punishment? The blind cat? Does her present misfortune emanate from her stubborn re-fusal to attend to the needy animal? Did she expend energy and good-will on cleaning up Bile because she is returning a favor and investing in him? Did she help Bile undress so he could shower and then wash his dirty clothes for the same reason? A blind cat is a blind cat; what can it do for her? And what endearments, to which only the two of them are privy, did she whisper in Bile's ear before leaving?

There are protean qualities to her current worries, which alternately take the shape of a fear that keeps pounding on the door to her brain or of one that she can now trace to a childhood memory. In her recall, she goes truant, and, instead of coming home, being a latchkey child on some of the afternoons when her parents returned late, she follows a road show. Then, just as she prepares to take a longer route home— not wanting to meet Zaak, alone at home, because he has seen her kiss another boy, a classmate, and she is fearful he might tease her— Cambara pawns her wristwatch for money to buy a ticket to watch the late matinee circus. She knows she will not come home until dark, but that does not seem to worry her either.

As it happens, her mother is about to organize a search party—in those days, not many households had telephones—and her father is about to go to the nearest police station and report her as missing, when she lets herself in with her key. Coming in from the dark outside into the part of the house where a bulb is burning bright, she looks like an alley cat that has just fled from a fight with a raft of foxes.

Now, mysteriously, the darkness of the night lifts all of a sudden, and the basement is ablaze with light, as if there were a skylight. Cambara hears her name called several times, and she follows the sound. Eventually, she emerges into the evening twilight and the flight of outside steps. She finds Dajaal waiting and saying, "Where have you been?"

Because she cannot herself explain where she has been, why or what has made her take the wrong fork in the road—if that is what she has done, and she doubts it—she keeps quiet, saying nothing, afraid that he might think her mad. She walks past him and gets into the car, using the front door, which she has found open. It does not make sense to blame it all on her bad sense of direction.

Just before moving, he asks, "Where?"

She says, "To the family property."

"Not to the hotel?"

"Later," she says. "Let's pick up my boys."

He starts the engine and lets it idle, his hand resting on his chin as though he is considering several choices available to him. Then he changes gears and moves speechlessly, as if saying what is on his mind will amount to nothing more than wasted breath.

She wishes she had the gumption to ask him what he thinks about Bile's dreams, which she suspects that Seamus will have shared with him. How might Dajaal interpret the dream in which Bile is in a stranger's clothes? For she has been in *his*, Bile's, when washing her own and waiting for them to dry. And if she had come out at Seamus's reentry into the apartment as he called out her name, he might have thought of the dream as uncanny fortuity, mightn't he?

There comes a stage in every story, Cambara reflects, when the protagonist is alone, afraid, worried, too exhausted, or too hungry to continue. Perhaps she has reached that point in her story. Is this why she is feeling queasy?

In the car, Dajaal driving, eyes focused on the road, she sits upright, looking ahead of herself, her hands in her lap, her fingers entwined, the thumb and middle fingers twirling her wedding ring, as if she is trying to remove it. She is having difficulties doing so, because it is too tight, the ring having set into the flesh around it and the joint having grown bigger over the years. She feels that she has come to the point in the story when the protagonist has changed from one state of being and hasn't made the full circle in which the metamorphosis is complete. She is lonely, fearful, and begins to envisage feeding on hunger itself.

Dajaal says, "My turn has come to thank you."

"Why is that?"

Turning to her, almost touching her thigh with his half-extended hand and withdrawing it just in time, he repeats, "Thank you."

Surprised, she asks, "What have I done?"

He replies, "Seamus told me when I called a few minutes ago on the phone about what you've done for Bile. We're both touched and very grateful to you. You've been exceptionally kind. Seamus describes you as a woman with a noble spirit, and he commends you. So do I."

"The pleasure to have been of small assistance has been mine," she says. "Not that I've done much, to be honest with you."

She observes, when she studies his face, that the heat mixed with emotion has made the veins on Dajaal's forehead stand out, so that they resemble serpents crisscrossed with deep furrows. How the years have plowed the fields of his head, leaving only thin wisps of hair with a lot of pluck.

"As for the masks, the props for your play?"

She sits forward. "Yes?"

"I've given the matter serious thought," he says. "You won't have anything to worry about. You produce your play the way you like it, and I will support you and provide you with adequate security for as long as it is in production."

Has someone else spoken to him to make him change his mind? If so, who? Bile can't have done it; he was in no condition from the moment Dajaal dropped her off until he came to pick her up. Unless they talked in the period between the moment she left the apartment and said her good-bye to Seamus and Bile, traversed the passageways of the basement, and met up with Dajaal. It is all very confusing. How long could she have been in the basement? Couldn't have been half an hour. Whoever did it, someone suggested that Dajaal reconsider his opposition to the use of the masks and moderate his views. Who? She has no idea. Does Dajaal's shift of position warrant her worry? The thought of it and what would happen if he did change it yet again gives her the shakes. She hopes that she will muddle through and come out the other end in one solid piece.

She says, "Very kind of you."

Dajaal continues, "Seamus, who at times knows Bile's mind better than I, not only because they have known each other for much longer and have shared their good and bad days, has intimated to me that Bile is of the view that we take a positive outlook on life, especially when it matters. And I agree with him."

She says nothing, judging what Dajaal has just said to be no more than smug waffling, if taken on its face value. She settles on waiting until he has committed himself to an unequivocal position.

He goes on, "Seamus and I talked after I had taken you to Bile's and later, when I was bringing him back. Again, we spoke after I waited long enough for you in the car park and you did not show up."

"I can't have been gone long," she says.

"Long enough for me to worry and phone Seamus."

She doesn't want to challenge him, but she doesn't think that the time between when she left the apartment and when she heard him calling her name was that long.

"Did you talk to Bile then, because he was there and having a meal with Seamus? Is that what you are saying?"

"From what Seamus relayed, Bile suggested a compromise. That you work on the basis of what he called 'a limited release' and that I moderate my earlier position and reconsider providing security for the specific site at which the play's 'limited release' is being staged," Dajaal explains.

"What do they mean by 'limited release'?"

Dajaal replies, "That it'll be for a couple of nights at a specific site and for a select audience. Small and intimate enough so we can take the temperature and work out what our future options are after the first night. From then on, we'll decide. If we think it is risky to give another performance, then we won't. This is a compromise with which I am okay. In fact, this was what Bile suggested all along, only I was putting up resistance. Now I've come round to accept it, because of your exceptional gesture of kindness."

Her eyes steady, she revisits in her memory the all-women evening do at Kiin's hotel. That too had a select audience of a few hundred likeminded women who, comfortable in one another's company, did outrageous stuff that might make a bald mufti wish he could borrow a wig and join in, carouse, cuddle, and delight in savoring the goods on display. She thinks that the plan might have a good chance of working. Dajaal's men at the gates, checking; no uninvited guests. Only for one night, or maybe two, and only for a select audience, for a start.

"Brilliant," Cambara agrees.

Dajaal's features assume a happier aspect: his cheeks rounded from grinning, eyes beaming. His relaxed demeanor has a curious effect on her: She is excited by their physical closeness, the warmth of his body so near and yet so far, inasmuch as she cannot imagine touching or hugging him without undue complications.

"You can trust Bile," Dajaal says.

"Bile has been wonderful to me," she breaks in.

"He's the gem of the lot, precious."

What lot? He has no equal, she is thinking. Then, surprise of all surprises: She has all too pleasantly and absentmindedly removed her wedding ring without needing to apply water, soap, or oil. That she has eased it off her ring finger as uncomplicatedly as she has is a bonus. From this instant on, she may no longer consider herself wedded to Wardi.

Dajaal, uncannily, goes on and, as if he knows what Cambara is thinking, launches into some sort of a sales pitch in praise of Bile. "You go anywhere, you won't find another man like Bile: generous, trustworthy, amenable to other people's ideas, and ready to make them his own for the good of everyone else. The poor man hasn't received back as much kindness as he has given. Alas, there is more sweetness to life than Bile has known."

Dajaal's high commendation of Bile's character is perhaps in keeping with the Somali tradition in which, before a suitor asks for the hand of his intended, an aunt or an elderly female relative does the rounds, visiting the blood relations of the young woman before any serious bid is made for the hand of the bride-to-be. This last, crucial move, the most important of the courtship act, falls to the men. Only, Cambara thinks, she is not yet anyone's bride. Moreover, she and Bile have not had the chance to talk about any of these matters; he has been indisposed. No matter. She can imagine nothing more challenging and more demanding than being in Bile's company. Needless to say, it is very sweet of Dajaal, who is a regular kind of person, to involve himself in Bile's well-being and to make as direct a bid for her hand as he has. It requires a man with a strong constitution to do so, and Dajaal has that and more, she assumes. In addition, he has an admirable loyalty and an enviable self-worth to embark on this most demanding of rituals.

He says, "Bile is the tops, no doubt about it."

She smiles sheepishly and looks away, telling herself that someone has probably used all the words that Dajaal has employed, in praise of Bile, to describe him. That is the trouble; in a sales pitch, one is selling oneself just as much as the item being promoted.

When he continues his patter of praise, Cambara says, "Enough. You're sounding as if you are speaking at his entombment. Bile is still with us and will live yet for a long time."

That shuts him up instantly.

In the silence, they both become conscious of the fragility of who joins them. Unfortunately Bile is not around to say to the two of them, as a parent might to two quarrelsome preteens, "Enough. Cut it out." It is then that it dawns on her that she and Dajaal are alike in their mad courage, the inimitable kind that can make a dent in Mogadiscio, a city that has fallen prey either to the machinations of the warlords or to the mysterious ways of mullahs' courts claiming their fair share of divine support. The only difference is that she sees nothing wrong in relying on Dajaal's bravery to do the dirty work as long as she does not bear witness or have firsthand knowledge of the perpetration of the violence. And it is obvious that he is doing whatever he is doing for Bile. She, like Bile, does not go anywhere near the scene of a crime where someone's blood is shed. Yet Bile cannot *not* know what is going on. Sadly, that is how societies function, thanks to a few dozen who get their hands soiled to their elbows with blood.

They avoid looking in each other's direction, Dajaal concentrating on his driving and Cambara absentmindedly trying to put on her wedding ring. They are silent like a married couple having their tiff. All of a sudden, she is alert to the change of scenery, and she pays attention to her surroundings, becoming aware of a young man, whom she soon identifies as Qasiir, Dajaal's nephew, approaching. This is the first of several checkpoints manned by the youths Qasiir has assembled, Qasiir, who now, raising his hand in recognition of his uncle, removes the roll of razor wire from in front of the vehicle. Three more stops and many exchanges of camaraderie later, they are at the gate, which opens to let Dajaal drive in.

Then Cambara hears someone rehearsing a text with which she is very familiar, because she has written it, in full voice.

As she pushes open the door to get out of the vehicle, she says, "Please accept my apologies. I didn't mean it to sound the way it came out."

"I would do anything for Bile," he says.

Just as she gets out of the door of the vehicle that Dajaal is holding open and before she has taken her first step toward the hall from which the rehearsing voice is emanating, her adrenaline rises to her head, almost depriving her heart of what it needs to continue its rhythmic beating. It moves her to listen with her full attention to the words she has written spoken with such eloquence. It is just as she gets closer that she senses an inconsistency in the delivery insinuating itself, for Gacal has become self-conscious, and he seizes. A pity, for his voice has left her impressed, sounding just the way she has always imagined it.

"Why has he stopped?" she says.

"No idea," Dajaal replies, standing close by.

Then a fly, noisy as a tropical summer in full swing, buzzes in front of her, hovering close to her eyes, and she shoos it away, after which she listens as Gacal picks it all up again, less hesitant, his words aimed at her but addressed to an imagined audience.

"Once upon a time, there was a villager who went out alone in search of his son and the half dozen cows that he took to the fields in the morning for them to graze . . ."

There is a pleasing gentleness to the voice, as if the speaker is aware that great expectations are borne in upon him and he is doing his utmost to fulfill them. Cambara is hopeful that given time and a bit of help and several hours of voice training, she will be able to iron out the unevenness that she can now detect, listening. Nothing is insuperable; she feels certain that she will be able to take care of this in less than a day or two, given the opportunity and Gacal's willingness.

She is silent and almost in a trance, pondering. His comment, "The boy is good," makes her stir out of her stupor.

It takes her a moment to regain her composure and longer still to find her voice. She says, "He has the timbre of a trained actor, Gacal has. Glad I've stumbled across him by chance."

"Where?"

"Turned up at the hotel where I am staying."

"What's his story?"

"Extraordinary."

And before he has the opportunity to elaborate on her meaning, she moves purposefully toward the hall, with Dajaal on her heels, as though making sure he will remain close to her, protect her from harm. They come to the gate, and she suddenly stops, her hand going up, knuckles ready but not tapping. It is as if she can't bring herself to believe her luck, and there is no wood to touch, the gate being of solid metal. Then she smells cooking coming from the courtyard: potatoes boiling, onions in a pan sizzling, a tape recorder playing a Somali song. Again, she hears the grown baritone of a boy who can easily train as a tenor, speaking.

"Please," Dajaal says, and when she turns he insinuates himself into the gap that has opened, bows deferentially to her, and, pushing the gate, says apologetically, "Please step aside."

He treats her like royalty. How long will this last? she wonders to herself. It can't, it won't, not for as long as she is with Bile. Maybe, all this gallantry is in lieu of the bouquet of flowers that a man courting a woman brings along and the dinners at restaurants to which he takes her. Besides, Bile is not all there, is he? Living in the abnormal times of a civil war means that this will have to do.

Entering, they find the armed guards sitting around the fire where SilkHair is tending to two pots, cooking. SilkHair says, more for the youths' benefit than for Cambara's or Dajaal's, "You'll have supper in a few minutes. Until then you may go and listen to Gaçal. We're having plenty of fun."

Cambara pats him on the head and says, "Well done," and proceeds toward the hall, where she is pleasantly surprised to find a stage: two planks that Seamus nailed together pronto, good enough for her immediate purpose. She says to no one in particular, "Seamus is a miracle worker."

Then they watch Gacal going through his routines, whatever these are meant to be, rehearsing and taking different lines in turn, now speaking as a grown man, now as the young cowherd who has been missing and whom the villager looks for just before nightfall. A latticework of shades—the ones in the outer rings light, those in the inner circles darker—overwhelms Dajaal and Cambara, who can only stare, confused, because they cannot make sense of it, at least not at first. But it does not take Cambara long to locate the source of the shades and work out that someone is playing with mirrors of different tones and of various color emphases.

"That's Qasiir, using a mirror to emit messages in codes," Gacal says. "That means all is well and there is nothing to worry about." Then he approaches, to welcome Cambara back with a hug, but hasn't the ingenuity to carry it through. He lapses into the voice of his proper age, a boy in his early teens. "It is fun, rehearsing, SilkHair cooking, Qasiir fooling with mirrors," says Gacal.

She is impressed with both boys for having taken the initiative themselves, a healthy indication that, if guided in the right way, they will be okay. "You're all doing very well. How marvelous."

Then he reverts to his own character, as she has so far sussed out. He retrieves a tape recorder from one of Cambara's tote bags, and he plays it for her. Cambara listens to a voice montage, her own mixed with Gacal's, and, superimposed on both of them, SilkHair's. She realizes that he has ruined her tape, which is a copy of another. Luckily, she did not bring the original. She does not reprimand him.

"How have you managed to mix the voices?" she asks, going closer to them, sounding sweet, charmingly maternal.

"By playing several tapes and recording our own song, Gacal and I," SilkHair says. "I am enjoying cooking too. We must feed them." He points at the young militiamen in shiftless expectation of eating a meal, regardless of who cooks it, since they won't.

Dajaal has had enough of this, and he is in no mood to indulge anyone. Just as Gacal joins them, Dajaal goes closer to where Cambara is standing. Mindful to be courteous to the two boys, whom she is pampering with her attentions, he speaks to her in an undertone, "In my job as a bodyguard and security fiend, I must have enough sleep. It's been a long day, and I need to get back. Please let's go. I'll take you and your two boys to Maanta, then show my face to Bile before I call it a day. Do you mind?" He goes back to the car and waits.

The boys have resumed rehearsing. She waits for a couple of minutes for the two boys to get to a point in their routines where she thinks they do not mind being interrupted, then she claps her hands together, now looking at Gacal, now at SilkHair, and applauds.

Then she turns to SilkHair. "Is the meal you were cooking for the armed youths ready? Because if it is, then we must head back, return to our hotel, where there will be food for the three of us."

When, after a few minutes, he says, "Cooked," she instructs him and Gacal gather their things and hers too, so they will all return to the hotel. They do as they are told as soon as the armed youth descend like hungry wolves on the pots, one or two of them almost burning themselves and quarreling greedily.

Then she remembers a joke she and her son used to share, because she is pleased with the way things have gone today and she is all game. She says, "Last to the car is the pig with the shortest snout."

And she breaks into a trot, half running. Gacal and SilkHair appear unimpressed, maybe because they find her humor about becoming the pig with the shortest snout a bit offensive. So they deliberately take their time, as if trying to wind her up, gather their stuff slowly, and then put on adult faces, silent, before they join her and Dajaal in the vehicle.

By then, Cambara is conscious of what they are up to, and decides to show them that she is no pushover. She says, "Boys, it's been a long day. We'll thank Dajaal in advance for his patience and generosity, and we'll turn in early, the three of us, immediately after we've eaten our suppers."

And that is what Cambara does: She turns in early, soon after her room-service meal. Too exhausted, she cannot bring herself to sleep. Restive, she switches on the lights to read, but her eyes close as if of their own accord, and her mind races off like a pampered child going out for a stroll with its mother, now running ahead of her, now behind her, and picking up memories and giving each of them a fresh once-over. Cambara examines in detail what her life has been like for the past few days, if only to determine what else she must do to make sure that she stays on course.

She thinks she has led too much of a sedentary existence since arriving, hardly exercising, her muscles atrophying. Thing is, though, her mind is alive—thank God for that; her family's property is back in her hands to do with as she pleases. She worries about Bile's descent into darker moods of dejection. She needs to devote equal time to the personal and the professional sides of her interests from this moment on. She dedicates several hours of the next day to decide how she will go about these.

Looking at the telephone, as though willing it to ring, she wonders when Raxma will call to give her the news she has so far gathered about Gacal's parents. Eventually, she falls asleep in the small hours but not before reminding herself that she needs to know just as much about SilkHair.

TWENTY-EIGHT

Cambara wakes up, dazed, to the ringing telephone in her room. She stretches her hand out to answer it, and, as she does so, her eyes still closed, she thinks, who can be calling at this most ungodly of hours? Perhaps Bile to thank her for the stupendous bunch of grapes she presented him with and which they shared with pleasure. But when she grabs the phone and then opens her eyes, mouthing the words "Hello, who is this?" she realizes that she is making two errors: one, it is later in the morning than she thought—probably about eight-thirty, nine o'clock; and two, she did not see him in real life or give and share grapes but in a dream, which the phone call interrupted.

She hears a confirmation of this in the distant voice of a woman who says, "This is Raxma with the latest. Are you up, ready to receive it?"

"Just a moment, Raaxo."

She gives herself a moment to look at her watch, which is by the bedside, sees that it is quarter to nine, and tells herself that it is time she has been up, eaten her breakfast, and asked after her two charges, to find out how their night has been. She sits up, rams a pillow behind her to lean against, and says, "I am listening, Raaxo."

Raxma's voice sounds closer, as if coming from next door. "I've rung around and am able to confirm much of what he has told you."

"You're a comfort to me," Cambara says. (The two friends alter each other's name—Raxma abbreviating Cambara to Cambo, meaning "apple," and Cambara changing Raxma to Raaxo, meaning "comfort."

"What time is it where you are? Don't tell me that you've stayed up to call me, because it is close to one in the morning."

"What won't I do for a friend?"

"I appreciate it, I really do."

"Anyhow," Raxma starts to speak, then pauses. "Gacal's parents, namely Qaali and Omar, lived in Duluth, Minnesota, until Omar found a two-year consultancy in Nairobi and the boy's mother, Qaali, moved to Ann Arbor, Michigan, to complete the remaining one-year compulsory coursework for a postgraduate degree at that university. Just before Qaali's departure for her fieldwork in anthropology in some faraway village in the Dogon country, the people whose traditional culture she was researching, she and Omar agreed on a date, in three months' time, when she would visit them in Nairobi for a break. From what I hear, they communicated as frequently as they could. In the part of Mali where she was stationed, telephones were unreliable and e-mailing was impossible, because there were frequent power cuts, at times for a week and more."

"Tell me what you know about her."

"Qaali has been described to me as a very determined woman intent on making up for lost time, in that she was determined to take her Ph.D. before her fortieth birthday. This was her second marriage, Omar's first. She had other children by another man; he had none, except their only boy. Add to this the fact that Omar was her junior by five years and the one with the job and the money. As a family, they often avoided the company of other Somalis, and they chose to relocate because of the adverse comments some Minnesota Somalis made about the gap in their ages and their respective incomes."

"I feel for Qaali, I like her," says Cambara.

"I knew you would."

"So they had no friends among the Somalis?"

"They had only American friends, who call her 'Precious,' a direct translation of her Somali name, Qaali. Here you have a Somali woman reinventing herself as an American. I suspect, too, that she may have put 'Precious,' not Qaali, on her U.S. passport, so we must keep that in mind when searching for her whereabouts," says Raxma. "Anyway, Qaali and Omar spoke Somali to Gacal, their son, and English to each other, and wanted to have nothing to do with this clan business, his side or hers, it didn't matter."

"I'm curious how you garnered this information?"

"Don't interrupt my flow. Wait until later."

"Go on."

"What was the last thing I said?"

"Nothing to do with this clan business."

"But they were nationalists, and they wanted to provide their son with a worldly perspective," Raxma continues, "and while he was still young and malleable wanted him to speak the language, learn about Somali culture, and pick up enough Arabic to be a useful tool for later in life. They saw the well-paid job in Nairobi as a godsend, for it would afford Qaali a number of years to devote to her studies; and Omar and Gacal would be close enough to Somalia to make brief visits. It just so happened that a fortnight before Qaali was due to visit, Omar bought air tickets for the two to make the first of what they hoped would be many trips. Omar was making a cursory reconnaissance, taking a good look at the city, deciding on a good enough hotel for them to stay in when the whole family reunited to spend four weeks together, after Qaali joined them in East Africa."

Cambara interrupts, "Come the week for Qaali's visit . . . !"

"No answer at home when she phoned, because by then they were in Mogadiscio," Raxma continues. "One thing you need to know is that she came to the nearest town to make the phone call, since none was available in the village where she was doing her fieldwork. So she stayed in the town for a couple more days, ringing Omar's mobile, his direct line at the office, his home in the evenings, and after several unsuccessful attempts, the school at which Gacal had been enrolled. She struck lucky there, the headmaster promising to look into Gacal's disappearance. He called him his star pupil, and said that the whole class missed him. Apparently Gacal was 'a charming kid,' He asked her to phone him in a couple of days. When Qaali did, he informed her that he had learned that her husband had gone to Somalia, intending to be back after the weekend and that no one had heard from or about him or Gacal."

"What did Qaali do?"

"She flew to Nairobi, a city unknown to her," Raxma replies. "She had little money and therefore found a cheap hotel for the night. The following morning she went to her husband's workplace, and they couldn't tell her more than what the headmaster had relayed to her, nor did they know anything more at the school when she called on the headmaster. She didn't bother asking the Somalis, of whom there are hundreds of thousands in Nairobi, putting up at every expensive hotel and frequenting the city's cafés, teahouses, and restaurants, certain that Omar would not have had dealings with them. Two days later, she took a twelve-seater, *qaat*-carrying plane to Mogadiscio in search of her husband and son, last seen when they were both well and planning to make a weekend visit to Mogadiscio."

"And then?"

"Not a word from her. Vanished."

Shocked, Cambara can't think of anything to say. She takes a deep breath, shifts her position in the bed the better to know what to ask. After a brief pause, she asks, "How have you gathered this information? To whom have you spoken?"

Raxma responds, "First I called Information, and got a Duluth number registered in Omar's name. When I rang, I spoke to a woman who denied knowing who I was talking about, but she passed me on to the estate agency from which she rented the apartment, who initially couldn't find either Omar's or Qaali's names as clients in their books. Then it transpired that they had her down as 'Precious,' not Qaali. Then I rang Information again, once I knew that she was a postgraduate student in anthropology at U of M, and I spoke to her head of department, her supervisor, and even the secretary to the department, all of whom answered my questions voluntarily. They had her first name as Qaali and her second as Precious, and used the two hyphenated. Insofar as the Americans are concerned, Qaali has disappeared in that large continent called Africa, and they have no way of knowing how to trace her. She isn't in Mali, at least not in the Dogon village where she is supposed to be doing her fieldwork. The last phone contact from her was when she rang the head of the department, but, because he wasn't there to talk to her, she informed the secretary that she might need an extension, because she was off to Nairobi and then Mogadiscio in search of her husband and son; she hoped to be back in a month or so. Alas, no word from her since that day. And then I spoke with the headmaster at her son's school in Duluth—he was the last to speak with her. And finally, I spoke with our friend Maimouna, who knows everything about international law and passports and such, and she was able to help me collect many of the details. I'm afraid she became obsessed with the story—but she was very helpful."

Cambara pauses to smile at the thought of their friend doing so much work. Then she asks Raxma for Qaali's and Omar's last names and other particulars, and, after giving her the hotel fax number, she asks Raxma to fax her photographs of both adults, if she can lay her hands on any. "The university can provide you with a mug shot, if there is nothing else."

"Are you sure you don't want to drop it?"

"While at it, give me their clan names as well."

"To what end?"

"To identify them, of course."

"Don't you have better things to do, my Apple?"

"No, Comfort. Not anymore. I am decided."

They laugh until their ribs ache.

"I prefer asking Kiin to intervene," Raxma says. "For one thing, she has much better connections than you; for another, she can get the Women's Network on board faster than you can. The network will be keen to give a hand. I'll talk right away to Kiin, whom I will get onto the business of tracing Gacal's mother," announces Raxma. "She and I are to speak tomorrow when she is due to update me and Arda on the progress of your affairs. Why don't you let me, since you have enough on your plate already?"

"Because Gacal is my precious little man and I adore him."

"In all seriousness, let Kiin intervene."

"I insist."

"How're things with you by the way?" asks Raxma.

"Can't complain; can't complain."

"Is that all you have to say?"

"Everything will be working out well," Cambara says. "Someone at the door," although there isn't. "Let's talk tomorrow or the day after. About this time. Either you call me, or I'll call you."

"Take care, Precious Apple."

The line disconnected, Cambara feels its dead weight and drops it. What do you know? she tells herself. Raxma and Kiin talk to each other often, and Arda is kept abreast of her daily activities. What other arrangements, of which she, Cambara, is unaware, are in progress?

After showering, Cambara orders room service. She does not have the heart to face anyone, least of all Gacal, the sight of whom will sadden her; Kiin, who is bound to ask her about her latest doings; and SilkHair, whom she meant to talk to today, but can't be bothered now to contact, in view of her current mood.

Breakfast consumed, she tries to read Flannery O'Connor's "Good Country People," but is unable to concentrate, turning the pages without retaining any of what she has read. Then the phone rings, and, answering it, she is connected to a male voice with which she is unfamiliar, Bile's.

"I've phoned just to let you know I am well."

He sounds top-notch, and they chat with extraordinary ease about this and that but never touch on what transpired at his place yesterday. He does not ask her questions about it; she does not allude to it at all. He refers, however, at some point, to his talks with both Seamus and Dajaal about the masks, and reiterates that the idea of "limited release," which has always been his, reduces the risk, as it does not rouse the enraged sentiments of the Islamists who oppose producing any play, with or without masks; and it will also not give ammunition to other injured parties who have lost out in the process of the reacquisition of her family property.

Then he asks, "When do we meet?"

"Tell me when," she says.

"I'll come and visit you at the property."

"Look forward to seeing you then."

The line off, she feels half livened up by a memory of her dream of the night before, in which she and Bile are alone, near a knocked-together shack. But they are very calm in themselves and sit in the sweet shade of a fruiting mango tree. They are eating grapes from a bowl, feeding each other in turn, their fingers touching as they do so, their lips, their eyes, their faces framed with traces of joy. Close by, two half-naked boys, in their preteens, are in the water, noisily splashing themselves and playing a catch-and-throw ball game, their contentedness apparent.

Then Cambara marks out the presence in the heavens of a medium-sized gray hawk surveying the scene from just above them for a long time before eventually alighting on a branch in another mango tree adjacent to theirs. The hawk nests quietly, and, as Cambara returns her attention to the goings-on, which are close to her heart, the hawk's short broad wings flap now and then, as if it might take off or perhaps it is reminding her that it is there, deciding on its next move.

And before she knows it, the hawk comes down, unafraid, landing noiselessly very close to where she and Bile are still feeding one another, touching, preparatory to lovemaking. Strangely, neither Bile nor Cambara seem to mind, once it becomes obvious to them that the hawk poses them no danger and is feeding on the fruit insects proliferating in their vicinity. When the two boys arrive, disporting themselves, wrestling catch-as-catch-can, dashing about, and frolicking, the hawk does not appear to approve, and, zeroing in on them, chases them away. Scarcely has she had time to wonder why when she notices that the hawk is raking in pursuit of a large-headed snake, which it secures with its mighty talons, dismembering it instantly.

It is then that a Dajaal look-alike approaches from the left to scare off the hawk, shooing it away with the accompaniment of untoward comments. The bird is not happy about being run off or having to abandon the dead snake in its disemboweled state. Cambara looks to Bile, hoping that he might intervene and persuade Dajaal not to interfere with the hawk or its exploits.

Bile does no such thing at first. He waits to see what Dajaal's intentions are and if he can interpret them. Dajaal gathers the snake with care, and, carrying its corpse, which is dripping with blood, away from his own body, walks over to where the two boys are romping about in the water, competing, and he throws it at them. The boys shriek with fright. They plunge into the water, staying under, only to surface at the deeper end of what looks like a lake. Gacal appeals to Cambara, "Please help."

Angry, Bile rises to his full height with such abruptness that he kicks over the bowl of grapes and spills its entire contents. He is enraged; he is trembling, at a loss for words. He stares furiously, in silence, at the figure that is no longer a Dajaal look-alike but a man resembling Zaak, even if he seems younger and a great deal healthier. Bile wants an explanation from Zaak's look-alike, but it becomes evident soon enough that the figure that bears a likeness, insofar as Cambara is concerned, to Dajaal and, insofar as Bile is concerned, to Zaak has none to offer. Whereupon, Cambara picks up a club to strike the figure, who takes off. She runs after him, pleased to be chasing him from the scene.

It is in the midst of this dream that the phone rings, startling her awake. She answers it, perspiring heavily, her heart racing like a hound in pursuit of a fox. She hears that Raxma on the line. "Just a moment . . ."

Now, Cambara doesn't know what to make of the dream, but she is delighted that, compared to an earlier one, in which there was also a foursome—Arda, Wardi, Dalmar, and herself at a dinner table having a dinner—no one dies in this one. She is also positive about her connection to Bile, whom she saw the first time early this morning in the dream and to whom she has now talked in real life

Out of bed, she changes into her work clothes—a denim shirt with snaps, a pair of jeans, and sneakers—and goes out of her room and down the stairway, feeling energized by the thought that from now on she will concentrate in equal measures, if that is possible, on getting to know Bile in as intimate a way as possible, on producing the play at whatever cost, and on helping trace Qaali, under whatever alias she might be using.

It crosses her mind, going down, past reception, to have the hotel send an e-mail to the BBC Somali Service five-days-a-week "Missing Persons" program, which benefits from the local support of the International Red Cross, asking that Qaali get in touch with Raaxo Abduraxman, a name made up on the spot, care of Hotel Maanta, for information about her son, Gacal. Then she leaves word with Irrid, the deputy manager of the hotel, that she is expecting a reply from one Raaxo Abduraxman about Gacal. One way or the other, she is sure she will get Qaali's message if it ever comes.

A moment later, roaming aimlessly, she finds herself at the café end of the restaurant, her notepad open, and she starts to draw up a list of her immediate needs. She has not gone far in composing it when the waiter arrives. Having served her in the room earlier, he brings her the usual—a bottled mineral water and a couple of slices of lemon on a saucer—and asks if she would like some more? She places her elevenses order: tea and biscuits. No sooner has he taken it down and turned to go than her memory of the dream of the night before, combined with her conversation with Raxma, above all Raxma's mentioning that she and Kiin are in frequent telephonic communication, wrings her withers for the second time. She sits, mulling over what to do. Faint with worry, she thinks that the only way out of this sad frame of mind is to act. She replays the talk with Raxma, then the dream, and scours the scenes for the second and third time in hope of appraising whatever possible interpretations there can be. Another thorough go-through—she also remembers Bile offering to visit—she affords herself the luxury of studying it from all possible angles, ultimately deciding that she had better move out of the hotel and into the family property.

This realization comes as a shock to her, so startles her out of her sense of calm that she is no longer able to go over the steps of the logic that have led her to this conclusion: Quit the hotel and take residence in the family house. Her stomach gurgles, babbling in the confines of her viscera, like a flushed toilet. Her agitated mood is tempered with a momentary self-control when she sees the waiter arriving.

He puts her elevenses before her: a pot of tea, biscuits, along with canjeera-pancake smothered in honey, and two slices of mango so sweet her mouth waters the instant she picks up the fragrance; the latter two she has not asked for, but she won't send them back, in case her charges come, as they often do. Cambara is of the untested view that even the waiter has figured out that she has the countenance of a troubled person and wonders if there is any point in looking away. No amount of gauging the intrinsic madness of moving out of the hotel—in which she has felt very comfortable and safe—and into the family property—in which she has never spent a single night, since her parents never thought of it as anything but an investment—can help her get a good barometer reading of her folly.

Nor can she bear the thought of the food: the tea looks undrinkable; the biscuits stale; the honey-smothered pancake too sweet; the mangoes hosts to their kindred flies and insects. She pushes them all away. A moment later, she pours herself a cup of tea, then unthinkingly puts condensed milk in it and some sugar, and stirs it. Now her demeanor is decidedly downbeat, and she is wondering why she has spooned condensed milk and sugar into her tea when she does not drink her tea that way and never has. She reasons that maybe these are part of the changes taking place in her, her deep sense of alienation taking root;

presently a stranger to her everyday self. What will her life be like in her altered circumstances?

Can it be that she wants to prove several points to herself? That she is moving out of the temporariness of a hotel into a house that is hers to demonstrate that she is just as committed to this country as the gun-toting youths, in whose direction she is throwing a come-and-get-me-if-you-have-the-guts gauntlet; that she knows that it will be a lot easier for her to work ceaselessly on the play and to provide the semblance of a home to the two boys if she moves out of the hotel into the property. Privacy is equally important here, for she will be in a position to host Bile, in the sense of looking after him, and get to know him more intimately without the prying eyes of waiters, bellhops, charwomen, the armed security at the gate, the in-house security, the deputy manager, other hotel guests—and Kiin. Not that she can ever hope to meet Bile without many others getting to hear of it. Maintaining one's privacy is a civil war casualty; people live on top of one another in ways they do not in peace times. No doubt, if she moves to the family house, she will have bodyguards, perhaps an outer ring of heavily armed security and inner in-house lightly armed day and night watchmen. She is far from sure that she will be safer or happier at her new home, but establishing a foot in the family property is as good a starting point as any campaign in which she has been involved, and she will launch it with a workable battle plan and a reliable safety net, never mind the deadly opponents that she may have to confront.

No sign of the boys today. What's bizarre is she doesn't ask about them, and the waiter, who has returned to collect the untouched tea, biscuits, pancake, and mangoes doesn't mention them either. He clears her plates of food without a spoken word, even if the disturbed expression on his face speaks volumes to Cambara, who is conscious of her irritability.

Then Kiin arrives with the gushiness of someone bearing a surfeit of tenderness; she is all questions. Effusive, she says, "It's all happening, isn't it?"

"I am moving out of the hotel into our house."

The idea is so unsettling to Kiin that she is not composed enough to ask her questions about Cambara's visit to ailing Bile; about the phone call from Raxma, who may have spoken to Kiin earlier before ringing her; or about Bile's purported suggestion that they invite a select audience to view the play, it being too controversial to be given a public viewing.

"I am moving into our house, which has been recovered, thanks to you and many other well-wishers' efforts. I feel that otherwise all your achievements will have been for nought, comparable, as a Somali pastoralist might say, to pouring milk on the thirsty sand of the Sahara."

Kiin stares at Cambara like someone whose center of conversational gravity has shifted to new shaky ground. Kiin fumbles among the wide repertoire of her wisecracks in an attempt to show that nothing will faze her.

She asks, "Do you think it wise to do so now?"

Cambara is selective in what she tells Kiin. She omits any mention of the dream and her conversation with Raxma, where the idea to move originated. However, she stresses the professional side of her keenness— "It'll be easier, I'll have continuity"—and then puts due emphasis on her monumental desire to show her gratitude to Kiin—"I'm moving into the house as a token of my appreciation to you and to all the others who have contributed to its recovery, above all you, Farxia, Dajaal, and the others"—and adds, "We'll have a party at the property just before we produce the play. How does that strike you?"

"But why?"

"I am itching to get down to the business of producing the play," Cambara says. Then she goes on, "There is a lot of work waiting for me. I need to start blocking the play, rehearsing, auditioning."

"There is time yet, surely?"

Impatient, Cambara cuts in and says, "It's all been wonderful staying here and enjoying your lavish kindness. Thank you very much; you've been all sweet and a boon to me, better than manna from any heaven, considering."

"Have you discussed this with anyone else?"

"No, I haven't."

"But why?"

She dares not underscore the bleak dreariness of her lack of privacy, her need to rely on others so she might perform the most ordinary of life's chores, aspects of Mogadiscio life that strikes her as utterly dis-heartening. An ancient unease returns. Will her moving into her house free her from these daily exigencies? Won't she become even more re-liant on others for protection? Kiin is silent for a long while, and Cambara watches her, her head buzzing with thoughts. Since it is char-acteristic of Kiin to precipitate an obstacle as she busies herself to re-move it, Cambara anticipates Kiin's initiative and preempts it with a single move in a sentence.

She says, "Given the choice, I would like to relocate right away, and for this I will require a bit of initial help from you."

Kiin is looking at her mobile, as though willing it to ring, or maybe she is considering whether to phone Raxma to suggest that she inter-vene. She replaces the phone in her handbag and says, "Name your needs."

"Your truck with armed escort, so I can move some of the stuff straight away," Cambara says. "I would appreciate it if you could or-ganize the purchase of a generator, a couple of beds and mattresses, a few pots and pans and other kitchen utensils."

"Consider it done," Kiin says. "What else?"

"Nothing else for the moment."

The edge of Kiin's voice is sharper. She says, "These are, as you put it, your initial needs. I am surprised that for someone relocating to a battle zone, abandoning the comfort and safety of a hotel and prema-turely endangering her life, you have no more items on your shopping list. Bodyguards, handguns, at least two battlewagons? Are you sure this is the extent of your requirements?"

"I am sure."

"No walkie-talkies or anything else?"

"I will keep my rooms here of course."

"Of course."

"And whenever our kitchen is not running, or if I get tired of eat-ing my food between rehearsals or scene takes, I'll be sure to arrange takeaways from yours."

"No problem."

"There is a lot to do," Cambara says, sitting forward in her chair, the front part of her body stretching as if at some point it will go off on its own, she is so eager to get up and go.

By way of urging her to follow her own instincts, Kiin, making the "Go, go sign," with her hand, says, "What are you waiting for?"

"When will things be ready on your side?"

"The truck, the deputy manager of the hotel, the head of our security, and the armed escort will be ready to take you in half an hour," Kiin says.

"Then see you down here in half an hour."

With Kiin gone to organize things, Cambara, now alone, is unable to square up to her necessities, which are in part determined by a matrix of theatrical and personal musts. Where to start? What to pack? What to do about the boys?

On her way to her rooms, the fires of enthusiasm, at the center of her being, suddenly start to dwindle. She is in a quandary, aware that she has been too hasty, but she is unwilling to change her mind. First off, she stops at the reception and brings wads and wads of cash in large U.S. dollar denominations out of the hotel safe, to buy a 2,000-kilowatt generator for her electricity requirements, a fridge of modest size, a queen-sized bed and two single beds, mattresses, bedspreads, sheets, bath and face towels, soap, and some food, including some vegetables, and if there is no supermarket with already packaged chicken, then a live one. She replaces the cash she is not taking with her and locks the safe.

Then she turns her attention to the matter of the clothes that she will bring with her, settling easily on a number of middle-of-the-road choices, neither too ostentatious nor too plain, plus the kind of work clothes she is now wearing, informal and chic. She takes good care to choose her nightdresses, just in case. "I hope I am not making the chickens hatch the eggs of the eagles," she says to herself. "In which case, too bad and too sad." Then she throws in two of the masks, one presumably for Gacal, the other for SilkHair.

In the unrelenting clutch of an oncoming excitement, more like an onset of flu announcing its impending arrival via a sneeze, Cambara hurries to gather a few things together and dashes out of the room to join Kiin. As she double-locks her rooms, she realizes that there are difficulties to do with living in several places—an apartment in faraway Toronto; the two rooms in the hotel; and now the family house—at the same time. She is already finding out that she will have to return to the hotel tomorrow for some of the masks, which she is leaving behind, advisedly because she has no idea how the head of security, Hudhudle, who appears to be a devout Muslim, might react to their presence in the truck. The suitcase she is carrying knocks weightily down the steps as she descends, the two wooden masks sounding hollowly; she lifts the suitcase higher to make certain she does not damage them. She is pitching forward when one of the bellhops offers to relieve her of it, informing her that Kiin is waiting for her near the truck, waiting to be loaded and ready to depart.

Kiin opens the door of the vehicle, the engine on and idling, to welcome Cambara in, just as the bellhop hands the suitcase to one of the armed escorts in the third row. The two friends are about to take leave of each other, Kiin preparing to wish her the best of luck, when Cambara's mobile phone squeals; she answers it on the second ring.

"Where are you?" asks a man's voice.

At first, Cambara does not say where she is, because she tries to figure out why she hears a touch of Gaelic in Seamus's English today, something she has seldom heard before. Has something made him nervous, worried, frightened?

"Why do you ask?" she says.

Seamus replies, "Dajaal, who left a message on my mobile, says that your family house was attacked last night and there have been casualties."

Kiin is curious, but Cambara tells her nothing.

Meanwhile Seamus continues, "Dajaal has just completed his mopping up exercise and has taken two seriously wounded militiamen from the attacking side to hospital, mere boys, as young as ten, he reckons." He pauses, and then he adds, "No one on 'our' side has been hurt."

Cambara says, "I'm on my way to the house, in a truck with armed escort. Please tell him that I am headed his way and would appreciate him getting in touch to keep us informed of how things are."

"I will have him expect you."

Seamus rings off. Cambara gives nothing away.

TWENTY-NINE

Cambara sits up front, next to the driver, half of her arm out of the window, her abject expression suggesting to those who know what she is doing that she is in all probability suffering from a belated loss of nerve.

Asked to explain why she is wearing a rueful mien, which is rather uncharacteristic of her, she might answer that she is not worried for her own life. What galls her is that she is not conducting her life alone, which is the noble thing to do. She is carrying out her elaborate plans in a cowardly way, driving headlong into a danger zone and taking along with her half a dozen youths and the deputy head and the security chief of the hotel, none of whom has anything to gain from this venture, her adventure. In addition to these, there are tagalongs Gacal and SilkHair, who mysteriously turned up as the driver put the truck in first gear and who jumped in with no idea where they were headed. Now they are two rows behind Cambara's, gabbing. She hopes that her reckless decision to move into the family home will not prove to be calamitous for anyone other than herself, because she will never forgive herself if someone else is hurt. Why isn't she worried on her own account? Because she's the one who left the comforts of Toronto and come to strife-torn Mogadiscio, and look where she has finished up? Eased her way into regaining the family property—not too bad for a mourning mother.

Her mobile phone rings, the suddenness of its tintinnabulation startling her and ending her private meanderings. Dajaal says, "Put your security detail on."

She spins around in alarm, behaving as if a hostage crisis is unfolding. She searches for guidance from the head of the hotel security. She passes the phone over to him, in the second row, and explains that it is Dajaal needing to speak to him.

"*Pronto?*" Hudhudle, the security chief, says and listens.

Under normal circumstances, she might be tempted to inquire why Dajaal's manners have gone walkabout, but she doesn't, mindful of the fact that she has already burned the candle at both ends, alienating Zaak first and now possibly Kiin by moving out when she has. She won't quibble over Dajaal's manners if he doesn't have the time to waste on the routine formalities of "Please" or "May I." She has added to the unusualness of the present situation by upping the risk by several notches. Moreover, his voice has sounded unstrung. Why hasn't he spoken to her and requested that she relay his message to the security detail? Is he very upset and doesn't wish to imperil their rapport, lest he say the wrong thing? If she didn't know him better, she might think that he considers her to be redundant because of her gender, given that war, which is men's, not women's, affair, can only be discussed with another man.

As she listens to the security man repeating some words after Dajaal, she acts as though unbothered, and pretends as if what is going on is of no concern to her and has little or nothing to do with her or her life. What instructions can Dajaal be giving that require Hudhudle continuously interspersing his responses deferentially either with "sir," or with similar phrases?

Cambara remembers a long time ago when there was peace in this country, when everyone knew their place in it and their responsibility for maintaining it. In the order and nature of things, you heard these forms of address, because Somali society was at peace with its collective conscience, comfortable in itself and proud of its station, perceived as being unique in Africa and the world at large. It's curious that she hasn't given much thought to any of this before now or hasn't associated these terms with an orderly way of living since moving into the hotel. Of course, it isn't that she has a wistful desire to return to a hierarchical, male-run taxonomy in which women occupied the lowest rung in the ladder. God forbid, no. It is just that she is nostalgic for a past in which your house was yours and you did not involve armed escorts to get it back or to get to it in the first place, and to live and sleep in it without having to park a battlewagon in several of its access points just to protect it.

"Here," she hears Hudhudle say, handing her mobile phone back to her but not before writing down a number on a piece of paper and then saving it on his handheld phone. Hudhudle will use the number in case of an emergency, she reckons, or in the event that it becomes necessary to get in touch with Dajaal.

She takes her phone back, mumbling, "Thanks," and stares at the equipment, maybe hoping that it will divulge to her the intelligence to which only Hudhudle is privy. She is aware that the information it has transmitted to Hudhudle may inalterably affect her life and the lives of the others in the truck if a battle were to erupt. If she hesitates to inquire what is going on, it is because she does not want him to speak to her in the belittling tone of voice adults employ with children; men with women; locals with foreigners to tell their addressee that there are certain life-and-death details with which she does not bother them. She keeps her counsel, remaining silent and deciding to let someone else do the asking. Strangely no one does, maybe because his men know that he will not oblige; and Gacal and SilkHair are blathering and setting each other challenges.

As the truck tumbrels in its forward motion—you would think its main aim is to rid itself of its passengers—the sinews of her face taut and stretched fully, Cambara journeys, in thought, back to her childhood, when her parents created a protective ring around her, keeping her deliberately underinformed "for her own good." She remembers traveling to Kismayo and then to Nairobi with her mother in her seventh year; mother and daughter were gone for over two months. Then something incredible occurred: She overheard Arda telling another woman neighbor, a day after their return, that she had taken her daughter, Cambara, to be infibulated. At first, Cambara asked herself why Arda was telling the brazen lie; she wanted to know what makes a respectable person, like her mother, resort to lying. Older and wiser, she would formulate it thus: What manner of society compels people to resort to taking refuge in falsehoods, disguising the nature of their drink in mugs, and investing in a myth of their own manufacture on the strength of which they murder their neighbors?

Cambara became a willing fellow liar when she repeated the same lies whenever any of her peers from the neighborhood or at school underwent the ritual of female infibulation, saying that her mother had hired a woman in Kismayo to perform it. The first time, Cambara lied out of loyalty to her mother; it was easier the second time, and she thought nothing of it; then she got used to telling the untruth until she almost believed it. She stuck to the false version, because she did not want her mates to tease her, describe her as uncircumcised, as impure. And of course, she did not want them to call her a liar. In the end, she made her mother's initial lie her own. And Cambara discovered over the years that she and her mother would repeatedly resort to deceiving to keep the fetishists of infibulations at bay; or to make it possible for Zaak to join her as her spouse, lies feeding lies. Not telling the truth becomes second nature to anyone who operates in oppressive societies; it is a way of avoiding a confrontation with the members of a society notorious for its hypocrisy.

The jolt resulting from the sudden stopping of the vehicle reminds her of her current situation. Hudhudle gets out of the truck and instructs everyone, save Cambara, Irrid, the deputy manager of the hotel, Gacal, and SilkHair to alight and to encircle the vehicle, and to wait for instructions from him. Not to be left out, however, Gacal and SilkHair elect to dismount, and they resume their teasing and fooling around, putting Cambara in mind of Roberto Benigni's film *Life Is Beautiful*. Hudhudle tells everyone that he will stay a few steps behind and that he will join them outside the family property. Then he dials a number, presumably to bring Dajaal up to speed about their present location and to tell him that they are doing as he has suggested.

Hudhudle says to her, "It might all seem dramatic to you, but you need not worry; there is nothing to fear. Dajaal and I view this only as a precautionary measure, a way of avoiding possible fire from wounded or laid-up snipers. You, Cambara, are to make yourself invisible. Lie on the floor, if you will. Please."

"Why do I make myself invisible?"

Hudhudle replies, "We're driving through yesterday's battle zone. We do not want any sniper to know that you are in the vehicle."

She thinks that ducking death is different from making oneself invisible. She wishes she had what it takes to daub herself with herbs and other juju smears that, as some folktales have it, render one invisible. Better still, she wishes she had been born into the clan family said to have the power of making themselves unseen, which they are said to do whenever they are warring against mightier foes.

It is when she hears his words, "Fear not, worry not, ultimately the victory is yours," that her heart goes pit-a-pat.

The vehicle still not moving, the engine still on, Hudhudle keeps the door open to make sure that she hauls herself down to the floor. What a discomfort it is as she jams herself, knocking her head then her knees against the protrusions of the vehicle, wincing and cursing at the inconvenience of it all. Then the deputy manager of the hotel, Irrid—so named because he had no front upper teeth, hence *irrid,* a door, in his mouth—follows suit; he lowers himself to the floor in the last row of the vehicle. Before shutting the vehicle door on them, Hudhudle says, "Good luck, everyone."

Then he walks the length of the vehicle backward, his weapon drawn and ready to fire. The driver changes into gear, going slowly and suppressing a chortle, amused to see that the sweetness of life can make a fool of the best of us. "What dramatic goings-on," says he. Even though silent, Cambara agrees with him.

The armed youths, meanwhile, fan themselves out into two groups and keep very close to the truck, giving it regal cover, with two of them ahead of it, guns raised and fingers on triggers, and some more on either side of it, having a good look around. SilkHair doesn't know what to do about his empty hands, he who has held guns, shot, and killed; Gacal, however, is crawling on the dusty ground, as he has seen in films, and smothering a laugh. The second lot of armed youths, who are trailing behind the vehicle, face the other way, skulking stealthily, as though on a prowl. Cambara compares this charade to the travesty of a one-vehicle motorcade in which a pontiff, a king, or a president is traveling, so many bodyguards gathered around one VIP, their drawn guns likely to cause mayhem if they go off accidentally, God forbid.

Irrid is breathing heavily. He says, "I wish I had gone directly to the Bakhaaraha market in the saloon car. Then I would have needed only a discreetly armed escort. As it is, I have a bad heart, and it feels as if death is closing in on it."

She says, "I had no idea."

Good breeding forbids her to speak of how she is penned up in a vehicle with such a heavy breather, with a bad heart. Not to pass out, she listens to the pitter-patter of her own heart, tapping to its rhythm, while having an earful of Irrid's sniffling. From the little she can see of the heavens when she looks up and through her side of the window, there are no clouds, only a large expanse of desolation.

The driver, his voice a little shaky, is saying, "I bet you had no idea what you were getting yourself into, dislodging a warlord from a property in which he has been raising a family."

She restrains herself from the temptation to disabuse him of the impression that she is afraid; she isn't, she might insist, not for herself. She overcame what she might describe as everyday fear when she buried it with her son, Dalmar. She doesn't know if it will make sense to him, though, that she feels guilty that they might come to harm. She senses a grave private unease and says nothing. It crosses her mind to lay all blame at her own door. Again, she doesn't speak, thinking, What's the point?

The driver laments, "Let's face it, and let's say things as they are. What will you do when Gudcur's men come for you, their guns blazing, and their 'technicals' firing bazookas? I hope we come to no harm ourselves today, just because we are caged in the same car with you."

Irrid says, "Don't say that."

Then they hear some banging on the vehicle, Hudhudle shouting, saying to the driver to stop. When the vehicle has come to a halt, and just before Hudhudle has pulled the door open, Irrid has a convulsive fit: "Please, please. Gudcur, I have nothing to do with any of this."

Hudhudle makes no heavy weather of Irrid's outpouring. He says, "Sit up, calm down, and hush, Irrid. Why are you behaving as if you've never smelled gunpowder? It is me, Hudhudle."

Cambara clambers up to her seat, embarrassed, as if she has been the one who has had the mild spasm. But she is relieved; her face says so. Then she spots Dajaal, who is carrying on like a military officer conducting a campaign with the help of a ragtag bunch of armed youths, telling them where to position themselves in the event of an ambush. He waves to the driver that there is no need to stop. Dajaal raises the boom himself, letting the vehicle pass. When the car comes level with him and the driver presses the button to wind down the window, Dajaal says to Cambara, without any preamble or word of welcome, "Bile is on his way here." Then he turns his gaze away, clearly indicating that he has nothing more to say to her.

She thinks, What else is there to say? What else is there to do? As she takes a surreptitious glance in the direction of Irrid, she remarks his residual sense of abashment, which lingers on longer than she thinks is good for the poor sod. Cambara derives comfort from reliving the scene in which she bore witness to Bile's soiled state, about which she will never speak. If only we'd admit to being weaker than we think. Weak we are born; weak we'll die.

Her sunken heart is heavier to carry than a foot that has gone to sleep, she tells herself, as she advances gradually into the house and then eventually into the hall, where she means, eventually, to conduct her blocking and rehearsals. Most likely not today.

Everybody helps in bringing into the house the two suitcases, and the small tote bag in which she had her toiletries, a packet of dried and sliced prunes, some raisins, and a few clothes; the suitcases are heavier and fuller, containing books, notepads, sketch pads, and only two of the miniature masks. SilkHair and Gacal supervising, she indicates that the tote is to go to her en-suite, never mind that there is no bed to speak of, only a mattress on the floor, soiled brown and full of tears. She prays that Irrid will return with the purchases before the end of the day. She has no idea where Dajaal is and does not recall seeing Qasiir when she was coming in the truck, maybe because she was on the floor and wasn't in a position to see anyone.

In the cool disquiet of the hall where she is alone for a moment, Cambara allows her imagination to soar to great heights so as to conquer her umbrage, overpowering it with her creative sanction, the license to do what she pleases in the family house, now that it has become hers. It is then that a couple of images come to her in the shape of a woman who has a lot of fight left in her and of another woman who will not cower at the sight of blood or at the sound of bullets passing close by. She wonders if the network of women will continue its commitment to giving her unconditional support if Kiin interprets her hasty move as unwary, thoughtless to the point of undoing all that they have done to recover the property for her. Will some of the women support her loyally, because of her determination to put up a fight, her fearlessness unequaled? She envisages living in the house—she has no idea for how long—and working in the service of peace and justice as the situation permits. Cambara pictures spending quality time with Bile, who, in her imagining, is enamored not so much of her as he is of the idea of a woman like her.

Then she hears small scuttles, similar to the sounds that rats make when scurrying to safety. She does not know where the noise is coming from, and cannot decide whether to look up at the eaves or toward the window, her pique, mixed with a worrying dose of fear, rising up for the first time since she alighted from the vehicle, from her viscera, as if to choke her.

"We are here," Gacal says.

She is relieved when she locates SilkHair and Gacal, approaching sheepishly. Why do children hide behind doors or pillars inside houses and delight in frightening adults? Although the two boys seem to be moving toward her, Cambara is of the weird impression that they are not gaining on her, the distance between them remaining unchanged. She urges them to get closer, and when they do and are within a meter of her, she says to them, "Please let's not startle each other."

Then she gives them hugs and, as she kisses them on the cheeks, in turn, remembers both the dream and her conversation with Raxma, from the combination of which the urge to move into the property has mysteriously sprung. She senses that even though neither has had a bath, SilkHair's day-old sweat has the hint of an adult's BO odor, as compared to Gacal's, maybe because Gacal's skin is less oily, and has something of an unchanged diaper smell to it. She deduces from this that SilkHair is probably Gacal's senior by two, three years.

She looks hesitantly around, the unfinished nature of the battle of the evening before beginning to haunt her. She realizes that her head is empty of original ideas that might help her to confront the situation at hand. Because she does not wish to allude to the attack on the house, she picks a neutral topic. She asks Gacal, "Where were you when I looked for the two of you this morning?"

Gacal is equivocal. "Here and there."

She asks, "Where is here? Where is there?"

"We went nowhere."

"He won't tell you, but I will," SilkHair says.

At Cambara's encouragement, it comes out that they went to see movies—SilkHair his favorite kung fu films, Gacal another blue flick. What bothers her is not that Gacal is being equivocal or refusing to answer her but that he is lying. Of course, she is aware that it doesn't mean that SilkHair's truth-telling is symptomatic of a more truthful nature; maybe he fancies that he can earn her affections that way, whereas Gacal is in a survivalist mode, behaving like a boy who had everything one day and none the next.

"Why, Gacal?"

Gacal's face loses its natural color, blanching with discontent. He wants to say something, but he cannot, as though fearing the consequence. She wonders, but does not dare inquire, how Gacal conducted himself in the situation of the night before. He is rattled. How much effect will Cambara's moving out of the hotel have on the two boys? Will it bring Gacal's reunion with Qaali, if she is alive, closer? SilkHair has known a tougher existence, doesn't mind trying his hand at cooking or fending for himself; he is eager to tell the truth, get on her right side. Gacal's difficulty in operating under this sort of condition is more recent, and he needs to adjust to his situation. On first meeting him, she suspected that the boy had attitude and that she would get used to it, and he to her.

Unprompted, SilkHair asks, "Shall I make a fire and then some tea?"

"Later. But tell me, when there is fighting and all the small and heavy guns are blazing, do you manage to sleep at all after things have quieted down and the attackers have withdrawn?"

"It is difficult to sleep," he says. "Your ears are full of noise, your heart of fear, and you are excited, and you want to talk, but you can't, because you do not know when or if the attackers will return. You don't want them to hear you. Sleep runs away, not daring to return for several nights. Then you stay up and another type of energy floods your body. You think you won't miss sleep, but when you do, you go crazy from sleeplessness."

"Where would you go in this house if you had no guns and they attacked?" she says to Gacal.

"I would hide up in the attic," Gacal says, "close to a water tank if there is one, or in a pantry. Not in the cupboard where clothes are hanging, for that is where they look for anyone hiding. At least, we did when we searched a house. If the fighting was brief, that is where I hid for a whole night, crouched by a water tank when the militiamen came to attack the lodging where my dad and I were staying. When no one was around, I would come down to the pantry. There is dry bread sometimes."

Cambara does not know what to do. She mouths the words "Oh you poor thing," but she can't bring herself to say them.

SilkHair is enjoying himself; that much is clear. He says, "What matters is to be patient and when you get the chance to kick their teeth in. Always good to chase them off. Never take any of them prisoner, you have to feed them."

"I won't know what to do," she admits.

"With the likes of Qasiir and his mates around, fighters known for their fearlessness," SilkHair, sounding like an old man speaking from experience, says, "you can relax. Just keep your mobile phone charged, and we can call Dajaal. Problem solved."

Then SilkHair turns to Gacal, his long stare focused on him in a forbiddingly communicative way; it is as if he is daring Gacal to contradict him.

"We are fine," SilkHair assures her.

She says, "I am not so sure."

SilkHair puts a physical distance between him and Gacal on the one hand and Cambara on the other. "Have you ever known any fighting?"

"Never."

SilkHair and Gacal look at each other in bafflement. She relives the commotion that Irrid created: The driver making snide remarks, in which he predicted that Gudcur's men would come, maybe after nightfall, gunning for her and determined to do their worst. The question is, which is better: to arm oneself or to insist, as she is wont to do, that they do not; and to hire gun hands until the conditions become livable.

SilkHair's excited voice awakens her from the brief trance as he says, "We know our lines. Shall we start rehearsing?"

"Maybe not now," she says.

"It'll pass the time, rehearsing."

"Yes, let's," Gacal says.

To SilkHair, "Where's the tea you promised?"
Gacal says, "I'll come and help make the fire."
SilkHair insists, "After tea, we rehearse."
"We'll rehearse after I've had tea."
"Promise?"
"Promise."
They rehearse; she waits for Bile to come.

THIRTY

Nothing seizes the imagination as relentlessly as fear does, Cambara thinks. However, even though she is fretful, she is determined not to permit the dread that she feels—which is only natural, given the circumstances—to cloud her judgment. Then she remembers the drift of a Somali adage that says that the mother of a coward seldom mourns the death of her child from impulsiveness. No matter. She will admit that she has been as foolhardy as a brave woman who has decided to tempt fate but who has had luck on her side up to now. From now on, no more harebrained daredevilry. She must get down to serious work to counter the onslaught of the panic beating in her heart . . . while waiting for Bile.

Cambara calls for an unscheduled pause in the resumed rehearsal, because she is making too many slip-ups in her directorial suggestions, repeatedly having to change her mind and contradicting herself. It is as if her heart is occupied, in part with consternation, despite her re-solve to abandon herself to repossessing the house, and in part by her eagerness to see Bile. She has just about whipped out her mobile phone debating whether it would be wise or not to ring him and ask when and if he is coming, when she hears the commotion of voices and then the arrival of a truck, most likely Irrid with the purchases. SilkHair and Gacal run off to join the excitement.

A couple of minutes later, Gacal reappears to report to her that he has seen the beds, unopened boxes of crockery, mattresses, a small midget fridge—"maybe for our room," he guesses—and lots and lots of other things. She is out of it, though, dejected in appearance, mild in her enthusiasm, whenever one of the boys comes to inform her of what he has seen. Looking at her sitting there, still, her gaze distant, you can't tell from her bearing what it is that she wants done.

There are comings and goings of the men bringing in the generator, a stove, the beds, the sheets, the mattresses, the bedspreads, boxes and boxes, creating a brouhaha. Only when decisions concerning where this item is to go and to which room that other item must be taken are to be made is she consulted, but she is indifferent. She will think about this later, she half shouts. Leave them where you like for the time being, she says, clearly annoyed with SilkHair, who is fired up and demanding that she give an answer right away. SilkHair feels put out and he walks away in silence to minister to his sulk in a corner. Just then Gacal returns, hanging out with the men bringing in the mattresses and pretending to work, and he spots SilkHair looking hurt. Asked what the matter is, SilkHair reminds his friend that they have forgotten to make the fire and the tea that they promised *her*. SilkHair speculates, "Maybe *she* is irritable, because she hasn't had her tea, the kick that some adults need. Like *qaat*."

The fire in the charcoal brazier ready for the tea, Gacal suggests they throw away the pan, all beat up and blackened by soot, in which they cooked food and boiled the water for tea the last time and open one of the boxes in which there is sure to be a new kettle. SilkHair doesn't agree, and the two of them, arguing back and forth, each giving their reason why or why not, go to Cambara to adjudicate. She says, "Do what you like. In any case, I don't want tea anymore."

Neither knows what to do or say. They look like two tomcats that have just been fixed, their faces drained of stamina. They slink away, giving each other a wide berth and avoiding any bodily contact whatsoever, as if they are sore. They make the tea and return to offer her a cup and ask if she wants sugar and condensed milk. Cross, she says, "Didn't I say I do not want tea?"

Irrid accepts a cup if it is on offer. Four spoons of sugar and some milk please. And biscuits, if there are any. He pulls a chair, clutching lots of chits in his right hand, receipts for his purchases in millions of the devalued local currency. Lacking somewhere else to spread them, he holds the one he is explaining about close to Cambara and lays out the rest on his lap. When he has gone on far too long for her liking, she says, her voice lackluster, "It doesn't matter. Give them to me, and I'll study them in my own time."

Then her mobile phone squeals: It is Bile at the other end, announcing that he is less than two minutes away from the property, Dajaal driving. Such is the animated change that takes place in her features, her boisterous movements, her spirited feistiness that Irrid, preparing to flee from the scene, searches unsuccessfully for a table, some surface anywhere on which to place his unfinished teacup. No longer the morose woman whom SilkHair and Gacal have slunk from, and no longer the woman with the moody take on the purchases Irrid has made, she is now vivaciously engaging the two boys—she wants them to join her at the rehearsal hall for them to resume their blocking—and thanking Irrid, warmly shaking his hand and politely requesting that he see himself off and give a handsome tip to the youths who've escorted him to and from the Bakaaraha market.

In an instant, the rehearsal is in full swing.

And Bile is spellbound.

Cambara can see that whenever she turns around, for he is seated way in the back of the hall on a hard chair, his legs outstretched, his expression that of a very contented man. He has taken a long look around, seen how much has been done, with a lot of input from Seamus, who has apparently kept him informed. He has been cursorily in the bedrooms, bathrooms, and kitchen and has satisfied himself that it will be a beautiful house when completed.

To her, he doesn't look anything like the man whom she saw yesterday: sick like a cat suffering from a bout of flu and soiled. For the life of her, she can't recall with any precision what it is that excites her about him. The times are confusing, and it doesn't help when you have to attend to too many life-and-death matters.

"Let's do this scene again," she says.

Gacal and SilkHair are at each other's throats, each blaming the other for not paying attention to his lines. They fight like two actors getting into a confrontation that is likely to ruin the chance of her working through the part of the text she wishes to solidify. Gacal accuses SilkHair of messing it all up for everyone; neither is prepared to listen to reason; their never-ending quibbles know no limits; and they take yet another unscheduled break, which gives her a chance to join Bile.

"You are very good, considering," he commends her efforts and stands up to greet her. They hug, and as they do so, she observes perfunctorily that all is well with him: hair combed, clothes freshly ironed, shoes polished, and fingernails scissor-trimmed, not nervously bitten off to the quick. He is having a good day.

"If only I had more time," she says.

"Gacal is excellent," Bile comments, his hand remaining within reach of hers but not touching or taking it, their closeness producing sufficient warmth to enliven the chemistry between them.

"He is a natural," she agrees.

"Where did you find him?"

"A long story, which is telling itself by the day, you won't believe it," she says. Then she pauses, this time taking hold of his hand and kissing him on the right cheek. Then she calls to the two boys to return to the stage, which they do a little unwillingly. She says to Bile, "Half an hour and we'll break for the day."

The moment they are on the stage, they become who they are: two boys seeking her attention and, knowing no better, scrapping to decide which will have the upper hand in a misguided tussle. SilkHair in particular is in an unpardonably sparring mood.

Cambara takes SilkHair aside, "Cut it out."

"I don't like that man at all," SilkHair says, then looks jealously over his shoulder at Bile.

"Why?"

"I've seen him before."

"Where?"

"At The Refuge that he ran."

"What did he do that you didn't like?"

"He was very, very strict."

"When was that?"

"I was younger, before I became a fighter."

"Why didn't you like him? Tell me."

SilkHair, she gathers from his response, saw Bile as a wizened old man with skin so smooth, manners so affected, that he fled and joined the first fighting force that might trust him with a gun.

They return to the stage, she pulling him, and they resume their rehearsal, Gacal performing his role very well, and SilkHair adequately. Then all of a sudden, SilkHair says, "I won't be a chicken, only an eagle. I must be one of the eagles; I am no chicken and won't be one. No matter what."

Not for the first time, Cambara takes the trouble to explain that a real actor, who is human, may on occasion represent a fictional character, say an animal, and that a child at times may play the role of an adult, provided one follows certain conventions. Her patience a little too stretched, she tells him that it is because of a convention that younger boys playing the roles of men older than their age sport a full beard and walk with a stoop. Younger girls wear the head scarves of older women, and they hunch their shoulders as part of the make-believe.

In a theatrical aside, Gacal, using the side of his mouth that is close to her, makes a snide comment: that SilkHair does not know the difference between playing the role of and being the character or the animal. Then he says aloud, more to impress Bile and Cambara and to goad SilkHair into further outrages, "SilkHair's problem is he does not know and does not want to say that he does not know."

"Say what you like, I won't be a chicken."

Determined to find the underlying cause of his obstinance one way or the other, Cambara asks SilkHair why he is unprepared to play a chicken, even though she has not assigned such a role to him.

"I am giving you advance warning that I will not play the role of a chicken," he replies. "No matter what."

"Why?"

"Because I do not want my mates the fighters to point at me and make clucking sounds, as if I am a chicken."

"Who says they will see you as a chicken?"

"Some of the fighters will, like Qasiir."

"But you don't mind being an eagle? And Gacal has no problem playing the chicken?"

"Because where I come from, my clan family owns everything, including the sky. Gacal comes from a family of farmers, lowly people who, like chickens, live on scraps, on other people's leftovers. They are as cheap as the dirt at which they pick."

"I think a brief pause is in order," she says.

As they disperse, in silence, she tells herself maybe the break will help her deal with the other hurdles of an artistic, text-related nature, although she doubts that she will be able to remove these obstacles until they are well into serious rehearsals, and even then may not be able to take care of the problems. Reading a text through the one time may not highlight or unbury all its inadequacies right away. This being her directorial debut, with the likes of SilkHair, she wonders how well her first attempt at playwriting and directing will work and how much rewriting she will have to do before she is happy with it. Written texts, she imagines, often require more than a read-through and much rewriting before the dialogue takes on its own life, independent of its author.

SilkHair goes off in a huff and sits away from everyone, on Seamus's toolboxes; Gacal finds a stool and is admiring a handful of the props, makeup paraphernalia, and other tools of her theatrical trade. Cambara, who walks over to where Bile is, wonders aloud when she might lay the groundwork aimed at making SilkHair and Gacal come to grips with the challenges that lie ahead of them.

"All will be fine, you'll see," Bile says.

Cambara has no heart to contradict his optimism, even if she is actually entertaining second thoughts about the whole thing. "Maybe I should put in more time, school Gacal in understanding the role he is playing. That it is not a chicken. I hate to make it sound so hoity-toity and literary and talk to him about metaphors and all that crap."

Bile struggles with a thought before saying "It's always novices who believe they know better. SilkHair strikes me as being used to fighting his way to the top. But you can't do that in life all the time."

She asks, "Do you remember ever knowing him?"

"I've seen lots of children in my days at The Refuge," Bile says. "He may have been one of the 'tourists.' We used to refer to them as such, because they would come infrequently when their families ran out of food, or when there was fighting in their area that displaced them. Am I supposed to have met him?"

"At The Refuge. You were too strict."

"And he left?"

"And joined a fighting force."

Now Bile and Cambara pay attention to the boys. They can hear their conversation, Gacal saying "I have no problem playing the role of a chicken. You become the eagle; I, the chicken. How about that?"

SilkHair, his index finger warning Gacal to stop provoking him, starts shooting arrows of venom now in Gacal's direction, now in Bile's, his hard look weakening only when it encounters Cambara's, and he turns back to Gacal angrily. "If you don't stop messing with me, I'll make you eat shit."

Gacal eggs him on with his sarcasm, saying "Oh please, please, SilkHair. Spare me. Don't hurt me; don't harm me. I'm quivering."

"I'm warning you," SilkHair says.

Standing, SilkHair towers over Gacal, his teeth clenched in anger at being provoked when he cannot do anything about it. His hands appear underutilized, as if they wished they had a weapon to use. Looking away with exasperation, he turns to observe that Cambara is watching every one of his moves intently. Cambara thinks that he'll need training in anger management, considering that he has been accustomed to falling back on the use of a firearm whenever he felt so inclined. He is clearly on a low, like an addict finding it difficult to kick the habit.

Gacal continues to incite him, saying "You haven't the balls, have you?"

"I said I'm warning you."

"Boys are boys," Bile says.

"Are they . . . always?" from Cambara.

In her wish to preempt further provocative exchanges, she settles on inaction, assuming that if she shows no interest to them, they will calm down on their own.

Perhaps boys are boys because people believe that it is healthy for them to tease, prod, and incite each other, she thinks, but I am wondering if these two are behaving in this way now and doing what they are doing because they are enjoying the closest yet to a normal life. A baby will weep its throat sore when hungry, but once it has had enough of its mother's breast milk, it will bite the nipple playfully and then laugh. Not before they have had their fill. Afterward, they fool with the food, spitting it, spilling it.

"Time to think of feeding the lot of you," she says, getting up and waiting for Bile to do likewise. "Two young cantankerous mouths to feed, not to speak of a guest with refined taste, I bet. What can I offer? No more than good intentions, considering the crockery in unopened boxes, the chicken still in its live form. There are veggies, yes. But I doubt there are spices or if Irrid remembered to get salt."

"We can order a takeaway," Bile says, following her in the direction of what he knows to be an unfinished kitchen, the old tiles removed from the wall and the new ones not yet here.

"A takeaway? Fancy that."

"First nights in new places are a challenge," he says. "Why don't we ring Dajaal, who can't be very far, as he is overseeing the security details around here, and he can bring back a meal from Hotel Shamac or from Maanta."

She considers the suggestion, fighting off an encroaching feeling of despondency that is activating her warning signals. For with shocking speed, unbidden, the thought of forever being dependent on someone—to drive her around, to mount checkpoints, to fix the fuse when the electricity fails, to fetch a takeaway—has reasserted itself.

"As long as you don't hold it against me . . ."

"Hold what against you?"

"I'll feed you from what we have in the house."

And she summons the boys, assigning the job of washing the vegetables to Gacal—to whom she says, "Make sure you wash your hands first . . . with soap"—and to SilkHair the chore of fetching the live chicken and the sharp knife she remembers using when cooking for Gudcur's children the second day she was here. SilkHair wants to prove to Gacal that he has balls, and so requests that he be allotted the honor of chopping off the chicken's head, and that Gacal should then forfeit the right to play the role of an eagle.

Bile says, "Never killed one in my life."

Gacal accepts the bet, and the two set their camp within view of Cambara and Bile, who start chatting, Bile agreeing that this is better than a takeaway any day. When he asks what Gacal's story is, having heard SilkHair's, she tells him the boy's heart-wrenching story and how she is trying now to reunite mother and son. She adds, "He is a 'tourist' in the land of misery in the sense in which you used the word earlier to describe SilkHair's probable status at The Refuge."

Then silence as the two boys work, SilkHair encountering no difficulties in swinging the chicken until he and it are both dizzy and then in chopping its head off. He even helps Gacal, who is a novice in the kitchen, to peel the potatoes and deal with the cutting of the onion without crying furiously, after which SilkHair starts to tell a story in which he boasts, rattling off his exploits as a fighter for the clan-based militia. He gives exaggeratedly gory details of what he has done to the enemy combatants, adding that it excites him to dice with danger, show that he is man.

Cambara then asks him to start a fire in the brazier and then fill two pans with water, one for Gacal's veggies and one for his chicken and to let her know when he has removed the feathers and the bird is ready to cook. She says for Bile's benefit, "Maybe I have prunes somewhere in one of my bags. A Moroccan chicken dish, the closest to *tagine* we can have at this place."

The two boys making very little noise and concentrating on their allocated chores, and Bile serene in her company, the evening appears majestic in its quietness, and she, but a woman who has it in her to take someone's measure and then do the good thing, even if she is also capable of settling accounts with those, like Zaak and Wardi, who are given to unbecoming behavior. She comes to realize for the first time in a while, that her rages toward Wardi, who at times she seems to have completely forgotten, and her disappointment in Zaak, whom she doesn't know if she will bother to invite to the private show at Kiin's, have gone. In their stead is a sense of elation.

Inching his way nearer, careful not to disturb her or interrupt their conversation, SilkHair stands for a few minutes in the periphery of her vision. When she motions to him to speak, he says, "Shall we?"

"Shall we what?"

"Start cooking?" SilkHair says.

She remembers that she hasn't looked for the prunes. In her travels, she carries prunes on the assumption that they help her digest her food better. That she hasn't searched for them up to now only means that she wasn't the cook. Up she stands and in she goes to a couple of rooms before she finds the tote bag in which they might be. Again, luck is on her side, because they are at the bottom. What's more, she brings out her shortwave radio, hoping to discover if the "Missing Persons" BBC Somali Service program, which airs at about this time, will broadcast her message signed with her pseudonym today.

She is happy she has decided that they eat together as a foursome here, for this has brought out so much fervor in the boys' wish to participate, and in Bile's desire to share their company as a threesome.

Back at the brazier, she says, "Let's!"

The communal cooking runs rather smoothly, and the two boys are in song, each taking their cue from the other's sterling performance, like the lines allotted to a professional actor at his peak. She derives immense pleasure from watching SilkHair, who is in a league of his own, and Gacal, who is a dab hand, like actors teasing the multiplicity of possible interpretations out of a single phrase. It seems, however, as if SilkHair has been cut from a coarser cloth, a touch too nervous, crude in his manner and seldom able to cotton on to his failing. She has had to remind him to wash his hands with soap and water, because he keeps wiping them on his dirty clothes.

Supper ready, she serves the boys and tells them to give them space. Too eager to be on their own, they take off, each carrying one of the new plates—SilkHair has insisted on opening the box—and tumblers full of water.

"How sweet of you to come," she says when they are alone, "on the first night that I've resolved to pitch camp here. You've been of immense help. Thank you."

He takes his first mouthful. "Good," he says.

She raises her glass, saying, "Sorry that we do not have anything stronger than water in a tumbler. Let's eat in celebration of peace."

An air of certainty prevails, with Bile commending her for motivating SilkHair and Gacal to take their cooking or whatever else they are doing seriously.

"I would like to audition for a part," he says.

"Would you?"

"Is there a part for an old man?"

"A villager. A wizened old man."

"Lend me the text?"

Time to listen to the "Missing Persons" program of the BBC Somali
Service. It takes her a long while to find the station, and when she does,
she discovers that the news is on. They listen to it, both feeling disheartened as they hear a nothing-good-comes-out-of-Africa litany.

Cambara says, "It is a pity the world doesn't come to hear of the very
many excellent things that are accomplished daily in different parts of
the continent by ordinary folks, achievements about which no one
ever learns."

"The news, sui generis, is about politicians and their doings, isn't it?"
Bile says. "Not about the ordinary person in the Midwest in the United
States; in a small village in Darfur, surviving the daily horrors; a fish-
erman in Sri Lanka; or a mother raising her children under difficult circumstances in Baghdad."

Cambara, confirming this and agreeing with the drift, adds that she
knows that you can have a good day and a bad day in civil war
Mogadiscio as you might in a small farming village anywhere. She goes
on, "Before I got here, I used to think that it wouldn't be possible to
enjoy a moment of peace in the company of a friend, with twilight
hours as breathtaking as the one on the horizon."

"You think you may stay here," he asks. "Long?"

"All being well, I might."

Just then, "Missing Persons" comes on. Cambara is surprised that
some of the people are searching for their cousins or half-brothers
after so many years of being out of touch. She can't imagine her and
Arda being apart for three days without one trying to phone or if possible e-mail the other. It is toward the end of the program that she hears
Qaali's name mentioned and her pseudonym, care of Maanta Hotel,
telephone number included, given.

"Let's hope Qaali or someone who knows her is listening to today's
program," Bile says. "For all one knows, she may be living close by, unaware that her son is here."

"Let's hope so."

"If I may add, please count on me to help too."

"Thank you."

"I mean it."

"I know," and she pats him on the hand.

They sit in the shadowy hour of twilight, like two lovers who have found quiet refuge in a corner of the night, away from the madding aficionados. She is tired from working her bones to exhaustion and feels she can do with a hot bath and pleasurable company. He is full of unexpended energy, the adrenaline of his enthusiasm having risen to greater heights.

"So what would you like to do?" Bile asks her.

She cannot find the courage to say what is on her mind, afraid that he might misunderstand her. For she wants to be in his company, never mind where—in his apartment and alone with him, at her hotel and in full view of many others, but she does not want to be sharing his bed. Not tonight.

"What are you thinking?" she asks.

"I've asked Dajaal to pick me up just about now and, knowing him, he will be showing up shortly. I can postpone his time of arrival, telling him to come later, or let it stand the way we left it."

"There is always tomorrow," she says.

The boys show up, carrying their cleaned-up plates, each willing to wash up his own as well as Cambara's, Bile's, and the pots. While they are busy with that task, Dajaal arrives on the dot.

Their parting words are not elaborate. She says, "Till tomorrow," deciding on when she hopes to meet him again.

He says, "Tomorrow."

THIRTY-ONE

A party is in progress.

Several of the roisterers are dancing to the latest Afro beat, and those not grooving are at the stand-alone barbecue spot helping with the grilling, in the pool swimming laps competitively, or simply whiling away the time enjoyably in their own way. It is early in the evening, and many of those present delight in being reunited to celebrate an event that means a lot to all of them.

There are about twenty or so revelers, among them Cambara, Bile, Kiin, Farxia, and standing behind the drinks table, wearing an apron, an elderly lady, an Arda lookalike, talking to an Unidentified Woman. Gacal and SilkHair are there, running errands, serving drinks, and performing odd chores, and there are also two girls, whom Bile introduces to the two boys. "Just come from Canada for a brief visit they are paying their uncles, Bile and Seamus. Cute, aren't they?" When asked the girls' names, he pauses hesitantly at first, then says, "One of them is called Raasta, the other Makka." Raasta is not eager to speak to either of the boys, whom she finds uninteresting because they are rowdy and won't allow her to concentrate on smearing the wooden masks with linseed oil. Makka is simply watching.

Cambara and Bile are at the shallow end of the pool, standing close to each other, talking. There is a platter floating between them, on which somebody has arranged a pattern of orchids, roses—some red, some yellow, and at least two white—and lilies. Kiin, distracted, is half listening to the Unidentified Woman, who is telling her about the tragedy that has befallen her, how her husband met his death at the hands of the militiamen who abducted him from the airport. Gacal arrives to put an intricate question to the Unidentified Woman, who politely declines to answer it, telling him, "Don't interrupt, darling, when I am speaking to someone else. Haven't I asked you not to butt in when you must not?" The Unidentified Woman isn't at all keen to deal with Gacal's question, on the assumption that it might lead them back somewhere she doesn't wish to return. At the moment, she is enjoying herself meeting some of the people who have helped to bring about her reunion with her son.

With the Unidentified Woman gone to apologize to Gacal, who seems put out, Kiin returns to being a voyeur watching Cambara and Bile discreetly cuddling; they are in a world of their own, and she follows them with her eyes, in silence at first. A little later, when she thinks they are being bashful, she encourages them to feed each other, now suggesting to Bile that he give an orchid to Cambara to eat, now proposing that Cambara feed Bile the red roses, now insisting that they pose while she takes suggestive photographs of them, the flash of the camera so bright they both close their eyes.

In the dream, there is an abundant fund of fellow feeling and a lot of gladness. There is joy all around. The women from the network come in ones, twos, and threes to pay their tribute to Cambara, to commend her for her efforts to bring genuine smiles into the eyes of many of the members. Everyone at the party—whether dancing, swimming, feeding each other on orchids and red roses, performing menial tasks, giving a hand at the cookout, or waiting to eat—is a willing partner in this hour of rejoicing, striving to contribute to the well-being of the entire community.

Arda looks on from close by, profoundly happy. This is quite evident, despite her self-restraint—her uncontrollable enthusiasm at being home after several years and finding that her daughter has achieved a miracle, through what, if she were a politician, she might call consensus building. She chats amicably with Gacal and SilkHair—the one wearing a white shirt, dark trousers, and a bow tie; the other in a dark shirt, and trousers the color of cream with the feel of linen—whenever they stop to engage her interest in the drinks they are carrying around on a platter, as waiters do.

Arda asks Gacal, "Where is this famous Irishman whom everybody wants me to meet? He is not around here, hiding, because he is too shy to be introduced?"

Gacal replies, "Seamus will be here, for sure, after he's finished building the stage for Cambara's play and given it its final touches. Imagine—he's built the stage and carved the masks all on his own, without any help from anyone."

"I want to shake his hand," Arda says.

"I'll tell him that if I see him," he says.

"I want to thank him too," she adds.

"No one deserves our thanks more than he does."

Then Arda comes adrift from her well-earned feeling of contentment and, becoming restless, moves away. Bored, she sprays passersby with Canadian dollars, according to a Nigerian nouveau-riche tradition in which the relatives or friends of a celebrant—the mother or the sisters, say, of the bride—paste cash on the foreheads of some of the invited guests and encourage them to keep the money, the better for everyone to remember the occasion. Amused, because he is not familiar with the Nigerian way of doing things, Gacal asks why she is sticking Canadian banknotes on the foreheads of the revelers. Arda replies, "My visit to Mogadiscio has coincided with my daughter achieving three unheard-of miracles: one, she has recovered our family property; two, she is producing a play; three, she has at last found a sentiment that has always eluded her—true happiness. I am so very, very delighted."

Then Arda pauses close to the swimming pool, taking in Cambara and Bile's doings. She walks toward them, maybe to say something disapproving. When on second thought she changes her mind and turns her back on them, Cambara and Bile interrupt their communing of their own accord, stepping out of the pool in their bathing suits.

It is Cambara's turn to occupy the limelight, and she does so by calling to Raxma, who has just arrived and whom she embraces most warmly, welcoming her enthusiastically to the city of their birth. Then Cambara presents Bile to the woman she describes "as my closest friend ever." Tired-looking, Raxma yawns and yawns before explaining that her journey involved a stopover in Nairobi.

"But why, Raaxo dearest?" Cambara asks.

"Cambo dearest, because I wanted to apprise the U.S. Embassy in Nairobi of Gacal's situation and to inveigle them to issue a replacement for his American passport so he may return to Duluth, if the idea takes his fancy."

"Any chance of this happening?"

"To this end," Raxma says, "I have brought with me affidavits signed by the Duluth police chief, another by a congressman, and a third by the headmaster at the school in Duluth Gacal went to, all of them attesting to Gacal's identity and that of the woman otherwise known as the Unidentified Woman."

"What did the consular officer say?"

"In a letter that I am carrying," Raxma says, "the consular officer at the embassy invites Gacal for an interview in which the boy will be allowed to present his own case."

"But that's wonderful," Cambara says.

Just then, Arda drags Cambara away and, for some bizarre unexplained reason, insists that her daughter submit herself to a thorough physical examination, more or less in public, one to be conducted under Farxia's astute supervision. They all wait in the anteroom to her clinic, anxiously silent like patients at a dentist's, as if in pain. After a few minutes, Farxia returns and she seems pleased with the result as she goes to where Arda, Bile, Kiin, Raxma, and the Unidentified Woman are all sitting, worried stiff. Elated, Farxia shows them a single printer-generated sheet, the kind that has perforations at the edges.

Joyous, Arda ululates, "Didn't I always say so?"

The sheet with the mysterious information about Cambara looks a bit more tattered now that it has been handled by several persons. It is straight in some edges and cut crookedly in some corners; it is passed from hand to hand. When everyone in the anteroom is satisfied, Arda calls to Bile, who is permitted to see the diagnosis.

Bile's verdict. "A clean bill of health."

"What do you know?" says Raxma sarcastically.

"My mother is nuts," says Cambara.

Then Cambara wakes up.

Bile says to Cambara, "I suggest we take a break."

It is past midday the following day, and Cambara, Gacal, SilkHair, and Bile are upstairs in the en suite bedroom, rehearsing. They are here because Seamus hasn't finished the much-needed carpentry and joinery work on the stage, and he has requested they find an alternative temporary place until the day after tomorrow, when he hopes to be done. Cambara has chosen the room farthest from where Seamus is hammering away with unprecedented fastidiousness. It is the only almost-habitable room in the house, the others being no better than dumps. But neither Gacal nor SilkHair has minded sleeping downstairs, since they have had the run of the entire house except for Cambara's room, which is under lock and key.

They've been rehearsing nonstop several hours every day—from soon after eight in the morning, following a quick breakfast, until the lunch hour, after which they take a brief break, no siesta, and then resume work, going over the text again and again. A perfectionist, Cambara feels there is still a lot of rehearsing to go through. Cambara is dead beat. To the trained eye of Bile, who takes pride in interpreting the delightful expressions on the face of the woman whom he adores, she looks battle weary.

It's become de rigueur, in the last couple of days, for Cambara and Bile to spend several hours with each other, with Cambara directing and occasionally rewriting and Bile, Gacal, and SilkHair rehearsing and learning their lines. At times, when Cambara invites them, they are joined by others, including Dajaal, Qasiir, and others who make walk-on cameo appearances as part of the crowd in a village, speechlessly watching as the principal protagonists act out their roles per Cambara's set plan. Plainly told, the latest version of the play is about an eagle raised from babyhood among chickens. He is made to fend for his food by pecking on the ground, in the dust—and therefore he thinks of himself as a chicken. A chicken who is the eagle's peer and playmate is hell-bent on sabotaging the idea of the eagle's finding his wings and flying, so to speak. The farmer who found the eagle several years earlier and who didn't mind the bird's cohabiting with the chickens now wants to retrain the eagle so he will become what he has never been— a bird able to fly. Cambara, in her rewrite of the original folktale from Ghana, has altered its drift—from giving a moral message, as folktales are wont to do, to being intense, provocative, complex, and a touch modernist.

"Time to take a break," Bile advises when he realizes that Cambara is not getting her way with the boys. Tired and hungry, they are tetchy, their back talk moody. She is exhausted too; so is he.

Although Cambara is discreetly aware of Bile training his keen eyes on her, she does not capitulate until the sharpness of his overpowering probe mixes with her desire to be alone with him in a room, not doing anything extraordinary, not even loving—just cuddling, snoozing. The look in her gaze softens a little under the scrutiny of his stare and a door to her heart opens, albeit in a tentative way. How marvelous to live close to someone whom you can wholly trust, whose companionship is never in doubt. But despite her exhausted state, in spite of the fact that her eyes are narrowing like the shutters of a shop at closing time, Cambara does not luxuriate in the warmth and affection she feels toward Bile, instead remembering the anger that has precipitated her arrival in the civil war city—her husband's treacherous behavior, which led to Dalmar's death and brought about her leaving him and Toronto to reinvent her place in the world. She wishes she could reciprocate Bile's charismatic advances, taken as she is with his calm approach to matters of the heart, never pushing, always concurring to withdraw at the slightest hint of bother on her side, or a change in her mood or perspective. She is cautious, as women must always be. Nor does she want to offer the impression of being too forward. She can't help being mindful of how first commitments lead one to a plateau of high expectations, only to abandon one in yet another snare. She would do well to pretend, if need be, that she is operating within the boundaries of tradition and remain within the parameters of acceptable behavior in the presence of Dajaal, Kiin, Gacal, and SilkHair. Seamus, she tells herself, is a person apart, a man in his own category, when one thinks of him in the context of local convention. Nothing she might do would ever disconcert him; he is a seen-it-all, done-it-all Irishman. All the same, it will not do for her to acquit herself with the deliberate calmness of a hard-to-get, difficult-to-know, impossible-to-love woman.

In her mind, she is staring at a door. Which key might open it to help her interpret the dream earlier? Was it a dream full of prophetic craving, in that it was very concrete—her mum visiting, the play brought to the stage, Raxma coming, bearing affidavits from the police chief in Duluth and calling at the U.S. Embassy in Nairobi, where she arranged for an interview with Gacal? Hopes raised and then dashed are a disaster. Must she interpret the dream as being no different from the daily, weekly, or monthly horoscopes one reads in the newspapers and magazines? She feels dizzy; the room she is in roams; she has no idea where she is and with whom until Bile speaks. Alas, she can't follow what he is saying—she is engaged with her worries.

He is most attentive to her, his bodily postures very deferential, quiet as a monk in a monastery at prayer time, highly indiscreet. His physical closeness helps her relive the telling pleasantness of their moments spent together, just as the world keeps speedily retreating. Imagine a world with Bile in it, but with no Dajaal. It is a kind of marriage, Bile's dependency on Dajaal, and Dajaal's protectiveness of his— for lack of a better word—employer. But when you work Seamus into this symbiosis, then you have problems of a different nature. She doesn't know if a relationship with Bile on his own, without Dajaal and without Seamus, will ever be feasible.

In Somalia, she thinks, one does not marry an individual; one marries a family, whose constituent units are hardly salutary in their symbiotic rapport with the couple, such is their economic interdependence. A family organized around blood is different from one built around the idea that circumstances determine its formation. She is not sure that she will manage to insinuate herself without strain into the ménage à trois. Somebody has to give, but who? Talk of hatching chickens, she muses, in the menacing vicinity of eagles about to prey on the eggs just laid.

She remembers committing several minutes to studying the photographs on the walls of Bile's apartment the one and only time she was there: photographs of Raasta just born; of Makka, wrapped up in a blanket, waiting to be found; of Bile, holding one, then the other; of The Refuge soon after it was established; of Seamus, with grease up to his elbows, fixing a generator; of Seamus with Bile, Raasta, and Makka; with Raasta and Shanta. No pictures of Dajaal and none of Shanta, save in the first two years following Raasta's birth. None of her husband, Faahiye.

Bile's mobile phone rings. He listens briefly, saying "Yes" twice and then announcing, "Lunch is on its way; it will be delivered soon. From Kiin's kitchen, with her kind compliments."

The monotony of work, work, and more work is broken with the pleasant arrival of Kiin, who delivers the lunch herself—a plain meal of fresh fruit, several large bottles of mineral water, and lots of lemon for the fish dish. Cambara has the pleasant sensation that Kiin has brought something with the lunch—a bit of news, maybe some gossip about Zaak, who knows? It amuses her to remember a quip ascribed to Norman Mailer, who is rumored to have said he couldn't vote for a man who hadn't the balls to cheat on his wife. Is Zaak capable of stirring a one-liner to life so others would repeat it?

"You and Bile are always working," Kiin says in a tone of voice that has a bit of why-don't-you-include-me envy in it. She serves Gacal and SilkHair, who need no encouragement from anyone to leave the adults to their wearisome talk. They take themselves as far away as they can, within reason.

"There is a role for you to play, Kiin," Cambara says, accepting the plate of food that Kiin is offering her. She mumbles her thanks, and goes on, "The main female protagonist in my play has good lines, and I am sure that you will do justice to them, even though you have never acted in a play. Do you wish to consider it?"

"I haven't the time," Kiin says, dishing a small portion of fish and salad for Bile, because he has indicated his small appetite by holding his middle and forefingers together just as she is doling out his share. "I am a single mother having to fight my in-laws daily for the custody of my two daughters, a manager of a hotel, and an active member of the network. When will I have the time for such a luxury—to learn the lines of a character in a play, rehearse repeatedly with you until I get them right?"

Cambara and Bile eat in silence, but they soon pay compliments to the chef and heartfelt thanks to Kiin. Several images from Cambara's dream at dawn flash through her mind, and at one point she catches herself smiling when she revisits the scene at Farxia's clinic What was *that* all about? A hidden reference to the lies mother and daughter told about Cambara being infibulated? What was the point of her being examined physically, and the result being passed on like gossip from one person to another?

Kiin says, "I've had a visitor today."

Neither Bile nor Cambara shows much keenness about this statement, assuming it to be an everyday thing. They do not inquire into the identity of the caller or the nature of the visit.

But when, elaborating, Kiin explains that the woman who came to the hotel earlier today said she wanted to talk to one Raaxo Abduraxman, Cambara sits up, jolted out of her inattention. Kiin then remarks, "I knew that there was something unusual about the woman as soon as she gave that sequence of the names."

Bile starts to display a little more curiosity—at the mention of the two names, he recalls that he has heard something vaguely to do with a family tragedy. It is nothing specific and about no one whom he has known or met. No matter how hard he overworks his exhausted brain, no clue presents itself. He also finds it curious that Cambara is silent, in the way of someone who knows the answer to a puzzle but won't speak it, so as not to spoil it for the others.

Bile asks Kiin, "What's unusual about a woman looking for someone called Raaxo Abduraxman? Do you know such a person?"

Kiin replies, "No such person exists."

"How do you know?"

"Because I know Raaxo to be the abbreviated version of the name of Cambara's and my mutual friend Raxma, and I know Abduraxman to be Cambara's father's name."

"What did you think then?"

"It's like a pseudonym, I thought of an author writing and not keeping his writing in a drawer but publishing it," Kiin says. "I thought that someone is telling me something while keeping it partially hidden from me. She was not a threat of any sort—a small woman, all skin and bone, haggard as hell and in someone's hand-me-downs, but not the begging kind. She had elegance to her careworn aspect, has known better days, I could tell, and was certain that all would be well with her and her world shortly if only she could get to this Raaxo Abduraxman. When I pressed her to tell me how she came by the name and she replied that it had been on the radio, I remembered vague mentions, of Raxma telling and not telling about Gacal and his mom, and of Cambara speculating about Gacal, but not getting me involved in the search for her."

"What did you do?"

"She is at the hotel, in your room, as it happens, most probably sleeping off a year of bedbugs, creaky mattresses, and other discomforts," Kiin says. "I felt you wouldn't mind if I lent her your room, since she is looking for you and you are looking for her."

"You haven't told her anything?"

"No."

"Why not?"

"It's not my place to do so."

In Cambara's thoughts, several images mix and match: meeting Qaali and liaising with her about Gacal and what might be done about him; encountering her mother, as she did in the dream; the thought of her mother arriving—"I've come to see your play, darling, I hope that I am welcome." Knowing her mother, however, it is in the realm of the possible that she might just turn up.

"Shall we go and meet my visitor?" Cambara says to Kiin.

"Let us."

When it is clear that Bile is inclined to stay behind, Cambara wonders aloud whether it would be easier for all concerned and wiser if Qaali were brought to the property, or if she, Cambara, should visit her at the hotel, with Gacal in tow. Kiin and Bile suggest that Cambara visit the woman, on condition that, once it is ascertained that she is the boy's mother—and it won't be difficult to do that—then the son and the mother are primed for the meeting. As to the question of how to minimize SilkHair's anxiety about being separated from Gacal, Bile says, "Leave it to me. I'll keep SilkHair entertained."

They exchange parting words as if they are going on a traumatic journey, Bile and SilkHair stepping out of the house to wave good-bye to the departing truck.

"See you when you get back," says Bile.

"No more rehearsal today," she says to SilkHair.

Kiin gives Cambara and Gacal a lift to the hotel. And it is as if Cambara is seeing him with different eyes—a child traceable to his antecedents. Is this why the idea of illegitimacy is so abhorrent to societies, because of this missing link to the starting point?

When they get to the hotel, Cambara and Kiin go their different ways, but agree to meet later for an update. Cambara encourages Gacal to spend half an hour or so with the youths whom he hasn't seen for a couple of days, promising she will call him. She goes up to the room alone, her anxiety level high and aware that she will have managed a coup with no equal if she brings this off, uniting mother and son.

Failure is no option. She knocks on the door out of politeness, even though she has the key in her hand. At her light tapping, the door opens. A small woman with drained features is standing in the doorway, anxiously waiting. Neither speaks. Cambara's thoughts race off like a well-looked-after pet, exploring what there is in the vicinity in hope of returning with interesting findings. Qaali lacks the courage that comes from knowing what to do or say. The room is not hers, and she doesn't know who the woman calling is and why they are meeting here.

This is when Cambara realizes it is incumbent upon her to speak first, as it is her room and world in which they are meeting. Besides, she has more information about Qaali than the other way round. True, they have never met before, but Cambara feels that she knows enough about the woman through the tragedy of her story, and to a lesser degree through Gacal, to give her a hug and a kiss too. Then she decides to speed matters up, and speaks as if they are late for a bus or a plane.

She says, closing the door behind her, and going past the petite woman, "If it is hard for me to know where to start, I can imagine how much more difficult it is for you to begin."

"My name is Qaali," the woman introduces herself.

"I know. Mine is Cambara."

"Not Raaxo Abduraxman?"

"No."

Qaali is the calmer of the two, considering—a woman who has known storms, dreams of hope turned to daily nightmares. Cambara is nervous, shaking, behaving in a manner that gives the wrong impression to Qaali, something she must put right immediately.

Her voice level, Qaali says, "Maybe you'll explain who you are and who Raaxo is and whether any of this has to do with my husband's death, or my son's life and his whereabouts. Please tell me why I am here."

Calmness becomes Cambara. "The news is good."

"What news? What are we talking about?"

Cambara sits down, motions to Qaali to do likewise.

Qaali says, "You have the advantage of knowing who I am, but I am at a disadvantage, because I don't know who you are. I know I've come in answer to the announcement, and that I bear grief and hope in equal measure."

Overwhelmed and yet able to speak, Cambara says, "Maybe you can tell me what went through your mind when you heard your name announced on the BBC 'Missing Persons' program."

As Cambara waits for Qaali to speak, her first thought is to look for a family resemblance between Gacal and this woman, Qaali. When Qaali begins to talk, her features grow more pleasant to the eye, even if gaunt; her voice is a delight to listen to, unrestrainedly rich, like the kind of yogurt to which a good chef might put any number of uses, fluid, malleable, and cultured.

Qaali says, "To a thirsty person, a mirage contains more water than whatever moisture there is under one's feet. It is very difficult to summarize the conflicting thoughts that went through my mind when I heard about the program. In fact, it wasn't I who heard it, but a neighbour whose children I coach in English; they are, as a family, waiting to join their family breadwinner, who lives in the U.S. One minute I saw my son and imagined holding him in my arms; the next minute, I told myself that I was to be the recipient of sad news, only this didn't make sense. Why would a woman ask me to look her up when all she has to dispense is the news of my son's death?"

"Let's talk of life, Qaali." The wells of her eyes flooded, her ears ringing with pent-up emotion, Cambara takes one decisive step toward Qaali. She picks her up and, throwing her arms around the small woman whom she must take care not to crush, says, "Your son is alive."

Qaali goes rigor-mortis rigid in Cambara's arms. She frees her bird-small body and raises one hand, palm facing Cambara. Qaali backs away, stiff and tense, not believing her joy, if there is any in her; as yet it is inexpressible. Her withering appearance belying her sense of optimism, she asks, "Where is my son?"

"Downstairs."

Qaali sits down with her hand under her chin, contemplative, then begins rubbing her eyes sore, as if trying to squeeze out at least one teardrop, given that Cambara's are runny with buckets of it, her nose sniveling. It appears that Qaali has done all her wailing, howling, cussing; there is no more weeping.

Her voice cold, she asks Cambara, "Who are you?"

Cambara pulls herself up, stops sniffing, and looks at Qaali, convinced that it is untimely to wipe her tears away, lest Qaali think of her as a paid mourner who weeps and wails at funerals. There is aggression, anger in Qaali's question; there is suspicion and pain in it as well.

"Who are you? Angel or devil?" Qaali says.

Cambara takes a long pause, breathing nervously, deeply at first then shallowly, until she can collect herself and gather her thoughts, thoughts she wears like a body tent. She emerges, wrapped in self-confidence, and tells Qaali her own story of loss, and then of her chance meeting with Gacal. She talks, and the longer she speaks, the more she feels the sine qua non to explain how it has all come out the way it has; what Gacal told her about his arrival with his father in Mogadiscio; how the taxi driver laid a trap, and how the attempt to rob them led to his father's death. Then Cambara relates her conversation with Raxma—also known as Raaxo, where the first part of the pseudonym comes from—and how her friend delved further into it; how the headmaster of Gacal's school in Duluth confirmed a significant part of the story. Cambara speaks on and on and continues talking until she sees the first teardrop, hears the first sniff, then Qaali's weeping, her eyes streaming so suddenly with so much liquid output that Cambara, who has now regained total control of her emotions, thinks of a tropical downpour.

She sounds weak as she asks, "Can I see my son?"

"Yes, of course." Cambara makes as if to leave.

"Wait," Qaali says.

Cambara does as told.

"Why did you do this?"

Cambara takes a few minutes to come up with an adequate answer to a question she hasn't asked herself up to this moment. She says, "I am neither an angel nor a devil. I am a mother, mourning. Like you. That's why I've felt for you from the instant I saw Gacal, why I've made it my business to pursue the course I have."

Meekly, Qaali says, "Thank you."

As Cambara is leaving, Qaali says, "Is it possible for you not to send him up right away? Give me a few minutes to get ready?" Cambara thinks of a lover preparing herself for her paramour. "You're a woman yourself and know what I am talking about, I am sure."

"Of course."

"And can I see him alone?"

"But of course."

THIRTY-TWO

In the rehearsal hall, which Cambara has revamped with help from Seamus, tirelessly loyal and more than willing to comply with almost all her refurbishing demands, there are the usual faces that have been a permanent feature of the scene.

Because of the large number of uninvited persons milling about, at times standing in her way and interrupting the easy flow of the rehearsal on account of their on and off susurrations, Cambara has asked herself if word has gone out that one can have fun sticking around here. She wonders who has spread the good tidings: that the property is an open house and that no unarmed person will be turned away as long as they are prepared not to make a nuisance of themselves. Rather than take heart from the interest others have shown in her efforts, Cambara tells herself that this is no cakewalk and that there is a lot to go through before she is satisfied with what she has achieved.

Of the usual crowd, there is Bile, her principal pillar, staunch supporter, frequent companion, and untiring consultant on the reconstruction of the text, who is reticent about offering advice in public on matters to do with the rewrites and acting with the discretion of a man who wants everyone to accord Cambara the deference due to her; Dajaal, who has been getting more directly involved in providing logistical assistance, shifting chairs and running errands, driving folks around whenever asked, and making himself available as a stand-in for the ScriptWoman; SilkHair, who has been left off balance by the new presence of Qaali in Gacal's life, which has resulted in Gacal showing less enthusiasm to eat with him, be with him, or remain a partner in disporting himself with SilkHair than he used to. Off-kilter, SilkHair has had to adapt to his enforced aloneness, often in a brooding, sulking mood, silent, withdrawn, wrought up over the slightest jab from Gacal or any hint of affront from Bile or herself. Cambara has observed that, of late, he has lost the wild, mischievous shine in his eyes. Gacal too is an altogether altered boy. You can catch him often lapsing into English at unexpected moments, as an indication of the difference his mother's presence has brought about. This way, too, he banishes SilkHair from his life.

There are also half a dozen young faces that she does not know, the majority of them female, who are attentive to detail, as students are, a couple of them taking notes. Cambara can't tell if they are journalists or theater directors in training. All she remembers is seeing two or three of these arrive with Farxia. There is also the daughter of Odeywaa, the shopkeeper, an acquaintance, through her parents, of Kiin, who has volunteered to fit the bill of ScriptWoman, even though this is the first time she is doing this sort of thing.

She can also count Qaali among those present, watching with interest and raring to help, but she is a cautious person, given to standing back and supplying even her interlocutors with sufficient breathing space, the better to know if she is imposing herself on them. Qaali, dressed in baggy shirts and trousers two sizes too large, which Cambara has lent her, has come along with Gacal. She and Gacal have spent close to fifteen hours talking, reconnecting, and getting reacquainted after their long, tormented separation. Gacal often looks in Qaali's direction when he thinks no one is observing him, maybe to make sure that she is still there. Every now and then, he even inflicts unnecessary breaks in the rhythm of the rehearsals by pausing right in the middle of a take, going to her, and whispering a son-to-mother secret in her ear. He continues not only to inquire aloud what she thinks of his performance, thereby irritating some of the others, most especially SilkHair, but also to barge in with comments that impose a moratorium on anyone else participating in their family injokes. Once or twice, mother and son have been driven back to the Maanta just to be there in what used to be Cambara's inner sanctum, which has now become theirs. Kiin won't hear of Cambara footing the bill, insisting, "The pleasure of providing free lodging to Qaali and Gacal is mine."

Kiin has been in and out the entire day, bringing food and other necessities, and putting her resourcefulness at Cambara's disposal. After lunch, she brought along her two daughters, intent on exposing them to the camaraderie that is part of creating theater. When not serving tea or busy helping in other ways, the older of the two girls sits close to Qaali, keeping a keen eye on the rapport between Gacal and his newly recovered mother in a manner clearly indicating that her mother has told her about what has occurred. Cambara, however, has, of late, discovered that Kiin is forbiddingly reserved, especially about the fact that she has not found roles for her daughters, as promised. She keeps resorting to either changing the subject or moving away on some pretext or other. No longer of the habit of deriving great joy from reiterating that it is through Raxma that she and Cambara met, something she has often done when being presented to a new person, Kiin has evaded making any reference to this link. Cambara isn't sure why. She wonders if Raxma has upset Kiin by keeping her in the dark about Qaali and Gacal or if there is some other more telling reason that will eventually come to light, something to do with her and Raxma. For it has occurred to Cambara that, as she saw in the dream the other day, maybe Raxma and Arda are planning to descend on Mogadiscio in time to watch the first performance.

All of a sudden, Gacal's voice reverberates across the hall as he gives a superb performance of a scene thought of as salient to the entire play. When he has done two more takes, and Cambara compliments him on his rendition, Gacal runs offstage and over to Qaali. He is so excited that he goes around hugging all those near him.

With everyone's concentration broken, Cambara wanders in the direction of the trestle table and the chair close to where the ScriptWoman is and stands there admiring the handiwork, not because it is very beautiful but because Cambara appreciates the gesture of someone providing her with a table that has sufficient surface for her to spread her papers and notes. She kicks gently at the trestle, as if testing the firmness of the wooden support. Then, carrying her stacks of paper and some notes in a folder, she walks over to the ScriptWoman to ask, "How are we doing?"

ScriptWoman is petite and very pretty at that: nose aquiline, skin *yussur* black, so dark it has a touch of blue to it. She is in an all-black blouse, dark blue skirt, and grayish head scarf. The smallness of her build and her choice of dark as a theme, plus the fact that her chin is weak, sets alight in Cambara the bizarre memory of having known this woman before. She remembers why: ScriptWoman distantly reminds her of Raxma, because of her friend's preference for all-black outfits. But whenever ScriptWoman speaks—she has stained teeth the color of brown curry—or walks—her footwear being of the cheap, leather-upper, rubber-heeled, ill-fitting kind—Cambara forswears never likening the two, thinking of it as a putdown of Raxma, who has a particular fondness for all-leather, stylish, Italian flat-heeled shoes, which she buys as much for their durability as for their comfort. Not necessarily expensive footwear but well made nonetheless. For the second time today, she wonders if the dream is dictating which of the many forks in the road her thoughts tread whenever they go off the beaten track. Now that she has seen her friend in the mien of ScriptWoman, she is bound to ask herself if she will see her mother, who was in the same dream, in the gestures of someone else.

Cambara suggests to ScriptWoman, who is reorganizing the un-numbered pages of the script, to put her marked-up script and her notes, some of which she used yesterday, on the center of the trestle table. She adds, "I will compare the changes made today to yesterday's when I have a moment."

ScriptWoman does as told: She puts the lot on the trestle table.

It is then that Cambara realizes that she does not know who brought the trestle or how it got here. Inexplicably, she feels put out, as if she were a conservationist disturbed at the thought of being responsible for the unwitting introduction into the environment of some alien vegetation detrimental to the survival of the local species. If this is my house and I live in it and will contribute so much money toward keeping it secure and safe, then it follows that I ought to know what pieces of furniture come in to it. But she has been remiss in paying close attention to what is going on.

She asks ScriptWoman, "Have you any idea who brought this trestle table?"

"The white man," replies ScriptWoman.

Seamus, she thinks. "When?"

"An hour before you returned from lunch."

"Did he leave a message?"

"Not with me."

"Do you know where he's gone?"

"I have no idea."

"I wish someone would know these things."

"I am only a volunteer," ScriptWoman says.

This is a new one on Cambara: a volunteer. She wonders to herself, but doesn't ask, if the young woman belongs to some civil society of some sort, like the Women's Network or some such, and if so to which? You need unpaid volunteers to perform many of the tasks that must be undertaken if Somali society is eventually to recover from its losses.

"You've come at Kiin's suggestion?"

"I've come with her, in her truck."

"How many others?"

"Half a dozen, all of us volunteers."

"Are some of the other women volunteers too?"

"I've been told they are."

Cambara looks around and observes these women's frenetic movements. Impressed and invigorated by what she sees, she feels heartened by the commitment of the young women, though she hasn't a precise idea what they are committed to. Maybe to peace and to the coexistence of the warring communities through collaborating on theater projects that are deemed beneficial to all.

Now she trains her intense eyes back on ScriptWoman and then, softening her gaze, smiles at her before ogling the trestle table, which Cambara assumes has taken Seamus a couple of hours to knock together, the hallmark of his benefaction. It is characteristic of every one of Cambara's new friends that each contributes his or her fair share in the hope of making a difference in her life here in this city. But where is Seamus? She is looking around, as if trying to spot him among those sitting way in the back of the hall, when a girl in her teens in a see-through *dirac* robe approaches her, bearing a kettle, very hot by the feel of it, and a mug. Who is she? The young woman introduces herself as "the TeaWoman" and asks if Cambara wants some.

"I would love a cup, yes."

TeaWoman raises the slim kettle with the long spout to a great height and then pours it, gradually bringing it down and then going up and down again in a half-moon arc, her hand steady, the curvature of her arm in a semicircle, mesmerizing.

Cambara takes a sip of it and, discovering it too sweet, winces. She says "Thank you," but doesn't tell TeaWoman that she takes hers without sugar. She puts it away and tries to get down to the business of imposing some order on the rehearsal schedule, seeing that Gacal is standing beside her, calmly waiting.

She motions to Gacal and SilkHair, who approach and indicate their eagerness to resume rehearsing. Bile is there too, humbly awaiting her command, his reading glasses balanced on the joint of his nose. After remarking that she has picked up the marked script and, turning the pages, murmuring to herself, receives from him a single sheet on which he has scribbled his notes.

"You'll see some more suggestions for word changes," he says. "You may need to think about them before we incorporate them. We can talk about them in a moment of calm."

Taking the sheet and adding it to the pile, she says, "Thank you, my dear."

Just as she is about to announce the resumption of the rehearsal and says which scene they will work on, she notices that neither of the boys is on the stage, where she wants them. Gacal is sitting with his mother, and SilkHair is skipping rope and showing off his athleticism to Kiin's two daughters. She claps her hands together, and they immediately join her on the stage. It is then that Cambara calls to Qaali.

"Qaali, dear?"

Qaali, smiling, turns to face Cambara.

"Here is the text of the play," she says. "I've hesitated for a long time to ask you to read the part of the wife. You'll see that whereas the parts for the eagle and the chicken and that of the farmer, which Bile will play, are closer to my idea of working text, this part needs a lot of rewriting. Will you volunteer for the part?"

Qaali takes the proffered text with both hands, her head slightly bowing. Cambara proposes a few minutes' break to give her a chance to read it at least twice. Then she hears a few snatches of conversation in the form of phrases that Gacal and SilkHair are exchanging as they egg each other on. It pleases her that the two boys have committed their respective parts to memory and can recite on cue when prompted. She knows that Bile has a problem controlling his ad-libbing, constantly improvising, his working script crawling with insectlike scrawls, especially SilkHair's part, which he has squiggled with chicken scratches. But that is the least of her worries. She is in a state of some high expectation, and her ears burn. She is in no haste to resume rehearsing, because Qaali is still reading and rereading the text.

Highly strung, she is anticipating that something unusual will happen. Touch wood, Bile has not been in low spirits ever since the two started to spend a lot of time together. He has also been an asset, ably ad-libbing several parts, now sounding like a mother in distress, now a preteen boy upset because his father has opted to alter the rules of the game plan. It has been well worth her while to recruit his services in an attempt to solve a theatrical cul-de-sac of sorts. She is grateful to him for suggesting that she add a new part: that of a narrator, designed to accommodate his expansive baritone voice.

Bile and Cambara find themselves standing close to each other. You can't tell whether it is totally by chance or through Bile's deliberate machination that their hips frequently collide. Maybe they are both experts at stealing private moments of intimacy in a public place, as they clasp hands, both cautious in the fluidity of the contact they make, ready to pull back. He, tall, slim, and very presentable, his eyes squinting as if a little impaired; his gaze conspiratorial, as though he knows something he is not prepared to divulge, secrets upon which their future happiness might depend. As rivulets of memories swirl inside her head, a breeze of emotion teases her heart. She thinks that the slight wind blowing into the open door that is her mind is the harbinger of good tidings of which Bile is the bearer. Alas, he won't speak of them. Is it the same reticence that she discerned in Kiin earlier in the day, which she misinterpreted in a negative way?

As Cambara runs her hand over the recently varnished trestle table, she asks, "Where is Seamus?"

"He is in the apartment, getting some much-needed rest," Bile replies. "Apparently, he didn't sleep a wink the whole night, busy setting things up for you. Then he came to the apartment and knocked together this table, which I see you are already using."

Then he whispers a for-her-ears-only mischievous suggestion. He laughs like a much younger man, covers his face with his hands, and then suddenly takes them away in the playful attitude of a child about to say "Peek-a-boo." Unbidden, he walks onstage and stands close to Qaali, in a way putting pressure on her and reminding her that they are waiting for her go-ahead.

When Cambara gives Qaali her cue, she also observes the eagerness on the part of Bile, Gacal, and SilkHair to resume rehearsing. Before a word is spoken, she restates the functions of space in the play. She stands in the forestage and for the first time requests that ScriptWoman read Bile's lines to her, the gist of which she recapitulates. But she is not entirely there, the enormity of her sense of anticipation of some event that is to happen or some person she is about to encounter being so huge that she has no idea what to do with all her nervous excitement.

Then she spots Kiin leading Raxma by the hand into the hall, small-boned Raxma in an all-black outfit of raw linen, her strides long, her chest thrust forward, her dark shawl falling off. She continues marching forward without bothering to pick it up. Cambara thinks that if Raxma is here, can her mother be far? Many questions come to her for answers, but she shrugs them off. When did Raxma get here? She can guess who picked her up from the airport. And where is she putting up? Why has no one told her about her arrival? She looks from Kiin to Bile, and Cambara has the unsettling feeling that they have both known of Raxma's arrival.

Buckets of emotion spill over, with tears of joy coursing down many a throat, Cambara blinking away the wet overflow, Raxma flashing a radient one, Kiin expressing her feelings with repeated hugs. Bile stands with the awkwardness of an amateur actor who does not know how or when to accept applause. Cambara, Kiin, and Raxma stand in a semicircle as if posing for a photograph. Sadly, because no one has remembered to bring a camera, the moment passes unrecorded.

Cambara says to Raxma, "Why are you in this most dangerous of cities?"

Neither the tone nor the phrasing is lost on Raxma, who remembers using these very words when the two friends met in Toronto and Cambara hinted at her wish to come to Mogadiscio and Raxma did everything she could to dissuade her.

Raxma is adept at taming her emotions with a momentary respite, an interlude in which she takes a good hold of herself. She says, "I am here for the world premiere of your play, come to support you and later to boast that I've seen it in the city that I still consider to be one of the most dangerous cities in the universe."

"Is Arda here?" Cambara asks.

From the way Raxma affects an air of surprise, Cambara suspects that her mother is already here and sleeping her jet lag off or is coming within the day. She knows that jet lag plays havoc with Arda's constitution.

"I haven't seen your mother in this blessed city, and have no idea where she is," Raxma says. "Do you know something we don't?" And she consults Kiin. "Kiin, are you hiding Arda?"

Kiin says, "I can confirm that I have never met the lady."

In the palpitations of her disquiet, like a pony racing to catch up with the afternoon shadow it has cast, assuming it to be its competitor's, Cambara tempers her impulses, training them on a faux pas. How can she forget to present Bile? The poor man is standing close by, bashfully looking from one of them to the other.

"Just a moment," Cambara says. "Here is my mainstay, apart from Kiin, my prop, my protector and guide. Here are Gacal and SilkHair, actors, rogues manqué, if you will. Aren't they cute, Raaxo dear? And here is Qaali. You know all about her, your input having been instrumental in contacting her, and we all thank you, dear Raaxo."

"A woman with the world at her feet," Raxma says.

"We'll have plenty of time to talk."

"We will, we will indeed."

Raxma and Cambara take their seats among the volunteers, and Bile, Gacal, and SilkHair take their respective positions onstage. After ScriptWoman prompts Qaali, giving her her cue, and the others resume reciting their roles, Cambara thinks that the downside of having the world at your feet is that you stand to lose everything if there is a giant earthquake.

With Qaali on her turn, Gacal is agog at first, worried perhaps that his mother may not make the required mark. What will SilkHair say to his mates if she fails to impress everyone? But she doesn't disappoint him, because she does a fairly good rendering of what she reads, going about it gently and sensitively, even if she hasn't had a lot of time to read the whole text thoroughly, much less study it with the care it deserves.

When it becomes obvious after repeated readings and several takes that Qaali is tired, and at times her voice breaks off like a dry stick from its parent tree, Cambara calls for a pause.

She says, "We resume in three hours, if that."

They separate into twos and threes, Raxma and Bile, finding a quiet dogleg away from the noises of ScriptWoman, TeaWoman, and the other volunteers. Cambara and Qaali spot their corner, where the boys serve them tea and let them be. Kiin is with her daughters, the older one volunteering as an assistant to ScriptWoman, the younger to TeaWoman.

Cambara, for Qaali's benefit, gives a summary of the story line of the play and, convinced that Qaali is a highly educated woman, decides to spare her an interpretative run-through.

Then the hall echoes with Bile's voice, calling Cambara and Qaali by name and announcing loudly, "It is time to begin again."

They come from different directions, all five of them, to converge on-stage, where they stand around expectantly waiting for something to happen, most likely for ScriptWoman to prompt Qaali, when Zaak, in his all-white Friday best, awaddle with an unhealthy aspect, his face meaty, armpits wet with sweat, forehead oily with fatty perspiration, his breathing heavy, insinuates his presence into Cambara's vision, shockingly dominating it. Held captive by the memory of the horrors he inflicted on her over the years she spent with him, never mind the nature of their relationship, and harried into a difficult fork in the road they journeyed together, including or rather ending with their fractious encounter the last time—and the only time he has ever been her host— she is undecided as to how to react or what to do. It ill-behooves her to be uncivil in the presence of two of her intimates, namely Raxma and Bile, not to mention so many strangers. Uncomfortable with his lack of bodily controls, he is duck-walking closer, wobblingly weak-kneed. She tells herself that it is not by chance but rather by choice that she has avoided him, not seeing or calling him. Then she hears the sound of approaching feet to her left, and before she has had the time or the opportunity to turn, Raxma is whispering in her ears. "Leave him to me."

Cambara says nothing; she stiffens. Bile, who knows of Zaak only vaguely, looks from Raxma, who is going past him, to Cambara, who is in a provoked disposition, and eventually toward the others, some of whom seem amused, some bewildered as they watch what is happening.

"Look who is here, Zaak himself," Raxma says aloud.

Zaak rolls to a halt and, his shirt sticking both to his back and front because of the ungodly dampness, maneuvers the upper part of his body and ultimately its lower part and his head with the slowness of a turtle taking a sharp bend in the road. Then he toddles forward, and Raxma, having stridden toward him, waits, with everyone watching. Cambara senses ripples of babble eddying forth, and, joining rivulets of whispers; these streams course down toward a tributary of popular disapproval.

Raxma says, "How're you doing, Zaak," her hand extended in the stiff manner of a warlord shaking hands with another in a photo opportunity imposed by the donor countries giving their starving nation food aid.

"Arda called me," he says as they shake hands.

"To say?"

"That I can find Cambara here."

"I am here too," Raxma replies.

"She said you'd be here."

There is a prominent tremor in his voice.

"Aren't you going to welcome me?"

"Welcome." The word passes his lips lifelessly.

They run out of things to say to each other. Raxma turns to Cambara, who settles on making her move, convinced that she can manage to keep him at a safe distance at the same time save Raxma unnecessary embarrassment. Cambara's best bet is not so much to offer apologies to Zaak and explain why she hasn't been in touch as to placate Bile's shattered self-containment. Bile might feel humiliated to bear testimony to her dealing crudely with her cousin, something he is not likely to approve of. Bile does not like the idea of Cambara and Zaak making fun of each other in front of so many strangers. He is of the old school, in which you do not tear into anyone, not least your partner or cousin, when others are around. She doesn't recall them ever discussing Zaak, although it is possible that Kiin may have filled him in. Cambara keeps a good distance, if for no other reason than that she doesn't want to be close to his foul mouth.

"What have you been up to?" Zaak says to Cambara, the portly words rolling out of his mouth in the manner of a roly-poly corpulently dancing across a round floor. "I am happy for you. You've achieved what you set out to do. Good for you, my girl. You've acted in a grown-up way, as I suggested. I doubt you would've recovered the property or gone on to produce your play if I hadn't pushed you when I did. I said so to Auntie Arda."

She says, "You abandoned me to my own fate, so I would act grown-up, is that it? You were rude to me so I would set myself higher goals and achieve them? That's a new one on me. Have you sold that to my mother?"

"And she bought it," he says. "Now why have you abandoned me? Why have you not been in touch to let me know of your successes?"

She says, "It is not that you need anyone's company when you have your bundles of *qaat*." Everyone nods their heads, appreciating the one-liner. But no one dares to laugh, except Raxma, who lets out a mild guffaw.

"When did Arda call you?" Cambara asks.

"Earlier today."

Whatever game her mother is playing, Cambara does not wish to let Zaak know that she has any idea where her mother is and hasn't been in touch either. This will only add more venom to her and Zaak's long-standing quarrels and will do nothing to improve their chance of making up with each other for the sake of Arda. There is time yet, though. She will question Raxma about Arda when they are alone later, and all will become clear.

"Okay, Zaak. Time I returned to work."

"I won't stop you," he quips and starts to turn away, feeling that he has darted back at her as much venom as she has thrown in his direction.

She says, "Did you bring along your bundle to chew while you wait? The way some of us bring a book to read when we are in the dentist's office?"

"You're being nasty," he says, grinning. "It ill suits a host to be wicked to your guests. Be nice to me when I am on your property. Please."

"Listen who's talking."

"Precisely," he says, looking around and trying to make contact with his audience, his winning smile spreading.

She has had enough of him; her voice says it all. "I have some urgent work to attend to," she says. "Could you give your coordinates to the lady with the writing pad?" and she points at ScriptWoman. "Since you've honored us with your visit to the property, I'll now invite you to the opening night of my play. You can sit in the front row, next to your favorite aunt Arda."

She turns her back on him fast and marches away toward the stage, where all the others are gathered, patiently waiting. It takes some time before a couple of them manage to wipe the grin off their faces and a little more before they are ready to resume their rehearsal. As Qaali steps forward to continue from where she left off, several eyes focus on the bulky back of a potbellied figure blocking what little there is of daylight with his fleshy plumpness. Zaak gone, Cambara sits next to Raxma, half listening to Qaali reading her part with more panache.

"Where is Arda?" she asks Raxma irritably.

"She's broken her journey in Nairobi, where she intends to sleep off the jet lag," Raxma explains. "We parted at the airport, she to take a taxi to a hotel, I to board my onward flight here. She'll be here early tomorrow. Kiin has offered to fetch her from the airstrip."

"That woman is going to be my death," she says.

"Take it easy, Cambo."

"How can I when there are Zaaks and Wardis?"

"Forget about Zaak; he is a fool."

"How can I?"

"Get on with your rehearsal, Cambo."

"Give me a minute." Cambara sits where she is, her eyes closed, as if this might afford her a look inside of herself, so that she might draw on her inner strength, which she is certain is there.

"Thanks, Raaxo," she says a few minutes later, ready to get on with her rehearsal. "You've been a darling. As always."

They soldier on rehearsing until late, by which time everyone is too exhausted, and the young women volunteers, including ScriptWoman and TeaWoman, have gone. Raxma takes over their jobs, moving about with formidable efficiency, never indicating for a single moment that she has arrived only a few hours ago. She won't hear of Cambara's suggestion that Dajaal drive her to Maanta. "Isn't that what friends are for: to be by your side when you need them? I'll be here until we are done for the day."

The next day when least expected, Zaak makes a dramatic entrance, walking ahead into the hall with a figure immediately behind him, he like the first of two vehicles tied to each other by an invisible rope, the one with its engine alive and running, as it pulls the other, namely the figure of a woman.

Zaak is carrying two heavy suitcases. He stops frequently, breathing heavily and wiping away the sweat just as often, halting altogether now and again, only to pick up now one suitcase, now the other, all the while conscious of the figure behind him, who is silently urging him to go on despite it all. As he comes forward, taking one foot at a time, pausing, and then continuing, everyone onstage falling silent and turning in his direction, Zaak seems to want to curse but dares not, again because of the figure goading him on subtly from behind. At one point, he puts down the weighty suitcases and then absentmindedly moves forward, tripping over one of them, awkwardly falling, and almost somersaulting. As he collapses into a heap, he makes an unearthly noise, something like lightning cracking, as if in pursuit of the thunder it is chasing across a cloudy tropical sky.

In contrast to Zaak, Arda presents herself well-groomed, bright-eyed, lively, and full of post–jet lag perkiness. She walks tall and large, swathed in an elegant frock of light cotton, the fan in her hand actively in motion, stirring the air about, the smile on her face obtrusive to the point of appearing false, especially to those who know her very well. Her skin brown, and, seemingly, too young for her age, she has a rested aspect to her, a jauntiness that borders on the nervous. In the scheme of things, she is upset, because it is Zaak who determines her forward progress.

The scene before Cambara strikes a distant chord in her memory, reminding her of one of her favorite plays, *Waiting for Godot*. The mystery, the despair, and the uncertainty of human existence, all of which she discerns in Zaak's and Arda's faces, bring to mind Samuel Beckett's Pozzo, who drives Lucky by means of a rope around the latter's neck. The day hasn't been kind to Zaak, whom, you can bet, Arda must have bullied and shamed in private on the basis of what Raxma told her. Now Arda is deliberately putting Zaak in his place in public, in the presence of the very same men and woman in front of whom he humiliated her daughter.

Raxma appears to be enjoying herself, watching the proceedings. Cambara, however, feels sorry for Zaak, thinking that the poor fellow doesn't even have a stool on which to sit, as does Lucky in *Godot*. As far as she knows, his transgressions notwithstanding, Zaak remains a nephew to Arda, and that means he is also of the same blood as hers. Maybe the midday heat, it being siesta time, the exhaustion pervasive, and the stress unbearable, is making Cambara start to see things, conjure up discordant images of a Pozzo-and-Lucky drama of desolation.

It's even clearer the moment they come near the stage where Cambara, Bile, Qaali, Gacal, and SilkHair are that there is bad blood between Arda and Zaak. Not only do they keep the same physical distance as before—Arda spurring him on, Zaak plodding wearily forward—but Arda is in a rage, and she wants everyone to know it. She halts all of a sudden, just as Zaak acts in a mutinous manner, refusing to take a step farther and also to lift the two suitcases. Arda says firmly to Zaak, "You've been rude, behaved in an unacceptable manner, hurled invectives in all directions whenever you've felt like it. It is time you apologized."

Only she doesn't name the person or persons to whom he must serve up a travesty of regrets. In addition, she handles him physically, pushing him out of the way, and rudely going past him toward the stage, where the others are gathered, watching in silence. When she reaches the stage, where Cambara is expecting her, with her arms open, her face adorned with a wide smile, Arda changes her voice. The vitriol that has oozed out with malicious intent when she talks to Zaak is transformed to sweetness, now that she is addressing her words to her daughter. They exchange remarks, neither moving toward the other.

"Done it, haven't you, darling?"

"Not yet, Mother."

"You have, my darling."

"There is a lot to do."

"You've done it. No question about it."

"Let's not tempt fate, Mum."

"In any case, come down and give your doubting Arda a hug and a kiss," and she motions to Cambara to come forward, "and tell me how you've managed to achieve all of this." In one sweep, Arda takes in the stage and the people on it, the hall and those in it. "All on your own. In spite of the numerous odds. Despite Zaak," and she looks at him.

Arda, to free her hands for Cambara's embrace, tosses the fan toward the stage in the attitude of an athlete who, winning the finals of a game, throws her racket into the admiring crowd. Bile has the fortune to catch the fan before it hits the floor; Raxma applauds. Cambara approaches, her heart racing, but she takes care not to collide with Zaak or stumble against the suitcases, which he left bang in the aisle

They hug, mother and daughter; they whisper in each other's ears, like two young beaux meeting after a long separation. Then each wraps her body around the other, Cambara finding it difficult to reach round her mother's waist, because of its dimensions. Her voice low and teasing, Cambara says, "We must lose weight, mustn't we?"

"That we will; that we will."

They turn their backs on everyone and walk out of the hall. It is not clear if Cambara means to show her mother the rest of the house or if Arda wants Cambara to herself for a couple of hours, in which the two might spend private time together and talk.

EPILOGUE

Three days later, at which point Cambara's days of work, more work, and more of the same, have extended into nights, and the nights into all-day affairs, she mounts the special performance before a select audience of mainly women. When not revising, rehearsing, or rereading and she is awake, she consumes lots of coffee to stay on her feet and spends her time, now in the company of Arda, who is ever so sweet; now Raxma, who is discreet and gently merging into the background, silent, unobtrusive; now Bile, with whom she is alone in the apartment to chill out and take long hot baths; and now Kiin, Qaali, SilkHair, and Gacal.

Raxma volunteers to do whatever is required of her, occasionally acting as ScriptWoman, recording the start and the end of the takes on the clapboard and penciling in the changes to the text as dictated to her by Cambara; at times, as TeaWoman; at others, accompanied by Dajaal, she goes to a part of the city she has not been to for more than fifteen years, because Cambara has requested olive oil for the wooden masks, since linseed oil, which is ideal for it, is not available. On another occasion, she is assigned to collect the costumes from the tailor. On her return, Raxma, appearing more desolate than either Arda or Cambara has known her to be, speaks of how she has borne witness to a skirmish in which two youths lost their lives right in front of her. "Felt like watching a horror movie live but on the big screen," Raxma says. "Only this was so insanely real, I couldn't bear the madness of it." To the question of how it all unfolded in front of her, she explains that teenagers got into an argument, for a reason unclear to her, and then all of a sudden started shooting at each other bang, bang, bang. Point-blank. No emotions at all. "As if they've done it for me to bear testimony." She sighs, then goes on, "I don't want to go out anymore. Enough. I am staying put; I feel safe here."

Where others might put questions to Cambara, gently probing, Arda stays decidedly in the margins, behaving differently from her usual self; she acts as if she has no opinions on any matter, no advice to offer to her daughter on any topic whatsoever. She is often heard saying "You know it better than me, darling. Who am I to give you counsel on anything after you've achieved what you have?" Nor does she have anything to say more particularly about Cambara's apparent closeness to Bile, even while others keenly watch the bourgeoning intimacy between them. Arda overhears the others talk of the amity flowering, their tongues wagging, some hinting at the possibility of a wedding, yet she makes no comment, either to Cambara or to the others, maybe because she does not wish a repeat of what occurred with Zaak—admittedly, her own mistake—or when her daughter married Wardi against her advice and they were alienated from each other. She doesn't want to mention Wardi's name or make reference to Zaak, knowing that she opposed Cambara's marrying the former, just because her daughter loved him, and imposed the latter on her—and what disasters they both turned out to be.

Curiously though, Arda takes to SilkHair, whom she has more or less put under her solicitous care. She talks of sending him to school somewhere to train as a mechanic or in one of the trades, provided he is up to the challenge and prepared to follow it through. She is on good terms with Qaali and Gacal, but alas there is little she can do to help them solve the bureaucratic muddle even though she tells them that she has spoken to one of her friends in the Canadian diplomatic corps. Both she and Cambara are relieved when Raxma informs them that she has been in touch with Maimouna, who is making representations with the U.S. consulate in Nairobi.

Arda and Dajaal get on well too; they discuss the security situation at length and the possibility of a sudden attack, which he shrugs off, describing it as "virtually impossible, considering." Then he continues, "I can understand your worries, which are the worries of an untrained mind. I am saying 'untrained' vis-à-vis security matters. Leave it all to me. Have no fear. We're okay as long as we stage the play for a special audience, masks or no masks. My worry is about giving a public viewing of the play with masks. Too risky." But from the way the two of them converse, Cambara feels that they are better acquainted with each other, more than they care to explain.

Arda takes to talking to Seamus more than to any of the others; he is less inhibited with her and he teases her. He tickles her memory to the extent that they exchange the jokes they knew in the day when Italian culture, language, and cinema were pervasive in their lives. She tells him some priest jokes, and he, for his part, cracks some 'peasant comes to town' ones, full of below-the-waist punch lines. Gacal is a constant listener to the ribaldries.

Bile, however, is more formal with Arda, very courteous, maybe as it behooves a future son-in-law. And Arda is ill at ease in his presence, maybe because of the age difference between her and Bile, potentially her daughter's future partner. She strives to show a relaxed aspect of herself to Bile. It's just as well that they are all very busy, Cambara seeing to the exigencies of the play, including makeup, and acting as an assistant to Seamus when it comes to lighting and stage management. Raxma puts herself forward to take on every other task with which Cambara charges her, her last assignment being that of a prompter; Seamus, in addition to his lighting and stage-managing duties, attends to the running of the generator; Bile, Qaali, Gacal, and SilkHair all do their jobs with absolute devotion.

Bile is unfailingly present at Cambara's side for most of their waking hours, steadfast in his supportive companionship, trustworthy in his offer of a large space in which she moves around free from all constraints. On more than one occasion, after everyone else has turned in, the two have gone together, and, too exhausted, she has dropped off into a deep sleep the instant her head hit the pillow in what used to be his niece Raasta's room. It is obvious to everybody that Bile, dejected in appearance when she is absent, is mad with longing for her. Things are such that he considers every activity that keeps them apart an unacceptable interference, a meddling into the *affaire de coeur*, and he hurts.

Overcome with anxiety, Kiin, in Cambara's presence, leads a spirited existence. She prays that everything will work out well for every one of her guests: that Gudcur will stay buried, if he is dead; that none of his minions will prove to be a nuisance; that Cambara will make a success of the play to which she, Kiin, is inviting a select audience and a few loyal intimates. But Kiin avoids saying anything when someone alludes to Bile and Cambara being an item, especially with Arda present. Given that she has helped bring forth the closeness, she is under the impression that it will be long-lasting. Raxma wears feistiness for her friend's benefit whenever Bile is not around, knowing that it will cheer her up and make working with her a lot easier and less acrimonious. Nor does she want to be drawn into the relationship either.

On the opening night itself, with butterflies taking residence in her viscera, Cambara's innards become a battlefield. She tells herself that a war has been won, which is all good and inspiringly welcome, but will the battle be lost?

The generator is on, and you can hear its humming noise from half a mile away. To ensure that there are no lapses in security, which Dajaal has planned very tightly, Seamus has run the cables all the way to the checkpoints. There are several inner and outer circles and a minimum of three checkpoints, the one farthest being manned by Kaahin, a close associate of Dajaal's, the second by Qasiir, and the one just before you get to the house by no other than Dajaal himself. All manner of communication gadgets are in use: walkie-talkies, a landline telephone at the property, and several handheld mobiles. At each checkpoint, there are men with machine guns hidden from view, the second security ring having the only "technical" as part of a show of force, if it comes to that. The phone keeps ringing whenever there are doubts about the identity of a person who has presented him—or herself—and whether this person has been invited. These are checked against the master list of guests, which is with Arda. Kiin is in continuous communication with all the parties concerned, considering that she has provided the names of the guests and their details in the first place. The play is being staged under the auspices of the Women's Network, which, as host, along with Hotel Maanta, has supplied the evening's refreshments.

In spite of the tension resulting from the tight security, there is a jovial atmosphere, with the guests behaving normally once they come through the rings, after being frisked, some having been asked what they think of as impertinent questions. Once or twice, Kiin has had to go in person to Dajaal's site of operations to sort out things. In all, only two persons have been turned away, because Kiin couldn't vouch for them or didn't know them well enough to allow them through. With no panic buttons pressed, Dajaal, Kiin, and Arda give the go-ahead that it may start when all guests have been accounted for.

There are altogether about twenty-five invited guests in the hall, only three of them men: Irrid and Hudhudle from the Maanta, and Odeywaa, the shopkeeper, husband to a very active member of the Women's Network, back from the National Reconciliation Conference in Nairobi just to see the play. There is another woman, a stringer for the BBC Somali Service in Mogadiscio, a pocket-sized woman, very intense, with a shrill voice when she speaks, with eyeglasses as thick as the nether end of a tumbler. She has a firm handshake and has the habit of poring over every statement Cambara makes with a view to analyzing and perhaps commenting on it. Cambara feels discomfited by the woman's probing eyes, and she can't wait for the chance to flee from the woman soon after Kiin is done with the introductions and the woman speaks of her interest in interviewing her and Qaali and Gacal. She reminds Cambara that it is thanks to her announcement on the BBC "Missing Persons" program that mother and son have been reunited. The head of the Somali Service wants a follow-up in the form of a live interview. Now she excuses herself and runs off to attend to new guests arriving.

As the curtain is prepared to rise on the minimalist stage and as Bile dons his mask and prepares to walk onstage, Cambara, excited, is full of fidget. She anxiously turns away, looking weary and acting as if she might flee from the hall. It is only when she hears Bile's baritone voice that she reinvests afresh her confidence, trust, and gratitude in everyone who has had anything to do with the play. And she remembers Bile assuring her—he is now onstage—that there is nothing to worry about, that the two boys will be all right, and that the crowd of villagers, none with a speaking part (all of them women recruited earlier in the day, and all given cash gifts by Arda), will be fine too. The action onstage is proving him to be correct.

Arda sits way in the back, her chair in semidarkness, chewing on the nerve ends of her guts, watching the performance from that viewpoint. Cambara, however, has insisted on not being in the hall now, scared that she might suffer a crack-up. After all, she has woven nearly every thread of her private, professional, and public life into the yarn that is about to be presented, with her directing it; Bile, Qaali, Gacal, and SilkHair acting in it; Kiin and Raxma volunteering to be in it. Failure of such a many-sided project will be difficult to take; she can't bear the thought of it at all.

Then Cambara's mind, in a way, walks out on her, as though in a bizarre daydream of the type seen when one is overexhausted and tense at the same time. She loses touch with everything that matters: She has no idea who or where she is anymore, what she is supposed to do where, and when she looks at the faces of the women and men sitting in the hall and watching her play, she finds she cannot name any of them. Nor can she put a name to her mother's or Raxma's faces, which look familiar but no more than that. Hence, away with her, since she won't be able to stand the tension gnawing at her guts in the first few moments. She sneaks away and goes to her rooms to have a few moments of quiet reflection. She wants to be alone, the first time she has been so for quite a long while, and where better to be by herself than a bathroom in which she does not think of herself as a guest or one that is in as good nick as Bile's.

She returns to the site, after recovering the self that earlier went on a walkabout, before the end of the play and finds Kiin pacing back and forth in the rear of the hall, busy keeping an eye on the guests, many of the women seated and by all accounts enjoying the story unfolding. Now that she is back, Cambara also keeps a close watch on the front row, trying to work out if she can tell whether they are as attentive as she might like them to be. She assumes that an author of a book, given the chance to study the body language of someone reading it, can in all likelihood figure out when the interest in it slackens off.

At some point, relaxing in view of the fact that there is rapt attention, with no one stirring in her or his seat, she remarks a change in the front row seating, noticing the belated arrival of a woman who was not there before. From where she is, because the light is so muted, Cambara cannot make out who the people are with certainty, cannot identify even those whom she knows, except the two men, namely Seamus, because he is white, and Dajaal, because of his military bearing, and because he is the only one standing close by, with his walkie-talkie faintly chattering. It is the woman to the right of Seamus that draws her attention. Cambara then thinks that there is something unusually familiar about the bodily configuration of the woman who is wearing a headgear with the purpose of disguising her identity. The woman has wrapped herself up in a shawl in a manner meant to put doubt into Cambara, to make her question her first judgment. No sooner has she recognized who it is and prepared to call to her than the breath catches in Cambara's throat, and she chokes on it. All the same, she knows that even though the light is faint and the distance between them is great, she can tell who it is: Maimouna, Raxma's and her mutual friend and lawyer. Maybe she has come to Mogadiscio not only to watch the play but also to represent Qaali and Gacal, on account of Gacal's lost documents? Maimouna, big, black, and very beautiful, is in the first row, with Kiin to her left and Farxia to her right.

Hers is the joy of an animal reuniting with its own kindred, and Cambara assumes her body into that of a tigress, keen-eyed, fast of pace. She takes the first few strides with incredible agility and speed, silently moving toward the front row. Kiin, in the meanwhile, is almost on top of her, holding her back, whispering to her that she is disturbing the audience. Kiin says to Cambara, "Later, later. Take hold of yourself and calm down. There is time yet; there is time yet."

Disregarding, Cambara moves impulsively toward the woman in the front row, not in the least clear in her mind what she will do when she finally gets to her: whether she will embrace her, welcome her, tell her how happy she is that she has made it to the opening night. But Cambara can't go farther, because the aisle is blocked off, with rows and rows of spectators having placed their chairs in a haphazard manner.

Several members of the audience request that she take a seat. Of course, they have no idea who she is, or why she is behaving this way, but it is obvious to them that she is disturbing their enjoyment, creating a racket and moving about as though she is mad. At least one of them believes that she is insane.

Eventually, Kiin leads her out of the hall, down the stone stairway, where they sit and she serves Cambara a hot drink. "I just wanted to say hello to her, tell her how pleased I am that she is at the opening of my first play ever."

At the end of the performance, which is universally described as a success, Cambara and her mother meet, and the two of them spend their first night together on the family property, joyous to sleep there and talk until the small hours of dawn.

A few days later, Arda gives a private party for everyone who has been sweet to or supportive of her daughter. Then Bile has a private audience with Arda, but no one gets to hear what the two have said to each other.

ACKNOWLEDGMENTS

This is a work of fiction, set against the background of events that took place in Mogadiscio. The characters in the novel and the incidents narrated in it are, however, products of my imagination. Any resemblance to any actual persons, living or dead, is coincidental.

In writing *Knots*, I have incurred many debts, some with people whom I am, sadly, unable to acknowledge, because I no longer recall their names or have never known them, and others with acquaintances and friends I met in Somalia, whose names I have decided not to mention out of consideration for their safety. I owe immeasurable gratitude to all of these people for helping me get a grip on certain aspects of the civil war in that country. I have made judicious analyses of what I learned during my research trips to Mogadiscio, and I remain responsible for the spin I have put on what they told me.

In addition, I would like to give a nod of thanks to my very good Milanese friends Edoardo Lugarini, Daniela Bertocchi, and Chiara (my godchild) for lending me their second home in the hamlet of San Sebastiano in Piedmont; to Jean-Christophe Belliard; to my hosts at the École des Hautes Études en Sciences Sociales in Paris, namely Michel Agier, Eloi Ficquet, and Maria Benedicta Basto; and to Clemens Zobel. Paris, in the spring, is very inspiring: *Merci!*

Among the many texts I have read, consulted, and borrowed from are Carlo Collodi's *Pinocchio*, in the translation of Nicolas J. Perella, who also wrote the introduction and notes (*The Adventures of Pinocchio*, University of California Press, 1986); Daniel McNeill's *The Face: A Guided Tour* (Hamish Hamilton, 1998); Martha Roth's *Arousal: Bodies & Pleasures* (Milkweed, 1998); Fatima Mernissi, *The Veil and the Male Elite* (Addison-Wesley, 1991); Peter Junge's *Arte da Africa: Obras-Primas do Museu Etnologico de Berlim* (the catalogue for an exhibition held in Rio di Janeiro in 2003–2004); and David C. Lohff's *Cyclopedia of Dreams*

(Running Press, 2000); and Robert Green's *The 48 Laws of Power* (Viking, 1998). My special gratitude to Ama Ata Aidoo for sending me, in electronic format, her *The Eagle and the Chickens* (Baobab Books, Harare, Zimbabwe); and to Christopher Gregorowski for his "retelling" of an African tale *Fly, Eagle, Fly*, illustrated by Nick Daly and with an introduction by Desmond Tutu (Tafelberg, 2000; the tale, in its written form, is attributed to James Kwegyir Aggrey, aka Aggrey of Africa). And finally, thanks to Our Dialogue, at http://www.ourdialogue.com/vl.htm.